The Lyric of Memory

The Lyric of Memory

Hilari T. Cohen

ISBN-13: 9781523400430
ISBN-10: 1523400439

For KHC, JSC, and DAC
because without you there is no music

Part One

I

Madeline Ellis woke up with a piece of a song rattling around in her head. This wasn't unusual. Sometimes she could fall back asleep and remember the chord progression in the morning, but experience told her not this time. This time she had to get up. The music was calling, making it impossible for Maddie to ignore the sound that only she could hear. She looked at the clock: 2:05 a.m.

With a deep sigh, she pulled herself out of the comfortable warmth of her bed and sat on the edge for a moment, getting her bearings as the tune spun its web through her brain. Giving in to the inevitable, she made her way downstairs to her piano, the full moon illuminating the room, and began the process that was so much a part of her, so deeply rooted and primal that she knew better than to fight it. She sat down on the piano bench, its soft leather well-worn and familiar, an extension of her body. She began to play.

Slowly at first, her fingers picked out the notes she had heard in her sleep. As she glided over the keys, the sound gradually changed, filling out with the lush fullness of melody that was the trademark of a Madeline Ellis composition. She had been creating music for as long as she could remember, at the beginning in fits and starts, then learning to read music as easily as she learned to read words, but with a more innate understanding. Her mother once said that Maddie had played music in the womb. Maybe she had. Maybe the notes were already with her then, before she had fully formed fingers to play with, before she had ears to register the sound. Whatever it was, and whichever way it happened, Maddie was born to be a musician.

She continued to play, stopping every so often to write down the complicated combination of notes in the book she always kept on the piano. By dawn she was finished. She looked out of the row of tall windows that faced the ocean. The early April sun was beginning its rise over the Montauk beachfront . . . inspiration framed by glass.

Yawning, Maddie went back to bed, hoping that when she returned to look in her notebook, the music she had just written would still be there, and that it would still sound the same. She could never be sure, because over the course of her lifetime she'd come to understand one truth: she could never be sure of anything.

When Maddie woke again, the bright light that seeped around the window shades told her it was well past noon. She'd have to force herself to stay awake if she didn't want to end up sleeping the day away. *Coffee*, she told herself. *Coffee cures everything.*

She threw an old gray sweatshirt over her pajamas and went downstairs, avoiding her notebook as she passed the piano. She knew she'd have to open it to check that she hadn't just dreamed the music, that the song was real. But that could wait for at least one cup of coffee to give her the courage to do so.

Once in the kitchen, Maddie worked effortlessly, humming the song she had heard in her sleep. As soon as the coffee was ready, she poured it in her mug and turned around—only to see the light flashing on the antiquated answering machine on her countertop. Maddie hesitated. People rarely left messages anymore, not since voice mail and texts had become such an acceptable form of communication. Sighing, she pushed the thought of her notebook away and hit "play."

"Hey, Mom. It's me." Her son Nate's voice came as a surprise. "You didn't answer my e-mail or the messages I left on your cell, so I'm hoping you hear this. I'm on my way out there; just wanted to give you a heads-up. Should be there before dinnertime. Hope you're home, or, come to think of it, I hope you're out somewhere great." He paused before ending with, "See you later."

Maddie really didn't remember when she had last checked her e-mail or even seen her cell phone. In fact, she didn't remember when she'd last been to the mailbox at the end of her driveway or to the supermarket, for that matter. Did she even have anything in her refrigerator to make Nate something to eat?

She had happily been living on peanut butter and Cheerios. It was always that way: when she finally got down to composing something new, she'd spend weeks hearing pieces of the music in her head, scarcely eating or sleeping, almost living in a trancelike state until the thing was out of her body and pieced together on the page. Maddie played the message again and then glanced down at her pajamas. If Nate was going to be here soon, she'd better get in the shower. The notebook would have to wait.

She had just finished dressing when she heard Nate's key struggling to turn the front door lock. She ran her brush through her long, curly hair. Once blond, it was now steely gray, almost silver in the dim light, but she didn't mind that at all. And she liked the small wrinkles around her eyes as well, because each line reminded her of how she had lived her life on her own terms. She smoothed the white cotton T-shirt over her faded jeans and practically ran down the stairs to greet her only child, nearly knocking him off his feet with a tight hug.

"Nate, I'm so happy to see you!" He looked better than ever, broad and strong, with day-old stubble on his chin, his sandy hair, long and wavy, resting softly against the back of his collar. He looked so much like his father once did that she had to remind herself that they were nothing alike.

Nate smiled and hugged her back. "You too, Mom. What's up? Where's your cell phone? I've been calling you for days. I know you use the Internet. Don't you ever check your e-mail? Do I have to fly out here just to speak to you? And what's with the door? I could barely get it open. When did you last use it?" His questions came in a quick-fire barrage, letting her know how annoyed he was with her.

"Sorry, dear, I'm so sorry. I just got caught up in a new piece of music and, well, you know the rest."

"I get it, but I'm not only your manager, I'm your son. And as your son, I worry. You do live alone, you realize? Maybe you should get a dog or something. I could probably train him to pick up the phone when it rings . . ."

"Very funny, wise guy. Okay, message received. Are you hungry?" Maddie asked to change the topic. *When*, she wondered, *had their roles reversed, making him the grown-up in their relationship?* "We can order some of your favorites from Gino's. Garlic knots, meatball hero . . ."

"It's useless to try and convince you to come out with me, isn't it?"

Maddie shot him a look that required no explanation. "So what's it going to be?" she went on. "Linguini with white clam sauce? Pizza? I have some good wine down in the cellar."

"Linguini sounds great. So does the wine. And after dinner we've got to talk."

"That sounds ominous. Is everything all right with you and Sophie?"

"Mom, please. Sophie is great. I'm great."

"So when are you going to marry that girl already? I could use some grandchildren. Almost all my friends have at least one."

Nate just looked at her with one eyebrow raised as if to say she better cut out the inquisition. "We—you and I—have to talk. I'm going down to get a bottle of wine. Or maybe two. Then I'm going to shower and change."

"What's so important that you had to fly cross-country to discuss it with me?" Maddie asked Nate's back as he headed toward the basement door.

"Shower. Wine. Talk. In that order."

She smiled despite the terseness of his tone. It was good to have him home, whatever the reason. She really didn't mind living alone, but when Nate was around she was always so happy. Maddie loved Sophie and enjoyed the rare occasions when she accompanied Nate from LA, but having him here all to herself was a real treat. She went back into the kitchen and picked up the phone to call the restaurant.

"Hey, Gino," she said when he answered.

"Maddie! How's it going? Ordering the usual tonight?"

"Make it for two—Nate just showed up!"

"That's nice. I'd drive the order over myself if we weren't slammed right now. Be sure to say hi from me!"

"Thanks, Gino." Maddie could hear him calling out her order to one of his chefs above the din before he hung up.

Forty minutes later Nate was back in the kitchen, his hair wet from the shower, wearing sweatpants and a T-shirt that had one of her old album covers silk-screened across the front.

"Where in heaven did you get that?" Maddie asked.

"A vintage shop in Silver Lake. Paid a bundle for it too. You're still a huge deal, Mom."

"Please, Nate. Don't start."

There was a loud knock on the mudroom door. She grabbed her wallet from a kitchen drawer. "Gotta get the food. Lose that last thought, okay?"

Nate busied himself opening the wine and muttering under his breath. Reaching into the cabinet, he pulled out two glasses and fortified himself with a heavy pour of the very expensive Barolo before Maddie came back into the kitchen with a pair of huge shopping bags.

"I told Gino you were home, and he insisted on adding a few things to the order. I think there's a salad and some tiramisu in here with your name on it. Guess I'm not the only one happy to have you here."

"Lucky me then," Nate said, bringing the bottle of wine and their glasses to the table. "Let's eat!"

Maddie unpacked the containers while Nate took out plates and silverware.

"This looks so good. Just like always, huh?" Nate asked with a smile.

"Of course. Gino is still the best around." Maddie put some linguini on the dinner plate Nate was holding and then forked salad into the small bowls sitting on the table. "You realize I was just teasing you about those grandchildren. I know you won't deprive me of the pleasures of grandparenthood forever."

Nate put his fork down and shot her the death stare he always used to give her when she nagged him to study in high school. Not that she should have worried that much—he'd done just fine through his undergrad years at Stanford and then when he got his MBA, all the while working for her. He was the best business manager she'd ever had—and she'd gone through quite a few of them after her divorce from Tom.

"Mom. Really? Like marriage worked out so well for you and Dad."

"Don't give me your crap, Nate. You'll be better at it than we were. After all, you've learned what not to do." She pushed the food around on her plate as she spoke.

"Well, because you're so interested, Sophie is busy with her fall collection. I'm meeting her in Paris in a few weeks while she shops for fabrics. Ombre silks, I think. Wanna come along?"

"Now you're just being mean," she said, only half kidding as she poured herself another glass of Barolo.

Nate set down his fork. "When's the last time you left the house, Ma?"

She scowled. "I don't know. And what difference does it make? I'm fine, and I don't need you to take care of me. Just handle the business, please."

Nate hung his head for a moment, then said, "Okay, Mom, okay." He took a large gulp of wine. "This really isn't going the way I wanted it to," he said, looking directly at her. "I have something important to talk to you about. And let me finish before you say anything, if you don't mind. I know how tough that will be for you."

Maddie felt a chilly draft sweep the back of her neck.

Nate drew in a deep breath. "You don't have to give me an answer right now. Just think about what I'm asking first." He moved to the chair beside her. "I feel bad that I didn't tell you this sooner, and for that I'm sorry." He pulled a black velvet box out of his pocket and popped it open. "I'm going to ask Sophie to marry me . . . and I don't want to hold the wedding here just because you can't leave the property."

Maddie felt the simultaneous shocks of joy and fear strike at her heart. Sitting up, she tried her best to remain calm while waves of panic crashed over her. Tears sprang to her eyes. "Oh, Natey, that's such great news." But at the same time she felt her world closing in on her, and it was a full minute before she was able to catch her breath.

"Ma? You're happy for me, right? And you'll come to the wedding, right?"

She choked back something that sounded halfway between a laugh and a sob. "Sweetheart, if a miracle happened and I could muster the courage to leave the property, which, by the way, I dream about, I would do it to make it to your wedding—"

"Oh, Mom." He smiled at her in relief. "I know that, I really do." He sat back in his chair for a moment, then gathered his strength to add, "And I've got one more request. At the wedding, well, I'd like you and Dad to sing together. For me and Sophie."

"Dear God, Nate!" Maddie stared at him, stunned. "Why ask me to do the one thing you know I can't? Anything else I could try to do, but not this!"

"I'm getting married!" Nate burst out, the son who had never raised his voice to her before. "I want you at my wedding, to be a real mom for a change and be there for me—hell, not just for me, but to join the rest of the living! In case you've forgotten, you're a legend. I am constantly reminded each and every day of my professional life that you and Dad influenced an entire generation! Your music is still played everywhere! Just last week I heard a new cover of 'Always in My Heart' by a young, hot band in a club in LA. Geez. Why can't you sing it at my wedding?"

"Nate—"

He shook his head. "No, Ma. I guess it's too much to expect that my mother, a member of the rarified rock and roll elite, would agree to do this for me, her only son. And what happens when Sophie and I have a kid someday? You'll only see your grandchild when we bring him or her to you? You won't leave New York to visit us in LA?"

"Cut it out, Nate. Now you're really playing dirty," she yelled right back, "invoking the one thing you know I want—another little you running around. That's just not fair."

"Wow, Mom. Wasn't it you who always told me that life's not fair and to get on with it anyway?"

"Well, you've got me there." Heart aching, Maddie assessed the look on Nate's face, a look she was all too familiar with. It was the same pleading stare Tom had always used whenever he wanted her to see things his way, back when they were just starting out, so very young and in love, when she still believed that anything was possible.

Nate took a deep breath. "Listen, Ma. I've done a lot of research and found a shrink who will come here and work with you on getting past your fear of leaving this beautiful prison you've built for yourself. If nothing else, let's just see if she's able to help you at all. You've got to try. Please," he begged. "Do it for me."

Maddie let out the deep breath she'd been holding in, knowing she was as good as sunk. "No promises, Nate. Let me think about meeting the doctor."

"What? Really?" He couldn't hide his shock.

She frowned at him. "But if you pressure me about singing with your dad, I won't meet the doctor at all. You'll have to have the wedding here if you want me to attend." She wondered if those words rang as hollow to Nate as they did to her.

"I suppose I'll have to accept that for now. At least I'll take it as a step forward." His cell phone rang, and Nate picked it up, looked at the number, and scowled. "I'm sorry, but I've got to take this. I'll go outside and let you do some thinking." Stepping onto the deck beyond the kitchen, he shut the glass slider behind him.

Maddie closed her eyes. *Nate married?* Was she relieved or frightened? It was what she'd always dreamed of, her son having a wife and children of his own, but now the thought made the panic rise in her throat. It was that old, dark cloud hovering over her, urging her to run, but once again she knew she'd only get as far as the property line.

Marriage.

And Tom.

Even now, when she brought back memories of Tom and all that had gone so horribly wrong, she'd be lying if she didn't admit that she had left a piece of herself behind with him in their loft in SoHo. And even though Maddie had made this new life years ago on the very tip of Long Island, she still had to be truthful and admit that there were times, on the coldest of winter nights, when she found herself remembering going out with Tom before Nate was born, bundled up, holding hands, picking up a copy of the Sunday *New York Times* and steaming hot bagels, heading home after a night in the studio. Recording their songs together used to leave them feeling wired and awake for hours, often until dawn the next day, making love over and over and then exchanging sections of the paper until they were tired enough for sleep. *A lifetime ago,* Maddie thought.

A little voice inside her head was screaming at her not to open that door again, not to agree to see Tom or to give in to Nate's plans of meeting this doctor, and especially not to perform live anywhere, not even at his wedding. But she would also be deceiving herself if she didn't admit that there was suddenly a small glimmer, the faintest murmur, and the nagging question of "what if?" inside her. What if she met with the doctor? What if she tried to heal herself of her fears so she could attend her only child's wedding?

She suddenly felt as if she was being backed into a corner. But if she didn't try to get out, she might lose Nate for good. She swallowed hard, recalling the desolation she'd seen in his eyes before he went outside. He hadn't said when he and Sophie planned on getting married. What if there was time enough for her to try? To do whatever it took in order to be there? It was bad enough she'd missed his Stanford graduation. She knew with sudden clarity that she'd never forgive herself if she missed his wedding. And neither would Nate.

But for tonight, it was all too much.

Maddie took her wine and went upstairs, knowing there was nothing left to say, leaving her son to clear the table and load the dishwasher alone.

Nate sat on a stool at the kitchen counter with a second empty bottle of wine while he considered going down to the cellar to retrieve another. But he knew he needed to keep his wits about him if he was going to have any shot at convincing his mother to sing with his father again. There were so many obstacles, not the least of which was her intense agoraphobia. He clearly remembered the last time she had actually left the beautiful beachfront property that was his childhood home. It was for his graduation from Montauk High School, and his father had made the trek to the east end of Long Island from Manhattan to attend with an entourage of hangers-on in tow.

To say that his very famous parents got along was like saying that oil and water mixed well: they would only be able to comingle for the briefest time before the heavy water, his dad, would start to sink, and the lighter oil, his mom, would float to the surface. Nate was that line in between, where the oil and water touched, but barely.

He wasn't the only one of his friends whose parents were divorced; he was just the only one who'd had his early life dragged through the tabloids because he, Nate Seymour, had been born into rock and roll royalty. Madeline Ellis and Tom Seymour were the voices of their generation, poets who wrote the most enchanting music together. Their early catalogue of songs still sold strongly a generation later; they were those rare musicians who had bridged the gap between mothers and daughters, fathers and sons.

The day Nate was born the world had stopped and paid attention. *People* magazine had published the first pictures of him at two days old, leaving Cornell Hospital in New York City, his dad buckling an infant seat into a black town car with darkened windows, his mom carrying him, just his little forehead visible beneath the blue knitted cap on his head and peeking out from the matching blanket he had been wrapped in. The way his mom told the story, they were followed by the paparazzi all the way home to their loft on Prince Street.

When the limo pulled up in front of the building, his father negotiated with the photographers to take one picture with the promise that after that they would go—but, of course, they never left. Nate always thought that this now famous lone photograph told a larger story, if one knew where to look. His mom and dad were clearly standing a little too far apart. For a successful duo supposedly happy being with one another, there was quite a physical distance between them. Nate was held close against his mother as Tom leaned away from them with his arms crossed over his chest. Neither of them smiled the way you would expect new parents to smile. Instead, you could tell they were only being polite for the photographers.

From his earliest memory, Nate could recall a similar army of paparazzi, each with a long lens and a flash, recording the most routine things . . . walks to the park, being pushed in a stroller, then toddling on his own tentative feet. His first days of nursery school, when the headmaster stepped out and shooed them away, only to find them back at dismissal.

But that was nothing compared to what happened when the Internet came along. It was then that the public's unquenchable thirst for gossip and scandal became a way of life. Apparently, or at least according to the Google search he'd done on his own history, every aspect of Nate's childhood and his parents' lives had been scrutinized. Everything right down to the part of their story that neither of his parents had ever talked to him about. On Nate's eighth birthday, a reporter for Page Six of the *NY Post* had caught Tom in a compromising position in a supply closet at the karate dojo where Nate's party was being held, and the picture had become a worldwide sensation.

Though only eight years old, Nate could clearly remember that there had been no coming back from that—his mom had packed up all of his things and a few of her own, hired a driver, pointed him eastward, and told him to stop only when they hit the Atlantic Ocean. They had left everything else behind: his dad, his childhood home, his dojo and friends. The only comfort for Nate at the time was that they'd left the annoying photographers and fans who'd dogged every step of his life until then behind as well.

His mother had bought an old, drafty Victorian house on the beach because, as she told him, she "needed a new project," something that only made sense to him years later when he, too, was an adult. It took a long time for Nate to distinguish between his mother's salty tears and the ocean's briny spray that battered the house during the endless storms that first winter. Even now, so many years later, a rainy day at the beach, one where the water churned and the sky was steely gray, brought Nate right back to his eight-year-old self, to the feelings of loss and despair, of guilt and remorse.

It was not as though his parents had ever brought him into their arguments, because they hadn't. It was, however, the feeling he had as a child, the one where if he hadn't asked for that party, if they hadn't celebrated it at the dojo, the photographer would have never snapped that picture and his family would have remained intact. A childhood fantasy, one that although he acknowledged as such, remained bittersweet.

Nate pushed himself back from the counter and cleaned up the remains of their dinner, all the while formulating in his head another way to help his mom overcome her fears and attend the wedding—and especially to sing for him and Sophie. His father had already agreed to it, and Nate had begun to hope that it might actually happen. While he often heard his mother singing when he came home for visits—usually while she sat composing at the piano—and her voice never failed to move him with its beauty, he had no memories of hearing his parents sing together. He'd only heard the old recordings of the time when they'd performed onstage with their band—something they hadn't done since he was a baby.

Nate shook his head, recalling how he'd first arrived at his freshman dorm in college to find nearly every girl on his floor putting a poster of his mom up on the wall of her room. It was the picture from the album cover she had recorded the year after they moved out of the city to Montauk. She had begun the arduous task of hiring contractors to fix up the house and had her concert grand piano delivered within days of their arrival. It was almost a race to see which would be finished first—the main part of the house or the album that seemed to pour out of her heart. She sat at that piano for hours on end, writing music with Nate playing quietly nearby. Even now he could clearly remember watching the mechanical workings of the giant instrument while lying on his back beneath it on the hard wood floor.

The photograph for that record cover had been taken at sunset, with Maddie, wrapped in the blanket that always rested at the foot of her bed, sitting on a dune staring out at the ocean. It was all pinks and purples and gold in tint, and Nate remembered the actual day of the photo shoot. It was late in August, and he was watching them work from the water on his boogie board. He'd befriended a bunch of surfers, and they'd adopted him as their summer mascot. They'd showed him how to navigate the dark ocean swells and had even taught him some basic surfing techniques.

He was watching his mom and the army of people it took to capture the perfect marketable image when he saw the surfers pull into the parking lot. Grabbing their boards, they headed down to the water only to stop short when they saw the commotion on the dune: the lights, the reflecting screens, and the tent that the hair and makeup people were scampering in and out of, touching up his mom's face after each series of shots. Nate could tell the moment the surfers recognized her. They started pointing excitedly, thumping each other on the back, and then began singing one of her songs, hoping to catch her attention. It was the first time Nate had ever seen her as someone else, someone other than his own mother.

When the surfers finally paddled past the cresting waves to the calm water where Nate floated on his board, one of them said, "Hey, kid. See that woman over there? You're probably too young to know this, but that's Madeline Ellis. She's like the greatest singer-songwriter of all time. I listen to her stuff every day. I can't believe she's right there on the beach!"

In that split second Nate almost blurted out that she was his mother, but he didn't. All at once he understood that if he told these guys who he was they would never treat him the same way again, and that would not be okay with him. He wanted to be ordinary, to fit in, to not be Madeline Ellis's and Tom Seymour's son. He might have only just turned nine, but deep down inside he knew better than to identify himself that way to his new friends.

At one point, his mother, who he knew had been watching him in the water, caught his eye. Without words passing between them he knew she recognized what he was doing and let him. The way she'd always had, he suddenly realized: shielding him from the pain and hurt of her life with his father, from the industry that had turned her into a superstar. And while he never had the inclination to create music himself, despite piano lessons, guitar lessons, and constant exposure to that world, he knew then that he would protect his mother and her career for the rest of his life. That was the strength of their bond.

Yet despite their closeness and his secret promise to look after her, Nate had been wise enough to know that he had to find his own way first, to break away from the impossibly long shadows cast by the fame of Madeline Ellis and Tom Seymour. So when it was time to choose a college, he picked the farthest location he could find. Being in California with his parents back in New York kept him sane. He loved them both, but by now, having tasted freedom, he could only take them and all the baggage that surrounded them in the smallest of doses. After graduation, he decided to stay out West, where, still feeling the pull of the promise he'd made as a boy and discovering that the music world had ensnared him after all, he set up shop as his mother's business manager—with her admittedly bemused but heartfelt blessing.

It was no surprise that he was good at what he did, and he gradually built his small startup company, Gramaphone, into a successful talent agency. He met Sophie when she was dressing the set of one of his client's movie projects, asked her out for a drink that turned into dinner. It was right then, between the appetizer and dessert, that he was thunderstruck by the undeniable attraction he felt toward her. He fell deeply in love, and quickly realized that he wanted to spend the rest of his life with her. Lucky for him, she had felt the same way.

Now, while he loaded the last of the silverware into the dishwasher and cleaned the crumbs off the table, Nate began to regret pushing his mother so soon after his arrival. On the long flight from LA he'd gone over his game plan repeatedly, knowing that he'd basically be requesting the impossible of her.

Over the past ten years all other attempts he had made to get his mom help for her panic disorder had failed, but Nate held out hope that the chance to attend his wedding, to sing for him and Sophie, would prompt her to finally see a therapist. Sophie was joining him here in just a few days, and he was planning to propose to her then. He could feel the pressure of the situation viscerally. His heart pounded in his chest; the blood rang in his ears with the knowledge that he had pushed his mom so hard and so fast.

Rinsing out the sponge, Nate wiped down the granite counters. Tired as he was from the day's travel and the wrenching encounter with his mother, he was too agitated to sleep. He drew in a deep breath, tied up the now full garbage bag, and took it through the mudroom and out to the shed for pick up the next morning. The cold, clean ocean air filled his lungs and helped to clear his brain. He would call Sophie, he decided, and worry about talking with Maddie tomorrow. Hearing Sophie's soft, reassuring voice would remind him that he was no longer the little boy whose parents couldn't stand to be in the same room together, and that when all was said and done, he had moved forward toward a future that was anything but empty.

II

Tom Seymour stood on the wide swath of concrete that served as the balcony of the Prince Street loft he still called home, coffee cup in hand, green eyes squinting against the sharp angle of the sun. It was just after dawn, his favorite time of day now, when the city was slowly waking from another night of endless partying and debauchery. Oh how well he remembered stumbling in at the crack of dawn himself, sky-high, feeling as though he was the king of the world.

He smiled somewhat sadly to himself. He sure could throw an epic party back then. The liquor was always top shelf, the drugs a reflection of whatever year it was. Quaaludes, cocaine, special K . . . he had tried them all, using them as long as they kept everything fuzzy and soft, time and responsibility suspended. *Yeah*, he thought, shaking his head. *The good old days.*

He lifted the mug to his lips and realized it was empty. Coffee was his biggest vice nowadays. *You're such a joke, Seymour*, he thought as he went back inside for a refill.

He had refurnished the place after Maddie fled with Nate, taking nearly everything with her but the bed they shared. But what had seemed so urban and hip to his younger self now felt cold and sterile. The angular, modern furniture, the abstract art, the stark grays and blacks the decorator had convinced him was a more masculine approach to the space no longer offered comfort. Sure, it was sleek, rockstar cool, but that just didn't define him in sobriety.

Tom looked down at the mug in his hand. It was faded from being run through the dishwasher at least a hundred times, but a bunch of pale pink flowers were still visible in an interlocking pattern across the front. It was one of the only things besides the bed that Maddie had left behind, and he cherished the thought that she had held it in her hands so long ago. As he rubbed the pad of his thumb along the well-worn ceramic pattern, a memory of her standing at the breakfast bar flashed through his mind. She was feeding Nate as he sat in his high chair, softly humming one of their songs to their son's delight, breaking into a wide smile when Nate would try to sing along with her. Tom closed his eyes to hold on to that image a moment longer before feeling it dissipate into the bright morning air, wishing he hadn't been such a fool, hadn't forced her to run.

In the fourteen years between the time Maddie had left him and Nate's graduation from Stanford, Tom had lived almost perpetually high, finally spiraling down into a rabbit hole of empty self-loathing. He had done all he could to erase any feeling, especially when it came to his ex-wife, sleeping with countless women, trying any substance he could find to numb the pain. From the moment they had met, he had been in awe of her, dazzled by her beauty and her talent, but in a drug-addled moment of poor decision-making at Nate's eighth birthday party, he had driven her away.

Years of therapy had finally made Tom understand that it wasn't this one transgression that had caused Maddie to leave, but a series of events over their lifetime together that had forced her to take Nate and flee. There had been brief periods of time when he was able to lay off the drugs and booze and thought he could make it work between them, when he believed he had the strength and discipline to take his ego out of the equation and allow her bigger talent to rightfully shine.

When they had started out together all those years ago, Tom had immediately recognized just how special Maddie was, how unique her music, and how much better he was with her around. Maddie had this ability to elevate him to a place where he still had faith that anything was possible, and in her absence, he had sunk to some dark places even he had never fully imagined could exist. He had finally, after drying out once and for all, and after all those years of expensive therapy, come to terms with the truth about himself: he was a fuck-up of monumental proportions.

As difficult as it still was sometimes, Tom had made the choice of sobriety in order to bring him one step closer to repairing the damage he'd done to those he loved the most. He had finally accomplished the first step of his plan: he and Nate had a relationship again, and while difficult, Tom had accepted that he had to move at Nate's pace, not his own. It hadn't been easy to rebuild that trust, but he had committed himself to the task, starting with small steps, flying out to California just to meet with Nate for little bits of time. He could recall that first conversation after he'd come through rehab, a full year after he'd made a fool of himself at a party at Nate's fraternity house.

"Why should I believe you this time, Dad?" Nate had asked sullenly. "You've let me down so many times before. You turned my graduation into a shit show. What's different now?"

It was an honest question, and Tom had winced at Nate's justification in asking it. His days of supreme overindulgence had culminated in a disastrous weekend at Stanford, starting at Nate's fraternity house, where a graduation party was already in full swing when Tom arrived fresh off the plane from New York. He'd spent some time talking with his son, but somehow had lost track of him, and after that, things had gotten hazy. He remembered drinking with abandon and doing line after line of coke with some of the frat boys, then fondling the naked breasts of a young woman who offered herself up to him because, as she told him, he was her mother's favorite artist. After a short while he forgot about Nate altogether and just let himself go wild.

At one point, someone handed him a guitar, and he ended up giving an impromptu concert. Problem was, no one wanted to hear the music he'd recorded after the band broke up. "Always in My Heart," they'd chanted, requesting one of his and Maddie's biggest hits. Enraged that even these young kids wanted to hear the old stuff, to hear only Maddie's songs, he'd smashed the guitar to pieces, and in the hushed silence that followed, he'd looked up to see Nate storm out of the room.

Hours later, Tom woke up in his hotel room, bleary-eyed and barely conscious, to find a nameless girl in his bed, her naked body sprawled childlike beside him. In the early light, she didn't look familiar, but even as strung out and powerfully hungover as he was, he knew he had brought her with him from campus. Dimly he recalled his offer of coke, her girlish giggles, his brief questioning if she was even of legal age—and the night of anonymous sex that had followed. But the most appalling memory, the one that had doubled him over with nausea right there in the bed, was the sight of Nate's disgusted face as he watched his father stagger out of the frat house with the girl pinned to his side.

He had flown directly from LAX to the Betty Ford Clinic and gotten clean, not just for himself, but also for Nate. Now, six years sober, he believed he finally had a handle on living authentically.

"I want you back in my life, Nate," Tom had told his son, his voice choked with emotion, the next time he arrived in LA. By then Nate was enrolled in graduate school to earn his MBA, and Tom had surprised him at the house he was sharing with some classmates. "I wasn't ready to live sober before, but now I'm fully committed to it—to you. I don't expect you to trust me, and I know I've got to prove myself to you. But give me a chance. Please. Because I'm gonna stop at nothing to make you believe in me."

Tom had been standing in the doorway as he said this, hand in his pocket fingering his ninety-day sobriety chip anxiously, waiting to see if Nate would recognize this clear-eyed and well-groomed honest version of himself, the person his son had never known.

To Nate's credit, he had listened, had taken the time to reflect, and finally came to understand that Tom was serious. They began to speak on the phone every now and then, and soon Nate was the one who initiated the calls. They met for lunch or dinner whenever Nate was on the East Coast, speaking tentatively at first, then with a growing sense of confidence. Meals turned into overnight stays; tension-fraught encounters turned to warmth and companionship.

They spoke all the time now and got together fairly regularly, either in New York or at Nate's place in Los Angeles, often with Sophie in tow. Buoyed by hope and the budding strength of his new relationship with his son, Tom knew it was finally time to make amends to the one person he had hurt the most: Maddie.

Sighing, Tom refilled his mug from the steaming French press, set it on the counter, and reached into his back pocket for his wallet. Every now and then he felt compelled to check the old newspaper clipping he'd carried around for years like a talisman. It was the *Rolling Stone* review of the opening show of their last ever concert tour, the one when Nate was just a baby:

"Madeline Ellis and Tom Seymour have hit the road, proving once again that Mr. Seymour is the most highly paid back-up singer in the music industry today. Ms. Ellis's talent so fully eclipses her partner's that he really doesn't need to show up at all. No matter: he seems to phone in his performance anyway . . ."

Tom had been so angry when the review originally appeared that he had cut it out to send to their publicist, hell-bent on firing the woman for allowing the piece to be printed in the first place. But instead he'd hung on to the clipping, using it as an excuse to stay angry so he could justify needing another fix, another drink. When he finally woke up in that California hotel room after the party at Nate's frat house, the nameless girl lying naked across his bed, he knew he had to face the truth. He was an addict, and he was living in his own personal circle of hell.

It was only after rehab that Tom was able to read the review differently and accept that the journalist had been right. He had been in such denial, thinking he was fooling everyone into believing he could handle the excesses he'd come to enjoy and that his talent, his songwriting were just as good as—maybe even better than—Maddie's. Now he kept that frayed, yellow paper in his wallet to ensure that he never forgot his unsavory past, to stay humble, and to keep his eye on the prize he was only now daring to hope he deserved: reclaiming the only woman he had ever loved.

As he ran his hand through his graying, shoulder-length hair, he thought about Nate's arrival at Maddie's yesterday and wondered if she had considered their son's request. When Nate had called him a few days ago and asked him to sing at his wedding to Sophie, Tom's heart had swelled with pride. It was the affirmation he had sought to know that Nate had fully put the pain of their past behind him, and Tom had jumped at the chance to honor Nate's request.

Nate had added that he was on his way out to Montauk to ask the same of his mother. Now Tom could only pray that Maddie was onboard as well.

Surely she'd agree? He himself had finally begun to write music again. It had taken years of being clean to feel confident enough to pick up his guitar, but he'd done it, and recently his agent, Bill Struthers, had gotten him a contract with a small new independent label. For the first time in longer than he could remember, Tom was excited about the future. He had poured his apology to Maddie out in song, and he wanted a chance to share that with her before it was released into the world.

The sun was beginning its ascent over the treetops of SoHo now. Tom drew in a deep breath of the early morning air. Sitting down on the low gray leather armchair facing the balcony, he closed his eyes to meditate, willing himself to relax, to put the thoughts of Nate's meeting with Maddie aside, to allow himself these moments of peace and reflection in the hope they would help him achieve some sense of calm.

Breathe in, breathe out, his internal monologue chanted repeatedly. But instead of quiet serenity, all he saw were pictures in his head of the past, of him and Maddie playing their music together, naive and enthusiastic, ready to conquer the world. Images of her, beautiful and naked in his bed, a tangle of arms and legs, intruded. He was the one who had ruined everything, having been too young, stupid, and arrogant to own up to it back then.

The intrusive thought told him there'd be no peace through meditation for him today. In addition he suddenly found himself thinking of the disturbing phone call that had come out of the blue from Emilia Parkson, his and Maddie's former backup singer, two weeks before, begging him to let her sing on his new album when he recorded it. He could easily replay their conversation in his head:

"Heard something from Bill about a new record deal, Tom. Can I come to the studio and sing backup for you? C'mon, baby. I'll stay clean, I promise," she had purred into the phone, sounding anything but. "We had such fun all those years ago. Let's make some more history . . ."

It was exactly that—their shared history—that Tom had worked so hard to put behind him. He hadn't seen Emilia since he'd been sober, but from the sound of it, nothing had changed for her. She'd surfaced periodically over the years with a phone call or text, looking to see if he would float her a loan or call a supplier to get her some drug or another.

And now? If his own experience had taught him anything, it was never to believe an addict. So even if she was still one of the best backup singers around, he knew he would never say yes. He couldn't put his own sobriety at risk again, and most importantly, he had no wish to see her, to be reminded of what she—what both of them—had done to tear him and Maddie apart.

"Emilia, how about I fly you out to Betty Ford first? On me. Please let me help you get well. Then I'll get you some gigs. I've met a lot of young musicians who'd kill to have your voice on their recordings."

"Sheesh, Tom," she'd slurred. "I have it all under control. And when did you get so old? You sound like my dad! Besides, what's wrong with a little fun now and then? You know me. I just like to blow off steam. I won't do anything to embarrass you, Tom. I'll stay straight through the sessions, promise."

He took a deep breath. "Em, no. I'm sorry, I can't—"

But she didn't let him continue. "Forget it. Just forget I called." Her voice was icy now, cut through with a thread of despair. "Damn it, I really thought I could count on you, of all people. *You know me.* I just need the money . . ."

"Emilia," Tom implored, "let me help you. I know how hard giving up the life is. I've been there myself—"

Again she'd cut him off. "Forget it, Tom. So sorry I even asked." And the line went dead.

Tom shook his head as the memory pierced his heart with true sadness. Wanting to help Emilia, he'd called her multiple times since then, but she'd never picked up.

Just remembering her desperate voice and the memory of what had happened between them so long ago made him feel as if the walls were closing in on him. Glancing at the clock on his phone, he had to restrain himself from calling Nate, to find out what had happened at Maddie's house last night. It was times like these, when meditation didn't bring him the calm he needed, that Tom badly craved a drink. Of course he had no alcohol in the house. Nor was he about to go out to find any. But he had to get away before the sweet siren of temptation began to swirl in his head.

Sighing, he pulled on a pair of jeans and a clean shirt and the Stanford baseball cap that he always wore to shade his face from anyone who might recognize him on the street. His home group twelve step meeting started in an hour, and he would make a point to take a brisk walk before he went. Maybe exercise could do what meditation could not: ease the ache of loneliness and the desire to self-medicate, to stop the pain, if only for a short time. Although he was pretty confident that he would not succumb, he wasn't taking any chances. Picking up his keys, he made his way out onto Prince Street and headed toward Grand Avenue.

Over the years Tom had found comfort inside the weather-worn stone church where the meetings were held, knowing that he sat in a place of no judgment. How could anyone judge anyone else here when all of them had their own personal versions of his story? Broken families, shattered marriages, failed careers, violence, and pain, with all of them working hard to stay clearheaded, to maintain their sobriety. Tom never stepped through the door without thanking that nameless young girl he'd woken up next to in that California hotel room, who unknowingly had pushed him toward redemption. Meanwhile he could only hope that she'd found her own way and was clean and in control of her life as well.

He entered the brightly lit room in the basement of the church to find that he was the first one there. The chairs were set up in their customary rows and the pitted, hissing percolator was brewing on the counter near the sink. Tom poured himself some coffee, the thin paper cup burning his fingers, and prowled the room as he sipped, looking at the religious artifacts on the walls without really seeing them.

He was about to take his customary aisle seat toward the back when his phone buzzed inside his pants pocket. It was his manager.

"Tom." Bill's voice was gruff. "Where are you right now?"

"In the East Village. Why?"

"Can you get uptown? I've got something to discuss with you, and I don't want to do it over the phone."

"Sure, Bill, I'll grab a cab. Is everything okay?"

"Just get here as soon as you can," was all Bill said before the line went dead.

Tom put down the coffee cup, said a quick good-bye to the arriving members he passed on the stairs. His anxiety mounted as the cab made its way uptown through heavy traffic. He tried to quash the uneasy feeling, but his heart was pounding by the time he hurried into the marble and glass lobby of the ultramodern skyscraper on Fifty-Second Street where his manager's office sprawled across the sixty-sixth floor. Once he exited the elevator, the receptionist quickly whisked him into the inner sanctum of Bill's office.

"Thanks, Jillian, and hold my calls please," Bill said, turning his attention to Tom. "You'd better sit down for this."

Tom's mind raced. He couldn't imagine what this was about, but he prayed like hell the small indie record label wasn't backing out on his new album. "What's the emergency?" he asked.

Even after decades in New York, Bill Struthers had never lost his Midwestern twang, and it was clearly in evidence now as he leaned against his desk and quirked a bushy eyebrow at Tom. He sighed heavily. "I don't have any other way to do this but tell you straight out. Emilia Parkson's dead. Apparent suicide."

Tom felt as if all the air had been sucked from the room. "What? That's not possible! I just spoke to her a couple of weeks ago! How?"

"Her roommate found her in the bathtub, unresponsive. The police are still there now. They found a crack pipe and a lot of drugs on the scene. Knowing Emilia, I'm willing to bet the test results will show lethal doses of meth in her system."

"Meth," Tom repeated, as though saying the word out loud would make it more understandable. Thank God he had given up all illegal substances before methamphetamine became the rage! He tried to swallow his rising nausea. "Fucking unbelievable," he said, his voice shaking.

"There's something else," Bill said quietly.

Tom looked up at him. Bill seemed to have aged ten years overnight. His craggy face and balding head were shiny with sweat, which he wiped away with a monogrammed handkerchief. "What? What more can there be?"

"A couple of weeks ago, Emilia stopped by looking for some session work. I stupidly told her about your new album, and she wanted in. I couldn't help her, Tom. Everyone in the business knows she's unreliable.

Christ, she was high all the time! And I owed it to you not to let her back in, not after what happened—"

"Please," Tom implored. "Don't even go there."

Bill wiped his brow once more. "I know, I know. Sorry. The thing is, she left a letter for Maddie with me. Told me she wanted you to be the one to give it to her in case she didn't return to pick it up herself."

Which she wouldn't be doing now that she was dead. A suicide . . . Tom groaned and dropped his head into his hands.

"I know this is a huge shock. Can I get you something? Water? Coffee?"

"No, Bill. I just need a minute. It's . . . unbelievable." Tom wiped his eyes with the back of his hand.

"I know. She just chose wrong, time and again." Bill stopped suddenly, and his eyes widened. "You said you just spoke to her? Did you have any idea—?"

"Oh my God," Tom breathed. "She must have called me after you turned her down. This—this is my fault!"

"Tom—"

"Give me a minute, Bill. Please."

Tom sat for a long while with his head in his hands trying to process the devastating news. Finally he was able to look up at Bill without weeping.

"This is not your fault, man," Bill said emphatically. "She needed help and refused to get it. Don't blame yourself."

"Easier said than done." Tom felt tears filling his eyes again.

Bill was silent for a moment, then picked up an envelope from his desk. "Can you get this to Maddie? Is that even possible? I know you two don't speak anymore."

"I'm going to make it my business to get it to her. That's the least I can do for Emilia."

"Okay, man. Please keep me in the loop."

Tom stood as Bill walked around to the front of his desk. The two men embraced.

"Take care, Tom. And if you do see Maddie, please give her my best. I may not be her manager anymore, but I still think about her all the time."

Tom smiled weakly. "So do I, Bill. So do I."

The moment Tom got home he went to his closet and threw some clothes and his running shoes into a bag as well as his toiletry kit and an extra sweatshirt. Along with meditation, exercise was his drug of choice these days. Keeping fit and strong was just another way of being in control of his life. He was in better shape today than he was when he first met Maddie all those years ago, and he was proud of himself for that. He could still turn women's heads now that he had his old spark back, his legendary charm refreshed and intact. He wouldn't dream of going anywhere without his running shoes—even on a mission as admittedly painful as this one was going to be.

When he was done packing, Tom stepped out onto the balcony, his thoughts on Emilia, his heart heavy. Above him the sky roiled with dark clouds. The wind had picked up, bending the bare limbs of the trees close to the ground, pushing the newly minted spring weather out of the way. He knew it would be colder in Montauk than here in the city. Anxiety rose in his chest, a persistent companion whenever he thought of his ex-wife. It scared him to think that Maddie could well refuse to appear with him at Nate's wedding, and the thought of the letter he'd tucked so carefully into his bag only made him feel worse.

Emilia. Oh God. Unable to help himself, he unzipped his leather messenger bag and pulled out the envelope Bill had given him. Emilia had simply written *Maddie* on it. Had she already known what she was going to do when she addressed the envelope, sealed it, and gave it to Bill? Could anyone have stopped her from doing what she'd done? Or had the overdose been accidental? She'd already sounded so out of it on the phone that surely his refusal to work with her hadn't made a difference?

Tom savagely shoved the envelope back in the bag. Whatever Emilia had intended, whatever she had written in that letter, she had unwittingly—or perhaps deliberately—forced his hand. For years he had wanted to see Maddie . . . to confess . . . to promise. But he had lacked the courage, aware from the few things Nate told him that Maddie was still unwilling to meet with him or listen to what he had to say.

Life, Tom had realized over the lonely years of his sobriety, was too short to live without love. But this was not something Maddie would want to hear, least of all from him. Still, this letter had given him the chance to at least lay eyes on her, the woman he had once loved, whom he loved still, but at what price? Would she have been informed of Emilia's death before he arrived or would he have to be the one to tell her? Would she hold him responsible?

"Help me, God," he whispered and was astonished at the words, the pain in his heart when he uttered them. He drew in a deep breath. Focus, he told himself sternly. For now, his goal was to get down to Penn Station to catch a train for Montauk. He'd call Nate on the way. As always, Tom knew he was cutting it close.

III

When Maddie opened her eyes the next morning, the first thing she saw was the empty wine glass on her night table. That would account for the headache now pounding at the base of her skull. She'd clearly had too much to drink, and that, combined with Nate's request to sing at his wedding, made her temples throb. The whole thing was ridiculous. She was not going to sing with anyone, especially not her ex-husband Tom Seymour. That ship had sailed long ago.

Cursing beneath her breath, she stumbled into the bathroom to rummage around for some Advil. It was crazy of Nate to expect her to get along with his father for any length of time. And it was simply impossible for Maddie to leave the comfort and safety of her house anytime soon. For Nate to put this on her now in an effort to have her sing at his wedding and make her believe that she'd never see her future grandchildren if she didn't get help, well, that was just plain cruel.

She struggled with the childproof top on the medicine bottle before finally wrenching it open and shaking out two capsules. Ducking her head under the running faucet, she swallowed them down with a big mouthful of water. Straightening, she realized she was trembling. What a way to start her day. She splashed more cold water on her face and ran the brush through her sleep-riddled hair, trying her best not to look too frightening for Nate. Drawing in a few deep breaths, she willed herself to be calm.

Once downstairs, she immediately realized that she hadn't needed to make any effort at all. Nate looked worse than she did.

"Hey," he groaned when she entered the kitchen. "I made coffee." His mug was sitting in front of him untouched. There was another bottle of Advil on the counter.

"I assume you have a headache too?" she croaked back.

"Brutal," was all he could muster.

"Advil and black coffee. Your dad used to call that the breakfast of champions."

He smiled thinly, and she smiled back, resisting the urge to tousle his hair.

They spent a few minutes suffering in companionable silence while she poured herself coffee and got busy making his childhood favorite, cinnamon toast. The familiar task helped to collect her thoughts, and she said, "Come sit outside with me. The ocean air always helps." She walked tentatively onto the deck beyond the kitchen sliders, then quickly lowered herself onto a chair that leaned against the outer wall of the house, afraid to go any farther.

Nate sat in the oversized wicker lounge chair facing the ocean. It was a cloudy morning, with a hint of chill in the air. Maddie watched as he tackled the toast, then licked the remaining sugar off his thumb. Taking a deep breath, he finally spoke. "I hit you with everything at once last night, Ma. I'm sorry. But at least all my cards are on the table now. Have you thought about singing with Dad?"

So he'd come out with guns blazing. Just like his father. Maddie took a deep breath of her own so she could answer calmly. "No, Nate. Just laying eyes on him again would be tough. Getting up in front of an audience—even if it's just your wedding guests—would be impossible. There's so much history surrounding our performances that I don't want to revisit, so much hurt. I don't need to go back down that road. Frankly, I'm not sure why he would either." Maddie paused, trying unsuccessfully to stave off her sudden curiosity. "What has he told you?"

"Not much," Nate replied, his gaze on the ocean. "It took us so long to repair our relationship, I think he'll do almost anything to keep the peace with me." Maddie winced at the pain in his voice. "I don't dwell on that anymore. I'm just glad that when his name comes up on my caller ID, he's sober." He turned and looked at her hopefully. "And this would be great for you too, Mom. Meeting Sophie's family, my friends, singing with Dad. It might just get you out into the real world again."

Maddie's headache was back, and she said more sharply than she intended, "First of all, you make it sound like I live in some alternate universe. I'm not a hermit out here, you know. I watch the news, I read the paper, and my friends come by for visits. I have a computer and shop online. You know that Gino delivers, so what more do I need?"

Nate stared down at his hands. "A life, Mom, a real life."

Angry tears pricked her eyes. "Ouch, Nate."

"The career you had—the one you could still have—is out there waiting."

He sounded so defeated but also, Maddie thought, resentful too. She couldn't bear the realization of what a burden she must be for him at times. Defensive anger rose to mask her despair. "So you want me to rejoin the rat race like you? Can't I just enjoy the life I've created here on my own terms? And since when did you become my judge and jury anyway?" She took a big swallow of her rapidly cooling coffee, trying to control her anger and the feeling that she'd been backed into a corner. "Did I mention that my last two albums went double platinum? I do have a career, you know. I sit behind that piano for who knows how many hours a day creating music." *Shut up, Maddie,* she warned herself. *You sound like a pouting toddler.*

"Mom, please." Nate sat forward in his chair. "Of course I know how well those albums sold. I like to think I had a big part in their success. I'm not questioning the depth of your talent, your commitment, your intelligence, or your lifestyle. I get it. You like it this way. But I really believe you're missing out on an incredible opportunity to reconnect with the world."

"Always the salesman, huh, Nate?" This time she smiled at him, seeing not only the man before her, but the boy he once was, putting on his best pleading look, regarding her with those big puppy dog eyes, trying once again to convince her why he really, really had to have that ever-elusive white Power Ranger action figure. She could feel her panic ebbing at the memory, and it gave her the strength to adopt a bantering tone.

"Reconnect with the world? Or help out your dad? That's the missing piece to this puzzle, Nate. He's got an agenda here. We just don't know what it is yet, right?"

"I have no idea." To her surprise, Nate sounded sullen. She seemed to have touched a nerve. When he looked at her again she was dismayed to see tears glistening in his eyes. "And what about me? You realize I've never seen my parents onstage together? Ever? Just some old documentaries on TV, where you and Dad create a frenzy with your music. Seems like half the world saw you perform as a duo, but not your own son. So is it too much to ask that you sing at my wedding?"

Maddie felt his words like physical blows. How could she possibly argue with that? "I need more coffee," she said weakly.

Tottering back into the kitchen to refill her mug, she tried to give herself a moment to reclaim her center. To stop her shaking. To stop the returning panic. The mounting anger.

Through the glass door she saw Nate walking down to the water. Relieved, she brought her mug outside and settled back in her chair. The ocean, she saw, was surprisingly choppy; a mirror of her internal struggle. Closing her eyes, she tipped back her head, trying to concentrate on the shifting sun on her face as it appeared from behind a cloud. A momentary distraction, that's all she needed. She took a few deep, calming breaths and realized she could actually smell the struggle of emerging spring, with its light scent of loamy soil mixed with the warming sand, a reawakening. The hoped-for feeling of calm began to wash over her.

There was nothing wrong with this safe haven she'd created—was there? If Nate hadn't come to her with all of this, she probably would never have thought of leaving the house on her own. But she knew suddenly that she didn't have a choice—and the realization was scary beyond belief.

She clearly remembered the first time she'd panicked upon leaving the house years ago. She and Nate had driven to Bed, Bath and Beyond to buy supplies for his freshman dorm room. They'd been wandering the aisles, checking things off the list he'd brought along, chatting easily when suddenly, from out of nowhere, she was hit with enormous waves of panic, so bad that she couldn't breathe. She'd been convinced she was suffocating, that she couldn't get enough air into her lungs. Her heartbeat accelerated until she heard the sound of her own blood pounding in her ears. Crushing pain had slammed her chest, and she'd clutched Nate's arm, choking out that she was having a heart attack.

Nate threw her in the car and sped directly to the emergency room at Southampton Hospital. She'd spent hours there while doctors ran test after test, all of them negative. Finally a young resident from the Department of Psychiatry wrote her a prescription for some sort of antianxiety drug as well as an antidepressant, offering all sorts of calming words about "just taking the edge off," but Maddie was having none of that. After all the years of being surrounded by a cornucopia of mind-bending substances while touring with the band and seeing what it did to others, she knew she'd never take anything stronger than an Advil. Deep down, she knew that she'd be okay if she could just go home.

And she was right. When a distraught Nate brought Maddie back to their house that day, insisting that he would postpone leaving for Stanford, she wouldn't hear of it. Surrounded by her familiar things within the walls of her own home, she was able to convince him that she was fine. Then she made him go, to fly across the country and begin a new life all his own.

She had been able to get out for a while after that fateful day, running her usual errands in her safe small circuit around town. At first she did her own shopping at the grocery store because Julia, the store's owner, would sit with her for a bit if she began to feel anxious. It was the same at the dry cleaners, the post office, and at Gino's. She knew everyone, and they knew her, all of them only wanting Maddie to be okay now that Nate was on the other side of the country.

But gradually things got worse. She began to feel panicky while driving the car and couldn't step out of it once she parked, becoming so short of breath that she feared she might pass out. By the time Nate returned home the following summer, she could barely bring herself to drive anywhere with him, but she kept up a good front by making light of her growing problem, telling him that she wasn't up to facing the summertime crowds, that she preferred the quiet of home. She suspected he really didn't believe her when she said she was fine, but she sent him back to school once again when Labor Day rolled around.

By Christmas of his sophomore year, they both knew she had issues that neither one of them could control, but Maddie didn't want Nate to feel responsible for her. She pointed out to him that she'd gotten really good at shopping online, had arranged for all of her food to be delivered, and that her closest friends had made it their business to visit with her at home. While it wasn't ideal, it had become a way of life, and Maddie insisted that she had adjusted.

Nate pleaded with her to see a therapist, but to no avail. Maddie no longer had the courage to fight her demons. She felt rudderless, afraid when she stepped outside her home and safe and protected within it, even happy most of the time. Why should she change that? Granted, not making it to Nate's graduation was painful, but the thought of leaving the house to fly cross-country had left her breathless with terror. Nate had said he understood, and maybe he had, because after that, throughout all the years Nate remained at Stanford for his undergraduate degree and his MBA, they just stopped talking about it.

At least until today.

Before Nate's arrival yesterday, her front door hadn't been opened in months, and she had thought her problem would just remain the unnamed elephant in the room, the way it always did whenever he came home to see her. Now, with all this talk about seeing a therapist and showing up at his wedding, Maddie knew things had changed, that Nate was determined to see her finally well again. How could she bear to disappoint him?

Feeling overwhelmed, Maddie blinked away the tears. She watched Nate step up onto the deck and lifted herself slowly out of her chair. "Can you bring in the dishes? I'm going to try to do some work."

"Sure, Ma." He sounded as tired, as spent, as she did. Though they hadn't exactly argued, their exchange, and all that lay beneath it, had been exhausting in intensity.

Maddie walked through the kitchen and down the hallway to push open the double doors, revealing the large, high-ceilinged music room dominated by the concert grand piano. In one corner sat a high-backed couch covered in a beautiful tapestry of jewel-toned fabrics, woven together in a way that made them look uniquely seamless. A pair of hunter-green leather wingback chairs completed the arrangement. Beyond the chairs was a large bay window with a seat covered in coordinating fabric to complement the couch, framed by butter-colored drapery tied back with a gold sash that pooled on the floor. The entire back wall was made up of floor-to-ceiling windows looking out at the churning sea.

It was a feminine space and spoke to exactly who Maddie was, both elegant and artistic. She sat down on her piano bench. Work was always her salvation, and she was glad now that she had her notebook waiting for her, that she had the desperately needed distraction of seeing if what she had written before Nate showed up was any good. She briefly looked over the music she had composed before she began to play, even though she didn't have to. She would always remember this composition without prompting, just as she knew instinctively that she had written something worthwhile. She could always tell when she had a special piece by the way she felt when she played it—and this one qualified.

The turmoil within her began to fade as her hands moved in rhythmic perfection, without effort; the sound was clear and infectious. For Maddie, the melody came first, the lyrics second. She was already formulating the ideas for what she wanted to express when Nate appeared beside her. She stopped playing and looked up at him.

He gestured to the piano. "That's beautiful. Is that what you've been working on?"

She could feel the tension seeping out of her. Neutral ground at last. "Yup," she said lightly. "I've finished the melody, now I've got to hone in on the words. Not like that's ever the easy part."

"Something tells me you've already got a plan worked out."

"Maybe a partial plan," she teased.

He was silent for a moment, clearly grappling with his own emotions. "So . . . are we okay here?" he asked at last.

For now, she thought. "We are, Nate. I'm happy for you and Sophie, sweetheart, I really am."

He smiled, clearly relieved. "Thanks, Ma. We can talk about the wedding details some other time."

When she smiled back, similarly relieved, he clapped his hands together briskly. "Okay, I'll leave you to it. I'm going into town for a bit, but I'll be back for dinner. In fact, I'll pick something up at the grocery store and cook for you tonight."

"To what do I owe this honor?"

"Let's just say it's in both our best interests if you keep working. I'll make something simple. I cook for Sophie all the time. She survives it. You can too."

"Okay, I'll risk it," she kidded, trying to further lighten the mood. "I have an account at the store, just charge it to me."

Nate gave her an odd look, and Maddie realized she had offended him when he said, "I can afford to buy groceries for dinner on the salary you pay me, Ma." And with that he turned and went out the door.

Maddie closed her eyes and listened to his car crunch away down the drive. Despite her and Nate's efforts to hide their feelings, she knew he was still shaken by their exchange out on the deck, as she was, and she could still feel herself reeling at the enormity of what Nate had asked of her. She ran her fingers over the keys, but found no solace there. The thought of Nate's marriage, her need to leave the house and "rejoin the real world," as Nate had termed it, terrified her—as did the unsettling realization that if she attended Nate's wedding, she would have to face Tom.

Again she tried to focus on the music, but her memories made it impossible to concentrate, so for the first time in many years, she began to play some of her older songs, the ones she had recorded with Tom. Her heart ached as the notes of the past surrounded her, bringing her back to a time that she could never really forget, no matter how hard she tried.

Part Two

IV

In the autumn of 1981, MTV had just been born, and most of the people Tom Seymour knew were still reeling from the violent death of John Lennon the year before. Music, ever evolving, had recently emerged from a decade of punk rock, bringing with it the nostalgic trend toward a quieter, softer sound. Word all around the freshman dorms at NYU was that Simon and Garfunkel were reuniting for a free concert in Central Park. Everyone was cutting classes to stake out a spot to hear the two legends sing together once more.

Although he hadn't met many fellow students yet, Tom knew he wanted to go, so he convinced his roommate, Gavin, a studious anthropology major from Ohio, to come with him. Normally Gavin wouldn't dream of cutting classes, but the way Tom had sold him on the idea meant Gavin had no shot of turning his charismatic roommate down. Tom Seymour was foremost a natural salesman, very used to getting people to see things his way. It was another component of his very big personality. With his dark good looks, deep green eyes, and athletic build, Tom exuded the kind of cool confidence that others wished they had, and Gavin was no exception. Hanging out with Tom opened doors to the social circles that almost every freshman on campus wanted to join.

At present they were walking toward the Christopher Street subway station, joining the raucous party heading uptown to the park. Even though it was only noon, the trains were packed with students. Stepping onboard, Tom immediately spotted a girl standing across from the doorway wearing a faded Paul Simon T-shirt tucked neatly into slim, worn jeans. She seemed so animated, her pretty face glowing with excitement, and the way she twirled her long, curly blond hair around one finger repeatedly was a major turn-on for him. Tom couldn't take his eyes off her.

He felt Gavin nudge him in the ribs. "Quit staring."

"Why? She's gorgeous."

Gavin shrugged. "Not my type."

But Tom felt inexplicably drawn to the curly-haired girl. And he knew he had to find a way to meet her even though the subway car was too packed for him to move. There was nothing to do but hang on and hope to catch her when she exited the train.

Just a few minutes later it screeched to a halt at the station and disgorged its passengers onto the platform.

As they climbed the steps up to the street and headed toward the Great Lawn, Tom tried to keep her in sight. He couldn't believe how many people were there. The crowd seemed to cover every blade of grass on the expansive meadow. The sky looked threatening, as if it would open up with sheets of rain at any moment and soak them all, but the air was crisp and cool. He and Gavin weaved in and out of the crowd as Tom kept the curly-haired girl in sight, and when she finally stopped to sit down, he stepped up next to her. When she suddenly turned to speak, he was caught off guard.

"Are you following me?" she asked warily, yet with the hint of a friendly smile.

"Um, uh, maybe, I guess." He didn't know what to say when the mere sound of her voice made all the nerves in his body tingle. "I saw you on the train and, well . . . are you a big Simon and Garfunkel fan?" *C'mon, Seymour. Is that all you've got?*

"Yeah, I am," she said, sizing him up with big hazel eyes. "I guess you are too." She motioned toward the crowd. "But then again, who isn't?" She smiled broadly, and Tom felt weak. "They're the perfect blend of music and poetry, don't you think?" she added.

"They're the first music I remember hearing at home. My mom played their records over and over after my dad left," Tom answered, hoping to find a way to ground himself in her presence.

"Oh, I'm sorry. Your parents are divorced?"

She had such an easy way about her. She disarmed him with her up-front manner and he couldn't help but respond honestly. "Since I was five. No big deal. I've had time to adjust."

"Still, that must have been rough, not having your dad around," she said, pulling a blanket out of her knapsack.

"No, he was around. He moved about three miles from our house in Scarsdale, and I saw him a lot. And their divorce helped me afford NYU. I got a great financial aid package, so it worked out in the long run."

"Well, that's one way to look at it, I guess," Maddie said with a wide grin. "You seem like you've adjusted just fine." She turned to the girl who hovered beside her. "Hey, Emilia, you want to grab one end of this?"

The other girl, with striking purple-tinted hair, had already struck up a conversation with Gavin about some sort of ancient ruins. Reaching for the blanket, still talking, she helped stretch it over a small square of lawn. The four of them sat down and continued their separate conversations.

"What about you?" Tom asked. "Family still intact?"

"Yeah. I'm an only child. My mom and dad own a hardware store up in Cape Cod. Wellfleet, to be exact. We're your typical small-town folk, I guess."

"So NYU must be a big change for you, being here in the city and all."

"Yup. But so far, so good." When she smiled, the corners of her hazel eyes lifted and seemed to open up her whole face for him to discover. The spray of freckles across her nose, the way her long eyelashes seemed to almost reach up to her eyebrows, her charmingly crooked bottom teeth. They spent the greater part of the next few hours just talking, leaving Gavin and her friend Emilia to fend for themselves.

By the time dusk settled over the park, the sky had cleared, and Tom took that as a sign of even better things to come. He'd already discovered that Maddie was all natural and thus intriguingly different from the girls who had attended Scarsdale High School. It was as though she was one half of a magnet, and he was the other, each being pulled together by a force greater than themselves. She was mesmerizing, and Tom felt himself falling deeply under her spell, not caring to resist.

When Paul Simon and Art Garfunkel took the stage, Tom and Maddie were swept away by the music. The Great Lawn became a cathedral, a sacred spot, with half a million people all singing together. Tom had come to New York to study music theory, but he couldn't imagine learning in a classroom what he experienced that night. Above it all, he heard the pure, sweet sound of Maddie's voice riding on the cool night air as she sang along, sending shivers up his spine.

When the concert ended, the four of them decided it would be better to walk downtown instead of fighting the massive crowd into the subway station. They headed east, turning onto Fifth Avenue by FAO Schwartz, walking past the windows of Saks Fifth Avenue toward the Forty-Second Street Library. At some point Emilia and Gavin broke away, with Emilia playfully telling Maddie not to wait up. Tom's heart swelled at the prospect of being alone with her.

When Tom and Maddie reached the lions that guarded the library building at the top of the massive marble stairs, Maddie stopped.

"Bet you don't know the names of those lions," she teased.

"Wait a second. You're not from the city. How do you know they even have names?"

"That's not the question, is it? Let me ask again: What are their names?"

"What do I get if I actually know the answer?"

Maddie hesitated. "Oh, let's see— How about the pleasure of knowing the answer?"

Tom took two steps closer. Lacing his fingers through hers, he pulled her toward him. "What if we up the pleasure stakes a bit?"

Maddie looked back with mock surprise. "To what exactly?"

"One kiss for each name," he replied, holding her now by the waistband of her jeans.

"Go for it," she said.

"Okay." He grinned at her. "That beauty on the south side, well, she's named Patience." He leaned in and gently kissed her on the lips and had to force himself to pull away after a moment. "And her sister to the north is named Fortitude."

"Oh wow," Maddie whispered as he leaned in for the second kiss.

Tom had never felt this attracted to anyone before, and her closeness, the warmth of her body against his own, made him go weak in the knees. She tasted so sweet, a combination of longing and desire, and the fact that she was kissing him back made him uncontrollably excited. He didn't want to let her go. He knew she felt it too, this strange pull between them. They stood there together oblivious to the city carrying on around them, people walking by without so much as a glance in their direction, as though they were a part of the iconic entrance to the building, frozen in time.

For Maddie, like Tom, the moment was life affirming. Earlier that same afternoon, she had looked out the window of her dorm room and seen that the weather didn't look likely to cooperate. But nothing was going to deter her from heading to the concert, especially not the threat of rain. She and her roommate, Emilia, had already decided to ditch their classes for the day and go early to stake out a good spot on the lawn. It was so exciting to be a part of something that was so quintessentially New York. She was such a small-town girl, and initially she had been overly concerned that she wouldn't fit in with NYU's fast-paced city life.

Manhattan was the furthest thing from her home in Wellfleet that Maddie could have imagined. She had been so nervous about making the transition to an urban school setting from the more laid-back life on the Cape, and she had counted her blessings when she met Emilia on move-in day. They had hit it off right away, becoming fast friends.

Emilia was a bright and bubbly music major who wanted desperately to be a professional singer. She had a clear, crisp voice and had already proved at dorm orientation that she was going to be the life of the party by getting up on a table and singing *Everybody*, a song she'd heard her newest obsession, Madonna, sing at a dance club in Chelsea called the Roxy. Emilia was a natural; she was born to be a performer. People gravitated to her and wanted to be wherever she was.

"See, Maddie. This is what I'm talking about," Emilia had said as they walked toward the subway, waving her hands in a grand gesture, as if she were leading a band. "We are so lucky to be here!" she exclaimed, tucking an errant strand of her waist-length eggplant-colored hair behind one ear. Black kohl eyeliner rimmed her top and bottom lids. She had multiple piercings on her earlobes, each adorned with a different stud or hoop.

For today's concert, she was a combination of the ultra-edgy Madonna and the virginal Brooke Shields. She had on ripped capri-length body-hugging black leggings, which she'd topped with a short black tulle skirt, a black bra that was totally visible under her cropped, off-the-shoulder lace top, and at least twenty-five black rubber bracelets lining her arm from wrist to elbow. Her hair was pin straight like Brooke's, almost school-girl-ish, except for the bold color. To make up for the fact that it wouldn't hold a curl, she held it back off of her face with a wide black lace band that had an enormous bow sitting three inches high off of her head, just like Madonna.

In the faded jeans and Paul Simon T-shirt she'd found in a consignment shop in Boston, Maddie felt as if she faded into the background, but she was okay with that. This was all part of the experience she'd expected when she enrolled at NYU.

"C'mon," Emilia said, grabbing Maddie's hand as they raced down the steps toward the turnstiles. "I think I hear the number one train now!"

Both girls dropped a token in the slot and pushed their way to the second set of stairs that would lead them down to the platform to catch the subway to the park. Emilia yanked Maddie onto the crowded car. She'd grown up in Manhattan, somewhere on the Upper West Side, and really knew her way around the labyrinth of the underground system. It was great for Maddie, because she felt safe navigating the city with Emilia.

"Hold on, and don't make eye contact with anyone," Emilia whispered into Maddie's ear. "You'll be a native in no time!"

Maddie felt the train sway as it sped through the various twists and turns of the tunnels that led them uptown. So many other students were in the crowded car with them that the buzz in the air was electric. But Maddie, remembering Emilia's warning, didn't join in the chatter and stared down at the floor.

Once they arrived at their stop, the crowd moved as one into the park, and Emilia led the way to find an empty spot for them to sit. When she stopped, Maddie felt a presence behind her. She turned to find a tall, good-looking boy with shoulder-length dark hair standing before her. He had the most intensely green eyes she'd ever seen.

"Hi," she said, instantly drawn to him. "I'm Maddie." With those brief words, she was lost in his gaze. She knew that he was talking to her, asking her about herself and showing some interest in her answers, but she was having trouble forming her thoughts. No boy had ever caused this type of pins-and-needles reaction inside her before, and she could only hope that her voice didn't falter and give her away. He told her his name was Tom, and he made her nervous because his close proximity caused a tightening in her stomach, a warm ache that spread down her legs.

The attraction between them had been immediate and palpable. By the time they were standing on the steps of the Forty-Second Street Library, all she wanted was for him to kiss her. She willed it as strongly as she could, trying to send him a signal, to let him know that she craved the touch of his lips on hers. When he finally did reach down to receive his prize for knowing the name of the first lion, the sheer heat of his body made her quiver. By the time he kissed her again, she knew that he felt it too. Even though she'd never done anything remotely like this before, heading to his bed was a foregone conclusion. She wanted to give herself over to him, body and soul. And she trembled when he finally took her hand and led her back downtown to his dorm room.

When Tom woke up on the morning after the kiss on the library steps, Maddie was breathing softly, her head against his chest. Tom didn't know if he believed in love at first sight, but looking down at her lovely, sleeping face, he also knew that he couldn't discredit the possibility. It was an exhilarating feeling, and he couldn't remember ever being this happy, this centered. He shifted a bit in the small twin bed, and Maddie started to stir, opening her eyes and smiling at him. He held his breath, wondering if she'd feel any regrets.

"Hey there," was all she said.

"Good morning," he said back. "What do you want to do today?"

She blinked and then smiled. "I don't know. It's too early to think about it."

"Let's not waste the day. Let's go out and do something special."

"So I guess this qualifies you as a morning person, huh?" she joked.

"I never really was," he responded honestly, *but you make me feel ready for anything.* Aloud he continued, "The sun is shining, it's Saturday, and I don't want to waste a minute. Let's go have some fun." He jumped out of bed and pulled his jeans on, rummaging around the floor for a T-shirt that wasn't too dirty to wear.

"No shower?" she asked.

"Later, when the dorm empties some." He grinned disarmingly. "Maybe we could shower together?"

"Hold on there Mister. Don't get ahead of yourself. I need to shower now. After that, I need coffee. Then we can embark on your day of adventure."

Maddie's blond, curly hair fell in a tangle around her shoulders. She couldn't have looked more beautiful to Tom if she tried.

"All right, but make it snappy. I want to have some fun!"

She smiled, threw off his comforter, and got out of bed. Pretending he wasn't looking while he pulled on his T-shirt, Tom feasted his eyes on her beautiful naked bottom as she put her clothes from the night before back on. She opened the door to his room and looked down the hallway. Empty. Thankfully it was still too early for anyone else in the dorm to be awake.

With Tom holding her hand, she tiptoed to the staircase and down two floors to the room she shared with Emilia. She didn't doubt for a minute that they would find Gavin there. Maybe the four of them could grab some breakfast together, considering that they were about to wake the other couple up.

As quiet as she tried to be once inside her room, the inevitable happened, and when she bumped against a chair, both Gavin and Emilia sat up in bed, none too pleased by the disturbance. Luckily Tom was able to charm them with numerous apologies and then coax them into spending the day together. Emilia and Maddie immediately headed into the common bathroom to shower, carrying their towels, toiletries and clean clothes.

The moment they were gone, Tom dramatically clutched his heart, turned to his friend, and said, "I'm in love."

Gavin rubbed his eyes and replied grumpily, "Don't be ridiculous, man. You're confusing sex with love."

"I'm not confused at all. I'm in love with her. I felt it the minute I saw her on the subway yesterday. I didn't expect this to happen, believe me. It just did."

"What are you smoking, man? No way it happened that fast."

"And you? Emilia? What do you think?"

"I don't think anything. We had some fun, I could easily hang with you guys today, but then I've got to get my ass to the library. I have a test on Wednesday, and I've done nothing about it. I need to study."

Tom grinned and shook his head. "I can't even think about school-work. All I can think about is Maddie. I don't really care about my grades anyway. I came here to make music, and I think she and I can be something special. Did you hear her sing last night?"

"Yeah. She sounded good."

"Damn right she did. So screw classes. We're going to work together."

"You can't be in New York without being in school," Gavin pointed out. "If you aren't careful, you'll find yourself back in the suburbs." He paused, shaking his head. "I can't go back, man, not there." He hesitated and then asked, "Can you?"

"Not gonna happen. I have a good feeling about this. Feel good with me."

"For this morning, if it includes getting some coffee, I will. Can't promise anything past that."

"That a boy. That's what I'm talking about!"

When Maddie and Emilia returned in their clean clothes and damp hair, the four headed to the West Village. They ate breakfast and then wandered in and out of vintage clothing shops before finally ending up in a used record store. Maddie and Tom eagerly began pulling out albums and comparing notes on which artists they admired most.

"Look!" Maddie held up a copy of Joni Mitchell's *Ladies of the Canyon* and started to softly sing "Circle Game." Tom joined in at the chorus, matching his harmony to her melody, and a small crowd began to form around them. The music soared, their voices blending as if by magic, and at the end of the song, the group applauded enthusiastically.

"You guys should take that on the road!" Gavin crowed. "You sound awesome together."

Blushing, Maddie shook her head. "I could never sing in front of a real audience. I'd be terrified. I was pretty scared just now."

"Really?" Tom gestured at the crowd that was starting to disperse down the store's narrow aisles, all of them still smiling. "Because I think Gavin's got a great idea. We could get a set together and try it out at an open mic night somewhere. There are clubs all over the city where we could sing."

"No way! I have an econ test on Monday and an art history paper to write . . ."

"Maddie," Tom said emphatically, "we have something special here, and you know it. Didn't you just hear us together? Those people loved us! I've got more than a few songs written that we could try out. Maybe we could earn a few bucks too. That wouldn't be so bad, would it?"

"No," Maddie said, sounding uncertain.

"Oh c'mon, Maddie," Emilia chimed in. "You guys sounded great."

"Just try it once and see what happens," Gavin added.

Maddie looked at Tom. He was so excited, so engaged, as if it was impossible for him to believe Maddie could turn him down.

She shook her head, sudden tears welling in her eyes. "I can't, Tom. The stage fright thing is real. I don't think I can stand up in front of strangers and sing. I get sick to my stomach just thinking about it. The only reason why I was able to sing here was because I didn't think anything about it. We just started and—"

"One thing at a time," Tom said, giving her that wide smile that had charmed her from the start. "Let's take it slow, learn some music together, and see how that goes. I have a whole lot of songs I want you to hear."

"So do I," she said quickly, unable to resist the idea of sharing them with him. He was so sweet and sexy and different than anyone she'd ever known back home in Wellfleet. And she had to admit that they'd sounded wonderful together. She took a deep breath. "Okay, if you wait until after my test. I have to get good grades or my parents will yank me back home to attend community college. And they never make idle threats."

"Deal!" Tom yelled and bent down to give her a kiss to seal the decision. Maddie felt the kiss sear her insides, wiping out her earlier anxiety.

"We'll start right now," Tom added jubilantly.

"Singing?"

"No, studying! You're going to ace that test, wait and see."

Later that afternoon, the four of them met at the Bobst Library stacks. Soon books were piled up on the well-worn wooden table along with empty coffee cups and discarded candy bar wrappers

After a while, Emilia took her leave, eager to find something more exciting to do on a Saturday night, and Gavin moved to a different floor where the quiet rooms were located. He was the most studious of the group, and he claimed that any amount of noise distracted him. Tom and Maddie worked in amicable silence until Maddie finally closed her textbook and rubbed her eyes.

"I think I'm toast. I can't imagine there's something I didn't study for that test, or at least I hope not," she said to Tom.

"Finally!" he replied. "I'm starving. Let's go get some real food."

"Sounds good." Maddie hadn't realized how hungry she was until he said the word "food."

They packed up their books and headed to the coffee shop on the corner of West Fourth Street and Sixth Avenue. Once in a booth toward the back of the restaurant, Tom pulled a sheet of paper from his knapsack.

"For the last hour while you were so intently studying, I worked up a playlist for us," he said.

"Seriously?"

"No time like the present. We should start rehearsing some of this after we eat."

"I need a minute to think about it," Maddie said, adding to the waitress who came by to take their order, "I'll have a grilled cheese, please, and coffee."

"I'll have the same," Tom said. When the waitress left, Tom leaned over the table and took Maddie's hands. "I'll give you a minute, but not much longer. I really want us to give this a try."

"I get that, but you clearly weren't listening to me earlier. I told you—I have terrible stage fright. When I was in high school I was in the chorus, and the teacher gave me a solo freshman year at the holiday recital. I was fine in the classroom, but once we moved into the auditorium for the dress rehearsal and I saw all those empty seats, I just froze. My teacher tried to convince me I'd be fine with a little practice, and I tried, I really did, but I just couldn't do it. The night of the concert I was shaking so hard I could barely breathe. I got clammy all over and thought I was going to faint. Thankfully one of the other girls could sing the part. It was all I could do just to stand in the chorus and sing with everyone else and not throw up. It was so awful. I still get scared just thinking about it now."

Tom listened, but was clearly undeterred. "Maddie, I can get you through that. Let's start small. We'll just head back to my room and go over the music. If you like what you hear, then we can work on your stage fright. I won't let you down, I promise." He held up one hand like a Boy Scout reciting the pledge, while his other hand squeezed hers.

Maddie realized she didn't know Tom well enough to believe him, but something deep in her soul told her to try. The waitress brought their sandwiches and coffee, and while she ate, Maddie thought about making music with him, singing with him, maybe even in front of other people, and not being afraid. She realized that Tom was right. They could start slowly and see if she was capable of putting the horrible memory of her high school chorus recital behind her and get over this irrational fear.

"Okay. I'll listen to the music, and if I like your songs, I'll try."

He smiled broadly.

"One condition," she continued. "You've got to listen to my music too, and be fair. You may like some of my stuff, and maybe we can give it a go as well."

"I think that's more than fair. It's going to be great!"

He grinned throughout the rest of their meal, and Maddie tried to quell the uneasy feeling in her stomach. As much as she wanted this to work, she couldn't help but worry that Tom wouldn't be able to solve this problem of hers. For his sake, more than her own, she desperately wanted it to work out. She was already worried about his disappointment if it didn't.

V

By the time the sun began its ascent the following morning, Maddie and Tom had already learned enough of each other's music to have an entire set prepared for open mic night. It was now Tom's mission to talk Maddie through her stage fright so that she'd agree to perform.

"First of all, we're going to practice this so much that you aren't even going to have to think about singing these songs. They will be so much a part of you that it will seem you've known them all your life."

"I do know some of them that well. I've been writing them, like, forever," she replied.

"Exactly. And the performance will be almost organic because you'll know the material that well."

"I don't think it's the music part that scares me, Tom. It's the people. The faces in the audience looking at me, judging my music, my voice. What if they don't like me?"

"That's just not possible, Maddie. I'm a tough critic. You're not just good. You're fabulous, and your music is insanely great. They are going to love you. How could they not love you? You are incredible."

She got up from the desk chair, walked across the room, and pushed him down onto the bed where he had been sitting. She kissed him all over his face and neck, and he responded with warmth and desire.

"Say it again," she murmured.

"You are incredible." He could barely get the words out. She left him breathless.

"No, not that. The part about my music."

He stopped kissing her and looked directly into her eyes. "Your music is special, Maddie," he said huskily. "Really special, and really good. You have something to say, and the melodies are haunting. My stuff is nice, but yours is the real deal."

"Do you mean that, or do you just want to get me naked?"

"I'm going to get you naked anyway," he laughed. "So there's no need for me to lie. I have you exactly where I want you!"

She sat up. "No, seriously. I still don't know how I'm going to sing in front of anyone else but you. I'm so scared."

Tom sat up with his legs crossed in front of her on the bed and took both of her hands in his.

"This is what we're gonna do," he said firmly. "You're going to maintain eye contact with me the whole time. You don't have to look at the audience at all, just at me. I'll keep you safe, I promise."

"Won't that look strange? Me just looking at you? I might as well have my back to the audience then."

"It won't really matter. Once you start to sing, no one will care what they're looking at, only what they're hearing."

"Are you sure?"

"I've never been so positive about anything in my life. It's all about the music, Maddie. The music is bigger than either of us. That's what the audience comes for, to be swept away by the sound."

In that moment, Tom could only hope that Maddie believed him. She looked so unsure, so scared. Which was crazy. He'd recognized right away that for her, singing was the same as breathing. A primal thing, almost necessary. How could anyone fear something that much a part of herself? He squeezed her hands. "Well?" he coaxed, giving her his signature Tom Seymour smile.

"Okay," she said, drawing in a deep breath. "Let's give it a try. But if I have to bail, you can't be mad at me. I really want it to work. I just don't know if it will."

"Believe with me, Maddie. We're gonna be huge."

And with that, they tumbled together onto the pillows, paying no attention to the beautiful sunrise spilling its golden rays over the rooftops below.

They didn't wake up until late afternoon, leaving the room only to grab some food at the dorm's cafeteria to bring back with them. They sang together late into the next night, practicing the songs for their set over and over until Maddie almost did feel as if she had been singing with Tom, performing these ten songs, forever.

The next morning she had to take her econ test, so she left Tom's dorm room early to shower and change into fresh clothing. Unlocking her own door, she was surprised to find Emilia in bed alone.

"Hey, stranger," the other girl said sleepily. "How was the rest of your weekend with your new boyfriend? Must've been good. I haven't seen you since Saturday afternoon."

Maddie felt the heat rise to her neck and face. "Tom convinced me to try an open mic night. We rehearsed practically all night Saturday after the library and most of yesterday." She sat down on the foot of Emilia's bed. "You know, there's something about Tom, something that pulls me in. But I don't want to get ahead of myself. We've only known each other a little while!"

Emilia stifled a yawn. "For a new guy, he sure hangs all over you. He couldn't keep his hands off of you in the library."

Maddie blushed again. "He seems great. It was really strange how quickly I felt connected to him."

"I didn't notice." Emilia grinned sarcastically.

Maddie let that one pass. "I really didn't come to NYU to find a guy. I came here, as my dad likes to remind me, for an overpriced education."

"So dish," Emilia said, sitting up. "Tell me everything, like, how was the sex?"

"I'm not the type to kiss and tell." Again Maddie blushed crimson, but she couldn't resist talking about Tom. "However, if I was, I'd have to admit we had a great time."

"I can't believe this. We go to a concert, you meet some hot music student, he turns out to be a songwriter like you, and you hit it off. In fact, your voices could be married already, they're that perfect together. What are the odds?"

"I know. I feel a little numb. And now I'm going to perform with him." Maddie shivered at the thought, which instantly dampened her mood. "Hey, where's Gavin?"

Emilia shrugged. "Dunno. I haven't seen him since the library."

Maddie stared. "But he didn't show up in Tom's room that night, or last night either. I assumed he was here . . ." She broke off. "So just a one-night thing for the two of you?"

"Seems that way. Oh, don't look so disapproving, Maddie! Gavin's a nice guy, but I'm not into a long-term thing. I'm looking to have some fun, and clearly so is he."

"Well, okay then. Sorry I asked." Maddie began to rummage through her clean clothes to find something suitable to wear to class.

"Hey," Emilia said, getting out of bed and padding over to give Maddie a hug. "I don't mean to be short with you. It's just that I'm a little bit jealous. Without trying, you met maybe the hottest guy on campus. He's cute, he's talented, and he's totally into you. Pretty amazing."

"Yeah, I guess it is," Maddie replied, smiling. "Now if I can only pass this econ test, my life will be just fine."

Emilia laughed. "You'll ace it, I'm sure. You're just that type of girl."

"From your mouth . . ." Maddie said on her way to the shower.

"Good luck," Emilia called after her, but Maddie wasn't sure if her roommate was wishing her well on the test, the open mic performance, or her newly minted relationship with Tom. All Maddie knew with a sudden shiver of apprehension was that she needed all the good vibes she could gather, because she wasn't sure about any of it.

When she left the classroom after taking her test and walked into the bright sunlight, she was surprised to find Tom waiting for her at the top of the steps.

"Don't you have class now?" she asked after he kissed her hello.

"I was too pumped up to go to class. I found us an open mic night spot."

Maddie was stunned. "Already?" A shiver ran up her spine. "It's not even noon. What was open?"

"The student union. I figured it would be best to try something small first before blowing your mind with a real club. If we can make it through a set in front of a jury of our peers, we can branch out. Let's get a buzz going about us first, a grassroots effort, if you will."

"That sounds reasonable, I guess," Maddie replied without much enthusiasm.

Tom practically leapt down the rest of the steps. "Who needs a marketing class? I already know what to do to get our music to the people!"

"When is this debut performance of ours?" Maddie asked nervously.

"Thursday. I wanted to give you time to finish that art history paper. It's due Wednesday, right?"

She nodded.

"Perfect. We'll have all day Wednesday and Thursday leading up to the show to practice."

"It's so soon," was all she could muster.

"No, it's not. It's three whole days from now. And you can finish the paper and then practice with me for a few hours each night."

"And what about classes?"

"Go to your classes. I'll get the word out about our set. It's going to be great, Maddie, you'll see." Tom's green eyes danced.

"What about you? Are you going to class?"

"Only if I have to. I'll make up the notes and the work. Promise. I want to put my energy into us. Let me do this thing, Maddie. I can handle it."

"If you flunk, it will be my fault. I can't let that happen. You've got to go to class."

He put his arms around her. "You worry too much, babe. I know what I need to do. You worry about you. I'll worry about us. Okay?"

Maddie didn't know what to say. It really wasn't okay with her—her strict New England upbringing put academic first. That little voice inside of her head wasn't the rule breaker that Tom seemed to be, and it made her very nervous.

"I'm only going to do this with you if you go to class. I won't be able to handle it if you crap out and have to leave school. Then where will we be?"

"School isn't the reason I'm here, Maddie. I know that now. Clearly it was so we could meet, so we could make music together."

"No, Tom. You're here to get a degree. What if the music doesn't turn out? Then what?"

He laughed, looking handsome and uncaring and oh so sexy to Maddie. "I don't think that way, Maddie. I believe in us and our music. I'm going to do everything in my power to make it work. Watch and see."

She realized it would be a waste to convince him otherwise, that he would do whatever he wanted anyway.

"Okay, okay, but please just go to class."

"Deal. But I don't have a class until three. Let's go to the union and check out the stage. You need to start getting used to the surroundings."

Maddie took a deep breath. This was happening. She was going to try to step onto a stage and sing. "I have a class at two, so we've got to make it quick."

"Whatever you say, Mad. We'll take a look around and then go, all right?" He took her hand, his handsome face close to hers. "Trust me."

Maddie knew that she would have to, because when she was with him, she could no longer trust herself.

It felt as though Maddie barely had time to catch her breath before Thursday night arrived. From the minute she had finished her art history paper, Tom had her practicing with him both on the stage at The Cellar Bar in the student union and in his room each night. She knew that the music was not going to be her problem; she had learned the entire set cold. It was the constant gnawing fear in the pit of her stomach.

As she got dressed that night in her most comfortable white T-shirt and favorite worn jeans, she looked at herself in the full-length mirror hanging on the back of her door. Maddie couldn't believe that she looked so calm on the outside when her insides were shaking. She wished Emilia was here to confide in, to help her deal with her growing anxiety, but Emilia, as usual, was already out with yet another guy she'd met on campus.

Maddie heard a gentle knock on her door. When she stepped back to open it, she found Tom on the other side, guitar in hand.

"This is it," he said, smiling broadly and looking breathtakingly handsome in a pair of well-worn Levis and a soft, blue flannel shirt, his white T-shirt peeking out of the collar.

Maddie fought off the instinct to bury herself under the blankets on her bed. A sense of doom gripped her. She felt as though she was on her way to face her executioner. She drew in the deepest breath she could and reached for Tom's hand. It was warm and by now so wonderfully familiar.

"Ready?" he asked, squeezing hers tightly.

"I'm as ready as I'm going to be. Let's go."

Tom stepped aside, and Maddie walked into the hallway. She heard the door click shut behind her, and firmly holding on to Tom, she walked to the student union building beside him, looking as calm and collected as she could, despite the fact that her insides were quaking and nausea bubbled at the base of her throat.

When she thought about it afterward, Maddie couldn't even recall a single moment of the walk from her dorm to The Cellar Bar at the student union. But she did remember that it was all she could do to remain upright. When they entered the building, Tom fetched her a glass of wine from the long wooden bar to help calm her nerves, but she could barely stomach the cheap, cloying stuff. He left her in a chair offstage while he went to do some last-minute tweaking of the sound system. She tried her best to follow his instructions, repeating the mantra they had created together over and over to herself. At one point she realized that she was actually saying the words out loud because one of the crew stopped to ask if she was talking to him. She no longer cared if she looked or sounded crazy; she just kept repeating the phrase that was meant to calm her.

"Trust in the music, trust in each other. Trust in the music, trust in each other." Tom came up behind her, and Maddie almost jumped right out of her skin. He put his arms around her, crossing them over her chest.

"Breathe in, breathe out. It's going to be fine."

"Easy for you to say. You aren't terrified."

"Only one of us can be terrified today. I'll pick another day." He swung her around and linked his fingers with hers, flashing her his most disarming smile.

"I'm going to try, really try. I just can't promise that I'll make it to the end of the set," Maddie whispered. "Hell, I don't know if any sound will come out at all when I open my mouth to sing." She felt her teeth chatter.

"You'll be fine. Don't look at the audience. Focus on me, just like we practiced. It will get easier as we go and the crowd warms to you." Tom looked so sure that Maddie almost believed him. She could hear people chatting with each other on the other side of the heavy red curtain and reluctantly moved with Tom to the center of the stage as the announcer stepped out to introduce them.

"Okay, get ready to welcome our next act to the stage . . . Madeline Ellis and Tom Seymour," the voice pronounced.

It was time.

As the curtain lifted, Maddie watched Tom pick up his guitar and play the introduction to their first song, one of those she had written. As he strummed the notes of the familiar melody, she lifted her eyes and found his gaze—and with it, her own voice. She was stunned to discover that as long as she looked into those warm green eyes of his, she wasn't alone. She was safe in some sort of weird protective zone they'd created together, a place where only the two of them existed. She could hear herself matching harmonies with Tom, feel herself swaying gently to the rhythm of the music. She felt strangely warm and comfortable held in the embrace of the melody, the serenity of the lyrics, the strength of Tom's gaze.

The audience sat raptly, as lost in the music as Maddie was, barely moving at all. At the end of the short set they were on their feet, stomping and clapping and begging for more.

Maddie was exhausted as one encore became two. Tom must have sensed that she needed a break, so he motioned the stage manager that they were done for the night. Maddie took a bow, heard Tom mutter a thanks and good night to the crowd, and the next thing she knew they were standing in the side alley outside the stage door in the cool night air.

"That was amazing! You are amazing!" Tom exclaimed, nearly jumping up and down on the cobblestones in excitement and then pulling her close to his chest for a series of deepening kisses.

Dazed, she finally stepped out of his embrace. "It felt like I was walking through a dream or something. I mean, did that really just happen? Did I sing onstage?"

"You didn't just sing, Maddie. You killed it out there! Didn't you hear that applause? We did two encores for chrissakes!"

"I just can't believe it. I've never been able to do that before."

"Now do you trust me? If you did it tonight, you can do it again."

Maddie hadn't thought about what being successful onstage would really mean. "Do it again? When?"

"As soon as I can set it up. I think we can make some money the next time we perform."

"Really?"

"Why not? The audience loved you . . . loved us. I can't wait to get back on that stage! C'mon. Let's get a drink and celebrate. We can listen to the other acts. I bet no one gets the reaction we did."

There was no way Maddie could refuse. She didn't have an early class the next day, and she had never experienced anything like what she was feeling right now. She was euphoric, and all because Tom was so thrilled with their performance.

They went back inside and sat at the bar watching the other musicians. Tom ordered a Jack Daniel's for himself and another glass of wine for Maddie. This time she didn't mind the taste, or the praise she received from some of the audience members who recognized them. People started sending them drinks in appreciation, but she didn't need the alcohol to feel high. Tom, on the other hand, accepted shots of bourbon and tequila, downing them with abandon, and his enthusiasm was so infectious that Maddie didn't even mind when he agreed to perform again over the weekend as an opening act for the headliner. Maddie had never felt so reckless and free.

She spun around on her barstool and suddenly spotted Emilia with her latest date at a small table against the back wall. Gavin and a few other people she knew from the dorm were sitting there as well. She got up and walked over to say hello, feeling slightly woozy from the drinks. When they saw her, they jumped up to embrace her, praising her voice and the music.

"I guess I better listen to Tom next time he's got a stock tip or something. He was so right. You have a boatload of talent, Maddie."

"That's so nice of you, Gavin, thanks. I was so scared to do this tonight. I can't believe people really liked us."

"I think that might be an understatement," Emilia said. "You guys blew the roof off this place. It was awesome!" She leaned in to whisper in Maddie's ear, "And if I thought Tom was hot before this, well, let's just say you are one lucky girl! Watch out—I just might make a play for him myself!"

Maddie stepped back, shocked by the hardness under Emilia's teasing tone. Emilia hadn't been around much of late, and she rarely mentioned Tom when she was. Since the start of the semester, Maddie had watched Emilia conquer one man after another, seemingly excited about putting yet another notch on her bedpost. She was one of those women who held some strange, hypnotic fascination for men, and there wasn't any doubt that she liked sex—and lots of it. Did Maddie now have to worry about Emilia being too interested in Tom?

The rush of uncertainty sobered Maddie fast. She and Tom had this brand-new relationship and now some success as a musical duo. Why would her roommate want to mess with that? She pulled herself together and smiled wordlessly at Emilia before returning to the bar. She slid onto the stool next to Tom and clutched his arm tightly. This feeling of jealousy over a guy was new for Maddie. *Maybe I'm overreacting*, she thought.

But hours later, as she stared at the ceiling of her dorm room unable to sleep, Maddie couldn't help but wonder as Emilia lightly snored across from her. It was the first night in a long time that Emilia had slept in her own bed. Maddie had been so happy until her interaction with Emilia at the bar. Now she felt confused by the way her relationship with her roommate had become so complicated.

Maddie had been a loner growing up, always retreating into the world she created with her music. She'd begun writing songs at a young age, expressing her feelings of isolation and her awkward adolescent longings. She had hoped that she could take her talents further, but after the debacle of her high school chorus performance she had thrown that dream away. She hadn't even auditioned for the Tisch School, the performing arts arm of NYU, when she applied there because she doubted her ability to overcome her fears of the stage.

Tonight Tom had changed all of that. With his charm and talent and his unbelievable determination and faith in her, he had accomplished what Maddie alone never could. Now that she knew she could sing in front of an audience with him, everything was different. She didn't dare think about it too much, but what if Tom was right? What if their music, their voices were special enough to build the kind of audience that might pay to hear them sing, to maybe someday buy their records?

Emilia turned over in her narrow bed, bringing Maddie from her thoughts. Kicking the blanket away, Maddie sat up, feeling as though there wasn't enough air in the room for the two of them. She threw on her robe and flip-flops, grabbed her keys off the desk, and slipped outside. The bright fluorescents in the dorm hallway hurt her eyes for a moment before they adjusted to the harsh, unflattering light. She headed down to the lounge area with its old, beat-up couches and chairs and sat near a large window facing Washington Square Park.

It looked so quiet and peaceful outside in the dark. She knew that there were drug dealers who made their living selling all sorts of stuff from the park benches, and she had been warned at orientation to avoid cutting through the area at night. She was tempted to find Tom and wake him, just to have someone to go out with, but she didn't. Instead she sat still in the battered armchair until the sun started to rise, reliving the evening and now and again trying to make sense of Emilia's comment about making a play for Tom.

Emilia knew perfectly well that Maddie and Tom were together. So why had she made that remark about a guy who was clearly involved with someone else? Did all girls do this and had Maddie just missed the memo, or was Emilia out of line? Maddie honestly didn't know, and things were no clearer as she watched the sun crest over the park. Gradually she became aware of the sounds of doors opening and showers running as the other dorm residents began to stir. Rising from her chair, she pushed all thoughts of Tom and music and Emilia away and headed back to her room to prepare for the day ahead.

That weekend Tom and Maddie played The Cellar Bar and again Maddie experienced preshow jitters, only not nearly as badly as the first time. The audience loved their set, and Maddie was able to relax enough to actually enjoy the experience a little. They opened for another student musician who offered to introduce Tom to his agent after the show, and the next thing Maddie knew she found herself signing a contract with a man named Jerry who promised to get their music heard beyond campus, to book them shows in bigger venues, and turn them into, as he said, "household names."

While Tom was off and running with the whole concept, it took Maddie longer to warm to the idea, mostly because she was still trying to maintain a decent GPA while performing four nights a week. Tom had basically—but not officially—dropped out of school. He didn't go to any of his classes or do the required assignments. He blew off his midterms and was trying to figure out a way to let his parents know that he was going to give music a shot full time when they paid him a visit.

As it happened, the Seymours heard about it before Tom had the chance to tell them anything. The son of a family friend, an upperclassman at NYU, had paid Tom's mother, Sara, a visit when he was home for the weekend and enthusiastically described catching one of Tom and Maddie's shows. He had also told her that Tom was dropping out of school to play music full time. Sara Seymour had immediately phoned Tom's father, and together they drove down from Westchester early one Saturday morning and took Maddie and Tom out to breakfast. Once they settled into a booth and ordered a round of pancakes, all hell broke loose.

"When were you going to tell us that you stopped going to class?" his father asked in a tone that Maddie found more frightening than if he had started yelling at the top of his lungs.

Tom nervously drummed his fingers on the table. "Um, I was meaning to discuss it with you both, but it's been crazy here. Maddie and I spend all our time playing The Cellar Bar. Our shows are packed. You should come check us out."

"Not a chance," his mother snapped. "We didn't agree to send you here for this. You were supposed to study music theory. I thought you wanted to teach someday."

"You know," Tom's father added darkly, "get a real job after graduation."

Maddie found it fascinating that even though they had been divorced for years, Mr. and Mrs. Seymour acted as a single unit when it came to their joint dismay over their son's apparent indifference to earning a college degree.

Now Tom's dad, Jack, turned his piercing gaze on Maddie. "Can't you convince our pigheaded son that he needs a college education more than he needs to be on a stage?" Without waiting for her to answer he appealed to Tom. "Take a leave of absence. You can keep the scholarship that way."

Tom's only response was to shake his head. His father, undeterred, focused on Maddie again. "How do your parents feel about what you're doing?"

Maddie gathered her thoughts before she answered. Tom's father was more than a little intimidating, and she wanted to choose her words carefully. "Honestly? I haven't told them. But," she quickly added, "I'm still going to classes and studying for tests. If we get really busy with performances, I'll have to rework my schedule, but I'm committed to getting my degree."

Jack glared at Tom from beneath bushy eyebrows while directing his comment to Maddie. "At least you've got your head screwed on straight. That's more than I can say for this guy here."

"You're being too hard on him, Jack," Tom's mother interjected.

"Sara!" Mr. Seymour's face turned an alarming shade of red.

Maddie realized that Tom's mother understood that Tom would remain unmoved by their argument. Her eyes, as green as Tom's, were determined, making it very clear to Maddie just where Tom had inherited his own strong will.

"If this is what he wants to do, let him." Sara turned to look at Tom. "But here's the deal. You lose your scholarship money and we can't help you out. It's state school for you then, not this expensive private university."

Tom reached across the table and took his mother's hand, and Maddie observed their unspoken connection. "Got it, Mom. That's fair. I promise I won't let you down. If we can't make something big happen in a relatively short time, I'll head to Albany and get a degree. I mean it."

"As long as you understand that I'm not happy about this," his mother said.

"That's putting it mildly," Mr. Seymour snapped.

His ex-wife ignored him. "Where will you live?" she asked Tom.

"I'll crash on the floor of Maddie's room if I have to. But hopefully it won't be a problem."

"How do you feel about that, Maddie?" Mr. Seymour demanded.

Maddie could feel herself turning red, and Tom kicked her under the table. The two of them were already sharing a bed most nights as Emilia had practically moved out for now, having recently taken up with a guy on another floor who had a single room. While they didn't know how long Emilia's current crush would last, they took full advantage of not having her around. "Oh, it won't come to that," Maddie said quickly. "But I'll help out any way I can."

In a gesture of defeat, Jack Seymour picked the check up off the table and opened his wallet. "Well, son, the next breakfast is on you. Let's see you actually make a living with that guitar of yours."

Tom spread his hands appealingly. "You need to have a little faith in me, Dad. Maddie and I, well, I think we're going to make it."

His father sighed. "Let's hope so. Although I hear Albany is beautiful in the winter . . ." He turned to Tom's mother. "C'mon, Sara. Let's go."

Despite their harsh words, divorced or not, they all clearly loved each other, Maddie thought, because Tom hugged both of his parents and walked them to the door of the diner, where he shook his father's hand and watched them step outside arm in arm. When he returned to the table, he ran his hand through his hair and tried to look uncaring. "Well, this just got real."

"Are you okay?" Maddie asked.

"Yeah, I think I am." He blew out a long breath, and then his signature smile returned. "I know I'm ready to make us famous. And, babe, it won't take long."

Maddie no longer doubted him, not for a minute. But she knew that she would need to hang on tight, because she was now in the center of the hurricane that was Tom. There was nothing to do but take his hand and believe in him the way he believed in himself.

VI

For Maddie, the next few months passed in a blur. She spent her time struggling to maintain her grades and get her schoolwork done while their agent, Jerry Simmons, a chain-smoking, whippet-thin bundle of nerves, gave them plenty of exposure and consistent work at The Cellar Bar in the student union. He also kept promising them a performance at what he called a "larger venue," but Maddie tried not to think about what that actually meant.

Her stage fright had not disappeared, but with Tom's help she was managing it better. He grounded her, made her feel safe, and when Maddie allowed herself to erase some of her doubt and to trust the bond she found in Tom's gaze, her world became ordered. With him by her side, the stage at The Cellar became more familiar, even comfortable, and after a time, they fell into a pattern of performances from Thursday night through the weekend, leaving Maddie to write papers and study for tests Monday through Wednesday.

By the time she registered for the spring semester, Maddie had learned to schedule herself better, without early morning classes, front-loading her weeks so that she'd have her weekends free. By March of freshman year, Maddie thought she had it all under control. And then Jerry called with what Tom considered incredible news—he had made good on his promise and booked them at The Bitter End, a historic club in the Village where all of Maddie's idols had performed at some point in their careers, including Bob Dylan.

"Maddie, do you realize when we hit that stage we'll be standing in the shadow of the greats?" Tom asked, turning her around in her desk chair to face him. She had been studying for her statistics midterm exam when he'd burst in with the news.

"Please, Tom, don't overplay this for me. I'm nervous enough." She bit down hard on the pencil she'd been holding in an attempt to quell her fear.

"Why? Our set is the same one we've been singing for months. The crowd loves it."

"It's just that I'm less anxious at The Cellar now. I know what to expect, and it's mostly the same people watching us at every show. They aren't strangers anymore. It's more like playing to friends," she said in a shaky voice.

"So I'll put the word out that we're at The Bitter End and they'll all show up. When you look out at the audience, you'll see all the same faces you already know. And more importantly, I'll be there. Look at me if you feel it's too much for you to handle, the same way we did when we started out. It worked at The Cellar, it will work anywhere!"

Maddie smiled weakly at him, not wanting to burst his bubble of excitement, but those old feelings of fear and insecurity were rising to the surface again.

Tom must have noticed, because he said gently, "We're meeting Jerry there tomorrow afternoon. He wants us to get a feel for the stage. Let's see how that goes and take it from there. Don't go into this thinking you can't do it. Believe that you can, and trust in me. We'll get through this together." He kissed her, threw on his jacket, and said something about getting a flyer designed on his way out of her dorm room.

Maddie turned her chair around to face the books and papers spread out on the desk. Statistics was a tough course, and she needed the full power of concentration to get through it. But even though she tried to focus, her brain was going in a million directions. She knew it would be useless to sit staring at her work when in this state of mind nothing would sink in.

Standing up, she looked around her. The room was a mess. Emilia had moved out to be with yet another new guy, and she had removed all traces of herself from the space. Tom had taken up permanent residence and it was their stuff that Maddie now saw strewn everywhere. Dirty laundry was piled high on the bed that had once been Emilia's, sheet music littered the floor from their late-night marathon writing sessions, and empty cups and plates from the cafeteria and takeout were stacked everywhere. Why not take one hour off from studying and clean up? If the space was tidy, maybe it would help her concentrate on her schoolwork, not on the terrifying idea of performing on the very famous stage at The Bitter End.

As Maddie cleaned, she began working through a new melody that had been rolling around in her brain for the last few days. By the time she carried a big bag of trash to the Dumpster in the dorm basement, she felt a gratifying sense of accomplishment. Not only did she like the new tune she was hearing in her head, she could see the floor of her room again.

Back upstairs, she began to sing out loud as she picked up her laundry. She didn't have lyrics in mind yet, but she knew that the melody was a love song; it just had that kind of romantic quality. Tom always teased her by saying that the best part of their relationship was the burst of creativity Maddie seemed to experience from being with him. The music had been pouring out of her of late, and with Tom's lyrics and arrangements, their sets at The Cellar had been selling out solidly night after night.

Still singing, Maddie picked up a pile of Tom's shirts and began tossing them in her laundry basket. A small scrap of paper fell out of one of his pockets, and she was about to throw it in the trashcan when she recognized the handwriting. Smoothing it out with her fingers she read:

Meet me in our spot between sets.

It was signed with an imprint of a mouth in crimson lipstick.

If the handwriting wasn't proof enough that Emilia had written the note, her very distinctive shade of lip color certainly was. What the hell? Maddie felt the blood rush to her head. Laundry be damned. The statistics test too. She picked up her keys and hurried out to look for Tom. He had some serious explaining to do.

By the time she tracked Tom down, Maddie felt totally out of control. She had never experienced anything like it before. Her heart was racing as fast as her mind, a jumble of thoughts and suppositions. Was Tom really seeing Emilia on the side? Was he just hanging on to their own relationship for the sake of the music, not for the love she thought they'd found together? And: Where could the two of them have met between sets? Her thoughts jumped from being sure that Tom was cheating on her to overwhelming guilt at the thought that she was about to accuse the man who was the source of her strength of being the worst kind of weasel.

As she made her way down the crowded street, she saw Tom coming out of the printing shop holding a big box. When he saw her, his face lit up.

"Hey, taking a break? The guy in the shop did me a solid and printed these up while I waited. Don't they look great?" He held out a sample of the flyer for their show at the Bitter End.

Maddie was too upset to speak. All she could do was pass him the note from Emilia. When he saw it, his face fell for a moment, but he recovered quickly.

"That crazy Emilia. She wants to sing backup for us when we finally record an album. We talked about it the other night between sets."

Maddie took a deep, calming breath. It didn't help. Her voice was icy as she said, "It doesn't seem likely you were talking shop, Tom. Clearly you've met with her backstage before, in your 'spot.'"

"Maddie—"

His placating tone infuriated her. "Looks like she left you a reminder of that 'shop talk' with the lipstick too."

"Don't be ridiculous," Tom said, pushing past her, handing out flyers as he started down the street.

She hurried to catch up with him. "Don't walk away from me, Tom! This is serious."

He spun around to face her. "What exactly are you saying, Maddie? That I'm cheating on you with Emilia? For chrissakes! You honestly believe I'd throw away everything for something as cheap as a quickie between sets?" He sounded truly indignant.

"That's exactly what I'm saying," she replied shakily even as doubt crept in.

"I would never do that to you, to us," Tom blurted. "I'm sorry that's what you think, but it's just not true."

It was as though a wall of some kind had risen between them, and Maddie wasn't sure if he was being defensive or telling the truth. "Don't you have studying to do?" he called over his shoulder as he continued down the street.

Maddie stood on the sidewalk, watching him walk away from her. She was more confused than ever. Emilia had made it clear on more than one occasion in the past that she was interested in Tom, and she hadn't seemed to care that Maddie had staked her claim on him first. Tom was charismatic, charming, and sexy—a combination that other women obviously found appealing. After every show Maddie watched them swarm the stage, hoping to catch his attention, but he'd never been anything more than polite, making it clear that he was committed to Maddie, to their music, their relationship.

Maddie tried to stop the frantic beating of her heart. Panic nibbled at the edges of her mind as she watched Tom disappear around a corner. How could she have been so sure, and how could he have so quickly made her feel as if she couldn't be more wrong?

Tears pricking her eyes, she walked into the park and sat down heavily on a bench. The brilliant weather had brought out hordes of students in a carnival-like atmosphere, everyone eager to shake off the long winter doldrums and welcome spring.

Two skateboarders raced by her, and as Maddie followed them with her eyes, she saw that a crowd had gathered around a small group of musicians busking under the arch that led into the park from the Fifth Avenue side. She got up to join them so that she could hear the music. Surely that would make her feel better?

As she got closer, she felt her heart skip a beat. They were playing one of her songs! And the crowd was responding—swaying to the music, clapping their hands, a few of them even dancing! Not wanting them to see her, Maddie hung back until they were done.

The applause was enthusiastic. Maddie thought the whole scene was surreal, but so exciting, and the only thing she suddenly wanted to do was tell Tom. As upset as she had been earlier, now she couldn't help but think that maybe she'd jumped to the wrong conclusion about Emilia's note. She wanted desperately to believe Tom, and remembering how coldly she had accused him, she felt a rising panic. What if he was so angry that he'd break up with her, end their musical collaboration before it really had a chance to go anywhere? She had to find him, to apologize, to make things right. She ran out of the park, away from the musicians, to find the one person she knew she was meant to be with. She only hoped it was not too late.

VII

When Maddie opened the door to her dorm room, she saw Tom sitting at her desk, a bouquet of daisies in his hand. All of the breath left her body, putting her off-balance. But she recovered enough to squeak out, "Hi."

He got up and crossed the room to hand her the flowers. "I know what this looks like, but it's really not what you think it is, I swear."

He looked so earnest, sounded so chagrined. She took the bouquet from him. "You didn't need to bring flowers," she said, looking around the room for an empty wine bottle to put them in.

"I didn't bring them as an apology, Maddie. I brought them because I realized that I should have been bringing you flowers all along. You are my everything. I need to make more of an effort to make sure you know that." He drew her into an embrace and kissed her deeply on the lips.

Though Maddie was tempted to melt into his arms, she pulled back and asked, "And just how do you propose to do that?"

"I plan on telling you every day how much you mean to me. I've come to rely on you for more than just the music, you've got to realize that, right?" He looked so sincere that her heart skipped a beat.

"I saw that note and got totally crazy," she confessed, relaxing a little. "I feel the same way about you. But Emilia has said things before . . ."

He took both her hands in his and stared earnestly into her upturned face. "I don't care what she said. All that matters is what we say, right here, right now. I'm in this for the long haul, Maddie, wherever it leads us, as long as it's together."

She felt her sharp anger at him dissipate. She wanted to believe him, had to believe him. She gazed directly into those intense green eyes, searching for a reason not to trust him, but couldn't find one. All she could see was Tom, the beautiful, brilliant man she'd come to love so quickly. Emilia no longer mattered. "Me too," she whispered back.

They fell onto the narrow bed together, and Tom spent the rest of the afternoon proving to Maddie that she was the only person in the world for him, kissing her, caressing her, making her feel special in the way that only he could. In his arms she felt her world begin to right itself, pushing their earlier argument to a dark corner of her memory.

Later that night, Maddie told Tom about the musicians she had heard playing her song in the park.

"Wow. That must have been amazing!" he exclaimed.

"It really was. To hear other people play the music you've written, to sing your lyrics, it's wild."

Tom said thoughtfully, "You know, I should talk to Jerry about booking us some studio time with the money we've made so far. We're going to need a band for that. Do you think those guys will be out there again tomorrow?"

"I guess, if the weather's as nice as it was today."

"Maybe I'll check them out while you're in class. We need some talent that will play with us on the cheap. Like for free. Maybe we can cut a deal for money on the back end if they're students looking to break in. And like it or not, we're going to need some backup singers."

"Not Emilia," Maddie said quickly.

"Okay," Tom said evasively. "Let's just see who we can get."

Maddie sat up in bed. "This isn't up for negotiation, Tom. I have an equal vote in this business decision. I say no Emilia."

He threw his leg over her body, letting her know just how serious he was about proving that she was his one and only. "I promise I don't have any feelings for that girl. I don't know how else I can prove it to you."

Maddie could feel him pressing his desire for her along her hip and considered letting the whole Emilia thing go, but then she said stubbornly, "C'mon, Tom. There's got to be a ton of other singers out there. Find them."

"I'll do my best. I promise. Now let me help you forget all about today."

Maddie lay back against the pillows but had trouble at first responding to his touch. All she could see was one image in her head: Emilia and Tom, hand in hand, sneaking off behind the stage to some unknown corner. It made her uneasy, and she couldn't get it out of her mind. But Tom was persistent, and she eventually succumbed, over and over again.

On Friday morning, Maddie met Tom at the front door of The Bitter End so that Jerry could introduce them to the club's owner, Paul Colby—a legend in his own right. First a manager, then ultimately purchasing the venue, he was a man short in stature but not in reputation. He had booked all of Maddie's idols—Bob Dylan, Joan Baez, Joni Mitchell—and here she was shaking his hand right outside his theater on Bleeker Street.

Tom had informed Maddie that they were going to do a quick run-through of their set to give her a chance to get a feel for the new surroundings and help quell her stage fright. She had all but conquered her phobia while performing at The Cellar. It was her second home now, and she was no longer afraid to face that audience and sing. But this would be different, and she was worried that this new crowd wouldn't give them the same warm reception they had enjoyed at school.

Paul Colby, an affable older man, opened the door to the club and walked them around the stage. It was small, with an exposed red brick wall that served as the backdrop for the performers. With 230 seats, it was almost double the size of The Cellar Bar. Maddie couldn't help but notice that the small tables crowded inside extended all the way to the lip of the stage. It was hard not to imagine the place filled to capacity, a thought that made her shake inside. When she glanced at Tom, she saw how excited he was to be there and only wished she felt the same.

"You guys do your thing, get comfortable here," Paul said. "It's going to be packed tonight, and you get only one shot to make it happen. There's always someone else coming on right behind you, so we've got no time for amateurs." Paul smiled reassuringly at Maddie. "Jerry tells me you guys are great. Can't wait to hear what you've got." Then he scurried away to check on a liquor delivery at the back entrance.

"Okay, you two. You heard the man. I'll be back for the show tonight." Jerry put out his ever-present cigarette in a small red ashtray on the closest table, turned, and bolted as abruptly as Paul had, leaving Maddie and Tom alone in the club.

Tom spread his arms wide, beside himself with glee. "This is so awesome, Maddie, isn't it? Look at us, playing The Bitter End."

Maddie couldn't move. Paul's words about having "only one shot" resonated in her, reaching deep into the heart of her fear. She stood near the stage between two tables, unable to take the step up to join Tom, who had started looking around for a stool for Maddie to sit on during their set. He was so intent on his search that it took a few minutes before he realized that she was still standing on the floor below.

"Get on up here with me, Maddie. Scope it out! Let's practice that new song you just wrote. Did we ever decide on a title? It was so late by the time we finished it last night, I can't remember." When he realized it would take more coaxing to get her to move, he jumped down beside her.

"Look at me, Maddie."

She lifted her head to gaze into his eyes.

"You can do this. What's our mantra?"

"Trust the music, trust in each other."

"That's right. It's worked before. No reason it won't work again. Now tell me the title of the new song."

"'Always in My Heart.'"

"Okay then. Let's practice." Smiling encouragingly, he took her hand, and together they climbed up to the microphone on the stage. He removed his guitar from its case and began to play.

As soon as Maddie heard the opening chords of the music she'd written, she felt some of her tension leave, but in the back of her mind she was well aware that at the moment no one was staring up at them from the seats below. Looking at Tom, she forced herself to become lost in both his eyes and the music, and it must have worked, because when the song was over, she heard a single round of applause coming from the back of the room. Paul Colby.

"Wow. What a great love song, and you two really look the part. You sold me! With a little professional arrangement and a few more musicians, I think you have a hit on your hands. Let me ask you something—are you happy with Jerry? Is he doing enough for you?"

"He got us this gig," Tom replied.

"Kid, the two of you could have walked in here on open mic night and I would have put you up on the stage with that song. Can he get you into the studio? Because if he can't, I can."

"Mr. Colby, I don't know what to say." Tom was doing his best to sound calm, but Maddie could sense the tremendous excitement surging through him—the same excitement she felt, only hers was sharpened with fear. "We'll definitely take you up on that offer. Can we record the song we just played?"

"Let's talk after the show tonight. I want to bring Jerry into the conversation. I've known him forever and don't want to do him dirty. But if he can't push you forward, I can."

Maddie was still shaking when they left the club, her thoughts racing, her anxiety mounting. All she wanted was to lie down in her safe little dorm bed and close her eyes, but she knew that even if she tried, she wouldn't be able to rest. It felt like a million jolts of electricity were traveling through her. Silently she let Tom lead her to a coffee shop where he insisted that she try to eat, but nothing seemed to appeal to her.

Tom, on the other hand, was ravenous. He ate his sandwich and then polished off the grilled cheese she'd barely touched. She wrapped her hands around her coffee mug, trying to pull the warmth from it deep into the center of her being.

"Maddie, it's going to be fine. Remember how nervous you were before the Cellar show? It's the same thing. You're not alone. I'm right beside you." He motioned for the waitress to bring the check.

"Be honest, Tom. This is so much bigger. You're talking about going into a recording studio and making a demo."

He looked across the table at her, his eyes burning with excitement. "Yeah. That's the end game. I want people to hear our music, to be on the radio, to play sold-out shows at Madison Square Garden. I want it all."

"Well, I'm not sure I do," she said quietly.

His eyes widened. "Are you kidding? We've been talking about this since the first day we sang together."

"I don't think so, Tom. You may have been talking about it. I've been thinking about how nice it's been to be able to share our music with each other and with our friends at school. I never saw myself on a stage as big as the Garden's. That thought makes me sick to my stomach."

Tom was silent a moment. She could see his jaw muscles working. "Can we do this show tonight and see what happens? We don't have to decide the path of the rest of our lives before I pay for lunch, do we?"

"No," Maddie whispered. "But I don't know if I can do this show tonight. I'm so scared."

Tom briefly closed his eyes and took a deep breath. For the first time Maddie saw how annoyed he was with her. But his tone was patient when he said, "What are we going to do to get you past this thing, Maddie? I'm here for you, always, but I don't know what else to do." He reached across the table and placed his hands over hers on her coffee mug. "Tell you what. If after the show you want to call it quits, I'll go out as a solo act. You won't have to perform ever again. But I truly believe you can do this. Trust me. I won't let you fall."

A few months ago, Maddie suddenly realized, those words would have made everything so much better. But ever since finding that note in his laundry, the word "trust" had been diminished for her when it came to Tom. She wanted desperately to believe him, to have faith in him, to be able to let go of everything that plagued her, but try as she might, it was impossible. Even if Tom was telling the truth about Emilia and nothing had happened between them, the protection he'd provided her onstage like a coat of armor now had a kink. If he had lied about Emilia, how could Maddie now believe he'd have her back during a show if she started to freak out?

The unsettled feeling was still with her hours later as she put on her standard stage attire—faded, patched jeans and a white T-shirt. She ran a brush through her hair until it fell in a tumble of blond curls around her shoulders. She was applying some concealer under her eyes to hide the dark circles from a serious lack of sleep when Tom burst into her dorm room smiling.

"Maddie, good news! I got you something to help with the anxiety." He pulled a small white pill out of his pocket.

"What the hell is that?" she asked.

"It's a 'lude. I got it from a guy I know on my old floor. It will relax you and get you through the show. By the time you wake up tomorrow, it'll be like you never took it."

Maddie put her hands on her hips. "No way, Tom. I'm not taking a pill you got from some strange guy."

"What's the big deal?"

"The big deal is that I don't take drugs. I don't know what that is exactly"—she gestured at the tiny pill in Tom's hand—"and I don't know what it will do to me, and I don't want it."

Tom winked. "Mind if I take it then? It's supposed to give you the best buzz, make you happy."

"Are you crazy, Tom? I need you there for me. If you take that pill, I'm not going to the club at all."

He shrugged, stuffed it back in his pocket, and showed her his empty hands. "Okay, I'll give it back."

"Promise me you won't take it before the show."

"You have my word." He leaned in close and gave Maddie a kiss. "Now let's go." Picking up his guitar, he opened the door for her. "Our fans beckon," he teased, trying to lighten the mood as he nudged her into the hallway.

Maddie took a deep breath, squared her shoulders, and walked with Tom the few blocks to the club. It was a beautiful night, clear, with more stars than she could remember seeing since leaving home. Maybe that was a good sign. If the number of twinkling stars in the sky was any indication, maybe someone up there was watching over her. She sure hoped so, because the closer she got to the club, the more fear she felt rising into her throat.

The place was packed by the time they stepped through the back door, with a line of people still snaked down the block. As they walked through the dark backstage area, Maddie thought her heart was going to explode from her chest. She repeated her mantra silently in her head, holding Tom's hand trying not to break their connection.

Tom pulled her through the darkness. Maddie could hear the act on the stage finishing their set to a lively crowd's appreciative applause. By the time Tom led her into the lights, she saw the crew breaking down the band's set to make way for them.

She hung back. "God, I don't think I can do this."

"Maddie—"

"I can't, Tom. Let me go!"

He tightened his hold. In the glow of the lights on the stage she saw the fierce gleam of his eyes. "You. Can. Do. This."

"Tom—"

He put a finger on her lips and locked his gaze with hers. "Trust me."

And before she knew it, they were being introduced, and Tom was playing the familiar chords she'd written. Maddie felt the heat of the center stage spotlight as she sat on the stool Tom had led her to and closed her eyes, afraid to look at the crowd.

Not until midway through the first song did she finally open them. To her amazement, she saw all of their friends from The Cellar Bar filling the front tables. Gavin was there, and so was Emilia, beaming up at her with unconcealed pride. Maddie let out a deep breath, focusing on the sense of safety and comfort she felt in the embrace of their familiar faces.

As they went through their playlist, Maddie's tension began to lift. Sensing as much, Tom caught her eye and winked. She smiled back, though she couldn't entirely relax. Even after their encore of "Always in My Heart" and the thunderous applause, she couldn't entirely shake the uneasiness.

She let Tom guide her through the haze as they exited the stage, where Jerry and Paul Colby hurried up to meet them.

"Let's step into my office," Paul said.

They were ushered down a narrow hallway into a small, dark room with record albums and cassette tapes on every surface. The four of them stood around the cluttered desk that dominated the space.

"You guys were great," Paul said enthusiastically. "Really loved your stuff. Jerry and I were talking. You've got to record that one you did as an encore—the one I heard this afternoon. What's it called again?"

"'Always in My Heart'," Tom replied.

"Yeah. You've got a real shot with that one. I think we can get you some radio play with it."

"When do you want to record it?" Jerry asked Paul.

"I'd like the chance to work out the arrangement a bit more," Tom said, adding quickly, "but we'll be ready whenever you tell us to be."

Maddie struggled to find her voice, shocked at Tom's quick response. They were nowhere near ready to record anything. "Don't we need to find some musicians first?" she asked.

"I have that under control. I've got a backup band in mind, Mr. Colby," Tom said, shooting her a look that said *please let me handle this.*

"It'll move things along quicker if you're a total package," Paul responded. "That will save us studio rehearsal time too. Come in polished, and we can lay down the tracks pretty quickly."

"What do you think, Jerry?" Maddie asked, hoping he'd save her from her own quaking fear.

"I think it's time for me to turn you over to someone who can get you to that next level. I'm more a booking agent, and I don't have Paul's contacts. I won't stand in your way."

Maddie was stunned. She looked over at Tom and saw that he was barely able to contain his excitement. Were they really ready for "the next level"? She could feel the heat rising to her face. To cover her nerves she blurted out, "Okay, Jerry. Thanks for everything."

"Really, Jerry, that's so generous," Tom said, shaking the older man's hand.

"Don't expect anyone else in the business to be that good to you," Paul warned. "It's ruthless out there. Jerry and I've known each other a long time. I'll take care of his end of this, don't worry."

Rummaging through some boxes on his desk, he pulled out two new Sony Walkmans and handed each of them one with a box of blank cassette tapes. "You've got to live, eat, and sleep this song. Record a rough cut of the tune and listen to it day and night. Make all of your changes and adjustments before you come to the studio. Time is money. You've got to get it down perfectly—it's your one shot. Understand?"

Tom responded immediately, "Yes, sir. We won't let you down."

"Good," Paul said. "Now go out there and meet your fans. Word of mouth is still your best marketing tool."

"I'm going to hang back and talk to Paul," Jerry said through the blue haze of his cigarette smoke. "You guys go. Good luck in the studio."

"Thanks, man, thanks so much." Tom took Maddie's hand and led her back into the narrow hallway. Right before they reached the interior of the club, he turned and kissed her warmly. "This is a dream come true. We're gonna make a record, babe. I can't believe it."

"Me either! And our own songs. It's incredible." Maddie could hear herself mouthing the words, but all she felt was dazed. It was happening too fast for her, yet she was afraid to disappoint Tom when he looked so deliriously happy.

As they made their way to the bar, people got out of their seats to shake their hands, clap them on the back, tell them how much they had enjoyed the music. Feeling almost disconnected from the attention, Maddie settled into a dark corner with a glass of wine, watching Tom work the room. He was masterful at charming people, making them feel special, pulling them into his world. Watching him, loving him, she suddenly thought she saw him reach into his pocket and put something in his mouth. She couldn't be sure, but it looked like the little white pill she'd refused to take earlier. Surely she'd imagined it? After all, she was overtired and emotionally exhausted.

It was well after midnight when she walked over to where Tom was chatting up a group of guys she didn't know. Emilia and Gavin and the rest of their friends from The Cellar Bar had left some time ago, and now Maddie tiredly put a hand on Tom's arm. "I'm going to head back. I can't keep my eyes open."

He pulled her in for a hug. "Do you mind if I stay? I'm so stoked. I know I won't sleep tonight. Besides, I'm doing just what Paul said—I'm talking us up!"

She couldn't help but smile. He was a bundle of energy and she just wanted to sleep. "Sure. See you later."

He kissed her and whispered, "Love you, Maddie."

"Love you too." As she turned to leave, she heard someone order another round of drinks. It was obvious that Tom was there for the long haul, and for a change, she really didn't care. All she wanted was lie down and close her eyes. She had no more room in her brain for worry, not one more shred of energy to think of anything but sleep.

By the time they were ready to go into the studio, Tom had worked his usual magic and convinced the group of young musicians Maddie had met in the park to perform for a piece of the profits should the record generate any money. There was a drummer named Ned, a bass player named Charlie, and a violinist who liked to be called Andre, although Maddie was pretty sure this was just some starving artist persona he'd adopted.

They were actually a pretty fun trio, and Maddie was immediately comfortable in their company. They showed her a lot of respect as a song-writer, praising the phrases and chords she'd created and calling them true works of art. During jam sessions and rehearsals they often added their own riffs to the music, strengthening Tom's arrangements and making the tunes flow easily with their harmonies. As it turned out, Andre played several stringed instruments and had a clear, strong voice, which served as a perfect complement to their own.

The only holdup was the fact that they were still looking to complete the band with a female backup singer, and even Tom hadn't been able to find anyone who was the right fit. Two days before their recording date, with time running out and the pressure mounting, Tom revisited the pos-sibility of asking Emilia. They were walking back to Maddie's dorm room after several hours of rehearsal when he brought up the subject. It had started to drizzle lightly, casting fuzzy halos around the streetlamps.

Maddie's heart sank. "How many times are we going to have this argu-ment, Tom? I'm not playing music in the same room with Emilia."

"But you guys are friends!"

"She has no boundaries when it comes to you," Maddie said stubbornly. "It's not fair to keep asking me if she can sing with us."

"Then what should we do? I'm open to suggestions, Maddie," Tom shot back. "We need another female voice to complete the arrangement I've worked out. You can't do it all, and I've looked everywhere and can't find anyone else."

"So re-arrange it with only my voice. Or let me record the backup portion separately and lay it over the rest. I just don't want her in the studio."

Tom stood still, ignoring the fact that the rain had picked up in intensity and was falling from his hair onto his shoulders. He let go of Maddie's hand and said darkly, "You are simply going to have to trust me. I am not now, nor have I ever been, involved with Emilia Parkson. I just know that her voice blends perfectly with yours and with the sound we have, for the record we're trying to create. Nothing bad will happen if she sings backup. But if we leave it alone and don't have that additional voice, well . . ."

Maddie stared at him. "Is that a threat, Tom? Are you saying that if I don't let Emilia sing with us and we fail, it'll be my fault?" Her voice shook.

"No, not at all. I'm just asking for some faith from you on this." Tom paused, running his hand through his wet hair in frustration. "And it will give you a chance to see that Emilia means nothing to me. I just want her there for her voice, that's all."

"But what about when we're not recording? I don't want her hanging around, chatting you up and cozying up to our band. She's like a bad virus—she'll move through the whole group of us, infecting us with her toxins."

Tom laughed out loud. "Isn't that a little overdramatic, Mad? Toxins? Really?"

He continued to laugh halfway down the block to the entrance of their building.

Maddie knew that she should trust her own instincts when it came to Emilia, but she also wanted to trust Tom. If only Emilia hadn't written that note, hadn't told Maddie that Tom was "hot" and she wouldn't mind making a play for him herself. Those things still stung. She drew in a deep breath and, with it, all the courage she could muster. "If I say yes, what's my guarantee that you only deal with her while we're in the studio? No after-hours partying. No corner-of-the-room hushed conferences. Everything you say to her is said in front of the group."

"If that's what it will take to make this okay for you, then fine. I'll keep everything between Emilia and me out in the open." Tom grinned at her, disarming as ever. "And why wouldn't I? I keep telling you I've got nothing to hide."

"Oh boy. I know I'm going to regret this."

"Yes!" Tom shouted.

Maddie covered his mouth with her hand and looked deeply into his eyes. "If I get the slightest hint that she's putting the moves on you again, I will pack up my sheet music and go. She can stay, but I will leave."

"It won't come to that, Maddie, really it won't." His heart was reflected in his eyes as he held the door open for her, and she found herself crumbling, as she always did around him. Still, she couldn't shake the feeling that she had just opened up a Pandora's box that would never be completely shut again.

VIII

Two days later they were in the studio, and from the very first take, it all jelled. Everyone felt it, from the sound engineer to the musicians, even to the janitor sweeping the hallway outside. Midway through the session, as Maddie looked around the room from her seat at the piano, she felt overwhelmed with joy. Her music was coming to life around her, swirling overhead, bouncing off the walls from the instruments held by her newest group of friends. Tom had been right: Ned, Charlie, Andre, and Emilia were the missing pieces that turned Maddie and Tom from a duo into a band. It was remarkable just how fast they had bonded, and the heady jokes were already flowing freely.

"Hey, man," Charlie yelled to Andre, pointing at the cap that perched jauntily on his long hair. "Paris called. They want their beret back!"

"Beret?" Ned questioned through his laughter. "I thought it was a Frisbee!"

Grinning broadly, Maddie turned her attention to Emilia. *So far, so good*, she thought, recalling the conversation the two of them had had the night before they starting recording. Emilia had called Maddie to thank her for the chance to sing with the band. She'd been bubbling over with enthusiasm.

"This is gonna be great, Maddie! I've got the whole track memorized already. You won't be disappointed."

Emilia never mentioned Tom during the call, and Maddie wanted to believe that she'd imagined the whole thing and that her fears were not real but rather a result of her stress over recording.

She was jolted from her thoughts when Tom sat down close beside her on the piano bench. He put his hand on her thigh suggestively and whispered in her ear, "Have I told you today how much I love you?"

Maddie felt herself melt. "No, but when we're done working, how about you show me?"

His eyes glinted in response, letting her know that they were on the same page, and when he smiled at her, she couldn't have been happier.

"You were right about everything, Tom," she told him softly.

He beamed at her. "Aren't I always?"

The groundswell of enthusiasm in the studio for "Always in My Heart" was enormous, and Paul was delighted with the finished track. He promised to make a few calls and see if he could get some radio play time for them, as well as booking them back into the club as headliners over the next two weekends.

The timing couldn't have been better. Classes were over for the spring semester, and everyone was looking to blow off some steam. The Bitter End was packed each night they played, and true to his word, Tom kept his distance from Emilia. The whole band worked the sets at the club because Paul wanted to be sure that the sound on the stage duplicated the radio release. Now all they could do was wait to see if any of his connections came through.

When it finally did happen, it was almost dreamlike. Maddie and Tom were in bed, sweaty from the late spring heat outside the dorm window and the efforts of their lovemaking. Maddie lay with her head on Tom's chest, his arms around her. The radio was set to WNEW-FM, the progressive rock station that broadcast the music they loved. They listened to "the night bird," Alison Steele, talk about a new duo and their harmonious sound. "I think you'll agree this is a great new band," she said as the opening chords of "Always in My Heart" drifted softly from the speakers.

At first, Maddie was too stunned to move, but Tom shot straight out of bed.

"Holy shit, Maddie! Paul did it. We're on the radio!"

"I can't believe it," she whispered faintly. "I wonder if the guys in the band are listening?"

"I bet they're at The Cellar. Should we go find them?"

"Definitely!" she answered, snatching her underwear from the floor, pulling her jeans and T-shirt on as quickly as she could. She was halfway out the door before Tom stopped her.

"Wait! I want to hear the end of the song. Let's see if she says anything else."

At that moment, the voice on the radio came back. "I love that new tune so much I'm going to play it again at the top of the hour. Tell your friends!"

Tom and Maddie looked at each other.

"Wow," was all Tom could say. He yanked the cord out of the wall and tucked the radio under his arm. "For insurance," he told Maddie. "I want to hear the song when she plays it again."

They practically ran the two blocks to the student union. Just as predicted, Andre, Ned, and Charlie were at their usual corner table with Emilia.

"Did you hear it?" Tom practically yelled at them.

"Hear what?" Ned asked.

"'Always in My Heart.' It was just on the radio!"

"No way, man," Charlie said.

Tom was already on his hands and knees looking for an outlet. He found one under the table, and the six of them sat, transfixed by the glow of the transmitter's soft light, willing the song to come on again. As promised, it played again. At first the group sat quietly, but soon they were all singing along. When it was over, there were whoops and high fives all around. Energized and excited, they all spoke at once.

"Hey, man," Andre said to Tom after they calmed down, "what's our next recording?"

"Yeah. We need to capitalize on this. When are we going back into the studio?" Ned asked.

"And a tour, man," Charlie added. "When do we hit the road?"

Tom sat back in his chair, grinning widely. "This is mind-blowing! I can't believe this whole thing is happening. Let's take tonight and just enjoy it!"

Maddie sat back, reflecting on this magical feeling of knowing they had truly become a band. Surely she would always feel this way, and the road to her future with Tom would always be this blessed.

And then she glimpsed what she thought was a pill bottle being passed from Emilia to Tom.

Maddie sat stock still, not wanting to believe her eyes. But she *had* seen it: an amber-colored vial with white tablets inside as it went from Emilia's palm into Tom's hand. He had his other arm draped around Maddie's waist, and because of the odd angle, she couldn't be sure of what she'd seen, but then she felt him bend down to put the bottle inside his sock, trying his best to control his motions so that she would remain unaware of them. Then he glanced at her out of the corner of his eye as if trying to determine if she'd noticed anything.

Maddie forced herself to remain calm. She certainly didn't want to ruin this moment for the rest of the band or publicly accuse Tom of something he'd promised her he wouldn't do. No, Maddie would have to think about how to handle this later, because right now, she was much too angry to formulate her thoughts.

When the band gathered the following week at their favorite coffee shop on West Fourth to finalize their next move, Maddie had done a lot of thinking, but she still hadn't decided on how best to deal with the situation. Tom had been so attentive and loving since that night that she wondered if maybe it was best to say nothing at all. Or was that simply the coward's way out?

She forced herself to pay attention to the talk around her.

"Andre, man, if you could play the mandolin on 'Back to Love,' it would really round out the sound we're looking for," Tom was saying as he bit into his club sandwich.

"I'd need some solid practice time, but I think I can do it," Andre replied while chewing. "I also know a guy who plays the harp if we need him."

"A harp?" Emilia asked. "Isn't that a little too classical for us?"

The sound of Emilia's voice grated on Maddie's frayed nerves. They had been together for long sessions in the studio over the last five days, and both times she had nervously watched for signs that either Tom or Emilia had come in stoned, but they hadn't. She'd also paid close attention to whether or not they arrived or left together, and that hadn't happened either. Both of them had behaved normally, exactly the way they always had.

Maddie had attempted to clear the air with Emilia after the night in The Cellar when they first heard "Always in My Heart" on the radio together, but Emilia had brushed her concerns aside.

"I am not going after Tom. You guys are together, I get it," Emilia had told her. "And our friendship counts for something, Maddie, you know? I'm grateful for the work, and I love singing backup for you. I could never imagine this happening when I first came to NYU. It's a dream come true, and I won't mess it up."

It's not that Maddie truly believed her, but she was glad to have gotten the issue of Tom and Emilia out in the open. Now, Maddie felt, if Emilia crossed the line, Tom would have no option but to cut her loose from the band.

Tom's voice brought her out of her own thoughts and back to the table.

"So why don't we practice some tonight?" he asked. "Meet at The Cellar at nine?" With the semester over, the campus club was dark most nights, and the manager was happy to let the group use the stage in exchange for the promise of future bookings in the fall.

"How long do you think it's gonna take?" Emilia asked. "I've got a date."

"A date?" asked Charlie. "Who with?"

"Yeah, Emilia, we're like your big brothers now. We want to meet the guy, make sure his intentions are good," Ned joked.

Emilia rolled her eyes. "Like I'm gonna bring anyone around to meet you two. What a way to scare him off. No thanks."

"Really, Emilia. You should let us meet him. You haven't been the most discerning judge when it comes to some of the guys you've dated," Andre observed. "Remember that loser who showed up at our last Bitter End show? That guy was so high—"

Emilia interrupted him with a loud laugh. "I don't need my dates vetted by you! Besides, it's just for drinks, Andre. No big commitment. Not like Tom and Maddie," she said and added, "How's the apartment hunting going, you two? Find something suitable yet?"

Maddie shot a look across the table at Tom. She hadn't said anything about moving in with Tom to anyone. Had he told Emilia?

Tom said quickly, "I've actually found something I want Maddie to see later. Who told you?" he added, obviously trying to head off a later argument with Maddie.

"Guilty," Andre said, then shrugged his shoulders. "What? Like it's some big secret you two are moving in together? Please. Why don't you just get married already?"

Maddie blanched. "I've rearranged my whole life switching to night school for this band next semester! I'm not ready to get married for it!"

"But think of the publicity we'd get," Andre laughed.

"I think we'll try living together first," Tom said sharply. "Let's save the marriage talk for another time."

"Dude, you've been living together in the dorm all year. Keep it real, okay?" Andre replied.

Tom shot out of his chair. The subject was clearly as uncomfortable for him as it was for Maddie. "I'm done here. Gotta go make sure everything's ready for tonight." He turned to Maddie. "See you at that apartment on Charles Street at three, right?"

She nodded. He threw some cash on the table. He had really saved quite a bit of the money they'd made playing at The Bitter End. "See you losers later."

There was an uncomfortable silence until, one by one, the other male members of the band left the table, mumbling hasty farewells. Maddie and Emilia were left alone.

"I didn't mean to upset you," Emilia said after a moment. "I thought everyone knew you guys were moving in together. It's really not such a big deal."

Maddie took a deep breath. "Look, Emilia, you've said some things in the past that make me question whether or not you can honor the relationship I'm in with Tom. He's off limits, plain and simple, as is everything about him."

"I heard you, Maddie," Emilia replied. "Not once, not twice, but multiple times now: leave Tom alone. You must think I'm a crazy nympho or something. Well, I'm not. Tom is all yours. Promise."

Maddie let out the long breath she'd been holding. "Thanks, Emilia," she said guardedly. "Look," she added, hoping to make amends, "I wasn't exactly a social butterfly in high school, and I'd really love to have the kind of friendship with you that I can put some faith behind, to know that you've got my back and I've got yours."

"Of course," Emilia replied quickly. "We want the same thing. I get that you don't trust me. That needs time. And I admit I was interested in Tom at first, and I was very jealous of you, but all that's changed. I care a lot more for the music you've written, Maddie. I think you're so talented and that I'm truly blessed to be a part of this crazy thing going on here." She reached across the table and took Maddie's hand. "Let's start over." She cleared her throat and broke into a wide grin. "Hi. My name is Emilia Parkson. What's yours?"

Maddie chuckled. "You know my name!"

"No, you've got to play along. What's your name?"

"I'm Madeline Ellis. Most people call me Maddie, and I write songs."

"Nice to meet you, Maddie. I think this is the beginning of a long, beautiful friendship."

"I'd like that Emilia. I really would." Maddie cautiously smiled back, hoping that this new, candid, and clearly sober Emilia was a person she could trust. Jumping in with two feet she asked, "So who's your date tonight?"

"Ooh, let me tell you about him . . ." Emilia said enthusiastically.

IX

Maddie heard the phone ring as she drummed her fingers on the beige Formica countertop waiting for Emilia to pick up on her end. It didn't take long.

"Hey there, Maddie. What's up?"

"I just got the architectural plans for the new loft in the West Village. You wanna come over and help me figure out where to move the walls?" she asked.

"Definitely! You know I love that stuff. And I have to fill you in on my date last night. This guy is *the one*. Give me a half hour. I'm on my way."

"Great," Maddie said, smiling into the receiver. "See you soon." As she hung up and looked around the little Charles Street apartment that she and Tom had shared for the last five years, she felt truly at peace. The band was successful, with a second album in the works to follow their platinum-selling debut record. Over the last two years they had done many successful college arena concerts, opened for bigger bands and now their first large venue tour as headliners was to start at the end of the month. At home, Maddie had created a cozy, warm sanctuary for Tom and herself, a place where the whole band liked to gather for impromptu meals and movie nights.

Even more importantly, in the time that had passed since that fateful Simon and Garfunkel concert in Central Park so long ago, Maddie and Emilia had gotten really close. Being the only female members of the band, they realized that it was important to maintain the bond that had grown between them. Their initial shaky relationship had finally blossomed into a cherished friendship.

Maddie and Tom had allowed themselves to spend some of their royalty money and together bought an unfinished loft apartment on Prince Street. They had debated the idea back and forth, both of them somewhat reluctant to make so large a commitment as a couple, although for different reasons: Maddie worried about Tom's increasing dependence on certain illegal substances, and he was growing more uncomfortable with her straitlaced ways.

Despite that, and believing their love for one another would make everything okay, Maddie and Tom were as settled down as any two rising rock stars could be, and the purchase of this home had made that fact all the more real for them both.

Now Maddie made quick work of setting out a dish of cookies for her and Emilia to share while they reviewed the drawings. Emilia, Maddie knew, loved junk food. No matter how hard Maddie tried to convince her to live healthier, Emilia always resisted, so every now and then, Maddie had to shut her eyes and give in. Shaking her head, she reached into the pantry and pulled out a package of Oreos, Emilia's favorite. Maddie prided herself on being a great hostess, so she kept them for occasions like this one. Just as she finished brewing tea and laying out her colorful linen napkins, the doorbell rang.

Emilia entered the apartment in a cloud of Calvin Klein's Obsession perfume, wearing a teal-blue one-piece jumper with a long black vest over it, a wide dark blue belt with a chunky silver buckle, high-top red Converse sneakers, and her violet-colored permed hair cascading midway down her back in a wild tangle of curls. Her outrageous outfits always made Maddie feel like she was invisible in her simple choices of jeans, T-shirts, and the occasional sundress.

"Let's see those blueprints!" Emilia cried, making her way over to the counter. "This space is going to be so great, and, ooh, Maddie! Oreos! You are the best!" She wrapped Maddie in a big hug.

Maddie smiled as Emilia, always a whirlwind of energy and enthusiasm, released her just as quickly and leapt to the counter to unfurl the blueprints. "Wow. This is intense," she said, studying the plans in front of her.

"Hold up, Emilia. Before we start redesigning the loft, tell me about this new guy you're dating," Maddie said, tucking her tame-in-comparison blond curls behind her ears.

"His name is Martin, and he's a photographer, this real brooding artist type," Emilia replied happily, munching on a cookie.

"Is he cute?" Maddie asked, bringing Emilia a mug of tea.

"In a skinny kind of way. He's got long brown hair that he ties back in a ponytail and dark gray eyes. He's just my type."

"Type? What type?" Maddie asked with a laugh. "You've gone after all sorts of men since I've known you. Have you started to discriminate?"

"Very funny. I like men, what can I say?"

"Are you going to invite him to a show so we can all meet him?"

"Well . . ."

"Better hurry," Maddie urged. "We're hitting the road at the end of the month for the whole summer. Will he wait around until you get back?"

Emilia looked down at her hands, a myriad of silver rings adorning her long, thin fingers. "I actually wanted to talk to you about that. What if he came with us for a bit, you know, hitched a ride, looked for inspiration? His photos are really cool, mostly in sepia and black and white. Real vintage looking. I think you'd like them," she added, biting into another Oreo. "There's room on the bus, right?"

"I don't know if that's a good idea," Maddie said hesitantly. "Don't you think the band will torture him? They tend to be so overprotective of you."

"Let me be the judge of that," Emilia begged. "If he's a keeper, he's going to have to get to know everyone, right? We all spend a lot of time together."

"That's true," Maddie agreed, now chewing contemplatively on a cookie while telling herself she was only eating it as a show of solidarity with Emilia. "Let me run it by Tom. I'll let you know what he says."

"Great. I really appreciate that." Emilia unscrewed the chocolate top from the cream center of the cookie in her hand.

"The road's never fun, at least not for me," Maddie admitted. "I really hate the live shows. And this tour is so big. I so much prefer studio work."

"You are so weird, Maddie! It's amazing how far we've come. We used to play those little dive bars, and now we're on this huge stadium tour. I mean, really, did you ever expect us to get this big?" Emilia asked, wide-eyed. "I get such a rush from the audience," she went on, "especially when they start to sing along with us. Don't you love it when strangers know the music, the words to your songs?" Her clunky silver bracelets sounded like music to Maddie as they hit against one another each time Emilia gesticulated with her arms.

"I do, but I still feel queasy every time I go out on a new stage. And the pre-show jitters are there no matter what I do." Maddie shrugged her shoulders to prove that it didn't really matter.

"I thought you and Tom had that mantra thing worked out. You shouldn't get this worked up anymore. Maybe you need to take something, you know, a Valium, to help blur the edges," Emilia said matter-of-factly.

"Tom offered me something at the start of all this," Maddie said coolly, "and it was almost the end of our relationship. No drugs for me."

"You are such a stick-in-the-mud! You don't have to do the hard stuff, but what's a joint or a Quaalude between friends?" Emilia batted her eyelids innocently.

Maddie knew from their shared time on the road together that pot and 'ludes were Emilia's current drugs of choice. "What do you think would happen if we all went onstage high?" she asked pointedly.

"I don't know. I never thought about it," Emilia said as she licked the Oreo cream.

She sounded so indifferent that Maddie felt compelled to reaffirm her own point of view. "It would be a disaster, that's what. Who would lead the band, remember the words, the set list?" Maddie knew perfectly well that drugs were always available, and she knew that everyone, Tom included, sampled a wide variety of substances whenever they toured—all of them illegal. Thankfully the police had never raided them backstage, or she surely would have been posting bail along the way for one band member or another. Still, it wasn't her place to tell them how to live their lives.

On the other hand, somebody had to be responsible. "We've got a growing reputation, a record contract," she insisted. "I'm not letting anything get in the way of all the progress we've made in this crazy industry. It'll only take one fuck-up to bring us all back down."

Emilia rolled her eyes. "I'm not suggesting—"

"Yeah, you are. You want me to try something when the thought of doing drugs would make me more anxious than I already am. You can take the girl out of a small New England town, Emilia, but you can't take the small New England town out of the girl."

"I know that, Maddie, but all I'm asking is for you to loosen up a bit." Emilia put down her tea and sat a little taller in her chair. "And not to judge me. I show up for work on time, and I'm always in tune. I never forget the words or the order of the songs. When and if I do, you have my permission to call me out, but don't worry so much about me. Actually, stop worrying about absolutely everything. I'm in complete control of myself, as are Ned, Charlie, Andre, and Tom. None of us has ever let anything interfere with our professional selves."

"That's true," Maddie said reluctantly. "But—"

"But nothing, Maddie. My indulgence is only recreational. I'm not the hardcore druggie you make me out to be. None of us are. So stop being such a drag."

Maddie drew in a breath. Emilia was right. Nobody in the band was ever anything but a consummate pro at work. So wasn't it unfair of Maddie to put her own set of moral values on them? Actually, she knew damned well it was.

She watched as Emilia separated the tops of four cookies from the bottoms and squashed two together, cream sides touching, before popping them into her mouth.

"What?" Emilia asked in response to Maddie's stare. "I don't think these cookies have enough cream. I like to double them up—or do you have a problem with that too?" she asked mid chew.

"Oh, I see. You're a grown-up now, huh, making creative decisions?" Maddie teased, breaking the tension that had been building between them. And with that, the two women fell into a fit of laughter.

As Maddie and Tom were turning down the blankets and getting ready for bed that night, Maddie brought up the subject of Emilia's new boyfriend.

"You're telling me she wants to bring some random guy she's dating with us on the bus?" Tom asked. "Does he have any idea what he's getting himself into?"

"No clue, but it seems important to Emilia to have him along."

Tom was silent for a moment and then shrugged. "If he's up for our kind of crazy, why not?"

"Are you sure? It's tight on the bus to begin with. Do you think adding another body will put us over? I mean, it's always close quarters in there."

"Didn't you say he's a photographer? Maybe he'll be able to capture some of what we do on film. If he's as good as Emilia says, we could have us an awesome album cover."

Maddie hadn't thought of that. Tom was always the one coming up with different marketing strategies to boost sales. It was definitely his strong suit. Lately she'd taken to writing more of their music, sometimes with Andre, while Ned and Charlie worked out the arrangements and Emilia filled in the harmonies. They had all fallen naturally into their roles, and she couldn't deny that this had helped make the band even more successful.

"And if the dude is cool with us, why shouldn't we be cool with him?" Tom continued, tossing Maddie's decorative pillows onto the small couch at the foot of their bed. "Besides, if it doesn't work out, he can always hitch a ride back to New York. It doesn't seem like a problem to me."

Tom was right. Why not?

"I'll let her know tomorrow," Maddie said, pulling the sundress she had been wearing up over her head. She cursed as her long, thick hair got stuck in the laced-up corset back.

Seeing her struggle, Tom said softly, "Let me help you with that."

Maddie waited, expecting him to set her free of the fabric, but instead she felt his hands caressing her thighs. It was very erotic not being able to see him, and she felt herself relaxing into the heat that only Tom could ignite within her. Five years later, he was still the one who made her heart race.

"Take my dress off, please," she implored, twisting this way and that.

"I love when you talk dirty to me," he teased, and with a quick motion he freed her, whistling appreciatively when he saw that she was wearing only her skimpy underwear beneath. He pushed her back onto the bed, kissing her neck while caressing her breasts. "We better make the most of this alone time, Maddie. The road beckons."

She didn't want to think of the road. She only wanted to think about how good he was making her feel at this very moment, how she wanted it to be just her and him, together, at home, making love. She closed her eyes, blocking out further thoughts. She was in the place she felt safest, with the person she loved most, and she planned to enjoy the rest of the time they had together before their professional lives got back in the way.

Two weeks later the band assembled at their usual meeting spot on the corner of Fifth Avenue and Washington Square Park, right outside the famous arch. Their roadies, Ernie and Sal, were already loading the luggage in the underneath storage bins of the bus. Both of them traveled everywhere with the band while another crew of roadies met them at each location, building up and then breaking down their sets.

Tom supervised everything, paying extra attention to the placement of the instruments and sound equipment that had been loaded earlier from their warehouse space into the two large trucks that were now preparing to leave ahead of them. Maddie and Emilia made themselves comfortable inside the bus, settling in for the first leg of their journey. It was a beautiful June morning, not too hot yet but with the hint of summer looming.

Maddie was sipping a large takeout cup of coffee, running through her last-minute checklist of the items she'd need for the road. It seemed inevitable: she always forgot the one thing she needed. It wasn't as though she wouldn't be able to replace whatever it was; she just hated the hassle of finding some random thing she'd left behind in a strange city.

On their first road tour of college campuses a few years earlier, she'd spent an entire winter without gloves because she'd left them at home. Each time they stopped, Tom implored her to buy a pair, but by then she'd become recognizable in the small towns where they played and was swarmed by fans whenever she walked down the street. She hated the fishbowl feeling of people watching her every move and had chosen to go without gloves instead.

The rest of the band was different, Tom and Emilia especially—they thrived on attention. Maddie was constantly overwhelmed by it, although it didn't surprise her anymore. She knew what to expect and now prepared list after list of her essentials, down to the coffee beans she preferred.

Emilia was sitting next to Maddie on the couch, but she kept staring out the window and jumping up to pace the aisle before sitting back down. After this had gone on for a good twenty minutes, Maddie finally said something.

"What are you doing?" she asked.

"Looking for Martin. He's late. I told him we were leaving at nine and that you'd never hold the bus for him. He'd better get here soon."

Maddie looked at her watch. It was 8:45. "He's got another fifteen minutes. Have some faith."

"Wait. Did you just try to be Zen about something?" Emilia mocked. "Did the earth just stop rotating on its axis?"

Maddie rolled her eyes. "Very funny. If Martin knows what time we have to go, he'll be here. At least he will if he's as into you as you've been claiming . . ."

"I'll be crushed if he doesn't show up," Emilia said after a moment. "Just so you know." She looked like she was about to cry, and Maddie suddenly felt bad. Pulling Emilia back down onto the couch, she gave her a comforting hug.

"Maybe he got stuck on the subway or something. We can always wait a few extra minutes."

There was a small commotion on the sidewalk as Tom began to usher the rest of the band onto the bus. He stuck his head inside and grinned at Maddie. "All here and accounted for. Everything is tucked safely away, and we're ready to roll."

Emilia opened her mouth to protest when Maddie saw that a strange man—presumably Martin—was standing behind Tom, somewhat blocked from Emilia's view. Maddie squeezed Emilia's hand. "Everything's fine," she whispered.

When Martin made his way up the steps of the bus, Maddie could see that he was carrying a large bouquet of flowers and a camera with a wide-angle lens on a strap around his neck. He was good-looking in a bohemian sort of way, although she found his long hair somewhat distracting. If he made Emilia happy, she figured, it was fine.

Emilia gasped as she caught sight of him, and in the next moment Martin was hurrying down the aisle toward her. Grabbing her by the waist, he bent her back in a big, showy kiss.

When he came up for air, he leaned over to Maddie and said, "Hi, I'm Martin. These are for you. A little thank you for letting me tag along with my favorite girl." He handed Maddie the flowers before turning to kiss Emilia again.

Maddie watched them, mesmerized by this very public display of affection. "Thanks, these are beautiful," she managed. "It was so thoughtful of you. Let's just hope you aren't sick of us by this afternoon!"

Martin grinned at her. "No way. I'm glad to be here. This will be a blast." As he spoke, he pulled Emilia along with him to one of the couches in the back of the bus.

When they pulled away from the curb, Maddie's thoughts turned to the summer before them and their largest shows to date looming on the horizon. Her stomach did a sudden flip-flop at the thought. She only hoped she could summon the courage to see this tour through.

When Tom finally sat down, she settled in next to him, practicing her deep breathing all the way over the George Washington Bridge, not stopping until they were midway to their first stop in Delaware.

By August, Maddie, Tom, and the rest of the band knew that the tour was a bona fide hit. They were sold out every night to crowds numbering in the tens of thousands and had started negotiating with their record label to extend the tour worldwide—dates were already being arranged to continue straight through to Christmas. For Maddie, the thought of all that travel was both thrilling and nerve wracking. There was talk of hitting venues in Europe, and if things worked out as Tom hoped, maybe they would have some time off around New Year's to celebrate in Paris.

It was the yin and the yang of it, Maddie thought: fear and exhilaration. They were making more money than she had ever dreamed, so much so that if she never wanted to work again, they probably could live off of the royalties from the music they'd produced so far. But Maddie knew just how unrealistic the thought of "retiring" was. She recognized how much Tom loved their fame, their success. And she was all too aware of just how much he enjoyed the attention of the groupies that showed up wherever the band went.

The other guys in the band were all single, and random women would magically appear backstage at every venue, scantily clad, their purses filled with all sorts of things to smoke or pills and other mind-altering substances to share. This unanticipated aspect of stardom was a constant struggle for Maddie to deal with. She hated being a jealous shrew or acting like a narc, and she wanted to be able to trust Tom, but ever since he had first offered her a Quaalude, ever since she'd seen him and Emilia pass a bottle of pills around, she had pulled on a certain type of mental armor to deal with it.

For Maddie this meant that she was getting better at ignoring Tom's enjoyment of the excess of alcohol and drugs constantly available to them, watching in silence as he often became drunk or stoned for much of the day, sobering up only when it was time to perform onstage at night. It was a vicious cycle, and it was the source of their greatest arguments, which were now happening with more frequency.

Worst of all, Tom didn't see what was wrong with some, as he referred to it, "innocent flirting" when it came to the gaggle of beautiful women who always surrounded him. He claimed it just made him more attracted to Maddie, but she considered it a form of cheating on their relationship, on her. While Tom no longer paid attention to Emilia, who seemed obsessed with Martin, he tended to eye each and every woman who crossed his path.

Maddie hated it, and in a rare moment alone before their show in Denver, she had confronted Tom after finding him sandwiched between two seminude women in their shared dressing room. When she entered, the two groupies scurried away like frightened mice.

Something inside her seemed to snap, and she felt the helpless as anger surged through her. "That's it, Tom. No more! I can't take it!" Her voice shook. "You're making me sick with your behavior. Either we're together or we're not. Choose!" Her heart was pounding in her chest, her face contorted with pain and frustration as she turned away from him.

Tom immediately came up behind her, placing his arms across her body, pulling her close to him. He spoke soothingly, in that charming voice that always seemed to disarm her whether she wanted it to or not. "Maddie, it's only you for me. I swear it. I don't know what to do to convince you. The others, well, that's just for fun."

"It's not fun for me, Tom," she spat.

He spun her around and tilted her chin gently with one hand, keeping his other around her waist. "It's you and me, baby. I love you. Only you."

Tom kissed her, and Maddie, hating herself, couldn't help but respond to his words, his touch. He was so unpredictable, and at this moment, stone-cold sober, he was the kind and warm Tom she knew—and still loved passionately. It was the other Tom, the drunk or drug-addled, woman-chasing Tom she hated. But even worse, she despised herself more for wanting him, for falling under the spell of the light, intoxicating kisses he was currently raining down her neck. He was her undoing, and she knew it. She just couldn't let go, couldn't gather the strength to leave him. Despite all the bad, she loved this man. She only hoped she'd survive being loved by him this way.

Two nights later they were in Los Angeles, running through a sound check at the Forum. Looking out over the darkened tiers of endless seats, Maddie was suddenly overcome by that all-too-familiar attack of preshow nerves. Dizzy and nauseous, she stumbled backstage, where someone tried to hand her a cup of the anti-anxiety herbal tea blend from the healer in Chinatown she always had with her. But Maddie had already drunk two cups, and she waved it away.

"Tom," she said faintly. "I need Tom."

Through a wave of nausea she heard his name being called. Someone, maybe Sal or Ernie, banged on the men's room door, while someone else rushed into the dressing room she shared with Tom.

"Sorry, Maddie—" Andre began, but by now the waves of nausea were rushing over her, and she knew there was no way she could keep the contents of her stomach down a moment longer. She rushed by him into the bathroom to throw up.

A moment later the door banged open, and Tom found her on her knees in front of the toilet.

"Oh, Maddie, really? This is getting old."

"I wish I could control it, Tom," she replied shakily, wincing at the coldness in his tone. "I really do. It's not as if I like being in this position," she added, motioning to the toilet she was bending over. She drew in a few deep breaths, then walked unsteadily to the sink, where she rinsed the foul taste out of her mouth and splashed cold water on her face. She pushed past Tom and went to sit on the small couch in the corner.

"I don't get it. You seemed to be okay at the beginning of the tour. What's changed?" he asked impatiently.

Maddie put her face in her hands. She hated the way he was talking to her, hated the all-too-familiar drug-dazed look in his eyes. She didn't know how to answer him. Granted, she had been handling her stage fright better when they first hit the road, but maybe the constant stress of seeing Tom stoned all the time, watching him barely make an effort to fend off one woman more beautiful than the next, had finally gotten to her. Why did she constantly allow herself to feel so threatened? And why had she gotten so sick just now? Usually the preshow jitters made her shake and sweat, not throw up. And her worsening relationship with Tom? Just thinking about it usually left her pierced through the heart, hurting in a way that left her exhausted and near tears.

Then it hit her. A random thought suddenly struck her like a wrecking ball. The one thing she had forgotten to pack in the rush of excitement at the beginning of the tour, the crazy thing she had ignored ever since then in the chaos of life on the road. *Her birth control pills.*

Panic swirled in her mind. This couldn't be happening—could it? It wasn't that she didn't want to have a baby; she did, someday, but while she and Tom were together, they had never made it formal, never gotten married.

The enormity of the possibility hit her like a blow to the heart. *The road is no place for a baby.*

Maddie realized she hadn't answered Tom's question. But she certainly wasn't ready to share what she suspected to be true until she was sure. They had two days to unwind in LA before flying back to New York—the bus ride was thankfully a one-way excursion. She'd need to hit a drugstore for one of those home pregnancy tests, and she'd need some sort of disguise to make sure she wasn't recognized when she bought it. As it was, the paparazzi made it impossible for her to have a private moment. They were everywhere, and she never knew when someone was going to jump out at her and shove a camera in her face.

"No answer?" Tom asked curtly.

Maddie's head snapped up, releasing her from her mental paralysis. "Cut me a break tonight, Tom," was all she could manage. "I'm tired. I want to rest here a bit before the show."

He looked at her for a brief moment before turning toward the door. "Sure, sweetheart," he said in what was clearly a sarcastic tone. "See you out there."

Maddie wasn't sure if she was hurt or relieved to see him go. She drew in a breath and fought the desire to weep. Exhaustion seemed to be creeping up from her feet, swallowing her body whole. She craved sleep, yet she couldn't clear her mind of her suspicions: Was she pregnant? Stretching out on the couch, she buried her head in her arms in an effort to shield herself from the world and waited for that dreaded moment when someone came to get her to perform for her fans, to be one half of the great Maddie and Tom show, to continue with the charade.

After three encores and a rousing, audience-fueled sing-along rendition of "Always in My Heart," Maddie couldn't wait to leave the arena. It wasn't her best effort, because she'd barely been able to find her voice while attempting to keep the persistent waves of nausea at bay. To make matters worse, she couldn't even center herself in Tom's presence, because he was flying high on whatever it was that he had ingested before they all took the stage. The whole performance felt hazy and surreal, and she was angry with herself for cheating her fans out of what they paid for.

To make matters worse, she found a message in her dressing room from their record label: the tour extension to Europe was set and would begin at the end of October. Maddie's heart sank at the mere thought of more travel, especially now that she was feeling so crappy. Tom and the rest of the band were pumped by the news about Europe. They immediately decided to celebrate by going out into the city and partying all night.

"Tom," Maddie said quietly above the din of the group's jubilation. "Tom," she tried again, louder this time, but still got no response. "Tom!" she shouted, and to her chagrin, the entire band turned to stare at her. She felt her knees trembling with fatigue and grabbed hold of the back of a chair to steady herself.

"What is it, sweetheart?" Tom asked with all the appeal of a snake charmer.

"I'm exhausted. I'm going to bed."

"Well then don't let us stop you," he replied flatly as he turned to shepherd the others out to the waiting limos.

"Wait a second," she said incredulously. "I need one of the cars to get back myself."

Tom shrugged. "Okay. Sam can take you and meet us later." He looked her up and down for a minute, as though he had another thing to add, but instead he turned and left her standing there alone. With tears welling in her eyes, she picked up her bag and made her way down the hallway and into the dark night. It was only when she was in the backseat of the limo that Maddie allowed herself to cry.

When the limo stopped at a red light, she noticed an all-night pharmacy on the corner. At this time of night there was less chance that she'd be seen by a curious reporter looking for a juicy story. So just as the light changed to green, she rapped on the glass divider and exclaimed, "Sam, do me a favor and pull over for a minute. I need to get something." She motioned to the flashing neon sign across the street.

"Are you sure you want to get out of the car?" Sam asked, surprised. Her dislike of public places was well known, especially when the band was near a concert venue after a show. "Tell me what you want, and I'll get it for you."

Maddie, thinking fast, forced an airy laugh. "I doubt you want to do my tampon shopping for me, Sam, but thanks." She paused. "Do me a favor and let me borrow that baseball cap you're wearing, okay?"

He pulled the limo over to the curb and passed her the hat without a word. She tucked her blond curls under it as best she could and stepped out onto the sidewalk. The air was filled with the scent of jasmine. As she drew in a deep breath, she was suddenly sure what the result of this test would be, and for the first time in a long while, she felt strangely calm. Maybe it was the jasmine; maybe it was the thought of carrying a baby inside her that made her feel this way. Whatever it was, she really didn't care.

Opening the door to the fluorescent glare inside the store, Maddie was relieved to find it nearly empty. Passing a couple of drag queens dressed for their night out in sequins and heels, she tucked her head low under the cap brim and into the collar of her jacket and marched over to the pharmacy, locating the pregnancy tests on a shelf near the feminine body wash and douches. Grabbing the first one she saw, she went to the cashier, keeping her eyes down and putting the only money she had on her, a fifty-dollar bill, on the counter. All she could think about was getting back to the car without being seen.

The old man at the register was clearly not a music fan, barely looking at her while making change and placing the box in a brown paper bag. Maddie took her package and went back to the car. The whole transaction had taken less than five minutes, and she drew in a large gulp of air, feeling less nauseous at last.

Sam dropped her off at the front entrance of the hotel, and when she expressed her thanks and handed him back his hat, he said, "I hope you sleep well, Maddie. That last show was awesome. Go get some rest!"

"Thanks, Sam," she muttered and took the elevator to the suite she and Tom shared to read the instructions inside the box. Once she realized that she'd have to wait until morning to take the test, she hid it under some clothes in her luggage. The last thing she wanted was for Tom to get back to the room and see the contents of the box before she had a chance to use it. She went to bed dreaming of the two blue lines on the little white stick that would mean she was pregnant, hoping that Tom's reaction would be as positive as the results she was so certain would prove her right.

X

When Maddie woke the next morning, she was happy to find Tom asleep next to her in their bed. She hadn't heard him come in, and while the band was infamous for pulling all-night parties after a show and Tom was always up for whatever fun he could squeeze out of them, she liked to think that he had returned not too long after she did. This morning she had no intention of dwelling on the thought of the groupies that may or may not have joined them at whatever club they'd gone to—at least not until she peed on the stick and knew for sure if she was pregnant or not.

She lay next to Tom for a moment, tucked warm and cozy against him under the plush comforter, trying to sort out her feelings. She had to acknowledge that she still loved the man sleeping next to her and probably would for the rest of her life. She just wasn't certain if she still liked him now that success had changed him so much. This tour had been illuminating for her, watching as Tom made increasing use of the veritable pharmacy that Martin, who had turned out to be Emilia's current dealer as well as her boyfriend, made available to the band. He seemed to have a connection in every city, and Maddie thought it truly remarkable that his photographs—an artistic chronicle of their cross-country adventure—were so good considering the fact that he was perpetually high.

Like the rest of the band. Thinking of them, Maddie suddenly realized how much she had been growing up and away from all of that so quickly on this tour. Moving so far forward, in fact, that she found herself without warning craving something else, something with a routine, something normal. She loved the music and she loved Tom, but all at once she knew that she could walk away from the rest of it right now.

The nagging thought that Maddie didn't want to face at the moment was what she would do if this pregnancy test was negative. She thought back to the callousness Tom had shown her when she was sick before the show, the way he'd tried to hide his impatience, and his readiness to allow her to return alone to their hotel room—again. How much more of this behavior was she willing to take?

Not now, she told herself fiercely. *Let those thoughts go.* The first order of business today was simple: pee on a stick.

She quietly padded into the bathroom on her bare feet, careful not to bump into anything that might make enough noise to wake Tom. She didn't want to be interrupted. Once she sat down on the toilet seat, she reread the instructions one last time. As soon as she was sure that the white stick was fully saturated with urine, she set it down gingerly on top of the box, flushed, and washed her hands, all the while looking at her watch to be sure to time the full ten minutes the instructions had directed in order to have her answer.

Funny thing was, it took no time at all for her to see the result: two distinct blue lines appeared almost immediately. She wondered if that meant she was farther along than she originally thought. Could she have conceived before they even left New York in June? She felt numb. She was going to be a mom.

Then the fear kicked in. What if Tom wasn't happy with this? What if he didn't want to have a baby now, or with her at all? How would his drug use affect the baby? Maddie shuddered. This wasn't something they had planned for, let alone ever talked about. Her eyes welled up as she collapsed on the toilet seat cover, her head in her hands. What would she say to Tom when he woke up? Should she just come out and tell him, or should she wait? Rehearse the perfect announcement?

She never got the chance to decide. Tom stumbled into the bathroom and found her there holding the white stick.

"What's that, Maddie?" he asked, bleary-eyed but coherent.

"Um, it's a pregnancy test."

He froze, blinked. "Are you serious? For you?"

"There's no one else here, Tom," she replied, realizing he was still half-asleep.

"Did you do it yet?" He suddenly sounded much more awake.

"Yeah. I did."

"So?"

"So it looks like I'm pregnant," she whispered, unable to meet his eyes.

Instantly he lifted her up off the seat and into his arms, kissing her hair, her cheeks, and then finally her lips.

"Maddie, that is crazy awesome! I am so excited! We're gonna be parents!"

She felt the weight of anxiety leave her body. "I was so worried you wouldn't want a baby," she said softly.

"Oh, Maddie, how could you think that? This is wonderful news!"

"Is it, Tom? Sometimes I honestly feel like we're not even heading in the same direction anymore." She crossed her arms over her chest and looked up at him. "The drugs, the drinking, the women. Nothing has changed, except that it's not just us now. We have to consider the welfare of our child going forward."

He stood still for a long moment, his green eyes holding her gaze. "Maddie, I love you. I keep telling you that. Those women you worry about aren't real. You're real. Our baby is real. I'll give up anything you ask of me. I swear it." He took both of her hands in his. "How could you think I wouldn't be happy?" He paused. "Wait. Are you happy?"

His words were a balm, what she wanted to hear, pushing her earlier doubts into a corner of her brain, and she started to cry in earnest. "Yes. So happy about the baby."

He hugged her and led her back into the bedroom. Sitting her down on the bed, he knelt in front of her.

"Well then, Ms. Ellis, there's only one thing to do. Will you marry me? How about a New Year's Eve wedding in front of the Eiffel Tower?"

Maddie was stunned. And then overjoyed. Maybe being married and having a baby would make all the groupies go away. Surely a wife and a newborn in Tom's life would send a strong signal to keep their hands off him? Everything, all of the women, the drugs, his ego that she had found unbearable ten minutes ago vanished, and in that split second she was willing to take the chance. Surely he would change, would go back to being the Tom she'd first met and fallen in love with, the man who was kneeling before her, the man for whom she was enough.

"Yes, Tom, I want to marry you," she whispered.

He stood up and pushed her back against the pillows, covering her with kisses and with his body.

"Is this okay? Are you feeling well enough to celebrate?" he asked.

His gentle tone and the concern on his face undid her. They spent the rest of the morning making love, stopping only to order a lavish room service breakfast. It was the happiest she'd been in months, and Maddie didn't want the feeling to end.

"When do you want to tell everyone?" Tom asked, seated at the laden breakfast table sipping coffee.

"Let's hold off until after I see the doctor back home. I don't even know when the baby is due yet."

"Do you think you'll be able to handle the European tour? Because if not, I'll cancel the whole thing. We can tour later, after the baby comes."

Maddie's heart warmed at his concern. "I really want to do it. Maybe what I thought was preshow jitters was really morning sickness."

"But you weren't throwing up in the morning. It was at night."

Maddie laughed. "I'm no expert, but I don't think morning sickness happens exclusively before noon. I think it can strike at any time."

"Well, that's confusing," Tom teased. "No matter. I think we should let the doctor decide. If he says it's okay for you to travel, great. If not, we'll put the whole thing on hold."

"Really?" Maddie felt the last of her doubts disappear. "I was worried you'd be disappointed if I couldn't do the tour. And by the way, the doctor's not a he. She's a she."

"And what do you think the baby is? Boy or girl?"

"No idea at all, and no preference either."

"I'm with you on that." Tom paused, looking at her with a softness she hadn't seen in a long time. "So what should we do today? I'm up for anything you want."

"I've been so tired," Maddie confessed. "Can we go down to the pool? Because all I want is to sit beside it and have a silly drink with a paper umbrella and a cherry on top."

Tom stood up and gave her a mock bow. "Your wish is my command, my lady. Except your cocktails from now on will contain fruit juice only."

"Sounds perfect to me!" Maddie took his outstretched hand and let him pull her to her feet. As he wrapped his arms around her, she closed her eyes, relishing the happiness she felt, the warmth of his care, the contentment and peace that she had begun to think she'd never reclaim.

An hour later they were poolside, Maddie under a wide umbrella, feet propped up on a lounge chair with Tom beside her. He'd positioned his chair close enough to hers to reach over and hold her hand, leaning his open book against his raised knees. Maddie kept her eyes closed, reveling in the warmth of the day and the peace she felt having Tom so close.

Eventually, one by one, the rest of the band found them, and the group sat in quiet companionship until Emilia, as usual, became restless.

"Are you guys gonna sit here all day?"

"Yup," was Tom's response.

Emilia gave him a quizzical stare. "Really? When did you become so sedentary? We're only in LA for another day. Let's go check out some clubs, get some drinks."

"It's barely two-thirty in the afternoon, Emilia. Maybe later?" Maddie replied.

"Well, I'm going downtown to see what kind of scene they've got here. Anybody else looking to have some fun?"

Only Martin seemed interested, and the two of them gathered their towels and flip-flops and walked off together.

Tom caressed Maddie's hand and whispered, "I'm gonna bust. I want to tell them. Please?"

Maddie whispered back, "I promise once we have confirmation from my doctor, you can shout it out to the whole world."

"Can I at least tell them we're getting married?"

Maddie sat up abruptly and looked at the rest of the band, Andre and Ned in the sun, Charlie and some of the crew in the shade, all asleep.

"Why don't we wait until after dinner?" she responded, wanting to hold this wonderful secret safely between them for as long as she could.

"Okay, okay, we'll tell them together later."

Was he sulking? Maddie's heart warmed, wondered how long it would take before her impetuous Tom blurted their secret to one or more of the band members.

"Thanks," she whispered, smiling at him. She felt his warm fingers squeeze hers and closed her eyes, allowing all of her worries and doubts to slip away.

She must have fallen asleep, because when Maddie opened her eyes again, she was alone at the pool. The sun was low in the sky, and she guessed it was approaching suppertime. Somewhat annoyed at Tom for having abandoned her, she sat up, and saw a note fluttering between the straw handles of her beach bag.

Went into town with the guys and didn't want to disturb you. Tom.

Maddie's heart sank. Even with the monumental news she'd shared with him this morning, he still couldn't spend a whole day with her, couldn't resist going out somewhere for a drink, to seek the attention of his fans. Why had she believed that things would change?

Blinking back tears, she gathered her things and stood up—a little too quickly. Dizziness overwhelmed her and she sat back down. Opening her eyes at last, she saw Martin and Emilia headed in her direction.

"You still out here?" Emilia asked. Not surprisingly, her words were slightly slurred.

"I must have fallen asleep, and everybody else left," Maddie said sullenly. "Did Tom catch up to you somewhere?"

"Nope. Haven't seen him." Emilia sat down unsteadily on a nearby chair. "We had a few drinks at a little folk club in town and now we're back," she said, stating the obvious.

Looking at her, Maddie suspected that she and Martin had had something other than a few drinks, but she didn't feel like confronting them about it. They weren't performing tonight, so it really wasn't any of her business. She glanced at her watch. "I think I'll go up and change. Our dinner reservation is in an hour at Spago's. I don't want to be late."

She felt steadier as she stood up and walked in her flip-flops to the hotel lobby. She was still somewhat dizzy when she got into the elevator, but at least she wasn't feeling nauseous at the moment.

Pulling out the key to their suite, she opened the door to an amazing sight. Tom had transformed their room into a tropical paradise, with great vases of roses and freesia, jasmine and hibiscus displayed on every available surface. He was waiting for her, freshly showered and dressed, hair still damp, holding a glass of amber liquid.

"I was starting to think you might spend the whole night at that damn pool," he joked. "But I'm glad you're here now." He took her beach bag from her, then handed her the glass. "Don't worry. It's sparkling cider. No alcohol."

Maddie took a sip. It was as refreshing as it was delicious. When she'd emptied it, Tom took her glass and set it down, then knelt in front of her.

"It dawned on me, Maddie, when I was sitting at the pool watching you sleep that I didn't propose in the way I should have earlier, so I hope you'll grant me a 'do-over.'"

Maddie smiled. "A 'do-over' isn't necessary. This morning was just perfect."

"Still, if you'll allow me, I'd like to make it more special." Tom took a deep breath. "Madeline Ellis, will you marry me?" As he spoke, he unearthed a black velvet box from his pocket and opened it for her. Inside, nestled in the red silk lining, was the biggest diamond ring Maddie had ever seen. It was at least a five-carat center stone, with smaller diamonds embedded in the platinum band. He must have gone to a jeweler while she slept at the pool.

Maddie was overcome. "Oh, Tom, that is absolutely beautiful. I love it." Tears welled in her eyes.

"Don't cry, Maddie. Put it on." He stood up, took the sparkler out of the box, and slipped it on the ring finger of her left hand.

Up close it was even more spectacular, a brilliantly white emerald-cut stone that spanned her finger from base to knuckle. It reflected so much light that it almost looked alive, shimmering and moving on its own.

"It's too much," she breathed. "It must have cost a small fortune . . ." Her voice trailed off.

"You're worth more than any diamond to me, Maddie. You are priceless," Tom responded, drawing her into his arms and lowering his head to kiss her softly on the mouth.

"But still . . ." she started, only to be silenced by another warm kiss.

Tom's twinkling green eyes met hers. "You do know we're stinking rich, right? This summer tour alone netted us over ten million, and the European leg, if we go, is just icing on the cake. We can afford it, and you should have it." His tone grew husky. "I love you, Maddie. No matter what's happened between us in the past, you've got to know that."

"I do, Tom." If she had any lingering doubts, now was not the time to dwell on them. She wanted this moment to be just for the two of them, no intruders. "Should we call our parents?"

Tom suddenly looked as shy as a schoolboy. "Well, truth be told, I called yours a little earlier. I wanted to do it right, to ask their permission first." He paused. "They said yes, by the way. So I guess it's time to tell mine. They shouldn't read about it tomorrow in the papers. Once the band knows, the world knows."

Maddie smiled back at him. "Okay, but no baby news. One thing at a time."

"I'll do my best to hold it in, but I'm busting with happiness. We really have it all, Maddie. We did it. The dream is ours now."

Looking down at the ring on her finger, Maddie considered his words. He was right. It would all turn out okay. Walking across the room to the massive carved desk, she picked up the phone. "I'm calling my mom first, then you call yours. Let's officially let this cat out of the bag!" she added gleefully.

Maddie still felt as if she was walking on clouds when she exited the limo in front of Spago's, Tom's hand resting protectively on the small of her back. Heads turned as they entered the restaurant, but Maddie kept walking, gripping Tom's other hand tightly as they were escorted into the private room reserved for them in the back. The rest of the band was already a round of drinks in, and no one noticed the huge stone on Maddie's left hand. Tom listened to their boisterous conversations for a moment, arms crossed over his chest, then picked up a knife and clanged it against the glass of Jack Daniel's that had appeared almost instantly when he reached the table.

"Ladies and gentlemen," he began, "I'm so happy to be here tonight with the people I love most in the world."

Silence fell as everyone turned to face him. "This tour has been awesome, and you are the people who make it so great. The only thing that could make it even more epic is this: Maddie and I are getting hitched!"

There was a moment of stunned silence before everyone started to whoop and let out enthusiastic catcalls. Emilia dashed over to Maddie, threw her arms around her, and then grabbed her left hand. "Lemme see!" she squealed. "Wow! That's some rock! They'll be able to see that from the back row at Wembley!"

Tom cleared his throat, and Maddie shot him a warning look not to let on that the European tour might not happen now. She was pleased to see his nod of acknowledgment in return.

"We need champagne!" Martin exclaimed. "Where's the damn waiter?"

As if by magic, the waiter appeared, and Tom ordered a magnum of Dom Perignon.

"Tom," Maddie whispered as he slid into the seat beside her. "That's the most expensive thing on the menu!"

"Only the best tonight," Tom responded, draping his arm over her shoulders.

When the waiter came back, he was joined by the sommelier and his small team of servers. The bottle was opened with a pop and a flourish, the fine crystal glasses filled and raised for Tom's toast.

"I am the luckiest man on earth. The woman I love has committed herself to me, and the best band on the planet is here to celebrate with us." Tom took a long sip, and the others followed.

Maddie only hoped that no one noticed that she didn't really drink her champagne, rather just lifted the glass to her lips and then quickly placed it on the table. She kept up that routine until Tom's glass was nearly drained and then slipped hers in its place and moved his next to her plate. When the waiter came to refill it, she motioned him to take care of the others first. It took some work, but she pulled it off throughout dinner, although she soon realized it no longer mattered. The rest of the band was pretty drunk, and no one was paying any attention to the fact that she was not.

After the elaborate dessert of flaming bananas Foster was finished, Emilia stood up to make a toast. "To my beshtest friend in the world," she slurred. "And to the guy she caught b'fore I could!"

Everyone laughed, but for Maddie, it signaled that it was time to wrap things up. She was bone tired and all she wanted to do was to go back to the big comfy bed in her hotel room. As Tom settled the check, she managed to catch his eye with a look that meant she'd had enough. Luckily he caught on quickly, making their excuses to the group.

"You lovebirds going back for a private celebration?" Emilia teased.

"Something like that," Tom replied, helping Maddie stand up. Everyone must have just assumed she was drunk from all the alcohol they had consumed and needed Tom's arms to steady her. In truth, it seemed to Maddie as if her morning sickness was going to plague her at night too. She was suddenly nauseous, and the room was spinning.

"Don't worry, we'll fill you in on what you missed tomorrow. Sweet dreams," Martin said as he ushered Emilia and the rest of the group out of the restaurant.

Once in the limo on the way back to their hotel, Maddie turned to Tom. "I'm sorry to keep you from the fun," was all she could muster, breathing deeply of the fresh air fanning her face from the partially opened window.

"Don't be silly. There's plenty of party left in me. I just don't need to go out tonight. I'm a family man now!"

Maddie managed to smile weakly and was happy to see the well-lit hotel sign appear in the distance. She hoped she'd be able to keep her dinner down long enough to get upstairs.

The limo finally came to a stop in the hotel's circular drive. The door was opened by a valet, and Tom stepped out first, offering his hand to her, coaxing her from the backseat.

Maddie stepped into a sea of flashing lights. Obviously the word was out, maybe from the staff at the restaurant—the tabloids paid well for this kind of juicy news—or maybe from an offhand comment by someone in the band overheard at whatever venue they were at now. All Maddie heard in the brief moment before Tom hustled her into the safety of the hotel lobby were shouts about their wedding date. Everybody wanted to know the same thing: when and where would the pop music wedding of the year be held?

For the first time, the noise and lights from the assembled reporters truly unsettled Maddie. How much worse would it be when she and Tom brought their baby along? Was it fair to subject an innocent child to this kind of scrutiny?

Maddie moaned as her stomach heaved. Instantly Tom tightened his hold on her and rushed her into the elevator to their suite and then to the bathroom.

He held her hair away from her face and murmured soothingly as seemingly everything she had eaten that night and more was expelled from her stomach. For Maddie, even though they had been together for five years, this whole thing seemed both newly intimate and utterly mortifying. Tom helped her to bed, took her clothes off, and tucked her in. He then climbed in next to her, stroking her hair and singing softly in her ear until she fell asleep. As she drifted off to the sound of his beautiful voice, she said a small prayer that it would always be this way: just Tom, the baby, and her.

Back in New York a few days later, Maddie's pregnancy was confirmed in the doctor's office. Maddie was almost three months along, and Deborah Adams, her OB-GYN, ran through a whole list of dos and don'ts for the next six months. She gave Maddie a prescription for prenatal vitamins and was about to send them on their way to book a monthly appointment routine with her staff when Tom asked one final question.

"Can we still travel? We're supposed to do a European tour that winds up around Christmas."

"Well," Deborah said thoughtfully, "that changes things a bit, but I think it should be fine. Let me contact one of my medical school buddies who lives in London now. I think she can arrange for care along the way, but if you have any problems, I want to know immediately. Oh, and the last trimester has a travel embargo. I want you back here after the middle of January at the start of your third trimester, understand?"

Tom let out the breath he'd been holding, and Maddie realized that the last leg of the tour had clearly meant more to him than he'd let on. "Of course, Deb. We'll be back right after New Year's, and I promise to take good care of her along the way. You have my word."

"Great." The doctor turned to Maddie. "You've got to understand your limits, Maddie. If you're tired, rest. I like to tell my new moms that they need to sleep now. Once that baby comes, your down time will be at a premium!"

Maddie smiled. She had no trouble with that since she already seemed able to fall asleep anywhere, anytime. After she and Tom stopped at the scheduling desk, she took his hand and walked with him out onto the street. It was a beautiful September day, the kind of weather that signals the end of one season and the beginning of the next. There was a hint of chill in the air, but it was a welcome relief to Maddie. The cooler, the better for her now. She was so much more comfortable sleeping at night with the windows open in their loft.

As they walked home, Tom turned to her and said, "Do you realize that it's close to the six-year anniversary of that concert in the park? Can you believe how far we've come?"

Maddie looked up at him, mirroring his smile. "I know. Big venue concerts, Europe, a baby. I never imagined all this."

"And I'm planning the wedding of the century for us. *People* magazine wants exclusive pictures and is willing to pay a bundle for them. It will be insane," he crowed.

"Don't go nuts inviting the world. Just the band, okay?"

Tom laughed. "You're kidding, right? It's got to be more than just the guys. I want to bring our families over, some of the management team . . ."

"And that will be enough. I don't want our wedding to be a circus, Tom. I just want it to be us."

He looked so mulish that she had to laugh. "Face it, Tom, I'll be huge by then. This," she said, patting her stomach, "won't be a secret anymore. Does *People* magazine really need to be there?"

But he didn't seem to share her amusement. "It's another way to sell records, to put people in the seats at our shows. Why do you care who knows? Let's tell the world now. We've got the doctor's confirmation."

Maddie tried to hide her sudden hurt. Did he honestly only think of her pregnancy as a way to sell more concert tickets? "I'm not ready yet, Tom," she said sharply. "It's our secret, our good news. I want to hold on to something that's just ours for a little bit longer, please?"

"We have to tell the band," Tom pointed out. "We're going to travel with them in tight quarters for the next three months. They're gonna catch on pretty quickly."

Maddie stopped short and held up both hands as if in surrender. "Okay. We tell the band on the plane trip over. But they've got to promise not to tell anyone else. I really don't want to deal with constant questions about the baby. The tour is the big news story, not me."

"Good luck with that, sweetheart," Tom said cheerfully as they headed down Prince Street and into the lobby, where he nodded hello to their doorman, Ralph. "Word's gonna get out sooner rather than later, and if you ask me, we should just roll with it. This kid, boy or girl, will have to deal with it too. We're famous, remember?"

Again Maddie realized how challenging it was going to be to raise a child in the glass house that was their current life.

"Maybe I'll retire," she said softly as they entered the elevator. "You know, from the road."

"That's just your hormones talking. Don't stress it now," Tom replied breezily.

Maddie looked at him. He truly had no idea how easily she could give up performing. She'd never really gotten over her stage fright completely, and the bigger the venue, the more she hated performing with all those people tightly packed together and staring up at her. She'd much rather keep to the background, and perhaps this baby would give her the perfect out. Maybe she'd just write the songs and let Tom do the rest.

"Take a nap, Maddie." Tom's voice was suddenly gentle, as if he could read her thoughts. "Let's see how you feel about this when you've gotten some rest."

She was too tired to argue, so she let him tuck her into bed, and before she knew it, she was asleep.

It wasn't long before Maddie realized that she'd need to improvise her wardrobe in the coming months. She didn't have any maternity clothes and didn't want to walk into any of the Madison Avenue or SoHo maternity shops where she would most assuredly be spotted. Instead she decided to try and get away with wearing some of Tom's shirts to hide her belly as it grew and wear only the slacks she owned with a drawstring or elastic waistband. Once they got to Europe, she would supplement her wardrobe. Surely her face wouldn't be as recognizable there.

On a distinctly chilly Halloween night, at what was appropriately the witching hour, the band assembled in a large hangar at JFK airport to board the private jet that the record label had provided for their flight to London. All of them were buzzing with excitement as the news hit that they were sold out in every venue. Adding to Maddie's anxiety about the stadium-sized shows they were about to play was her mounting confusion about her relationship with Tom.

Even after he put that gigantic ring on her finger several weeks ago, the constant barrage of adoration from his female fans hadn't ceased. They appeared everywhere, scantily clothed, overly perfumed, leaving scraps of lacy underwear or lipstick-smudged notes for him wherever he went. There was no amount of reassurance he could offer Maddie, even though he remained attentive to her needs, bringing her small snacks throughout the day, making sure she had an extra pillow to rest her head on when they traveled, and telling her how much he loved her. Maybe it was the raging pregnancy hormones, but all Maddie could see was her rapidly expanding waistline, bringing every insecurity she had about her own appearance to the forefront. She was sure Tom would give in to the temptations around him sooner or later. In her mind, it was just a matter of time.

After the plane had reached cruising altitude, the in-flight entertainment programs flickered onto the screens, and Maddie watched as a flight attendant pushed a drink cart toward the back of the plane. Tom put his hand on her knee. "Are you thirsty? Would you like a soda?"

"I just want to sleep," Maddie said, yawning.

He smiled and pulled the blanket she'd laid on her lap more tightly about her. "Then rest. I'll be back."

She smiled as he kissed her brow. It was nearly one a.m. New York time, and she was exhausted. As she was about to close her eyes, one of the record company executives who accompanied them wherever they traveled sat down in the seat vacated by Tom.

"Hi, Maddie."

Maddie sat up reluctantly. "Hey, Paul, how have you been?" she asked politely, wondering why he'd sought her out instead of joining the raucous party that was cranking up in the rear of the plane.

"I'm great, Maddie, thanks for asking. How about yourself?"

"I'm fine," she replied.

"So when's the baby due exactly?"

Maddie stared at him in shock. They hadn't even told the band yet! How in the hell—? "What?" she croaked.

Paul patted her hand. "Don't worry. I haven't told anyone. My wife was in the waiting room of Dr. Adams's office when you came out with Tom. She's due in December."

Maddie didn't know if she should be relieved or annoyed. Was there no privacy left for her anymore? "Wow. Good for you guys," she said politely. "I'm due in March."

"Have you thought about what you want to do after the baby comes?" he asked.

"Not really," Maddie said, suddenly wary.

"Well, the label is talking about your next studio album and backing that up with another tour—much bigger than this one."

Maddie could only stare at him.

"We want to send you guys to Australia and Asia."

"I really haven't had a chance to process *this* yet." Maddie waved her hand over her stomach to further acknowledge that what Paul's wife had surmised was, in fact, true. "So there's no way for me to know what the next step will be. I think Tom and I need to discuss our future plans before we let you make them for us."

"Of course, of course," Paul said quickly. He paused for a moment before going on. "You know, Maddie, some of us would like to see you do a solo album. If you look at the sales of the group's records, it always seems to be the songs you write that climb the charts. 'Always in My Heart' has basically become an anthem for an entire generation."

"Thanks, but no," Maddie said at once. "Tom and I are a team."

"Whatever you say." Paul stood, his attention drawn to the loud applause coming from the back of the plane. "Will you look at that guy?" he said with a laugh.

Maddie turned to see that Tom had taken over the beverage service and was pouring drinks for everyone with a flourish.

"He sure knows how to have fun." Paul winked at her before heading down the aisle to join them.

Maddie was glad to be alone. Paul's suggestion that she record a solo album had shocked her even more than his revelation that he knew about her pregnancy and that he wanted the band to tour Asia and Australia. She had never once considered recording anything as a solo artist and felt embarrassed not to have realized that her label kept tabs on which songs sold more—the ones she wrote versus Tom's songs. And why should those statistics matter, just as long as the group kept bringing in the millions of dollars in record and ticket sales that lined the pockets of all involved?

And what would Tom do if he ever found out what Paul had discussed with her? He was so touchy about things like that. Suddenly cold, Maddie pulled an oversized black cashmere sweater out of the large tote bag by her feet, slipping it over her head to cuddle into its familiar warmth. Tucking the blanket back around her, she leaned her head against the seat.

Maddie had always known that Tom's ego was huge, but she had decided some time ago that in the realm of their business, this wasn't such a bad thing. Admittedly it had been the driving force behind their partnership from its earliest days. He was the one who had believed in their talent, who had pushed her out on the stage, who had promoted the hell out of them back at school, and remained hungry for more, even to this point, when success was clearly theirs. Over the years she had come to understand Tom better and knew for certain that this was the type of blow that could push him past the edge of reason. If he ever found out that the label wanted a solo album of Madeline Ellis music, well, that would most assuredly be the end of them. He just wouldn't be able to take the hit.

Maddie ran a hand over her stomach, thinking about their baby. She couldn't let that happen. Not now. Not ever. It just wasn't worth the risk of losing Tom and the family that they were about to become. She closed her eyes, concentrated on her breath, and willed herself to sleep.

But she still felt uneasy about the situation when their flight landed at Gatwick airport and they were shuttled by bus to their hotel. Perhaps that's why she immediately agreed when Tom asked if he could gather the band together in their suite and share the news about the baby – their original plan was foiled by her extended nap on the plane.

Tom didn't waste any time: "I know we just told you guys that we plan to get married on New Year's Eve in Paris. Well, here's another bombshell for you—"

"Lemme guess," Emilia squealed. "Maddie's pregnant."

Tom shot a dark look at Maddie as if to ask if she'd spilled the beans before the group had assembled. Maddie's eyes widened at the accusation, but she let him know with a cutting glance that she had done no such thing.

Regaining his composure, Tom said weakly, "Wow, Emilia. Didn't know you were psychic."

"Whoa! I was kidding. Wait a minute . . . are you serious? Are you two going to have a baby?" Emilia asked, turning to Maddie.

"In March," Maddie replied with a smile. "And you are all going to be godparents!"

"Holy shit!" Martin yelled. "That explains the quickie wedding at the Eiffel Tower, huh?"

"I would have asked Maddie years ago if I thought she'd say yes," Tom shot back. "Our baby just gave her a good enough reason not to say no!"

"But the tour . . . are we still playing all the scheduled dates?" Emilia asked, looking crushed.

"Yes, we are," Maddie assured her. "I'm fine, and the doctor says as long as I rest enough between shows everything will be okay. I just need to be back home by mid-January. Everything else will just fall into place."

Apparently the shock had worn off, because suddenly everyone was talking at once and rushing to hug Maddie and shake Tom's hand. Maddie's happy smile concealed her inner turmoil. *It's all good,* she thought, *as long as Tom never finds out about Paul's conversation with me.*

XI

The last morning of 1986 dawned cold and bright in Paris. Gingerly negotiating the damp, uneven cobblestones, a very pregnant Maddie browsed the farmers' market aisles in the early morning light, stopping now and then to marvel at the beauty around her. The sharp, ever-present scent of Gauloise cigarettes mingled in the chilly air with the yeasty smell of freshly baked bread as vendors set up their stands of colorful produce and flowers. Water taxis made their way along the Seine River across the street from where Maddie stood, and the sun reflected brightly off the majestic zinc rooftops that dotted the city. Maddie had already fallen in love with Paris and was delighted that Tom had planned for them to be married in a place that was both terribly romantic and special.

The tour had picked up speed as they traveled across Europe over the past months, breaking attendance records in London, Amsterdam, Rome, and Barcelona. The craziest thing to Maddie had been the visits from other rock stars who came backstage after the shows. Elton John and Sting had showed up at Wembley, and in Dublin, Madonna, who was playing there the night after them, asked to meet her.

Maddie smiled at the memory of Emilia stunned speechless when she got to shake her idol's hand, but for Maddie, all of it had remained surreal. Focused on her pregnancy, she didn't really care that they were now part of an elite group of musicians who made an impact, as Tom loved to point out to her, and were becoming wealthier with every city they played. Tom loved each and every minute of the fame and attention, but he had stayed faithfully by her side, day and night.

Wanting to prove to her just how serious he was about their marriage, he had insisted on planning the entire event himself. Maddie had balked at first, but secretly felt touched that he would want to do this for her. He made her feel cherished, and she had to admit she liked being at the center of his universe. He had promised to keep tonight's wedding tasteful, simple, and small, with family and closest friends only, and so she happily turned the task over to him. Wanting to surprise her, he hadn't shared too many details of the ceremony and reception with her, whispering only, "Think of the day as a gift to unwrap, one hour at a time."

The celebration had begun at their last show a week ago, right here in Paris. Tom had secretly flown in both sets of their parents and assorted other family members as well as those of the rest of the band. At the last encore, he had brought them all out from backstage to sing "Always in My Heart." With tears in her eyes, Maddie had barely made it through the chorus, overwhelmed by love and, for the first time ever while onstage, complete serenity.

On Christmas Eve, Tom had hosted a huge dinner for everyone associated with the tour and their families in the hotel's private dining room. And somehow, on Christmas morning, Tom had arranged for a tree to be delivered and set up in their suite, beautifully appointed with custom ornaments and magnificently wrapped presents for everyone. As the sparkly paper flew off the boxes and gifts were opened and shared, Maddie had to admit it was the loudest, most raucous, and happiest Christmas she'd ever celebrated.

The best present Tom had given her, however, was the strength of his word, and she had held on to that tightly. For weeks now, there had been no drug use, no women flocking around him after the shows, and he had cut back on his drinking dramatically. She could not imagine ever being happier than she was at this moment in her life. She felt truly blessed.

By now the sun was rising higher in the cloudless blue sky, and Maddie began to feel hungry. There was no sense in waiting to eat with Tom: his bachelor party had been held the previous night, so she knew he wouldn't be getting up anytime soon. Humming to herself, she left the farmers' market and sat down at a small table at an outdoor café. The weather had warmed, and Maddie had dressed in layers under an oversized wool coat with a brightly knitted scarf tied neatly around her neck. Once the waiter came to take her order of a croissant with butter and jam and a pot of jasmine tea, she took off her coat, loosened the scarf, and sat back to people watch.

The sidewalk was nearly empty; it was still early enough in the day for most Parisians to be in bed. Maddie liked being part of a smaller crowd because it meant there was more of a chance that she could sit there unnoticed.

Or so she thought. Out of the corner of her eye she caught a glimpse of a photographer lurking near the wall that kept the Seine River back from the cobblestone street. He was a thin man with a hat pulled low over his eyes, but there was no mistaking the camera around his neck. Then she saw another man with a long lens standing behind a tree, and another leaning on a car parked farther down the street, and while they were keeping a safe distance, they made her feel uneasy. Surely she was mistaken? But before she could even pull her scarf up to cover her face, all of them moved as if on cue toward her. Others appeared seemingly out of nowhere, and then they all broke into a run, gesturing and calling her name as flashbulbs popped and passersby turned to stare.

Before Maddie could panic, her waiter appeared in front of her, deliberately blocking the photographers' view. Ignoring their shouted protests, he yelled at them in rapid-fire French and shooed them away with the long white apron around his waist. But the paparazzi were relentless, and he uttered an oath as he grabbed Maddie's arm, picked up her coat, and helped her quickly into the café.

"Mademoiselle, *s'il vous plait*." He motioned her to a corner table away from the windows before disappearing into the kitchen. Maddie sat down and forced herself to breathe calmly. When the waiter returned, he carried a complete breakfast of croissants, sliced ham, fruit, and spread, which he delivered with a flourish.

"Merci beaucoup, merci beaucoup." She struggled with her high school French, trying to express her gratitude.

He was about the age of her father, and now he smiled at her in the same gentle manner. "'Always in My Heart'?" he asked. *"Ma chère, c'est une très belle chanson!"*

"You are too kind, sir." She offered him a small bow of her head to bridge the language gap.

He smiled back even more warmly. *"Profitez de votre petit déjeuner. Je ferai un sortie qu'ils restent à l'exterieur."*

Maddie guessed from the waiter's hand gestures that this wonderful man was going to disperse the paparazzi while she ate, and for that she was grateful. She savored each and every bite, drank two pots of tea, and finally settled back with a sigh.

"Oh Lord," she whispered as she suddenly realized that now she'd have to leave the warmth and privacy of the café. She'd been gone long enough, and she didn't want Tom to worry in the event he woke up and found her missing. Sighing, she pulled a large stack of francs out of her coat pocket and left it on the table. As she pushed back her chair, the waiter reappeared, took her wordlessly by the hand, and led her through the kitchen. He opened the back door and peered out before stepping into the alleyway with her.

"Si vous allez à la fin et tournez à droite, ils ne sauront pas que vous êtes allés." He gestured with his hands to make her understand that she was to walk straight to the end of the alley and turn right, avoiding the swarm of photographers still gathered at the front of the restaurant. Maddie was so touched by his concern that she stood on tiptoe and placed a quick kiss on his cheek.

"Je ne vais pas oublier votre gentillesse, monsieur," she said with a smile.

"Mon plaisir," he answered warmly and closed the kitchen door behind him.

And to think the French had a bad reputation of being unfriendly! That sweet man had saved her from the type of scene that would have most assuredly ruined her day.

When Maddie reached the end of the alley, she peered around the corner before stepping onto the sidewalk. No photographers! She was able to make her way back to her hotel unnoticed, slipping past the doorman and into the elevator. She unlocked the door to their suite as quietly as possible, but Tom was in the shower, singing loudly. She thought about stepping into the steamy water with him, but before she could undress, he had turned off the spray and entered the bedroom with a fluffy towel wrapped casually around his waist.

"Good morning," she said. "I never expected you to be up this early. That's why I went out and had breakfast alone. I figured you'd sleep in after last night's debauchery."

Tom grinned at her. "You know what I've learned recently? When you don't overindulge, there's nothing to sleep off. Besides, I've got too much to do today. We're getting married tonight, Maddie!"

"I know," she said, positioning herself in front of him to give him a hug.

He leaned down to kiss her, and before either of them realized it, his towel was on the floor, they had fallen onto the bed, and three hours had passed.

Afterward, feeling sated and happier than she could remember, Maddie drifted off to sleep, her head on Tom's chest. When she woke up, he was gone. She lifted herself on one elbow and saw a note on the nightstand with a bunch of fragrant yellow freesia tied with silk ribbon resting on top.

Maddie—

It would be bad luck for us to spend the rest of the day together. I'm not sup-posed to see my bride on our wedding day, so meet me at the base of the Eiffel Tower at 7!

Tom

She lifted the flowers to her nose and inhaled their sweet scent. Her cheeks warmed as she thought of their lovemaking, of Tom's insistence that he handle every detail of the wedding, of his thoughtfulness in leaving her flowers and a note. Dared she let herself believe that their life would always be this way, with Tom so attentive to her needs and excited at the prospect of impending fatherhood? He kept telling her that they had it all, everything they'd ever dreamed of, and in response she had relaxed, dropping much of her defensive posture over the last few weeks of the tour. It felt good to be in a place of such peace.

Still smiling, she glanced over at her wedding dress, hanging gracefully from the highest spot in the room: the valance above the large, cathedral-shaped window. The gown was almost Grecian in inspiration, with multiple layers of beige and gold chiffon held together by a jeweled collar, falling over her growing belly in soft waves, certainly not hiding the fact that she was about to enter her third trimester. There was a long, flowing wrap to wear over the dress studded with beautiful crystals hand sewn with delicate gold thread. It shimmered in the light, and whenever she had put it on during fittings she had felt so special, so loved.

Maddie knew that a whole team of women was preparing to descend on her in a very short while to do her hair, to apply her makeup, and to ensure that she was ready at the appointed hour. She wanted to look her best on her wedding day, not for the uninvited yet unavoidable photographers and paparazzi whose snapped images would be shot instantly around the globe, but for Tom.

Knowing that her mom, Emilia, and the rest of her family would soon be stopping by, Maddie set the flowers down and focused on some fleeting moments of quiet. Walking into the living area of their suite, she picked up her guitar and sat down on the sofa, lightly strumming the familiar strings. In a flash of inspiration, she wrote a song, one that had been bubbling around in her head for a while, not whole until this very moment.

As she played the bridge over and over she immediately knew that this melody would be an organic step forward in the progression of "Always in My Heart," only more mature, like Maddie herself. She had the song finished in less than an hour, taking the time to chart it out on blank music paper.

Just as she added the title—"Forever with Me"—at the top of the page, she heard a knock on the door. Tucking the papers carefully into her guitar case, she took a deep breath to ready herself for the gaggle of women waiting in the hallway. Okay, Maddie thought, she would graciously accept that they were determined to transform her into the bride of the year. But the most important thing was the baby. Happy in the knowledge that she had the most perfect wedding gift to bestow on her soon-to-be husband, Maddie gave her belly a loving pat before she opened the door.

Glancing in the mirror one last time before leaving for the ceremony, Maddie couldn't help but smile. There was no doubt about it: she was glowing. And why not? It had been an afternoon filled with laughter and love. Emilia had taken her role as maid of honor and only attendant seriously and had made sure that Maddie ate some of the tea sandwiches she'd ordered from room service. Emilia had poured champagne for Maddie's and Tom's mothers and told them story after story of their antics on the road. Emilia had kept the tone light and breezy, and the afternoon had flown by.

Now, as Emilia arranged the gold and crystal wrap around Maddie's shoulders, she leaned in to whisper, "I'm so happy for you. You deserve this, my dearest friend."

Looking directly into Emilia's eyes, overjoyed to see how clear they were tonight, Maddie drew her in for one last hug. "Thank you, Em. I'm so lucky to have you as my maid of honor; did I tell you that already? But even more, I'm so glad we're in this life together."

Emilia's eyes welled up, and Maddie wiped away a lone tear that trailed down her friend's cheek. "No crying! You'll ruin your makeup!"

"Okay, okay," Emilia said. "Is everybody ready to go?"

There was a chorus of feminine whoops, and they all surged toward the door, but not before Maddie remembered to step out into the hall and ask Sal, one of the roadies, to bring along her guitar.

As soon as the elevator doors opened onto the lobby, what seemed like thousands of flashes went off in front of their eyes, blinding them. Voices clamored for Maddie's attention, and she turned away, still unable to see. Luckily three of her roadies, working as a security detail for the night, swept in and safely deposited Maddie and Emilia in the waiting limousine.

The heavy doors closed and silence descended. Blinking, Maddie spotted their flower bouquets on the seat next to them, and suddenly the whole evening's plan became very real. Her heart surged with happiness. Riding through the streets of Paris, she saw fans crowding the curbs with signs, waving to her and shouting good wishes as they drew closer and closer to the Eiffel Tower.

When the limo came to a halt, Emilia gave Maddie a tight hug and a kiss on the cheek and stepped out of the car first to the excited shouts of the crowd. She moved out of the way quickly, and Maddie's father reached into the car to offer his hand. He looked so different in his stylish black tuxedo and bow tie than he did in his usual faded jeans and denim work shirt, so distinguished, befitting the good man Maddie knew he was. She held fast to him as she emerged to the roar of her fans. Squeezing his hand, she turned briefly to acknowledge them.

The weather had gotten colder since she'd visited the farmer's market that morning, and she marveled at how many people were bundled up braving the chill because they truly wanted to be a part of her very special night. As she walked with her father into the base of the Eiffel Tower where the ceremony was to be held, the crystals on her wrap shimmered, appearing to dance as they reflected the hundreds of flashes from the photographers' cameras. Tom had repeatedly told her that they were rock and roll royalty, and while Maddie had always laughed at him, it was exactly how she felt at this very moment.

Looking up, she caught her breath. Tom must have hired an army of people to transform the space at the bottom of the tower into a whimsical fairyland. Countless varieties of sweetly scented flowers and small twinkling lights lined the aisle. A red carpet marked her path to the altar, where Tom stood looking so handsome in his white tuxedo jacket and dark pants. He had a single daisy pinned through his buttonhole, a symbol that took Maddie's breath away. She immediately realized that he was sending her a message from their past, from the day in the dorm when she had accused him of cheating on her with Emilia. They had come so far, and Maddie knew in that moment that he wanted her to understand that he was hers and hers alone now, from this day forward, for better or for worse, forever.

It was the single most romantic thing he had ever done for her in all of their years together. Locking eyes with him, Maddie sent him a silent message that she knew with absolute certainty that she'd never love anyone else. She was his and he was hers, and that's the way it would stay.

The ceremony itself was officiated by Bertrand Delanoe, the mayor of Paris. Fortunately he kept it short, as Maddie's advancing pregnancy made it hard for her to stand for any length of time. After they exchanged vows, Tom swept her into his arms for a long kiss, which was greeted with cheers from their assembled guests. They headed back down the aisle together, Maddie's shimmering wrap catching the light as she walked with Tom to the private elevator that would take them to their reception at Le Jules Verne, the restaurant high atop the tower.

The moment they were alone, Tom turned to Maddie and asked, "How have I done so far, Mrs. Seymour? Is this a fairy-tale wedding or what?"

"Better than I could have dreamed," Maddie breathed. "I feel like a princess. Thank you." She stood on her tiptoes for a kiss that lasted until the elevator glided to a stop.

Then Tom said with a gleam in his eyes, "Wait until you see what else I have planned."

The doors smoothly parted, and Maddie gasped. Paris was laid out at her feet beyond the enormous windows, a twinkling light show below them and a sky full of stars above. There were tables set with crisp white tablecloths, highly polished silverware, and sparkling crystal glasses. Hundreds upon hundreds of roses in the palest peach and apricot hues spilled out of vases on every available surface. It took her breath away. She turned to Tom and whispered, "I don't know what to say. It's spectacular. "

"I know," he said gleefully. "We only have a few seconds before they let the rest of the guests come up." He drew her into his arms and held her tightly, leaning in to kiss her deeply on the lips. Midway through their embrace, Maddie felt the baby kick.

"Tom!"

"Oh, Maddie," he breathed, "my family—" Resting one hand on her belly he kissed her again, not letting her go until the elevator doors opened and their jubilant guests descended upon them.

As the evening wore on, Maddie realized that Tom had left no detail unattended, right down to picking the set list for the wedding band to play. He had gathered a large group of local musicians together for the night, an all-star ensemble playing alongside their own band. After they cut their rose-covered, multi-tiered chocolate buttercream wedding cake, Tom asked Maddie to come up and sing.

"Okay," she said at once. In a room filled with their most cherished friends and loved ones, she felt no fear.

After they performed "Always in My Heart" together for their delighted guests, and in a moment of sheer joy, Maddie picked up the guitar that Sal had brought for her and asked someone to bring a chair up on the stage for Tom. She sat him down and in front of all of their guests said, "Tom, I love you so much. This has been the most beautiful day of my life. I wrote this as a wedding gift for you." And then she played "Forever with Me," the song she had written in their hotel room earlier, her voice strong and clear, full of love.

For Maddie, it was almost an out-of-body experience. As her eyes scanned the crowd, she could see that she had their rapt attention. It confirmed what she already knew: this song was special, and it was going to be a huge hit when they recorded it.

But when she turned back to Tom, she suddenly froze. He was sitting stock still as he listened, staring at her with eyes that pierced a hole right through her heart. She knew at once that something was wrong, horribly wrong. She knew him far too well, and suddenly she felt sick, the bile rising to her throat. What was it? What had she done?

By the time she strummed the last chord, their guests were surging toward the stage, cheering and calling her name. But Maddie had eyes only for Tom, who hesitated for a moment too long once she finished singing before standing to hug her stiffly and then slip away to the bar.

Surrounded by adoring family and friends, Maddie watched Tom down one drink and then another and realized that something had shifted between them. She had no idea what it was; she just knew that she didn't know how to regain their equilibrium.

At some point, not even sure what time it was anymore, Maddie searched for Tom, desperately wanting to take back her impromptu performance, climb into their hotel bed, drag the blanket over them both, and fall into a deep sleep. But she couldn't find him, and when Maddie's mother saw her daughter's panicked look from across the dance floor, she signaled her husband. They quickly pushed their way to Maddie's side, bundled her up in her shimmering wrap, and asked one of the security men to bring around a car to escort them back to the hotel.

The moment they were seated in the limo, Maddie's mother put her arms around her while her dad told the driver to take them to the service entrance of the hotel, knowing there would be reporters waiting out front.

"Where's Tom?" was all Maddie could say as they sped off into the darkness. "Where did he go?"

Neither of her parents answered.

"Please tell me what happened," Maddie persisted. "What was wrong with the song I sang?"

"I don't know, Maddie," her mother finally answered. "It was one of the most beautiful you've ever written."

"I've never heard your voice sound so sweet. It was magical," her father added.

"Then why didn't Tom like it? Why did he leave?"

Again they had no answers.

Once inside the elevator headed to Maddie's suite, her mom asked, "Do you want to stay with us tonight, sweetheart? Tom might need some time alone."

"No, Mom. Thanks, though."

"What the hell happened?" her dad repeated, voicing the thoughts that were racing through Maddie's mind. "I thought that song was terrific."

"I did too, Dad," she whispered.

"Well if you ask me, he's got some explaining to do," her father replied gruffly.

"Let them work that out themselves, Kyle. They're married now," Maddie's mother said in her blunt New England way.

They waited for Maddie to unlock and enter the suite, and once inside, she turned back to kiss them both before shutting the door. "Tom?" she called hopefully. Her heart sank at the silence that greeted her. Never in her life had she dreamed that on her wedding night she'd go to bed alone. Tossing her glittering wrap on the floor, Maddie wearily stepped into their bedroom and switched on the light. She gasped at the sight of the rose petals scattered in a heart-shaped design on top of the down comforter. Tom must have arranged for that in anticipation of their first night together as husband and wife.

That's when Maddie broke down in tears.

Maddie slept for most of the flight back home, but whenever she was awake, she stared unwaveringly at the platinum and diamond band on her left hand. Lost in her own thoughts, she was startled when the pilot announced over the PA system that they had begun their initial descent into JFK. Fastening her seat belt below her large middle, she glanced over her shoulder. Tom was somewhere in the back of the plane, having one last drink with the band before the flight attendant stowed the bar cart.

Tears pricked her eyes. Ever since their wedding night, he'd been so distant. His silent withdrawal whenever she asked him what had happened told her that she would only make matters worse if she didn't drop the subject. Hard as it was, she had decided to wait until they were alone in the privacy of their own home.

Home. It was all Maddie could think about, and now they were so close.

When the pilot's voice came back on asking everyone to take their seats for landing, Tom plopped down next to her, drink still in hand, waving off the flight attendant who was trying to pick up the stray glasses and trash.

"Hey," he said offhandedly, though he refused to meet Maddie's eyes, "the guys can't wait to get back in the studio. There's talk of pulling together a live album from this tour."

Maddie stared at him. "Studio? I'm not going into the studio, Tom. Look at me! I'm so big I can barely walk. You promised me a break, and I'm going to hold you to it."

"You wouldn't have to do much. Everything is already in the bag from our performances, hence the *live* album. It's really just a lot of remixing, choosing the best tracks. Being pregnant doesn't stop you from listening and pointing to the track you like best, does it?"

"Tom—"

"C'mon, Maddie, help me out." His fingers drummed restlessly on the rim of his glass. "The label is pushing me hard on this."

"I don't care." Her voice shook.

"By the way, when were you going to mention that they want a solo album out of you?"

Maddie's breath caught. She turned quickly and scanned the back of the plane where Paul and his boss, Russell, were sitting together deep in conversation. They must have said something to Tom. "I wasn't interested," she whispered, "so there was no need to mention it."

"Oh really?"

"What the hell is wrong with you, Tom?" Maddie blurted, her voice breathless with tears. "You've been a miserable bastard ever since our wedding reception. A completely different person from the man who left our hotel room all excited to marry me." *So much for waiting until they were home to start arguing.*

He gave a curt laugh, still refusing to look at her. "Okay, whatever. We've got three months before the baby comes, and all you need to do is get in the studio and lay down the track. We can add 'Forever with Me' as a bonus. It's a classic Madeline Ellis tune. Got your stamp all over it." There was no mistaking the sarcasm in his tone, venom like in its delivery.

"I wrote it for you, Tom," Maddie said, her voice quavering with hurt. "I don't care if we ever record it."

If Tom heard what she said, he chose to ignore it. Lifting the glass to his lips, he finished the rest of his scotch in one long swallow and stuffed the empty glass into the plush leather pouch attached to the seat in front of him. "All the more reason to record it. We'll make millions, and the world won't be denied another killer song of yours, Maddie. Heaven forbid that should happen."

"You're drunk," she spat.

"Don't I wish," was all he said before he closed his eyes and turned away from her, effectively ending their conversation.

Winter had begun to recede, and the wind, once biting, was now softer, warmer. Maddie and Tom had fallen into a strange new rhythm, working on their live album for a few hours each day and then going their separate ways, leaving Maddie to put their loft in shape for the baby. She was glad for the distraction and worked hard to have everything ready before her due date. She had purchased an antique crib and changing table and begun to buy little onesies and pajamas, folding them into neat piles and storing them in the chest of drawers she had found at a craft fair in the West Village. Her mother and Emilia had thrown Maddie a baby shower, and the generous gifts she'd been given by the wives of the record company executives had rounded out the rest of the things she would need once the baby was born.

Tom's lack of interest in readying the loft for their baby wounded her deeply. He spent most of his time at the studio and barhopping with the band after the day's work was done. There was no doubt he was drinking hard; all of his earlier promises were now effectively broken. The relative peace Maddie had known in the weeks leading up to their ceremony was gone. When she looked at their wedding pictures, she could clearly tell which ones were snapped before she sang to him at their reception. All of those showed her the man she loved. The ones taken after reflected the cold, icy blankness that was so much a part of the stranger he was now.

On a spring like day two weeks before her due date, Maddie could no longer resist the warm breeze blowing softly through her bedroom window. Although walking was cumbersome and she tired easily, she slipped on one of Tom's old button-down shirts and a pair of black leggings—the only things that still fit her—and took a stroll along the perimeter of Washington Square Park. Here the flowerbeds were full of bright yellow crocuses pushing their way toward the sun. Maddie paused to admire them, then sat for a time on a bench and watched the passersby, a cap pulled low over her brow to avoid being recognized. Feeling happy and unfettered for the first time in a long while, she bought a bouquet of fragrant daffodils from a street vendor, then started for home.

She was halfway down Prince Street when she suddenly doubled over in pain. There was a warm rush of water between her legs. Dizzy and gasping, she leaned against a phone booth, waiting for the contraction to pass.

She managed to limp to the lobby of their building before the next wave of pain hit, radiating from her back across her stomach. Maddie whimpered, dropping the flowers on the polished floor.

"Miss Maddie!" It was Ralph, their doorman, hurrying to take her arm. "It's the baby, yes?"

She could only nod.

"It's okay. I'll hail a cab."

"Thank you," she managed.

"I will track down Mr. Tom and send him to the hospital right away," he promised as he led her outside to a waiting vehicle.

Maddie was in too much pain to do more than give him a nod of thanks.

Despite the fact that her labor had come on so suddenly, it still took over sixteen hours for Nathan Ellis Seymour to be born. Tom didn't show up until Maddie was well into transition, although she had been asking for him repeatedly as the contractions increased in intensity.

"Maddie!" Suddenly he was there, staggering into the labor suite just in time for the birth. When he bent over to kiss her, she smelled the alcohol on his breath. Nauseous and in pain, she closed her eyes and turned her head away. Through the haze that surrounded her she thought she felt something inside her heart shatter. Tears leaked from her eyes as she was told to push.

But from the moment Dr. Adams put Nate in her arms, from the very second her little boy caught her pinky finger in his tiny fist and held on tight, Maddie forgot everything. The pain, the hurt, the impossible state of her marriage to Tom. No matter what, she and Nate would be okay. She loved him from the moment she saw him . . . her precious son.

Once Maddie was settled into her room she quickly drifted off to sleep. When she opened her eyes again, she saw Tom sitting in the big armchair in the corner cradling Nate and singing softly in his ear. For the briefest moment she forgot the trouble between them and smiled. He looked up at her, blinking back tears, and whispered, "Oh, Maddie." And then he got up and handed Nate to her, and as she looked on, frozen in disbelief, he disappeared into the night.

Without mentioning where he'd been, Tom returned three days later when Maddie and the baby were ready to be discharged from the hospital. Maddie knew that he'd returned a number of times to see Nate because she had heard the nurses discussing how sweet he was with their son, but he hadn't stepped into her room once to see her.

While struggling alone to recover from the birth, Maddie's sadness had turned to anger. The fact that Tom could treat his wife, the mother of his child, this way made her both bitter and resentful. When he finally came to bring her home, Maddie said curtly, "If it's not too much to ask, can you please deal with the photographers? The nurses have told me they've been camped outside since I got here. Nate doesn't need that kind of attention when we leave."

"It's taken care of, Maddie," Tom said coolly. "I don't want Nate unduly exposed either. They get one shot, and then we go home. They've promised us a few days of peace after this."

"Really? How'd you arrange that?"

"If nothing else, I'm still a great negotiator. Now are you ready to go?"

With the nurse's help, Maddie got painfully into the wheelchair while Tom waited impatiently in the doorway. They rode down to the lobby in silence. At the entrance, Maddie saw that the circular drive was crammed with reporters holding microphones and cameras. A large number of devoted fans had gathered as well, some waving signs reading "Welcome, Baby Nate," others shouting their names, trying to get them to look up for a picture.

The nurse helped Maddie out of the wheelchair. Holding Nate close, Maddie stood blinking in the sunshine while Tom posed behind her, arms folded across his chest. Maddie could only hope that the many cameras clicking away would miss the fact that Tom Seymour and Madeline Ellis were standing a bit too far apart for a couple who were blissfully happy, as their record company wanted the world to believe.

In the haze of new motherhood, Maddie couldn't keep track of Tom's comings and goings from the loft. There were times when he'd stumble into bed stinking of booze and weed and sleep until late afternoon the next day. Then he'd spend a few minutes alone with the baby, singing to him softly while changing his diaper, before heading out again. Often, when she got up in the middle of the night to calm her crying son, she'd trip over some of Tom's dirty laundry, strewn haphazardly wherever he'd removed it on his way to their bedroom. Throughout Nate's first weeks her own sleep cycle was irreparably disrupted, and she was no longer sure if it was daytime or nighttime because Nate barely slept two hours at any one stretch.

Between breastfeeding him on demand, changing countless diapers, soothing Nate when he was fussy, and trying to shower once in a while, it was all she could do just to get through the day. She often found herself watching Charlie Rose on PBS while feeding Nate, only to drift off and wake up in the same spot in the broadcast as it repeated itself in the middle of the night.

Her mother had offered to come and help, but Maddie didn't want her to be exposed to Tom's objectionable behavior. She knew how angry her parents still were about the wedding, and Tom was lucky he hadn't been around when they came to see their new grandson in the hospital. The last thing Maddie needed in her sleep-deprived state was a showdown between her acerbic New England mother and this silent, hostile Tom.

But one brilliant spring morning, with a soft breeze blowing through the open windows of the loft, Maddie could no longer bear her isolation. She had slept a few hours the night before, and at the moment Nate seemed quiet and content. For the first time since bringing him home from the hospital she felt energetic enough to take him outside.

She dressed Nate in an adorable tie-dyed onesie under a pair of faded denim overalls and was delighted to find that she could actually pull on her regular-sized jeans for the first time since giving birth. She was still a little puffy around the middle, but she was able to disguise what remained of her pregnancy belly with a loose cashmere pullover in palest yellow. As she ran a brush through her wildly long hair and applied some mascara, blush, and lip gloss, she realized that she actually looked human again. She packed up the diaper bag and attached it to the handle of the dark blue Perego carriage, gently put Nate inside, and tucked a lightweight blanket around him.

She took the elevator down to the lobby and then remembered: the photographers. Would they still be lurking outside? A number of them had been hanging around the few times Maddie had taken Nate to the pediatrician for his newborn wellness visits. With Ralph's help, she'd been able to slip out through a service entrance and into a waiting cab, but this was an unplanned outing. She hoped she hadn't made a mistake.

As the elevator doors slid open, she cautiously peeked out and was relieved to see no one in the lobby. Ralph was in his usual position near the front exit, and she called out to him.

He hurried toward her. "Good morning, Miss Maddie!" he boomed. "So nice to see you downstairs! Looking good!" He had delivered so many packages and take-out meals to her over the last six weeks that she wondered if he had ever expected to see her emerge from the loft again. He was clearly surprised to see her standing there in the lobby dressed in something other than her oversized sweatpants and stained T-shirts.

Maddie's heart warmed. "It's nice to see you too! Is it safe to go outside? Are the photographers still there?"

Ralph laughed. "I think they gave up a few weeks ago. We all thought you were never going outside again. You've given them the slip for now."

"Great. I'd love to walk over to the studio without being hassled."

"If they do show up, just call me before you head back. I'll be ready." He strode over to the large reception desk and reached underneath, withdrawing a heavy wooden baseball bat. "They won't bother you or Nate on my watch!"

Maddie laughed. "You're my hero, Ralph. Thanks again." Adjusting Nate's blanket, she stepped out into the sunshine. To her relief, Prince Street was nearly deserted. Everyone was probably enjoying the glorious weather at the park. Maddie breathed in the fresh air and felt her spirits lifting. It had been far too long since she'd been outside or exchanged words with other adults. She couldn't wait to get to the studio and show off Nate and maybe even hear some of the album that Tom had all too often reminded her the band was busy mixing without her.

As Maddie neared Broadway, the street became more crowded. People went in and out of the stores and restaurants or sat at tables at the sidewalk cafés, enjoying the weather. Car horns blared, taxis sped past, and Maddie breathed deeply in contentment as she started to feel the rhythm of the city around her. She had always felt at home here. People may have recognized her pushing the carriage, but surprisingly no one bothered her—New Yorkers were often cool that way.

Rounding the corner of Prince and Broadway, Maddie saw the studio up ahead and felt a major sense of accomplishment. She had successfully navigated her first solo trip with her baby, and she chuckled softly at the thought. It was both ridiculous and hysterical for a world traveler like herself to think that a short six-block walk would mean so much to her, but in that moment, it really did.

She opened the tall glass door and pushed the carriage in ahead of her, then walked down the tiled corridor that led to the studio. She entered and waved to the curly-haired young receptionist, who, clearly startled to see her there, dropped the magazine she'd been reading. "Maddie!"

"Are they in room A or B, Sherri?" Maddie asked.

"Let me tell Tom you're here. Hang on—" Sherri reached for the phone.

"Don't bother. I've got this," Maddie replied cheerfully, already pushing the carriage down the dim corridor toward the mixing booths. She peeked into the first studio, but it was empty. As she neared the second, a young woman suddenly burst through the door, pulling her blouse back on as she almost crashed into Maddie. A cloud of patchouli oil lingered after she was gone.

Maddie stood there for a moment trying to catch her breath, then pushed Nate's carriage through the door. There he was, sitting alone at the mixing board. "Who was that woman, Tom?" she asked, struggling to keep her voice even, to keep the hurt and anger from showing on her face.

"What woman?"

Maddie immediately noticed that in his haste to cover himself back up, Tom had misbuttoned his shirt. She propped a hand on her hip. "Really, Tom? You want to pretend you weren't just half naked in here with a stranger?"

"C'mon, Maddie," he replied. "I'm just trying to get this record out. One of us has to work, you know."

She closed her eyes and struggled to contain the rage rushing through her. From his stroller, Nate whimpered in his sleep, forcing her to regain her center. Squaring her shoulders, she cleared her throat and tried to look uncaring. "Where is everyone?"

"The session was called for noon. They aren't here yet," Tom replied.

"So you came in early for a little extracurricular activity?"

Tom leaned back in his chair, infuriatingly calm. "I don't even know what that means, Maddie. You must be hallucinating from lack of sleep."

His tone, his words, enraged her. She clenched her teeth. "Yeah, well, one of us has to care for our son."

"Whatever."

Maddie's anger deflated. Tears pricked her eyes. This wasn't what she had envisioned for her first excursion outside with Nate. *Calm, Maddie, stay calm. For Nate's sake.* There was no sense in trying to reason with Tom. She struggled to speak past the lump in her throat. "Can you play me some of the tracks you've completed?"

For what seemed like the first time in weeks, Tom's expression softened a bit. "Sure. Let me cue something up." He passed her a set of headphones, and she sat down next to him and placed them over her ears, all the while keeping an eye on the carriage. Tom pushed a few buttons, and the music surrounded her, full and lush, swirling inside her head. She could hear their vocals, the instrumentation provided by the band, and then something more—the audience singing along with them.

The effect was breathtaking and took her right back to Wembley Stadium, where the song had been recorded toward the beginning of their European tour. She looked up at Tom, deeply moved, to find him watching her. She smiled, and he smiled back, but it didn't reach his deep green eyes. Her own eyes again filled with tears.

Worse than the memory of the half-naked woman nearly running her over in the corridor was this feeling that he already drifted away from her, and she didn't know how to bring him back.

"Tom—" Her voice was thick with tears as she pulled the headphones off. "I wish I'd never—"

The door burst open and Emilia rushed in, a tornado of nervous energy, long hair matted and wild, a riot of purple and pink streaks sticking out in every direction. She stopped, pivoted on her impossibly high boot heels, and then squealed aloud.

"Maddie! What are you doing here? Oh God, it's Nate! Can I hold him?" She moved toward the carriage, but Maddie stopped her before she could reach in and lift the baby out.

"Emilia, wait, he's sleeping . . ." Her voice trailed off. She hadn't seen Emilia since Nate's birth, and she was shocked by her appearance. Emilia's once beautiful skin appeared pale and blotchy. Her pinpoint irises signaled the ingestion of one or more of the illegal substances she'd grown so fond of. Looking at her stained blouse and inappropriately short, wrinkled skirt, it dawned on Maddie that Emilia had not been home from wherever she'd been the night before.

"I won't wake him, I promise," Emilia said much too loudly and reached into the carriage again.

"No!" Maddie said sharply, and Emilia, stunned, backed away. "I don't mean that you can't hold him, Em," Maddie said hastily. "Please just wait until he wakes up. This is the biggest break I've had in weeks."

"Oh, okay then," Emilia replied coolly. "I need coffee anyway. I'm gonna run to the bodega on the corner. Are you staying today, Maddie? Are we finally going to lay down the track for 'Forever With Me'?" She flailed her arms and paced, clearly agitated. "We won't be done until we record that, and I'm dying to get away on a real vacation."

"I'd love a coffee, if you don't mind," Maddie said quickly and watched as Emilia pushed through the door. "Wow," she murmured sadly.

"She needs rehab, not a vacation," Tom said coldly. "She's been out of control ever since Martin left her."

"What? Martin? When? Why didn't you tell me?"

"I did. You just never seem to be listening when I talk to you anymore."

"If I hadn't been so wrapped up in Nate, I might have seen this coming," Maddie said, ignoring the jab.

"My point exactly. So give in and hire a nanny, Maddie, please. You'd be more involved with the band, and you might even get your own life back on track," Tom said impatiently.

"It's *our* life, Tom," Maddie snapped. "And we've been over this. I didn't have a baby so someone else could raise him. I want you and me, together, to give Nate the most normal life we can, despite all of this crazy—" She fell silent and gestured around at the expensive recording equipment covering every inch of the room.

"It's not normal to be stuck at home day after day when we can easily pay someone to watch Nate for a few hours." Tom scowled at her. "For God's sake, Maddie, bring a nanny with you to the studio if it makes you feel better, but we've got to finish this album. The whole idea was to move it out quickly, to capitalize on the tour's momentum. You're holding us up, and some of the guys are starting to get tired of waiting. They're talking about taking on other gigs, and we're going to lose them. How much clearer do I need to make this for you?"

Tears burned in Maddie's eyes, but Tom, staring angrily at the ceiling, didn't notice. This whole morning had taken an awful turn, Maddie thought, worse than anything she could have imagined when she first stepped into the warm sunshine feeling so full of anticipation.

An outer door slammed, and Maddie gathered herself as best she could. She said quietly, "I'm here now. Let's lay down the track and be done with it."

"Finally," Tom growled just as the other members of the band began to file in.

"Maddie!" Andre exclaimed when he saw her. "You've returned to the land of the living! So happy to see you!" He engulfed her in a bear hug.

"Hey, man, move over," Ned said, pushing Andre aside to embrace Maddie warmly. "We've missed you. You look great! Are you ready to record?"

Maddie felt a surge of emotion overcome her, making her realize just how much she had missed working with them. And then Nate, almost as if on cue, woke up crying to be fed.

What the rest of the world outside of the studio never knew was that when the smash hit "Forever With Me" was recorded, Nate Seymour was nursing at Maddie's breast. But if Maddie listened really carefully to the master tape, she could hear her son cooing softly in the background, and despite the turmoil in her life, that one small detail always made her smile.

XII

The album was their biggest seller ever, going triple platinum just two weeks after its release, with "Forever With Me" becoming their second number one hit, climbing the charts in record time. But there was little joy for Maddie in its runaway success. During the album's meteoric rise, Tom spent more and more time out of the loft just to avoid dealing with the deepening rift between them. He often came home stumbling drunk—or not at all. There was a stretch just before Nate's first birthday when he disappeared for three weeks, and while a large part of Maddie worried, another part felt relief: there were no arguments when Tom was gone.

They had fallen into some strange sort of uneasy dance, one where the partners couldn't find their rhythm, couldn't get in sync, causing them to continuously bump into one another, all sharp elbows and plodding feet, movement without grace. At least Nate kept Maddie busy. He was an active infant who had taken his first steps at ten months, and at a year he was toddling through the loft every chance he got. He was, Maddie told herself often, all the joy she needed.

She wasn't sure why, but the record company executives, so insistent on having her record a solo album before Nate was born, had backed off. She hadn't heard another word about it, and for that she was grateful. She wasn't sure about the future of the band either. After their last recording session, well aware of Tom and Maddie's estrangement, they'd all scattered, taking on other projects but promising to reconvene if either of them wanted to do another album. Maddie knew deep down that if she never recorded another song or performed live again, she'd be just fine. She had more money than she could spend in one lifetime. All she wanted now was the chance to raise her son in the most stable environment possible.

She thought often about taking Nate up to the Cape and starting over there, but she was afraid of feeling as if she had failed her family, with their tough New England stick-it-out-at-all-costs attitude. Besides, she loved living in New York, and though it pained her to admit as much, she couldn't bring herself to leave Tom. Despite how little they saw of each other and how far they'd drifted apart, she couldn't deny that she still loved him and held out hope that he would come back to her. Surely Tom would realize that Nate was so much more important than the drugs, drinking, and other women he now pursued. And surely he'd leave that world behind to become the father their son deserved.

It was near midnight on a hot and humid stretch in mid-August 1988. Steve Winwood's voice, playing softly through the speakers from a top forty radio station, competed with the quiet droning of the air conditioner. Maddie hummed along as she straightened up the loft. Her hair was piled high on her head, and she was wearing a white cotton sundress that she hadn't completely buttoned after feeding Nate before bedtime. There were toys strewn in every possible corner and dishes in the kitchen sink. As tired as she was, she knew that if she left anything till the morning, nothing would get done. Once Nate was awake, the nonstop action just started all over again.

The song ended, and Maddie turned off the radio. Tackling the dishes in the sink, she began humming a new tune she'd recently begun hearing in her head, the first song she'd come up with since Nate's birth. She was concentrating so intently that she didn't hear the elevator ping to announce its arrival. The front door banged open and she turned, startled, to see Tom on the threshold.

Maddie's eyes widened at the sight of him. His face was drawn, and he had lost a few pounds since he was last home. His jeans fit loosely around his hips, and his T-shirt was soaked with sweat that darkened the imprint of their first album cover prominently displayed across his chest.

"What the hell?" she burst out. "What are you doing here?" Her hands flew to the front of her dress, attempting to do it back up.

The gesture wasn't lost on Tom, whose eyes narrowed. "Last I looked, this was where I lived. My name is still on the deed, isn't it?"

"That's not what I meant. You're never here anymore. I'm just surprised to see you, that's all."

"Why would I want to be here when that's the type of greeting I get when I walk through the door?" Tom's tone was scathing. "It's not like you want me here anyway. I came to see Nate."

"At midnight?" Maddie folded her arms across her chest, determined not to let him see how much his coldness still had the power to hurt her. "He's sleeping. And that's the way I'd like to keep it, Tom, so please keep your voice down."

"I'll just look in on him before I go to bed, if you don't mind. He's my son too."

She took a deep breath to swallow the angry words she longed to shriek at him. "I didn't say he wasn't. I just asked that you wait until morning to rile him up before you leave again."

Tom moved to the sofa, sweeping toys to the floor before sitting down. His expression was mutinous as he looked up at her. "I'm not going anywhere tomorrow. I've got nowhere I need to be, and we've got to talk about our next album."

Maddie tried to hide her shock. Was Tom out of his mind? Had he forgotten everything she'd been telling him since Nate was born? And as for his implication that he was staying here overnight . . .

"There's not going to be a next album, Tom," she said coldly. "I haven't written anything for a while."

"That's interesting. I thought I heard you humming something when I came in. And the next album? Clearly some details got past you when Nate was born. We've got a contract that says the next album is due at the end of the year, and it's legally binding. At this point we'll probably deliver it late and have to pay penalties."

"What are you talking about?" Maddie's voice rose. "I'm not going back into the studio, Tom, so if that's why you're here, you're wasting your time. I'm not leaving Nate with a nanny for days on end just for the sake of any album!"

Tom shrugged. "Then ask your mother to watch him. You've got work to do." He pulled off his boots, tossed them into the middle of the living room, and walked into their bedroom, slamming the door behind him. Maddie stood looking after him, grappling with her temper, telling herself not to react to his outrageous behavior. But when she heard the shower turn on, she stormed after him.

Bursting into the steamy bathroom, Maddie flung the shower door open, not caring that the spray got her wet. She was so angry that at first it didn't even register that Tom was naked.

His grin was devoid of warmth. "Miss me, Maddie?"

She blushed hotly as she glanced down at his body, hating herself for the familiar longing that crept deep into her core at the sight of him. She stammered, "Tom, I don't care what you say. I'm not going into the studio while Nate is this young."

"I'm open to suggestions then," he said, moving the soap around his body suggestively. "The label isn't going to wait until Nate goes off to college. Neither is the band. It's now or never, and I'm not letting you ruin all of my hard work putting us on top just because we had a baby. Maybe you haven't noticed, but lots of women have children and still work. It's not 1953 anymore, sweetheart."

He turned off the water, pulled a fluffy blue towel from the warmer, and brushed past her. Maddie grabbed his arm before he could leave the bathroom and swung him around to face her.

"My, my," he drawled. "It's been a while since you couldn't keep your hands off me."

"I want to know why you're being such a prick. What the hell is the matter with you?"

"I'm not being anything, Maddie. And we're not having this conversation again. Now if you don't mind," he said, removing her hand from his arm with a look of disdain, "I'm going to sleep." He walked over to the bed, flung his towel to the floor, and slipped between the sheets, still dripping wet.

Maddie stood there for a moment, incredulous. She had no idea what to do. She definitely didn't want to continue arguing with him, but she wasn't going to relent. And now he was in her bed. *Naked.*

Resisting the urge to weep, Maddie padded down the hallway to Nate's room. Before their son was born, Tom had insisted that she put in a trundle bed for the nanny he had hoped she would hire, and while Maddie had initially fought the idea, she was glad for it now. Pulling back the blanket, she slipped between the cool, crisp sheets. Though exhausted, she lay with her eyes wide open, feeling angry and hurt and utterly alone. She tried to convince herself that everything would seem clearer in the morning, that the light of day would help her figure out what she needed to do about the recording contract and the cruelty of Tom's behavior. The fact that he thought he could show up any time he wished and make himself at home in her bed—and that she had let him—had to stop.

Eventually she closed her eyes, but her mind continued to race, caught up in the uncertainty of what was to come. And when she finally fell into an uneasy doze, she was besieged by bizarre nightmares where she was running toward some unknown place that scared her even in sleep.

The next thing Maddie remembered was waking up in an empty room. Nate wasn't in his crib, and she panicked. Stumbling into the kitchen, she stopped short when she saw Tom and her son sitting together. Nate was smiling ear to ear and bopping up and down in his high chair, covered in mashed banana. There were Cheerios strewn all over the floor. Tom was sitting in a chair next to Nate, strumming his guitar and singing softly to him in his melodic voice, something about a beluga whale.

It was the normalcy of the scene more than the relief washing over her that caught Maddie off guard. It was almost dreamlike, something she could only imagine would ever happen. Tom's entire demeanor seemed different, unguarded and familiar. Almost as if they were back in college again, before their runaway fame, before their estrangement. Her heart ached with the memories.

And then she heard Nate say "dada." Tom's head snapped up, and she saw the shock in his eyes.

"Oh my God, Tom," Maddie cried, utterly disarmed. "Did you hear that? He's never said that before!"

"At least someone here still cares about me," Tom replied. Putting his guitar down, he leaned over to give Nate a kiss. Then he looked at her, his expression reverting to the disinterested one Maddie was so used to seeing nowadays. "Coffee? I couldn't find the beans."

She looked at him: his hair still tossed from sleep, his handsome face made sexier by its thinness and the shadow of a beard. She had to remind herself not to be taken in by this moment of intimacy. She tried to recall his ugly words of the night before, but in that moment, she couldn't. All she could do was ask, "Hawaiian Kona or Columbian Sumatra?"

"Whichever you're drinking. I'm easy," he said in that infuriatingly indifferent tone he'd been using with her for months now.

"*Sure you are,*" Maddie muttered under her breath, her mood souring as she busied herself with the coffee preparation. Leave it to Tom to ruin the stunning wonder of Nate's first word.

Behind her she heard Tom let out a sigh. "Can we talk like adults, Maddie? Please? We've got a lot of ground to cover, so let's call a truce, okay? I'll start. Sorry about last night. I was really hungover."

Maddie slowly finished the coffee prep, trying to calm down, to keep her thoughts from racing back to the long list of grievances she wanted to fling into his face. She didn't want to fight with him, and with Nate right there, babbling in his high chair after saying his first word ever, it seemed all the more important that they try to get along. She drew in a breath and turned to face him. "Sure. What's up?"

Tom spread his hands. "The album, Maddie. We owe the record company an album. There are all sorts of penalties to pay if we don't deliver, not to mention the people who depend on us for work. You remember the band, don't you?"

Despite her best efforts to remain calm, Maddie couldn't help but bristle. She closed her eyes and turned away, but the old, familiar anger was already surging into her heart, an uncontainable tide. "Of course I remember," she snapped. "I'm not the one who's out every night with another nameless groupie; I don't drink myself sick or snort cocaine or do whatever else it is that you like to do. I'm here day in, day out, taking the best care of Nate I can."

She looked over at their sandy-haired little boy feeding himself the cereal still clinging to the tray of his high chair, his round, adorable face and chubby little hands covered in banana goo. *Some truce*, was all she could think.

"I'm not asking you to be the morality police here, Maddie. I'm asking you to come back to the studio. Let's lay down some new tracks and be done with it."

"Be done with it? Really? One more album and then we're done? Seems I've heard that before. It's the same old argument, Tom."

"Well, the label will probably want to back the record up with a tour . . ."

Maddie didn't know whether to laugh or cry or throw the coffee pot at him. "Exactly," was all she could manage. She pulled Nate out of the high chair to rinse him off at the sink. Realizing it wasn't going to be easy to clean him there, she carried him into the bathroom on her hip and turned on the taps in the tub. Tom trailed behind them.

As soon as she set Nate down on the tiled floor and pulled the sticky pajama top up over his head, he escaped, running into his bedroom, banana-covered hands and all. Maddie looked at Tom. "In case you were wondering, this is how I spend my days now."

She made a move to brush past him, but Tom caught her arm and said with unexpected gentleness, "Let me."

Maddie turned to pour a capful of baby bath bubbles in the tub and checked that the water was warm enough. She was throwing some toys into the bath when Tom returned with their squirming child.

"He's fast," Tom said, smiling at her warmly for the first time in what seemed like forever.

"Tell me something I don't know," she said, refusing to soften. Lifting Nate from him and deftly removing his diaper, she put him in the sudsy water. Then she turned back to Tom. "Do you really think we can take this baby on the road, Tom? City after city, late nights, you and all those women, the drugs, the drinking? Sorry, but I'm not exposing our beautiful boy to all that crap."

Tom refused to be baited. Instead he grinned at her, that sexy grin she'd never been able to resist. Damn him. "Stop with the drama, Maddie.

We can make it happen any way you want. We can tour slower, take more days off between gigs, make less stops if that's what you need us to do."

"Let's forget about Nate for a minute," Maddie snapped. "What about the rest of it, Tom? Do you know how humiliating it is for me to watch you go out and do God knows what with God knows who night after night? And don't promise me that it won't happen when we both know you don't mean it. No more, Tom. I'm done."

His smile faded and anger sparked in his green eyes. "You really don't have much choice, sweetheart. The record company has us by the terms of our contract."

Maddie was about to wash the banana out of Nate's hair, but instead she whipped around to face him. "That's where you're wrong, and that's where we're different," she said furiously. "I'll pay the penalties. I won't go back on the road, Tom. Not ever again." She turned back to Nate and began singing to him, ignoring Tom completely as he stormed out of the room.

When Maddie came out of the bathroom with Nate dried and freshly diapered, she was astonished to find Tom in the kitchen. She had expected him to leave the apartment, and yet here he was sitting at the counter sipping coffee. When Nate saw Tom, he gurgled and extended his arms, and Maddie had no choice but to relinquish him to his father.

"Hey, buddy," Tom said softly. "What do you want to do today? Spend some time at the park?"

"It's supposed to be over one hundred degrees this afternoon, Tom. Not safe for him to be outside," Maddie said tartly.

"Then in the spirit of our supposed truce, why don't we go to the beach?" he replied.

Maddie hid her surprise by remaining stiff and unmoving in the doorway. "And the dozens of photographers who camp outside our front door can come too, right? One big happy family."

"So we'll hire a car and give them the slip. What do you say, Maddie? Let's have a family day. You agreed we'd try to be civil with one another, remember?" He motioned toward Nate. "For the baby's sake? And maybe a change of scenery will help you think more clearly about what we've got to do."

Maddie realized he was serious. "And just how do you think that going to the beach will change my mind?"

"You love the beach. I think you just need to see that traveling with Nate is something we can accomplish together." Tom stood up, shifted Nate onto his hip, and took both her hands in his big one. "I'd like to give it a go. How about you?"

Maddie was startled by his touch and the hot rush of blood that reached from her toes to her neck. She stepped back quickly, pulling her hands free. "I'm not so sure."

Was it her imagination, or did he look hurt? "Let's talk about it later, okay?" With Nate still on his hip, he walked across the kitchen to pour two cups of coffee. He smiled as he handed her one. "Let's start over. Truce for a day?" he asked again, adding softly, "I mean it this time."

Maddie felt her resolve slipping away. She knew how much Nate would enjoy a day at the beach. "Okay. But how can we do this and not be mobbed? I don't want Nate exposed to overexcited fans or have his picture taken."

"Let me make a few calls. I think Russell at the record label has a house in Montauk. Maybe he'll let us use it for a few days."

A few days? Maddie nodded even as her heart began to pound nervously. She hadn't spent more than a single day with Tom in so long that she wasn't sure what to make of the whole idea. She went into Nate's room and began to pack some clothing and toys along with diapers and his beloved blanket. She was glad for the distraction, glad for the chance not to have to think.

Tom came in a few minutes later to tell her that a car was coming to pick them up in an hour. All she needed to do was be dressed and ready. "I'll watch Nate in the meantime," he added.

Maddie was amazed to find out how much she could accomplish in an hour when she had help with Nate. She was able to clean the kitchen and pack her own bag in record time and even managed to finish another cup of coffee before the phone rang. It was Ralph letting them know that the car had arrived. Tom put the bags in the elevator while Maddie strapped

Nate into his stroller, and together they went downstairs to brave the barrage of flashbulbs that Maddie had come to expect whenever she stepped onto the street. Sometimes she wished that she never had to leave the safe confines of her home. It would be so much easier that way.

Two and a half hours later they pulled into the driveway of a beautiful multilevel beach house off Soundview Drive in Montauk. Maddie had never been to the very tip of Long Island before, and she could hear the ocean as they stepped out of the car. It made her feel like a young girl again, growing up on Cape Cod. Nate had slept practically the entire drive, and Maddie and Tom had been able to negotiate a partial settlement between them regarding their future plans.

"If you promise to keep the recording studio free and clear of any extraneous personnel"—Maddie had looked accusingly at Tom as she said this—"I will come in and record for a few hours each day once we have all the songs written."

"And we'll find a nanny to watch Nate while we work. Someone old and gray, okay? No nubile Swedish chicks," Tom teased.

The idea of a subsequent tour was still up for discussion, and they were in the midst of it when Tom opened the front door of the house.

Maddie gasped. It was the most beautiful place she'd ever seen. The living and dining area were one big open space, painted a beautiful butter yellow with glossy white trim. There were soft, plush couches covered in a tan tweed pattern with oversized accent pillows in an abstract kiwi-colored print. Through the expansive French doors that led to a large deck she could see the ocean shimmering just below the house. Spectacular.

Nate squirmed in her arms, and she was somewhat afraid to put him down, not knowing what damage he might cause, but she knew he would not be contained much longer. "Let's change and go down to the ocean," she suggested, struggling to hold on to him. "This one needs to burn off some energy."

"Great. I'll throw on a bathing suit and watch him while you put yours on."

Tom picked up their bags and walked up the short flight of stairs that led to the bedrooms. One of them had a crib in it, and he dropped

Nate's things there. Maddie followed and was happy to see a matching dark cherry wood changing table set up as well. "I didn't know Russell had kids," she said.

"I didn't either, but I guess if this is a place where his family gathers, then someone must. Lucky for us. I didn't really know how to put together that portable thing we brought with us."

Maddie chuckled and put Nate down. Opening his overnight bag, she pulled out his bathing suit and sunscreen. It was a battle to get him to sit still long enough to be readied for the beach, but she ultimately got the job done, placing a small Mets cap on his head to shield his eyes from the glaring sun. "Let's go find your dad," she said, lifting him up and walking down the hall.

There were four other bedrooms on the second floor, each with its own bathroom and design scheme. One was clearly for a little girl, with its pink and purple bedspread, matching curtains, and a large dollhouse in one corner. Maddie closed that door as she passed by so that Nate wouldn't be tempted to do any damage to the delicate toys it contained. She most certainly didn't want him left alone with the array of Barbie dolls she saw on one shelf—they'd be destroyed in no time.

There was another room with a queen-sized bed and large windows that faced the front of the property and a matching one across from it. The master suite was at the very end of the hallway up a short flight of stairs, where Maddie found Tom standing at the window staring out at the ocean. The room was enormous, almost the size of half of the first floor. There was a tiled fireplace on one wall, a giant bed against another, and two walls of wraparound glass facing the Atlantic. It took her breath away.

Tom turned and winked at her. "Pretty amazing, huh? I think this is the perfect place for us to ride out this heat wave, don't you?"

Maddie noticed that he had put her luggage down next to his. Was he expecting her to sleep in the same bed with him? It had been so long since they'd been together that it took her a minute to figure out that they hadn't had sex in almost a year. She blushed at the thought, and to cover her nervousness, she said, "Somebody's got to do it, might as well be us! If you take Nate downstairs, I'll change. Hopefully we can hit the beach unnoticed."

"We're not in the Hamptons, Maddie. Russell told me the people here are much more laid back, less impressed with celebrity, and that they respect their neighbors' privacy."

"Sure hope so. I don't remember the last time I swam in the ocean. I can't wait." All at once she felt as excited and happy as a young girl. Rummaging through her bag, she pulled out her two-piece suit. She really hoped it still fit—she hadn't bought anything new since Nate was born, and it hadn't seemed necessary to buy beachwear as she'd never expected to make a trip like this one.

She waited until Tom and Nate were downstairs before she stripped off her sweaty sundress and put on the bathing suit. The bottom was okay, but the top was tight, an apparent side effect of breastfeeding her son. Throwing a T-shirt over it, she ran downstairs to make the most of the family time that awaited the three of them while the truce with Tom held.

Needless to say, Nate loved the water. Maddie and Tom sat together for most of the afternoon while their son dug for shells and emptied bucket after bucket of cold water on them. Not until the wind picked up, bringing a chill as it blew in off the ocean, did they gather their belongings and head back to the house.

While Tom took Nate upstairs for a bath and clean pajamas, Maddie rummaged around the pantry to figure out what to make for dinner. She was sunburned, tired, and blissfully happy. Humming to herself, she pulled out a box of pasta, fresh zucchini, and ripe red tomatoes.

"It was nice of Russell to call ahead and have his caretaker stock us up," she said when Tom appeared wearing a faded T-shirt and rolled-up blue jeans with a freshly bathed Nate, hair still damp, in his arms. "The refrigerator is filled with all sorts of produce, milk, cheese, and juice."

"He also left instructions for how to get into his wine cellar and encouraged us to open any bottle we find interesting," Tom said. Settling Nate into a booster seat at the kitchen table, he went down to the cellar while Maddie cut Nate some juicy peach slices and waited for the pasta water to boil. The fresh air had made Nate hungry, and he was making quick work of the fruit when Tom came back upstairs holding two bottles of red wine.

"Which one would you prefer?" he asked.

Maddie hesitated. She'd love a glass of wine after nursing Nate later, but she knew from experience that Tom would finish the rest of the bottle on his own. It had been such a pleasant day, and she didn't want his drinking to ruin the good mood she was in, or affect their fragile truce.

"Maybe we shouldn't open any."

"Don't be ridiculous. Russell was adamant. We wouldn't want to insult him."

"It's not that. It's just . . . well . . . you aren't you when you drink too much."

Tom scowled at her, and Maddie realized she had offended him. "I'll only have one glass, if that's what you're worried about. Don't make a big deal out of this."

"Do you promise?"

"Scout's honor," he replied, putting his hand over his heart.

Maddie hid her relief by turning back to the stove. It certainly looked like the truce was going to hold. Dare she drop her guard altogether? The thought was so tempting, so tinged with the hope of happiness, however brief it might be. "Okay. I'll have a glass with you after dinner. I've got to feed Nate first."

"Perfect." Tom glanced at both labels before saying, "I'll open this one and let it breathe. I bet it'll taste pretty spectacular once it takes in some air."

Tom pulled a corkscrew out of a kitchen drawer while Maddie began slicing the tomatoes. By the time the pasta was al dente, she had the sauce ready, and they sat down at the table to eat. After a few bites of his rigatoni, Nate began to whimper and rub his eyes. It was obvious that he could barely keep his head up. Maddie lifted him gently out of his seat. "Leave my plate there. I'll finish it when I'm done putting him to bed."

"Sure. I'll wait for you. I'll be on the deck watching the sunset."

She brought Nate over to Tom for a good night kiss and then bounded up the stairs. There was a beautiful wood rocking chair in the room next to the crib, and she sat down and cradled Nate's head to her breast. She knew it wouldn't be long before he was too old for this nighttime ritual, and she realized how sad she'd be to give it up.

A half hour later, Nate was full and drifting off in his crib. Maddie turned on the baby monitor, picked up the portable receiver, and headed down to the kitchen to be greeted by a breathtaking sunset right outside the French doors: violets and pinks streaked across the darkening sky while the waves crashed ashore in a rhythmic lullaby. Tom was sitting on the deck holding a glass of wine. Maddie stepped outside to join him, overcome with a sudden feeling of well-being.

"Is he asleep?" Tom asked softly.

"Almost immediately," Maddie responded. "It must have been the sun and all this ocean air." She drew in a deep breath herself.

"Is it all right for you to drink this now?" Tom asked, handing her a delicate- stemmed glass. "It's pretty tasty."

She lifted the glass to her nose and sniffed the warm, earthy scent, then took an appreciative sip. "You're right. It's delicious." It only took a little bit of wine to make her feel woozily relaxed, all limber and fluid. "Are you still hungry?" she asked.

Tom looked at her for a long moment, as though he was measuring his response. "I am."

Maddie felt herself blush. *What was the matter with her?* She told herself that he meant he was hungry for the dinner she had prepared, nothing more. "I can bring our plates out here. It's so lovely and cool, and it'd be nice to watch how many stars come out tonight."

"That sounds great," Tom replied. "But you sit. I'll get the plates. Thanks for cooking, by the way," he added when he returned with the bowls of pasta.

"It's my way of saying you were right about running away to the beach for a bit. I don't know if it's a day in the sun, the wine, or the setting, but I feel so relaxed. I'm glad we came."

Tom smiled back at her. "Me too."

They sat in quiet companionship while they ate their dinner. Maddie's glass was empty, and Tom refilled it, leaving his own empty.

"You really aren't going to have any more?" Maddie pointed to his glass.

"I don't want to upset you or ruin this moment," he answered. "When I called a truce, I meant it."

"Thank you," Maddie said softly. Then, hesitantly, she added, "Look, Tom, I'm not your mother. I can't presume to tell you what to do. But I do know that you without copious amounts of alcohol are preferable to you drunk."

"I like to drink, Maddie, I can't lie. It helps blur the lines for me. It makes me feel I can do anything, like my talent is real and limitless."

Maddie blinked, astonished. "But, Tom, it is. We've been so successful. We have a beautiful child. What else do we need?"

He looked right at her as if he wanted to say something but stopped himself. Then he shook his head and said heavily, "There's always more, Maddie. I want our name, our brand, to live forever. I want Nate to be proud someday of the work we've done, the music we've made. I don't want to stop yet."

Maddie took her glass and walked over to the railing, watching the moon rise in the sky. "It's not that I don't love the music, Tom, because I do," she said, facing away from him. "I love writing songs, sharing them with you. I just don't like that life anymore. Having Nate changed everything for me. I want us to be a family, to have times like today, to be able to be enough for one another, just *us*."

She heard him draw in a deep breath, and when she turned around, he was standing right behind her.

"If you're referring to those other women, they meant nothing to me, really nothing. I'm not proud of it, but there were times when I just wanted mindless sex and you didn't." Tom ran his hands through his hair. "I drink too much, Maddie, and it clouds my judgment."

"But why? What makes you behave this way, running crazy, coming home mean and nasty?"

She could see the conflicted emotion in his green eyes. "I have no answer that will make you happy, Maddie, and really, we called a truce, and I want to live up to that. Let's not argue." He leaned down and kissed her lips, and for the first time in what felt like forever, and despite his words, she was lost.

Tom took the glass out of her hand and put it down on the deck before he gathered her in his embrace. When he kissed her again, she knew there would be no resisting the pull between them. She felt the fiery burn in the core deep down within her, the rush of adrenaline from her heart to her toes, running through her veins in sheer need and desire.

When Tom reached for her hand, she gave it to him without hesitation, following him up the stairs to the master bedroom, allowing him to pull her shirt up over her head as they went into the bathroom. He turned on the shower, stripped down to nothing, and removed the bathing suit she still had on.

At first Maddie was somewhat shy, afraid that the extra five pounds she still carried from her pregnancy would make her unattractive to him, but Tom's ragged breath when he looked at her told her otherwise. He opened the door to the oversized stall and pulled her under the water with him, kissing her all over and taking his time to show her just how much he was still attracted to her.

It was all Maddie could do to stay on her feet as his hands swept her body with lavender-scented soap. All of her pent-up desire pushed the hurt aside, and she let herself believe that everything would be okay, that they would make it past the pain they had inflicted on each other. She was, after all, a romantic at heart, Tom was her Prince Charming, and she wanted to hold on to the hope that he had at last found his way back to her.

In the morning Nate was up with the sunrise. Maddie heard him babbling in his crib and walked down the hall, changed his wet diaper, and brought him back into the master bedroom. When Nate saw his father, he clapped his little hands together. He was so excited to have Tom there that Maddie knew she had to try to make this relationship work.

She set Nate down gently on the bed, and he immediately crawled onto Tom's sleeping body and lay down on top of him. Maddie grabbed the camera from the diaper bag and quickly snapped a shot before Tom realized what was happening. As he woke, he shifted his arms to wrap Nate in a giant hug, causing him to laugh. Tom said, "Now this is the kind of wake-up call I could get used to!"

"It's the best, isn't it?" Maddie said, loving the sight of them together this way. "If you watch him, I'll make coffee. Come down when you have your fill of cuddling."

"I don't think it'll be me who wants to let go first." Tom laughed. "We'll be down soon."

Smiling, Maddie made her way to the kitchen. She put coffee beans in the grinder, boiled water for the French press, and cut up more peaches for Nate to eat while she assembled the rest of their breakfast. She didn't even realize that she was humming the bridge to her newest song when Tom came in with Nate.

"Wow, Maddie, that tune is infectious. I love the sound of the hook!"

She blushed. "I just started working on it. I don't have a lot of time to write anymore, as you can tell."

"Well, that's one you've got to finish. I'll take Nate down to the beach after he eats if you want to work on it."

"I do, but I don't want to miss out on any time with the two of you. I'll finish the song, I promise, but not this morning. It's our last full day here."

"Okay. But we need to figure out a way for you to have time to write when we get back."

"Does that mean you plan on sticking around?" she whispered.

Tom cleared his throat. She could have sworn he suddenly felt shy. "If you'll let me. I mean I really do want all of this—" He gestured to Nate, who was now sitting in his booster seat covered in peach juice.

Maddie bit her lip. "I'm sorry, Tom, but not if it means you come and go at will. You're either all in with us or not."

"I can only promise to do my best, Maddie." His voice was husky, his green eyes reflecting his inner struggle. "There's a lot of temptation for me in the city, I admit. But I also know how much I have to lose if I fuck up again. We can record another album, we can limit the tour dates, and we can give it another go. I love you now, forever, and always. Please believe me."

Maddie felt her doubts melting away. Her husband was pledging himself to her again. He looked so sincere, and she was drawn back to their time at school, when their relationship was new and they were both so very young and innocent. The open honesty they had shared when they first met was gone, she knew that, but if there was any glimmer of a chance of having Tom back, she owed it to Nate to try. All she needed to do was say yes. She took a deep breath. "I want to believe you, Tom. Tell me you'll do right by us."

He stood and wiped away the tears that sprang from her eyes. "Thank you, Maddie," he said and took her in his arms. "We're a team, baby. We'll make it. I'm sure of it."

They spent another wonderful, restful morning at the water's edge. After lunch, Nate fell asleep on the beach towel Maddie had spread under an umbrella on the sand. Sitting beside him, Maddie closed her eyes and suddenly found herself surrounded by the music that had been crashing around in her head for the last few weeks. All at once the song came together for her. She heard it: start to finish, over and over.

She had never really questioned her creative method; it was inborn and undeniable. Journalists had often asked her where the music came from, how she worked, why she wrote, but she always found it impossible to explain. It was as if she was simply the conduit for the magical process that she could not seem to describe other than to say that the music just took over her mind and forced her to write it down. Tom understood, because he had watched it happen so many times. She knew that his process was so different from hers, more tenuous. He could struggle over a chord or phrase for months. That never seemed to happen to Maddie; the music seemed to pour out of her naturally.

She opened her eyes and turned to Tom, who was listening to something on his new Walkman. It was much smaller than the original ones they owned, and the sound quality had improved. She had to shake him to get his attention.

"Tom, I think I need to go inside. I finished the song in my head, and now I want to put it down on paper."

His eyes widened and he broke into a wide smile. "That's my girl. Go ahead. I'll keep an eye on Nate." He put the earphones on his lap as if to prove that he wouldn't be distracted from his task.

"Thanks. I won't be long. If Nate wakes up, there's a green sippy cup of water for him in my beach bag."

"Green sippy cup, got it," Tom said, shooing her away.

She picked up her flip-flops and hurried back to the house. Since she didn't have any blank sheet music with her, she wrote the chord progression down on a legal pad she found in a kitchen drawer, along with the lyrics that had been part of the completion of the song. The whole process took less than twenty minutes.

As Maddie set aside her pen and folded the paper, the house phone rang. She jumped, having all but forgotten that the real world existed outside her door. At first she wasn't sure if she should answer it, but by the fifth ring, she did.

"Hello?" she asked tentatively.

"Maddie? Hey, it's Russell. How's it going out there?"

"Russell! We really can't thank you enough. Your home is really beautiful, and you're a great host!"

"I'm so glad to hear that, Maddie. Tom told me you guys needed a break from the city. Are you heading back tomorrow?"

"Unfortunately, yes. If you ask me, I'd stay in Montauk forever. I really love it here."

"Yeah, well, work calls. Remind Tom that the studio's booked for Monday and the band will be there. And, Maddie, we can't wait to hear what you've got for that solo album of yours."

Maddie was stunned into silence. *Solo album? What solo album?*

"Tom hinted it was going to be pretty special. But of course we already knew that." Russell chuckled.

Maddie head spun. She'd never agreed to a solo album. Tom must have signed her up for this. That's why he had showed up unannounced the other night, then brought her out here, seduced her, lied through his teeth while he charmed her—and Nate!—all for a solo Madeline Ellis album.

Maddie, you stupid, stupid fool! Shit! She had known, of course, that Tom had negotiated a new deal with the label just before Nate was born, but had he made a deal on a solo album too, signing away her right to refuse without her knowledge? Because she *had* refused—she couldn't have made that clearer to him, to Russell, and to Paul. Would he do that to her? *Could* he do that to her? Once back in the city she'd need to call her attorney . . .

"Maddie? Are you there?"

Mind racing, she steadied herself before answering. "Sure am, Russell. I'll tell him. And again, thanks for everything."

"My pleasure. Don't miss the food at Gino's, by the way. He's a young chef from the city who's taking Montauk by storm. You'll love his restaurant. Very family friendly."

"Maybe we'll try it tonight," Maddie said woodenly. "See you Monday." Hanging up, she wasn't sure if she was furious or hurt or both. She just felt numb, as though a bucket of cold water had been splashed in her face. She stood still for a long while, just breathing, waiting for her heart to stop racing.

Once calm, she realized she'd have to think this through carefully, to do what was best for her, for Nate. Slowly she formulated her plan. If Tom had indeed signed an agreement with the label that meant she owed them a solo album, she'd record it, and she'd be sure to include her very best work. She would live up to her part of the contract in order to protect Nate and her own good name at all costs, because it was now apparent that she could never count on Tom to do that for them. She would also need to shield her heart so that Tom would never fool her like this again.

They took Nate to Gino's that night for dinner, and if Tom noticed a shift in Maddie's behavior, he didn't mention it. He kept up his end of the conversation, not even flinching when she told him about Russell's call earlier that afternoon.

"So you're okay with the solo album, Maddie? I wanted to tell you, but after Nate was born, well, you weren't exactly ready to hear it. He took all of your concentration, your attention."

Maddie was silent.

Tom paused and then went on in a pleading tone, just as she knew he would. "The executives were relentless, Maddie. They wouldn't sign the band to a new deal without it."

She took a long sip of her Chianti. "I had a baby, Tom, not a lobotomy. You could have come and explained it all to me when it happened."

"I was under tremendous pressure, Maddie, and you and I weren't exactly on good terms. You know how tough Paul and Russell are when they double-team you. It was the only way I could ensure the band stayed together. Everybody was being offered side deals, and I wanted to lock them down."

"And what did you get out of the deal, Tom? What was the sweetener?" she asked coldly.

He dropped his gaze from hers. "They guaranteed us three more albums together. And I get complete creative control."

"Three?" She nearly choked.

"Yeah," was all he could manage.

Maddie drained her wineglass and motioned to the waiter to bring her another. "So now that I know, what's next for us, Tom? Do you really plan to live at home?"

She hardened herself against his hopeful expression as he reached across the table to grab her hand. "If you and Nate will have me."

Nate will have you, Maddie thought. *That's the only reason I'm still here right now talking to you. And considering letting you come home with us. Because Nate needs a father. Because he needs you.*

Shit, shit, shit.

"And the last couple of days, the things you said . . . the sex," she added tonelessly. "Did it mean anything at all to you?"

"Maddie, I love you. I always have, and no matter how fucked up I am, I always will. I'm trying to keep us together."

"Wow, Tom. Do you really believe your own bullshit?"

He sat back in his chair, clearly stunned, but, being Tom, recovered quickly. Maddie watched as his eyes took on that pleading look and his voice grew husky with emotion. "I'm telling the truth, Maddie. You and Nate are my world."

The waiter returned with her wine, and instead of responding, Maddie drank it as quickly as she could. That night, for the first time, she was the one who got rip- roaring drunk while Tom remained stone-cold sober.

Maddie woke up the next morning to find the temperature had dropped during the night and that she had a pounding headache. She stumbled downstairs for coffee and watched Tom and Nate playing with a soccer ball on the deck outside the kitchen while she drank it. When he saw her, Tom scooped Nate up in his arms and came inside to hand her a bottle of Advil. "How's your head?"

"Been better," she replied dully.

"Take two of these with some black coffee. It's the real breakfast of champions," he joked, attempting to lighten the mood.

But Maddie wasn't amused. She popped two pills, took another swig of coffee, and went back upstairs to pack. An hour later a car arrived to drive them home to their Prince Street loft.

Once there, the unspoken tension between them remained, settling over them like darkness. They spoke only when the subject involved Nate and fell into an unsteady rhythm, one of them always leaving the room as soon as the other entered, passing Nate off as they went. They slept in separate beds, each made their own way to the studio to work and ate their meals in silence. Maddie thought of it as a cold war, and obviously Tom did too, but out in public, through an unspoken agreement, they practiced détente so the world would never suspect a thing.

And despite their unhappy arrangement, they managed to release Maddie's solo album to both critical acclaim and staggering sales. The song she had finished on the beach, "That Certain Summer," stayed on the charts for a full year while they toured the country, Nate in tow.

The success of Maddie's album seemed to be the final blow for Tom. While Maddie shuffled through her life in a protective daze, focusing on Nate, always Nate, Tom retreated into a world of his own. All of his earlier promises to her were broken. The creation and production of the three albums he'd committed them to record fell solely on Maddie's shoulders while Tom effectively vanished from her life, and she struggled to keep their careers relevant and the record company happy—again all for Nate. Meanwhile she watched and said nothing as Tom spiraled down into a place even she could not have imagined.

Though he still lived with her and Nate on Prince Street, though they remained coldly civil for the sake of their son, she knew from the rest of the band, from her parents, and from the tabloids that Tom was always high, drinking way too much, and flirting with every woman he saw. He hadn't contributed a thing toward the band's next album.

They managed, thanks to Maddie's exhaustive efforts, to release two of the three records by the time Nate entered grade school. But the third one was delayed again and again, because Tom simply couldn't stay sober long enough to write songs with Maddie. Their magic had always been a blend of their musical talent and poetic lyrics, but they hadn't penned a note in over a year. They kept a group of musicians and backup singers waiting as well, and instead of taking other gigs, the most loyal band members professed their support for Maddie while the rest clung to the hope that one day Madleine Ellis and Tom Seymour would record another huge hit and that royalties would line all of their pockets once again.

It turned out to be a long wait.

On the morning of Nate's eighth birthday, Maddie awoke to the sound of rain. Pulling on a warm sweater, she went into the living room, bypassing the empty guest bedroom in which Tom slept whenever he came home—which wasn't often nowadays—to finish wrapping the last of Nate's gifts. The bicycle he had begged for sat off to one side, a big red ribbon affixed to the handlebars. Maddie had arranged for it to be delivered late last night so that he'd wake up and find it this morning. She'd been anxious about Tom stumbling in drunk in the wee hours and waking Nate, but fortunately that hadn't happened.

"Mommy?" At the sound of Nate's sleepy voice, she hurried into his room to find him sitting up in bed, still half-asleep.

"Happy eighth birthday, sweetheart! Bet you can't wait for your party later! Do you want to come see your presents?"

Nate threw the covers off, stood, and stretched in his Mighty Ducks pajamas before running to give her a hug. A second later he was past her and in the living room, whooping aloud over his new bike. Maddie's heart swelled as she watched him ride it around the oversized loft. *Just for the day, forget the impatient recording executives and his absentee father,* she told herself. *Just enjoy Nate.*

"Can we get dressed and go outside, Ma?" he pleaded. "Can I ride my bike to the dojo today?"

"Afraid not, sweetie. It's raining."

Nate rode over to the large floor-to-ceiling window that looked out onto Prince Street. He had asked that his birthday party be held at the karate dojo he attended several times a week, a place where he had made a number of friends over the past two years, friends who didn't treat him as a kid with superstar parents and a sensei who demanded just as much from him as anyone else.

"What if it stops raining before the party? Can I ride it then?"

"Who's afraid of a little rain?" Tom's voice boomed as he entered the loft, shaking the rain off his coat and then tossing it across a chair, not caring that the fabric beneath became wet as well.

"Dad!" Nate screamed in excitement. "Come see my new bike!"

Maddie watched as Tom folded his son in his arms. She looked anxiously for signs that he was drunk, that he smelled of other women, or God knew what else. He was dressed in worn jeans and a faded blue sweater, and at first glance, he looked utterly, reassuringly . . . normal. But she knew better than to judge him on his appearance alone.

"Tom," Maddie said sharply, "it's not a little rain. It's teeming."

"There's your problem, Maddie. Always seeing things half empty instead of almost full."

"Really? I'm not the one who gets Nate's hopes up that he can ride to the party on his bike. Not in this weather." She took a step closer, and her eyes narrowed. "And take a shower. You stink like the garbage you were out with last night."

"Just love those homespun New England expressions of yours, dear. Loosen up a bit, huh?"

"What is that supposed to mean?"

"You're the smart one. Figure it out." Tom set Nate down and gave her a mocking smile. "Always know where I've been, eh, Maddie?"

Maddie shook her head, refusing to rise to the bait. She could only hope that he would indeed get in the shower and not collapse on her bed. Once asleep, there'd be no waking him, as she well knew, and she wasn't about to have him miss Nate's party—much as she wanted him to.

After putting the torn wrapping paper from Nate's smaller gifts in the garbage and cleaning up the breakfast dishes, Maddie began to feel somewhat calmer. She could hear the water running in the shower and was thankful that Nate, distracted by his new bicycle, hadn't noticed anything amiss between his parents.

"Look at me, Ma! Is it time to leave for my party?" Maddie turned to find Nate dressed in his white karate gi, the new stiff green belt tied tightly around his waist. He threw a few practice punches and kicks, clearly proud of his latest accessory, and Maddie's heart swelled as she looked at him. He was a great kid, despite his famous mom and dad, despite their rocky relationship.

Even at eight years old, Maddie knew that Nate was well aware that he didn't have parents like other kids at school. His dad didn't go off to work every day in a bespoke suit, sharply starched custom-made Egyptian cotton shirt, and imported silk tie. He wore ripped jeans and T-shirts, and his hair brushed his shoulders and fell down his back. He was seldom home, while she almost always was, often spending days on end at the piano composing in her pajamas, barely stopping to eat or sleep, ordering take-out lunch and dinner for them. Nate never complained or made comparisons to his classmates. He just accepted the bizarre rhythm of his life with gentle ease.

"Should I see if Dad is ready?" Nate asked now.

"I'll do it," Maddie responded, wondering what was taking Tom so long.

She went into their bedroom and heard the water running in the bath. What on earth was he still doing in the shower? As she went to pull the blanket over the bed in an effort to neaten up the room before they left, she spotted a used hypodermic needle, a burned votive candle, and one of their small acrylic kitchen cutting boards on the night table. They hadn't been there before Tom showed up that morning.

A chill ran down her spine. Maddie knew about the drinking and the recreational stuff, but if he was now doing serious drugs . . .

Nate's voice calling from the hallway interrupted her shocked thoughts. "C'mon, Mom, I want to go!"

Maddie threw everything from the night table into the trashcan by the bed.

"One minute, honey," she yelled back. She went to the bathroom door and cracked it open. A wall of steam washed over her.

"Nate's anxious to leave, so we're going ahead of you. Just meet us at the dojo."

"Yeah, whatever," came Tom's response.

She shut the door behind her and quickly left the room.

"Let's go, Nate. Dad will catch up with us in a little bit." She grabbed her keys out of the bowl on the small hallway table, quickly pulled the gate of the elevator open, and rode down with Nate to grab a cab on the corner.

Thanks to the weather, there weren't any paparazzi in the lobby or out on Prince Street, but somehow they must have caught wind of Nate's party, because they were camped out on the sidewalk in front of the karate studio. Before exiting the cab, Maddie tugged Nate's rain hood tightly over his head and, putting one arm around him, elbowed her way through the crowd and past the two burly security men she'd hired to stand at the door. As much as Maddie had hated to do it, she was determined to ensure that only Nate's invited guests made it inside.

Shaking the rain off and hanging up their coats, they were immediately surrounded by Nate's classmates and friends. Andre and Charlie were there as well, and Nate hugged them happily when he saw them. As Nate had requested, the party would begin with a black belt demonstration of board breaking and sparring, followed by a lesson for all willing guests. While the sensei gathered the children on the mats, Maddie looked over the refreshments and then turned to join the other parents.

"Hey, Maddie."

Maddie looked up. "Hi, Emilia, how are you?" *More importantly, what are you doing here? Who invited you?*

Emilia shifted uncomfortably from one impossibly high heel to another. "Where's Tom?"

"He's on the way. Did he tell you about Nate's party?"

Emilia nodded. Looking at her closely, Maddie was taken aback by her appearance. Her eyes were bloodshot, with dark rings underneath her lower lashes. "You okay? You look exhausted."

Emilia kept glancing over her shoulder at the door to the dojo. "I'm sorry. Didn't sleep so well. I think I'm coming down with the flu." She sniffed a few times and dabbed a tissue at her nose. "So is Tom gonna be here or what?"

"He was still in the shower when Nate and I left." While Maddie and Emilia were no longer as close as they had been before Nate was born, Maddie suddenly needed desperately to confide in someone. Taking a deep breath she blurted, "I found a used needle next to the bed this morning,"

Emilia blinked. "What?"

"A needle," Maddie repeated, her voice dropping to a whisper. "I'm terrified to think what that means. But it would explain why he's not writing. I'm starting to really worry that this album will be more than delayed. I'm not sure we'll get it out at all."

"Umm . . . Maddie . . . let's not jump to any conclusions. Maybe there's a reasonable explanation for what's going on."

Maddie was rendered speechless by this flippant reply. *A reasonable explanation?* Was Emilia joking? Or so high that she'd lost sight of reality? Over Emilia's shoulder she suddenly saw Nate gesturing to her frantically, indicating the empty space on the mat beside him.

"I'm sorry," Maddie said guardedly, "I have to go." *Please,* she thought, crossing the room to Nate's side, *don't let Tom embarrass our son in front of all his friends when he gets here. And please, Emilia, don't do anything to humiliate me in front of these women, either. Please leave their husbands alone . . .*

Maddie watched the karate demonstration with unseeing eyes, applauding when Nate applauded and cheering when he cheered. All the while she watched the entrance of the dojo, but Tom did not appear. Emilia, too, had vanished; a quick glance told Maddie that she wasn't sitting with the other women—most of them the mothers of Nate's guests—in the chairs set up by the refreshment tables.

When the sensei called the children to the floor for their lesson, Maddie headed toward the ultra-chic group of moms, aware that she needed to be polite. If there was any piece of parenthood she hated, this was most certainly it. Making small talk with other mothers from Nate's private school, especially these women who specialized in competitive childrearing, was the worst thing anyone could have her do.

"Hi, Maddie," a perfectly groomed, thin blond woman with perfect small white teeth called to her. "It's such a great thing you're doing here, having this kind of party for Nate. I mean, he could have probably asked you for a private concert for his friends or something. This is just so, so, well . . . average." She seemed proud of herself for finding just the right word.

"Nate loves it here, loves the sensei and the lessons. It was a natural fit." Maddie was about to move away from the tiny blonde when she heard a small commotion at the front door. Turning around, she saw that Tom had arrived.

His effect on women never ceased to amaze Maddie. Wherever they went, he immediately charmed every woman in the room. Today was no exception—every one of the moms who a moment before had seemed eager to tell Maddie just what they thought of Nate's "average" party now rose and headed toward him. *Like a stampede*, Maddie thought.

Just then the pizza deliveryman appeared through a side door, and Maddie grabbed the wallet out of her bag to pay him. As she waited for him to make change before giving him a substantial tip, she caught sight of Emilia leading Tom to a far corner of the room, talking nonstop while he listened with an impatient look on his face. She breathed a sigh of relief. At least if Emilia could keep Tom occupied he wouldn't hit on any of the other mothers there.

The room quieted down for a while as the kids devoured their pizza, and before Maddie knew it, the sensei was carrying in the large chocolate ice cream cake she had ordered, fully ablaze with candles and sparklers. She looked around for Tom but didn't see him, so she started singing "Happy Birthday" without him.

Maddie was gratified when everyone else joined in, even the grinning sensei and the other moms and dads, with Andre and Charlie contributing a charming harmony. The applause that followed was genuinely enthusiastic, and tears pricked Maddie's eyes as she saw the joy on Nate's face.

An expectant hush fell as Nate leaned forward to blow out the candles—a silence that was broken by a sudden commotion toward the front of the dojo. There were shouts and a curse, and all heads turned as a pair of strange men who Maddie could only guess were paparazzi burst through the front door. The security guards, one of them waving a night stick, followed close behind them, with one of the guards yelling out, "In here! I saw them go in here!"

One of the photographers threw open the door to what Maddie knew was the supply closet. After every lesson, Nate and his fellow karate students were expected to pile their mats neatly inside, though it would be empty now, with all of the equipment currently in use out on the floor.

As the door opened, the other photographer pressed his camera to his face—and captured the image that was suddenly exposed for all of them to see: Emilia on her knees in front of Tom, whose pants were gathered around his ankles . . .

Despite the collective gasp from the other adult guests, it took Maddie's brain a moment to register what she was actually witnessing.

"It's that piece of shit Martin!" she heard someone yell, and in what seemed like slow motion, she saw Andre leap across the room to make a grab for the camera just as the security guards caught the man by the collar and wrestled him out into the street. Through the dojo window Maddie saw that it was indeed Emilia's old boyfriend Martin—though she barely recognized him. He was emaciated; his once long hair was thin and greasy, his face gray, his eyes haunted. And he still had the camera . . .

"Maddie!" She turned and saw Charlie steering Nate toward her through the crowd. Nate! Instantly the strange pressure in her chest and the feeling that she was about to faint lifted, and she knew she had to get herself and her son out of there.

Grabbing Nate, she threw his coat over his head and made a dash toward the town car that she had prearranged to be outside waiting to take them home. Pushing past the security men and ignoring the photographers' shouted questions about Tom and Emilia who had been exposed to all in the dojo, she ran to the car, pulling Nate, who was crying by now, into the backseat.

"Why do we have to leave, Mommy?" he wept once the driver slammed the door behind them. "I didn't get to eat my cake. And where's Daddy? Why didn't you wait for him?"

Thank God, he hadn't seen . . .

"Prince Street, Ms. Ellis?" the driver asked, ignoring the press of bodies around the limo, the flash of cameras, the pounding of fists on the window.

"No," Maddie gasped. "Get us out of here, please."

"Where to?"

Maddie didn't know. Couldn't think. Escape. Get Nate as far away as possible from this place and the unthinkable consequences she knew would follow. "East," she croaked.

"Beg pardon, Ms. Ellis?"

"Go east," she repeated. Where? Again she didn't know. Then words seemed to come from deep inside her: "The Long Island Expressway." She cleared her throat, forced herself to speak more calmly, aware of Nate's frightened eyes on her. "Just head east, and don't stop until you run out of road."

"If I do that, we'll hit the ocean, Ms. Ellis." The driver was teasing, having seen Nate's tears and perhaps aware that the paparazzi storming the limo seemed more insistent than usual.

The ocean. Suddenly Maddie remembered Montauk. With its isolation and beauty, it might just be the perfect place for them to hide.

Part Three

XIII

Nate gripped the steering wheel of his rental car tightly as he drove into town, eyes darting between the road and the heavy gray clouds lowering on the horizon. Snow had begun to fall, leaving a thin white layer on the lawns and treetops. Where had *that* come from? Hadn't he been sitting on the deck with his mom this morning, drinking coffee and nursing a hangover?

Nate hadn't paid any attention to the weather since his flight landed at JFK the day before. *Shit.* But who could blame him for not checking the news since then?

Dealing with his mother had been bad enough, but he hadn't counted on the one specific stress he had avoided since his high school graduation ten years earlier, which was the last time both of his parents had been in a room together: His father's train was due at the Montauk station any minute, and his mother had no idea that she was about to be confronted with the man she had vowed never to see again and, before last night, had no reason to believe she'd ever have to. It was as bad a nightmare as Nate could imagine, only this time, he was the center of the storm in more ways than one.

When Tom had called Nate only an hour before, he was already on the train heading east to Long Island.

"Nate, I know this is crazy, but I have to see your mom. It's important."

Nate had hidden his shock behind what he hoped was a calm, reasonable response. "Dad, she'll never agree to that right now. She hasn't even decided about the wedding. We talked about this. I told you I had to ask her myself. You being here will wreck any chance I have of convincing her."

"I know I promised to wait, but something's happened. One of her oldest friends has died. I just found out this morning." Tom cleared his throat on the phone, and Nate got the horrible feeling that his father was close to tears. "I've got to tell her myself, so please, Nate, pick me up at the station and let me try. Or at least bring her with you and we can talk in some neutral place. A coffee shop maybe."

"Oh, Dad, Mom will never—"

Tom interrupted, "I know it will take a lot to convince her to see me, but I have to do this right."

"No, Dad, that's not it." Nate drew in a deep breath.

"Oh." There was a long pause. Nate could hear the sound of the train clattering over the tracks. "You mean the agoraphobia."

"Yes," Nate said softly. "It's the same old story."

"Does she see a therapist? Is she getting any help?"

"I've finally found someone who will come to the house. If Mom will allow it." Last night Nate had had reason to hope she would. But now? With his father on the way, unannounced, unexpected? And thoroughly unwelcome?

There was another long silence, then Tom said quietly, "You've done a good job keeping your mother's problem under the radar, son. I don't know how you've managed it."

"It hasn't been easy, Dad. It was hard work convincing the label to avoid having Mom tour to support the albums she's released. I played up the stage fright angle, and with her history, I was able to sell it. No one—not the record company or the tabloids—knows the whole truth."

"How have you kept the paparazzi from camping out in front of the house all these years? They'd have a field day if they knew the real story."

Nate allowed himself the ghost of a smile. "They've never been able to get past the neighbors. They're our best allies. Any stranger found near the property gets the crap kicked out of him or is run off by the local police. It's like a no-fly zone or something."

Tom let out a whistle. "All these years I believed what I read in the press. I just figured she always hated to tour, so it all made sense."

"Then my plan worked. I hope I'm as lucky in convincing her to sing at the wedding."

"I'll do my best to help," Tom replied.

Then stay away, Nate had wanted to shout at him, but just then the train must have entered a dead zone, because the phone disconnected suddenly. Tom hadn't called back.

Now, as Nate turned into the small parking lot in front of the station, he knew it was almost time to continue their awkward conversation. He could hear the train clanging as it approached.

Despite the chilly wind and steady snowfall, the reality of his father being here in Montauk suddenly made Nate feel overheated and uncomfortable. Was this what the beginnings of panic felt like? Is this what his mother experienced?

There were few riders off-season, and Nate recognized his father as soon as he stepped off the train. Nate was gratified to see that Tom had aged well since he had last seen him in LA. The hair that peeked out from under his baseball cap was fully gray now, but his shoulders were still broad, strong. Despite his bulky jacket, it was clear that Tom had been working out.

"Dad, over here!" Nate shouted through his open window, snow falling on his hair.

Tom's face broke into a wide smile. "Hey, Nate. Thanks for picking me up on such short notice." Opening the car door, Tom got in, throwing his small leather bag on the seat behind them. "Wow. It's good to see you," he said heartily, reaching over to grab Nate in a quick embrace, clearly trying to diffuse his anxiety. "It is definitely colder here than in the city. And this snow! Hope I packed enough warm stuff."

"I'm sure you'll be fine. It's great to see you, Dad."

"You too, Natey."

Nate smiled at hearing his childhood nickname for the second time in twenty-four hours.

"How's your mom?" Tom asked.

Nate's smile faded. "Pretty off balance. I've given her a lot to think about. Your showing up isn't going to help," he added.

"I know, son. But I have to see her."

"I remember, Dad. Somebody died. Who—"

"A friend. Someone we knew a long time ago."

His father's voice was so filled with pain that Nate was stunned into silence. "Dad—" he eventually managed.

"Don't, Nate. I have to talk to your mother first. And I'm going to need your help to make it happen."

"I know," Nate said miserably.

After a pause Tom asked, "I'll need to find a meeting around here."

"I'm sure they must have some. Let me see . . ." Nate pushed some buttons on his phone to Google the answer. "They do. Every morning at the Lutheran church on Main Street."

Tom put his arm around Nate's shoulder. "It's gonna be okay, Nate. I'll deal with your mother. And we'll get through this together. I just want you to know how proud I am of you for supporting her all these years. I'm sure it wasn't easy. And I'm thankful you're trying to get her the help she needs now."

His hand tightened on Nate's shoulder. "I know how much you want your mother at your wedding, but if she's adamant about not singing, please back off and let me handle it. It's not worth risking your relationship with her, and we both know I can't possibly make things worse between us. So if you strike out, I'll bat cleanup, okay?"

Nate smiled at the baseball reference. Spring training may have just started, but with snow falling and winter holding on, a relaxing day at Dodger stadium with his father seemed like a distant dream. "It's a real long shot, Dad. You know Mom—agree with her or get out of her way. Now let's get you a hotel room. You didn't give me enough time to make a reservation."

While Nate was away on his grocery run, Maddie sat composing at her piano. She had finally returned to the song she had been writing the night before Nate had surprised her with his visit was playing a continuous loop in her head. As she made small changes to the melody, she began to think about the larger picture, the arrangement, which instruments she would need to flesh out the full sound that for now only she could hear.

It was like putting the pieces of a puzzle together, and Maddie knew she really wouldn't be able to rest until it was done, but all the talk about Nate's wedding and the thought of singing with Tom—hell, just *facing* Tom—was so distracting that she found it unusually hard to concentrate. It was simply outrageous to believe that she and Tom could be civil to one another again, or at least polite enough to walk their son down the aisle, let alone join each other in performing for Nate and Sophie and their guests.

Just thinking about it made Maddie more than uncomfortable. Who could have known that after she'd told that limo driver to head for Montauk after Nate's disaster of an eighth birthday party that she and Tom wouldn't see or directly speak to each other again for years?

For two decades, Maddie had communicated with her ex-husband through her divorce attorney, Marvin Stein, a man who more than made up for his wiry appearance with his sharklike instincts and ability to eviscerate his opponents. Marvin had made quick work of the details, and seven months after moving to Montauk, Maddie and Tom were divorced. Marvin had his assistant, Sandy, a veritable bulldog in her own right, act as the go-between for the twice-a-year court-appointed visitation weeks when Nate would travel to the city to stay with Tom. Brisk and efficient, Sandy would pick Nate up and drop him off, refusing to carry messages or share impressions or gossip for either one of them, thus ensuring that Maddie and Tom were separated completely by more than the miles between them.

Marvin had also set up a system with an entertainment lawyer he worked with to handle all of Maddie's business dealings so she didn't need to bother with Tom on any aspect of their musical relationship, including the remaining album due their label after their split. When Nate finally graduated from Stanford and expressed an interest in managing her career, Maddie, surprised and gratified, had willingly turned everything over to him, confident that he would guard both her vast fortune and her musical legacy.

And now Nate was asking that she reunite with Tom, in song, no less, at his wedding to Sophie. Remembering the last time she'd spoken to Tom, Maddie shuddered. They had run into each other briefly, inevitably, at Nate's high school graduation. Tom had arrived with another nameless bimbo on his arm and didn't bother to hide the fact that he'd started drinking long before the commencement ceremony started, making their encounter exceptionally tense and unpleasant. If it hadn't been for Nate, for the love she had for her son, Maddie would have left the graduation as soon as she saw Tom there, but she didn't. She had toughed it out as best she could.

From the day she'd moved with Nate out of the city and away from his father, Maddie had made it her mission to ensure that her son had as normal a life as possible. She joined the PTA, contributed cookies to the bake sales, hosted sleepovers, cheered him on at little league games, and drove everywhere in carpools. Knowing she had to play the role of both parents for Nate kept her going—until the day she realized that he didn't need her in that way anymore. By then, leaving the house just hadn't felt important or even necessary.

Maddie had been fine since then. Really. The mere hint of reopening that wound and dealing with Tom again was more than she could bear to think about because she had made her peace with her choice in life. She certainly didn't want Tom back in it now.

Maddie shook her head, realizing she was too distracted to compose for the moment. In the kitchen she grabbed a cup of coffee and headed out to the small recording studio she had added onto the edge of her property, just to see if there was anything she'd need to update or supply before she summoned her old band out to record her new song. She had built the studio after finishing the renovations on the house, wanting to have the ability to stay close to home while Nate was still in school.

The studio had professional-grade recording equipment and was big enough for her band to fit in comfortably while working on new music. Maddie had eventually added two bedrooms and bathrooms to ensure that her band members always had a place to stay if they missed the last train back to the city or were too tired to drive back if they rented a car.

Maddie knew that not everyone wanted to come all the way out to the end of Long Island to work when Manhattan was such a big lure. It always surprised her when people actually asked to stay over, but it delighted her as well. Montauk, while at first a safe refuge from the glaring lights of the paparazzi and gossip columns, and of course from Tom, had become her home. It was quiet in comparison to the city, especially in the winter and spring.

The summer brought its share of tourists and sun-lovers, but Maddie didn't mind. She had a large piece of property, and it was very private, surrounded on two sides by tall beach grass and steep dunes, and with the ocean in her backyard, there was never a real problem with trespassers.

After a few years, the paparazzi had given up on her, finding more current and interesting—and especially accessible—celebrities to harass. They had labeled her a recluse, and Maddie had never cared. Her closest neighbors knew who she was, but more importantly, they were incredibly protective of her. They did their best to allow Maddie the privacy she craved. It was a tight-knit, exclusive community of the very wealthy, which made it important for everyone to keep strangers at bay.

If she kept on her prescribed stepping-stone path, Maddie could make it out to the studio cottage from the kitchen of her house without panicking. She walked quickly, minimizing the amount of time she spent outside in the open, shaking from a combination of cold air and frayed nerves.

Reaching the front door, she felt under the window box for the key. She had put it there years ago for some of her favorite studio musicians who had a habit of showing up in the middle of the night, long after she was sleeping. They knew that she never minded if they let themselves in, helped themselves to the large and varied supply of food and alcohol she kept in the kitchen cabinets, just as long as they were up and ready to work when she joined them the next day.

That trust had been built over the years with her band, and most of them were fully aware of what had transpired in the dojo so long ago and how it had destroyed both Maddie's marriage to Tom and their career as a duo. None of them ever mentioned the topic, and thus they were always welcome. If one of them needed a place to crash, he or she knew where to find it.

Maddie looked up at the sky before unlocking the cottage and was surprised to see snowflakes falling from the lowering clouds. She'd been so wrapped up in Nate's arrival and her new song that she hadn't paid attention to the weather at all. Stepping inside, Maddie switched on the TV and was startled to see that a Nor'easter was headed their way. An unexpected late-season storm meant she'd better put in an emergency call for a grocery delivery. Despite Nate's promise to get the necessities for tonight's dinner, Maddie didn't know how long they'd be stuck in the house, and she was running low on both milk and coffee. Her calls to him went straight to voicemail, the cell service probably faulty due to the storm. She hoped she hadn't waited too long—in the off season, the stores that remained open did so on sporadic schedules, so she crossed her fingers and dialed the grocery store on her cell phone. She was totally relieved when she heard Julia pick up on the other end.

"Hey, thank the Lord you're still there. It's Maddie. I need a few things . . ."

After a lengthy conversation with Julia about the storm, Maddie felt pretty confident that she'd ordered enough food to make it through any impending natural disaster.

"You just call me if you need anything else," Julia said. "I'll bring it over in a jiff."

Maddie was smiling when she hung up. Living out here in Montauk had brought her back to her small-town roots. She knew all of the shop owners, always asked after their families, really cared about her neighbors. It mattered to Maddie that she belonged to the community and that no one was impressed by her fame.

Knowing Julia would be stopping by fairly soon with her groceries, Maddie quickly checked that all the studio windows were tight and that the heat was on low to prevent the pipes from freezing. Turning off the lights and locking the front door, she replaced the key in its hiding spot before cutting back across the property toward the warm glow of her kitchen.

The snow was falling more heavily now, and she hugged her arms close around her shivering body. The surf was building, each swell pounding against the beach in ominous warning. Generally, Maddie didn't mind a good storm; since being confined at home for days on end was her comfort zone to begin with, she was immune to cabin fever.

Once inside the house, she let out the breath she'd been holding and closed the glass slider against the strengthening wind. Then, with a contented sigh, she headed into the pantry to pull out some ingredients for tollhouse cookies, Nate's favorite.

By the time Nate and Tom pulled into the parking lot of Gurney's Inn, the only hotel in town still open, the snow was falling fast. As they crossed the chilly lobby to the registration desk, they were forced to step around a variety of large electrical cables and bulky black cases.

"What's all this?" Tom asked.

"I don't know." Nate took a closer look and recognized the equipment as camera cases. A crew must be shooting a film or commercial somewhere in town. There were a lot of people crammed in the bar across the lobby, and they didn't look like they were going anywhere anytime soon. He told himself this was no reason to panic.

Approaching the young woman behind the desk, Nate put on his broadest smile while Tom hung back a bit, his baseball cap shading his face. "Hi there. We were hoping to get a room for a few nights."

"Wow, I wish I could help you," she replied, "but we're overbooked. The trains just stopped running with this storm coming in, and no one can get back to the city."

Which was exactly what Nate had feared. "Are you sure? Can you double-check?"

"I don't need to, sir." She gestured to the bar. "I just booked that whole crew, and they're stacked three in a room. The storm's moving east, and Penn Station is already shut down. Portions of the expressway are closed too."

"What the hell?" Nate burst out. This was worse than he'd thought.

The young woman nodded importantly. "You better get where you're going and stay there. This is a huge Nor'easter. They're saying to expect as much as two inches an hour. And it's supposed to snow well into tomorrow. Sorry we can't accommodate you."

Great. Now what the hell was he supposed to do? If he and his mother had spent less time butting heads yesterday and drinking all that wine, maybe this storm thing wouldn't have slipped completely off their radar screen.

"Thanks anyway," Nate replied politely before crossing over to Tom, who was now leaning against the far wall near the front entrance, overnight bag at his feet.

"Hey, Dad," he said, quickly shifting gears, "turns out this storm is the real deal, and it's coming in fast. They have no rooms for you, but I have another idea. C'mon."

"What other idea, Nate?" Tom asked, following him back out to the parking lot. The snow was coming down harder now, making the pavement slick. He opened the car door and threw his bag onto the backseat before shaking off the snow and sitting down, stamping his feet against the rubber floor mat.

"You're not going to like it, but it's an emergency situation. I'm going to sneak you into the cottage."

"Cottage? What cottage?"

"Mom's cottage. She's got a recording studio out back with a couple of bedrooms. You can lay low until I can convince her to meet with you, now that you're here."

Tom stared at him. "Sorry, Nate, that's delusional. How are you going to keep my presence a secret until she agrees to see me? Not that she's ever going to agree anyway."

"Dad, you're the one who came here to see her. To tell her about whoever died. How is staying at the cottage any different?"

Tom dropped his head in his hands. "I don't know, son. I just thought we'd keep things on neutral ground. Take things slow. But if she finds me in her cottage, who knows what might happen?"

Sure wish you'd considered that before you got on the train, Nate thought, frustrated and, yeah, as nervous as his father at the thought of what Maddie would do when she found Tom staying uninvited on her property. "We're out of options, Dad. You can't stay in the hotel, the train isn't running, and no way am I driving you back into the city in a Nor'easter, even if the roads were open, which they're not."

"Fuck," his father said.

Nate drew in a deep breath and let it out again in a cloud of icy vapor. "It'll be okay. I'll sneak you in and keep Mom occupied so she won't notice. Then all I'll need is some time to break the news before you come tell her whatever it is you need to say. Depending on how that goes, we'll work on her together about the wedding. Okay?"

"Okay," Tom ground out, sounding thoroughly unconvinced.

Obviously he was beginning to realize the stupidity of his impulsive actions, Nate thought, but there was no pleasure for him in that knowledge.

"We'll make it work," Nate said grimly and turned on the car's heater as the wind picked up, sending a chill down his back. At least he thought it was the wind. It might just as easily be his fear of having his mother find out that he was stashing his father in her cottage. This was going to be a huge gamble, and Nate could only hope it all worked out in their favor. Otherwise there was going to be hell to pay.

XIV

Julia had dropped off the bags of groceries and then hurried back to her truck, telling Maddie that the roads were quickly becoming impassable. Maddie worried about Nate as she put the food away and then pulled out the flour, brown sugar, and chocolate chips Julia had brought. She had wanted to make the cookies together with Nate the way they used to when he was a boy, but he had finally gotten a signal and called shortly after Julia left to say he'd made it to Sunrise Highway but that the going was really slow and he wasn't sure how long it would take him.

"Don't worry, Ma," he'd added before hanging up, "I'm safe and being cautious."

Maddie smiled at his words, the ones he'd used ever since he'd first learned to drive and she had made him promise to call whenever he was going to be late. She'd gotten him a cell phone on the day his license arrived in the mail, and even as a teenager Nate had been extremely responsible about staying in touch with her whenever he was out.

Maddie set to work making the cookie dough. She was humming the melody to her new song and mixing the dry ingredients together when she thought she heard a car coming up the driveway. But when Nate's key didn't turn the lock in the front door, she dismissed the sound as nothing more than the wind.

Once she added the wet ingredients to the dry ones, she watched the batter coming together under the paddle of her electric mixer. While waiting for it to blend, she walked down the long hallway and turned on the front-porch lights. Through the swirl of windswept snow she was surprised to see Nate's car parked in the deep powder that was now covering the gravel drive. There was no sign of him anywhere.

"What the hell?" Maddie said out loud. She thought about going outside to look for him, but the idea of actually turning the antique bronze knob and opening the front door was too overwhelming. She fought the fear that rose in the pit of her stomach and walked shakily back into the kitchen—and was surprised to see Nate stepping through the sliding glass door.

"I thought I heard you out front," she said as he shook a layer of icy flakes off of his coat and hat. He stood in a small puddle of melting snow, his boots already off, his socks sodden.

"You did," he smiled. "I knew you'd be less than thrilled to have me leave a trail through the house, so I walked around back to leave my wet things in the mudroom."

"Then why did you come through the kitchen door?" Maddie asked.

"Because the mudroom door was locked." Nate hoped she'd buy that excuse, because he'd avoided that entrance simply because the cottage was visible from there.

She smiled at him. "Thanks for your thoughtfulness, Nate. I appreciate it. Guess what I'm doing?"

Nate glanced at the counter and smiled back, more from relief that she hadn't noticed his detour to the cottage. "It looks like you're making my favorite cookies."

"Yup. Ready in fifteen minutes. Do you want some milk with them?"

"I'd rather raid the wine cellar, if you don't mind. The ride home was pretty gnarly for this California boy. But I do have the ingredients for dinner." Nate held up a wet paper shopping bag. "I'll change my clothes and get started."

"Great," Maddie said. "I like the idea of warm cookies and wine for dessert on a snowy night. Let's start a new tradition!"

"Let's!" Nate responded over his shoulder as he headed down the stairs to retrieve the wine, praying that the snow would continue to fall long enough to cover the footprints he and his dad had made when they snuck around back.

In the guesthouse, Tom settled in for what was sure to be a long night. He and Nate had worked out a plan: Tom was to stay in the bedroom in the back, using only a flashlight to find his way around and keeping the front of the cottage dark. At least the cottage was warm and cozy, decorated with framed photos of its construction and bits of folk art that Maddie must have purchased locally. There were a lot of maritime pieces: intricately built model sailing ships and paintings of whales and colorful varieties of fish. Everything was done in navy, red, and white, making Tom feel overly patriotic, at least for the moment. In the cabinets he found some peanut butter and crackers, and helping himself to the bottled water in the fridge, he settled in for an impromptu dinner.

As Tom crunched his way through a sleeve of saltines, his eyes fell on the numerous bottles of liquor set out on a highly polished wood table in the living room. Heavy, cut-crystal glasses sat beside the full bottles of his favorites, Jack Daniel's and Glenlivet 21. Tom swallowed hard. Although he'd been sober for six years, he hadn't managed to garner the courage to face Maddie again until now, when the letter from Emilia had forced his hand. Not surprisingly, he suddenly felt anxious, and he quickly pulled his chip, a souvenir of his sobriety, and his phone out of his pocket and placed them on the table in front of him. His lifeline.

He'd make the call to his sponsor, Ryan, if he felt it was necessary, but for now, he took a long pull from the water bottle and continued to work his way through the jar of organic peanut butter, as though the sweet, thick spread would help feed his courage as well as satiate his hunger.

When Tom opened his eyes the next morning, he was greeted by a spectacular winter scene. The snow was piled in pillowy drifts up to the windowsills, while the flakes continued to swirl in the air, settling atop one another so serenely against the backdrop of the violently pounding surf. The sky was still a chalky gray, and Tom wondered how long he'd be able to count on the steady snowfall to conceal his presence from Maddie.

He made his way into the kitchen, found the coffee beans in a ceramic jar and the grinder in a cabinet, and got busy with the French press on the counter. With the water in the kettle heating on the stove, he thought about what Nate was trying to do for him, enabling him to finally speak to Maddie face-to-face after all the lost years. Tom's nervousness rose as the memories threatened to swamp him. There were times in the past when Nate had come to stay with him on his twice-yearly court-mandated visits that Tom could barely recall. The drugs and alcohol had done their damage, and not remembering most of Nate's childhood remained one of his biggest regrets.

He hadn't been a good father, plain and simple. He had put his own needs before his son's, and for that, he'd never forgive himself. He took a few deep breaths. *Center yourself, Seymour. At least for today you've got more in the plus column: although tempted, you didn't touch a drop of Maddie's booze.*

The whistling kettle brought Tom back to reality. As he poured the boiling water over the coffee grounds, he wondered if Nate would be able to fabricate an excuse to come out and check on him. Rummaging around the kitchen, he found some bagels in the freezer and butter and raspberry jam in the refrigerator. At least he wasn't going to starve to death waiting for his son to appear.

While his bagel toasted, Tom flipped on the TV set, glad to see that the cable wasn't out. He desperately needed a distraction while waiting for Nate; there was too much snow outside to consider going for a long run. The storm update was given by a tired-looking weatherman who clearly had been up all night reporting. And while the rest of the world had apparently known this Nor'easter was headed their way, once again Tom had been too wrapped up in his own troubles to notice.

While tossing and turning in the back bedroom the night before, he had thought a lot about Nate and the wedding that lay in his son's future. But mostly he had thought about Maddie and wondered, for the very first time ever now that he had stepped into her private world, if he had played any role in her agoraphobia. Was there something from their shared past that he'd missed along the way, something more than the stage fright that had plagued her back then? Maybe there was a connection between the two; maybe his pushing her onstage to perform had contributed to her problems today?

Or was it the things he had done to her after? The cruel way she'd been dragged into his downward spiral of addiction no matter how fiercely she'd fought to keep their infant son out of it? Tom only had bits and pieces of memories of those days: the record deal he had signed behind Maddie's back and then crapped out on, the grim descent from booze and pills to coke and worse, and the resulting end of everything when he'd ruined Nate's birthday party at the dojo. That was one thing he'd never forgive himself for. The field day the press had made of it after Martin—the man Tom had welcomed onto their first big tour just because Emilia and Maddie had asked, a man Tom and the band had come to consider a friend—had sold that terrible photo to the tabloids. Even now, after decades of drinking and drugs, after further years of intensive therapy, the humiliation and pain still made him wince whenever he thought of it.

His toast popped up. Relieved, he pushed all thoughts of the past aside and busied himself preparing his breakfast, drinking Maddie's coffee, and waiting for Nate to make an appearance. It was going to be a long day, and Tom settled in to wait.

Nate came into the kitchen to find his mother pulling her famous baked French toast out of the oven. It smelled incredibly good, and he felt more than a little bit guilty. He was deceiving her while she was doing her best to make him feel comfortable in his childhood home.

"Good morning, sunshine," she said. "How did you sleep? Did you hear the wind howling last night?"

Nate looked at his mother, standing in front of him in her oversized pink and white flannel pajamas, her curly hair spilling wildly down her back, and he felt immediately overcome with tenderness, protectiveness. He pulled her to him and whispered lovingly in her ear, "I didn't hear a thing. I conked out from the wine—it must have counteracted the sugar in the cookies!"

"Then you'll need to refuel," Maddie teased, hugging him back. "French toast and coffee should do the trick."

Turning, she put a small blue pitcher of warm maple syrup on the counter and motioned for Nate to sit on one of the tall stools at the center island. Then she brought him a plate of the French toast and filled his mug with steaming coffee.

Could she make him feel any guiltier? Or more anxious about what the day would bring? Determined to face the inevitable as soon as possible, Nate cleared his throat. "Are the shovels still in the shed? I'll start to dig us out after breakfast."

"No need," Maddie responded. "The plowing service will be here as soon as the storm heads out to sea."

"A plowing service?"

Maddie's lips twitched. "I know my limits, Nate. Once you moved out, along with your muscle power, I needed to make certain adjustments."

Nate put his fork down. "When do you think they'll be here?"

"No telling. They'll need to plow the main roads first. Why? Is there somewhere you need to be?"

"No, no," Nate said a little too quickly. "It's just that I could use the exercise."

"That's a bad way to exercise, sweetheart. You're not a teenager anymore."

"I'm not an old guy on Lipitor either. I'm still young enough to shovel," Nate teased, trying to cover up his fear of having Tom exposed when the snowplow arrived and before he'd adequately prepared his mother for the shock.

"Well, I'm glad you're not," she continued. "More coffee?"

"Yes, please," he answered. While her back was turned he snuck a peek out at the cottage. It looked still and serene. His father was obviously following orders by staying toward the back of the house and out of the sight-lines of Maddie's kitchen. "So what do you have planned for today, Mom?"

"I'd like to polish up this piece of music I've been working on. It's serendipity that you're here, you know. I've arranged for the band to come out to record it with me."

"What?" Nate's heart seemed to jump into his throat. "When?"

"As soon as the snow stops falling."

"But—but the trains aren't running," Nate said quickly.

"Doesn't matter. They always rent a car, and we'll be plowed out soon enough."

Nate forced himself to quit stammering. "So when do you think they'll be here?"

"Tomorrow or the next day. I'm not sure exactly when. It depends on when the snow stops falling, but I want to be done fine-tuning the music before they get here."

"It will be great to see them," Nate said, trying to sound enthusiastic, but failing miserably. Thankfully his mother didn't seem to notice. In fact, she seemed inordinately cheerful this morning.

"I know they'll be thrilled to see you too. It'll be fun having all of you out here together!"

Fun wasn't the first thought that came to Nate's mind. He was going to have to work fast.

"Hey, you cooked breakfast. I'll do these," he said, bringing the dishes Maddie was reaching for to the sink. "You get to work."

"Thanks, sweetie. I appreciate it." She gave him a quick kiss on the cheek as she made her way to the music room.

Nate smiled, but all he could think of was how angry she was going to be with him in a very short while. As he rinsed the syrup off of the silverware, he realized he had to let his dad know that the launching of their plan had just gone into overdrive. He needed to check on him anyway; make sure the cottage heater was working and that there was enough food in the fridge. Since his mother always got lost in her music, there was a good chance he could slip out to the cottage and be back in the house before she even noticed he was gone.

Nate quietly hurried up to his room to pull on an old pair of Timberland boots. Luckily they still fit. He layered up with a T-shirt, a long-sleeved polo, and a sweatshirt, then made his way down to the mudroom and, with a hat, scarf, and gloves on, trudged out to the shed to look for a shovel he could use to make a path from the back door of the house to the front walk of the cottage.

Hearing the hurried scrape of a shovel right outside his door, Tom peeked cautiously out of the window to see Nate hastily flinging snow out of his way as he waded through the drifts between Maddie's house and the cottage. Tom's first instinct was to go outside and help him, but he thought better of it—what if Maddie saw him? Or had Nate talked to her already?

When Nate reached the porch, he and Tom locked gazes through the front window. Nate motioned quickly for his father to open the door. Tom did so, and Nate pushed his way inside.

"That looked like hard work," Tom commented. "I would have loved to help you out."

"Not a good idea," Nate responded.

Tom frowned at him. "What's wrong, Nate? Where's your mom?"

"She's finishing a new piece. She'll be occupied for a while. Everything okay out here?"

"It's fine. Have you talked to her yet?"

"No. I thought I'd do that when she's done composing. Are you warm enough?"

"Nate—"

Stepping farther inside, Nate looked past Tom's shoulder into the kitchen. "Do you have enough food?"

"I don't need anything out here, Nate, thank you." Tom kept his voice even, though his heart suddenly felt as if it would break. It was obvious from Nate's behavior that he'd asked too much of the boy. Why the hell hadn't he realized as much sooner? Confronting Maddie was something he should have spared his son, and he thrust his hands deep into his pockets to resist the urge to put his arms around him. He cleared his throat. "Go back to the house, Nate. I'll deal with your mother. I should never have involved you in the first place, and I'm deeply sorry."

"It's not that, Dad."

"I just didn't think things through," Tom went on. "I should've calmed down after talking to Bill. Should have waited before calling you."

"Dad, listen," Nate interrupted. "It's okay, really. You need to know—"

Over Nate's shoulder, Tom saw the front door ease open. A blast of icy air rushed inside. Damned wind, Tom thought, and moved to close it. But then it opened farther, and Tom froze when he saw Maddie, bundled up in a puffy parka, silver curls spilling out of her knit hat, standing on the threshold.

He must have made an involuntary sound, because Nate whipped around, and the three of them stood in a silent, stunned standoff until Maddie finally found her voice. "Tom Seymour. What the hell are you doing in my studio?"

"I asked him to come, Mom," Nate said quickly.

"That's not true," Tom put in. "I—"

Maddie turned her back on him. Her voice was like ice. "This is my home, Nate. I'm the only one who gets to decide who comes to visit me."

"Yes, I know, but—"

She held up her hand to silence him and turned away from his pleading eyes, the same ones that had gazed at her when at ten years old he had broken a brand-new window with his baseball. When he had failed a test in school. When he told her he was moving to California to attend college—thousands of miles away . . .

"Maddie, please hear me out," Tom broke in. "This isn't Nate's fault. I didn't tell him I was coming until I was well on my way. I needed to speak to you about something. I didn't mean to end up here, but I got stuck in the storm, and the hotel ran out of rooms. Don't blame Nate. His intentions were good."

Realizing he was rambling, Tom stopped speaking and glanced at his son, who stood frozen before him. Here it was, the one thing Tom knew that Nate dreaded most: a nightmarish replay of his childhood. His parents were standing in the same room together, his father desperate, his mother furious. From the look in Maddie's eyes, there would be no talking to her now.

"I'm sorry," Tom whispered, and he didn't know if he was apologizing to Maddie or to Nate or summing up in one word what a pitiful fuck-up he was.

"Mom," Nate said in a voice barely above a whisper, "I know seeing Dad here is a tremendous shock, but—"

"Nate, it's okay," Tom interjected. "Go back to the house. There's no need for you to make excuses for me."

"Dad, please. Stop talking." Nate drew in a breath and turned to Maddie. "Mom. Can we sit down like adults and discuss this?"

Maddie glared at them both, then took a closer look at Tom. He was older than the last time she'd seen him, certainly, all gray now, but no less imposing. Still handsome, she noted before a sudden bolt of clarity made her realize that he was sober. In fact, he was looking at her with eyes so clear and green that she felt an immediate, overwhelming urge to reach up and touch his face. Instead she made a small, wounded sound and snatched the knit hat off her head and pulled the zipper of her jacket open.

"Okay," she snapped. "I'll sit. But that's all."

Tom recognized her discomfort immediately. "Come into the kitchen, Maddie. I can make us some tea. You don't have to talk to me if you don't want to, but there are some things I need you to listen to."

"You're offering me tea in my own house?" Maddie snapped. "This is ridiculous." He saw the heat rising to her face as she continued, "And you have *nothing* you can tell me now, Tom. We haven't spoken a civil word to each other in years, and we're not about to start. I want you out of this house right now."

"Mom," Nate groaned.

"Five minutes, Maddie, that's all. Then I'll go. I promise."

"*You promise?*" Maddie shouted. "You promised me a lot of things, Tom Seymour, and I—"Over his shoulder she suddenly caught sight of her son's anguished face. Instantly some of the fight went out of her. As angry as she was with Nate, this situation wasn't his fault. Tom had always been a master manipulator.

She inhaled deeply, closed her eyes for a moment, and struggled for a calm she wasn't sure she could attain. At last she said, "No tea. Five minutes, and then I'm going back to my house. Once the trains are running, you'd better get back to yours."

Tom looked at Nate. "Go finish shoveling the walk, son, please. I'd like the chance to speak to your mother alone."

Nate looked over at Maddie as if seeking her approval, but Tom was already pushing him gently toward the door. "It'll be okay," he whispered into Nate's ear as he nudged him outside before turning back to Maddie. She hadn't moved, hadn't said a word, only folded her arms across her chest, her eyes fixed elsewhere. He drew in a deep breath and began, speaking a little too quickly because he was afraid she'd cut him off before he could even begin.

"He's a great kid, Maddie. You did an amazing job raising him on your own, and that's the most important thing I want you to know. I plan on spending the rest of my life trying to make up my absence to him. I'm happy and proud that Nate and I have already come as far as we have."

He continued in a rush so she couldn't interrupt him. "Secondly, I am sorry, Maddie. I'm so sorry that I hurt you, that I allowed myself to get so deeply self-involved that I couldn't finish what we started all those years ago. But things are different now. I'm different. I've been sober for a long time."

His words seemed to snap Maddie out of her trancelike state. "Is that right? Just like that I'm supposed to believe you're truly sober now? I've been down that road with you before, Tom, and it's gonna take a whole lot more to get me to buy what you're trying to sell me. And it wasn't just the alcohol or the drugs, Tom. It was—oh God!" She broke off and pressed her hands to her face. "Why am I even bothering with this? With you?"

"Maddie—"

"No, Tom. No!" She put her hat back on. "I'm going home now. I'd like to say it was great seeing you, but it wasn't."

"Maddie, just hold on a minute. Please." Tom opened his overnight bag and pulled out the letter he'd been charged to deliver to her. "This is for you."

She turned the envelope over and immediately recognized the scrawled handwriting as Emilia's. "What the hell is this?"

"I'm not sure. Emilia asked that I give it to you."

"Well, tell her no thanks. I don't want it."

Tom stuffed his hands into his pockets, indicating that he wouldn't take the letter back. "I wish I could do that, Maddie, but it's not possible. Emilia's dead."

Maddie's head snapped up. "What? How?"

"Just the way you would have imagined. Overdosed and drowned in her own bathtub."

Maddie gasped and put out her hand as if to stop Tom from saying another word.

"Maddie—"

"No, Tom, no! I've got to go." Still holding the letter, she turned and fled the cottage, not looking back, not stopping to speak to Nate pacing up and down the walk. Tom watched as Maddie slammed the house door behind her, leaving their son standing on the path in what seemed to Tom the most familiar dilemma for the child of a divorce: indecision. Which parent should he comfort first?

Wanting to spare him that pain at least, Tom opened the door and called to him. "Go on, son. Take care of your mom. We can talk later. Now that I can stop hiding out, I'll finish shoveling the walk."

"Just stay inside, Dad," Nate yelled back. "Mom's got a crew coming to do that anyway." He gave Tom a weak little wave and headed toward the house.

Tom waited until Nate was inside and then shut the cottage door. He stood still for a moment, his pulse running double-time from the mere sight of her. Was it possible that she could be even more achingly beautiful than he remembered? Was it possible that he really was still in love with her?

God, yes. And that was the last thing Tom needed. That Maddie needed. Once safely inside the walls of her fortress, it might be best if she never emerged again.

"Yeah, that went real well, Tom," he muttered out loud, collapsing on the sofa with his head in his hands.

Nate, meanwhile, had opened the back door and stepped into the house to find his mother sitting on the floor of the mudroom, still wearing her coat and hat, sobbing uncontrollably.

"Mom?" He could barely speak, shocked as he was by her crumpled form.

She looked up at him with tear-stained cheeks. "Nate, please help me stand up."

He gently lifted her and then eased her onto the built-in bench against the wall. She tried undoing the laces of her boots, but was too blinded by tears. Her sobbing scared him. The last time he could remember seeing her cry was in the limousine on the way out to the East End after his eighth birthday party.

"Mom?" he asked again. "Are you okay?"

"No. No. No. Not okay. Help me take these boots off."

"All right, stop trying. I'll do it," Nate said gently.

When he'd pulled them off, he watched as she threw her hat and gloves on the bench, picked up the letter Tom had given her, and, in stocking feet, went into the kitchen. She walked to the center island and pulled the cork from one of the bottles of wine still sitting out from last night's dinner. She took a glass out of the cabinet and poured it full, taking a long gulp before realizing that she was still wearing her coat. She steadied her hips against the granite counter and removed it, one arm at a time, leaving it on the floor where it fell. Stuffing her cell phone into her back pocket, she then grabbed her glass, the bottle, and the sealed envelope, and headed wordlessly upstairs.

The next thing Nate heard was the sound of her bathtub being filled. He stood at the doorway between the mudroom and the kitchen, not really believing what he'd just witnessed. She'd left her coat on the floor. It was a small thing for someone else, but a huge anomaly for his own neat freak of a mother. She always knew if you moved a decorative pillow so much as a quarter inch out of place on the couch. She used to tease him in high school that he'd never get away with throwing a party after she'd gone up to bed. It was not in her nature to leave anything out of its proper spot.

But what had upset her like this? Had his father told her about the band member who died? Or was it merely the sight of him that had set her so far over the edge? Either way, it didn't seem likely that they'd agree to perform together at his wedding, let alone even attend it together.

Nate took off his own bulky jacket and wet boots, picked up his mother's coat, and went back into the mudroom to hang them on the wall pegs. He then trudged up the stairs. His mother's bedroom door was closed, and Nate could still hear the water running. Tears pricked his eyes, and he sat down, his back against her door, to wait.

Maddie sat in the tub, sobbing, wishing she'd brought more than the half-filled bottle of wine into the bathroom with her. She felt like drinking until she passed out, then realized that the idea of doing that in a full bathtub was sure suicide. Irony or coincidence? she wondered, considering the way Emilia had died.

The shock was giving way to utter grief and a sense of finality. And to the old, familiar feelings of betrayal, of violation, not just by her ex-husband, but also by her ex-best friend.

Maddie lay back, closing her eyes until her breathy sobs stilled. Only then did she sit up and, carefully separating the flap from the back of the envelope, begin to read:

Dear Maddie,

I know this apology will never make up for what happened at Nate's birth-day party, but I have to try, so here goes: I'm the one who let Martin into the dojo that day. I was still hung up on him, and when he asked if I'd sneak him in to take some exclusive photos of Nate's party and then promised to cut me in on the profit when he sold them, I bought into it. I needed money for drugs, and I'd do anything for a fix, including seducing Tom for cash.

That's what happened, Maddie. It was all me that day, not Tom, and it only shows you how low I went: sheer prostitution. I never dreamed Martin would take that picture or betray me, you, everyone in the band, by selling it. I tracked him down and pleaded with him not to, but he wouldn't listen.

I can't tell you how sorry I am that I was so desperate, so strung out that I would do anything just to feel something. My career was finished after that day, Maddie. Karma is a bitch, and it was what I deserved.

I'm so sorry, so eternally sad. I love you, Maddie, and miss you more than you can ever know, my very dear friend. Please, please, don't allow my mistakes, my past to ruin everything for you going forward.

xo,

E

Maddie read the note over and over again. It wasn't dated. When could Emilia have written it? Years ago but never had the nerve to send it? Or just before she got into her bathtub? How would she ever know? Emilia was dead. Maddie couldn't reply to this letter, and all at once she wanted desperately to speak to the woman she had once considered her closest friend.

The bathtub. Maddie was suddenly shivering violently, and not just because the water had grown cold. She set the glass and bottle on the tile floor and quickly wrapped herself in a towel. As she stepped out, replaying Emilia's words in her mind, her cell phone, sitting innocently on the edge of the tub, began to ring. She hesitated for a moment before answering it.

"Hello," said the voice on the other end. "Is this Maddie?"

"Yes, who is this please?"

"Maddie, hi. I'm Dr. Jennings . . . Sasha Jennings. I got this number from your son, Nate. I specialize in patients with agoraphobia, and he thought I might be able to help you."

A chill went up Maddie's spine. Talk about timing. How did she know Nate hadn't just called this woman when she ran up the stairs, wine bottle in hand?

"I don't know, Dr. Jennings," Maddie said coolly. "I haven't been able to leave my property in a very long time, and I'm really not bothered by that small fact as much as my son seems to be."

"I understand," the doctor replied. "But I'd like to have the chance to come out and meet you, tell you a little about what I do, and if you're interested, perhaps we can try to work together. It's a big world out there. Maybe you'd like to see it again."

Maddie was silent. The voice on the other end of the phone asked, "Are you still there, Maddie?"

She hesitated. Despite feeling a desperate need to speak to a professional, to try and sort out all of her jangled emotions, she was pretty sure that she was beyond help. "I am. Sorry. I'm just trying to . . . Are you local?"

"No, I'd come out to you, though."

"You'd have to," Maddie replied dully.

"I'm in Huntington, and normally I'd be able to get out there in the next day or so, but the weather has made that impossible."

"Okay then," Maddie said, relieved. "Why not call me in a few days?"

"Well how about this," Sasha said. "Today's Thursday." Maddie could hear pages turning; probably the woman's date book. "Let's meet on

Monday. That should give the plows the weekend to do their thing. Nate sent me the address. What time is good?"

Backed into a corner, feeling vulnerable and sad and, yes, maybe a little bit drunk, Maddie heard herself agreeing to one o'clock.

"See you then," the doctor said cheerfully before she hung up.

Maddie put her phone down on the sink and stood for a moment wrapped in the bath towel, letting the warmth of the radiant heating under the tile floor erase the chill she'd felt since hearing Emilia had died. Maybe it was for the best that she'd agreed to see the therapist. Maybe it was time to see if she had what it took to attend Nate's wedding. To deal with her ex-husband and to understand that the true impact of Emilia's note would take days before she internalized it completely, that she would think about the words, the apology, before she decided how to deal with forgiving someone who was no longer there to hear what she wanted to say.

And then there was the matter of Tom so close by in the cottage. It had been a shock to see him again, and she had to admit that her proximity to him had shaken her deeply. She didn't want to think about it, but couldn't stop herself from questioning why it was that she hoped she'd see him again before he left her property.

When she stepped out of the bedroom, her hair piled on top of her head and wearing a sweatshirt and sweatpants with warm, fuzzy socks, she nearly tripped over her son sitting on the floor in the now dark hallway. It was much later than she imagined and she realized that she needed to put something together for dinner.

"Nate!"

He scrambled to his feet. "Hi, Mom. Um, how was your bath?"

"Fine. What are you doing?"

"I was worried. You were so upset."

"I'm fine. I always am, aren't I?"

"No, Mom, you're not," he said, anger taking over from the relief of seeing her emerge from her bedroom obviously unharmed. "And neither am I. Do you think I wanted to sneak around this way, hiding Dad in the cottage? Watching you cry like your heart is broken?" He followed her as she went down the long back staircase to the kitchen. "And what was that letter Dad gave you? Who was it from?"

His anger seemed to spark a similar emotion within her. "You are not a part of this, Nate," she said more harshly than she intended. "This is between me and your father."

"C'mon, Mom, are you really going to shut me out?"

"Yes, I am. There's a lot of history here that doesn't concern you."

"History or secrets, Mom? Sounds like secrets to me. And it is too my concern. You won't have anything to do with my father, but your careers are intertwined, and I manage yours. I need to know what's going on with you." He was red-faced and obviously upset now.

Maddie stood perfectly still for a long moment before answering him. "I have always done what I thought was best for you, Nate. When the court ordered me to allow your father visitation, even when I didn't want you to go, I let you, because I thought it best that you know your own father, worrying the entire time what crazy things you were being exposed to, what confusing things you may have seen, praying you'd make it back to me in one piece. I kept a roof over our heads, sent you to the best schools, made sure you had every tool you needed to help you succeed. And now you're saying I shut you out? What else should I have done? Tell me."

Nate swallowed hard. "Oh, Ma. It's just that I walk around with big pieces of the puzzle still lost to me. Like what made you leave Dad specifically when I was eight? And who wrote that letter he gave you? Dad said somebody in your old band died. I know them all, don't I? So who was it from? What am I missing here, exactly?"

Maddie pushed past him into the kitchen, refusing to cry, refusing to acknowledge his pain. She'd not be able to bear this otherwise. "Nate, I'm sorry. It just doesn't concern you."

"Okay, so maybe it doesn't! But my wedding does, and now that Dad's here and he's given you that—that letter, can the two of you maybe focus on *me* for a change?"

His words cut Maddie to the quick. Stone-faced, trying to control the sobs rising in her throat, she busied herself pulling together the ingredients for an impromptu meal, walking back and forth between the stainless steel Sub Zero and the center island countertop.

"Mom." Nate's voice quavered. "Can you please look at me? I'm really trying to get some answers here."

"I'm sorry, Nate!" she exclaimed. "I'm so sorry, but there is no repairing this relationship."

"I'm not talking about a relationship! I stopped wishing for you and Dad to get back together years ago. I'm just hoping to get you out of the house again, to attend my wedding, and something tells me it won't happen until you work out whatever it is that stands between you two."

"Oh, so now you're a psychologist or something?"

"Mom, please."

She knew she'd hurt him, and she hated herself for it. But she was afraid to speak, afraid to so much as open her mouth again, knowing that she'd never stop the sobs from escaping the moment she did.

Nate looked down at the array of food she'd gathered on the glossy granite counter. He scrubbed at his eyes, cleared his throat, and said huskily, "How about this, Mom? Dad's here. You're here. I'm here. Could we all be together just for a meal? It would be a dry run, sort of. If you can do this with him, maybe you can survive his company at the wedding. Is it too much to ask that I have my parents together for just this once?"

Was it? The truth was that if Maddie said no to having Tom in her home for a sandwich, she would forever be the wrong one instead of the wronged one. But then her home would never again be the safe haven she'd created for herself, the no-Tom zone, a place where he'd never been, never touched anything.

Nate reached across the countertop and took her hands in his. "Dad's been sober for six years, Mom. And I'm here with you. Nothing bad will happen. I just want to see what it would be like for us to be together, if only for a meal. Please."

Maddie felt her resolve weaken. She was always taken aback when Nate did something that made her realize he wasn't a kid anymore. It was a shock each and every time it happened and an acknowledgment of the passage of time that literally took her breath away. And now that she'd had a little bit of time to process the shock of having Tom so close, she couldn't help but admit to herself that she was curious. She let out a deep sigh and collapsed on one of the stools at the counter.

"Oh boy, Nate." She took another deep breath. "All right. But only because you asked." She paused and then added faintly, "I hope I don't regret this later. Go ask your dad if he wants to come in for dinner."

The look on Nate's face told Maddie that he had never expected to convince her. In an instant he was in the mudroom putting on his coat, hat and boots before she could change her mind. In no time the back door slammed, and he was gone.

To keep the roiling emotions at bay, Maddie busied herself building a fire in the kitchen hearth. It was another luxury she'd afforded herself when she remodeled the house all those years ago. There had been an old fireplace that the previous owners had boarded up, and it was a true labor of love to restore it to its original glory.

Maddie had even gone so far as to research the type of tile that had been used when the house was first built: beautiful blue and white Delft ceramic florals, which she'd tracked down and imported from Europe for the fireplace surround. She had matched a heavy wrought-iron grate to the tiles, fashioned with a similar design of intertwining leaves, making it the centerpiece of the room.

When she lit the kindling and the logs caught up in a blazing fire, she felt somehow stronger. Her insides had stopped shaking, and she felt truly warm for the first time since getting out of the bathtub. As she heard the outer door to the mudroom open, she grabbed the wine bottle on the island countertop and stowed it under the sink. She wanted to believe that Tom was sober, but she certainly wasn't about to put temptation in his path—or ever truly trust him. Those days were long behind her. She took in a deep breath and prepared herself for what was to come.

XV

Maddie felt a sudden rush of cold air sweep across her sock-clad feet, sending a jolt down her spine. Nate was back with Tom. As much as she tried to convince herself that she was doing this for her son, deep down she realized she had selfish motives as well. She couldn't deny what she had felt when she first pushed open the cottage door to discover Tom inside. She'd been shocked to discover that the familiar flutter of excitement, of primal attraction that had first drawn them together was, unfortunately, still there. Seeing Tom again despite their years apart, regardless of her hard work to convince herself that she hated him for what he'd done to her, to their marriage, to Nate, had caught her entirely off guard.

Maddie busied herself setting out plates, napkins, knives, and forks, deliberately facing away from the mudroom—as if not seeing Tom walk into her house and back into her life would really make any difference. She heard their banter, the happy lilt in Nate's voice as they made their way inside. Bracing both palms on the counter as if to hold on to what was hers alone, this house, this haven she'd created, she drew in a deep breath.

"Hey, Maddie," she heard Tom say softly. "Thanks for inviting me in. It really means a lot."

She smiled to cover her mounting anxiety. "Yeah, well, Nate asked, and I have trouble saying no to him."

"Okay, I get that," Tom replied and turned quickly to take in the wide expanse of the kitchen with its warm tones of yellow and blue and the spectacular hearth with its now blazing fire. "Wow. You always had flair with color, Maddie. I see that hasn't changed. This is truly beautiful."

"Thank you," she said stiffly, refusing to allow that one compliment to undo her. At one time Tom had known her better than anyone else on the planet. How could that possibly still be true? Her feet felt leaden, making it difficult for her to move until Nate pulled out one of the stools at the counter and motioned for her to sit.

"Mom collected most of the pieces here locally. I can remember being a kid and going to estate sales every weekend. We must have rummaged through centuries of junk to find these treasures, right, Ma?" Nate asked, clearly trying to bring her around to a safe topic, easing her way into this awkward reunion.

She let out the deep breath she'd been holding. "Yes, we did. But we had fun, right?" She smiled at him weakly.

"Some of the time. A couple of those houses spooked me, though. Like the ones with horsehair-stuffed furniture, remember? I thought I could smell the dead horses!"

Maddie felt herself thawing a little. "I remember. And I told you it was just the old, musty air because all the windows were shuttered. But we found some good stuff for sure."

"You certainly did," Tom said with forced heartiness. "Do you have more antiques throughout the house?"

"We do!" Nate answered before Maddie could. "I'd be happy to take you on a tour after we eat. I'm starving."

"If that's okay with your mom, I'd love to," Tom said.

They both looked at her expectantly, and Maddie knew she was sunk. Nate seemed so happy to have his father here despite the fact that he was clearly anxious—as anxious as she was and as Tom seemed to be. She couldn't deny him the chance to show Tom the rest of the house. But after that she'd insist he go back to the cottage. She simply didn't trust having him here.

"Sure, Nate, if your dad is really interested. And I'm sorry you're starving. Dig in. It's nothing fancy; I just threw together whatever I could find in the fridge."

"Looks like a feast to me," Tom replied. "And it's nice to eat in a real kitchen for a change. I eat out way too much."

"Cooking was never your thing," Maddie said, and regretted the words as soon as they flew out of her mouth. She really didn't want to talk about the past. "Neither of us really thought about cooking back then," she added lamely. "I only learned how when Nate was young and we had to survive on more than peanut butter and canned soup."

"Yeah," Nate added, his mouth full of tabouleh salad. "But the real change came when Mom discovered the Food Network. That really stepped up her game."

Maddie smiled. "Who knew I was such a visual learner? Watching those chefs prepare a whole meal in a half hour changed my life."

"I'm not surprised," Tom said. "Think about it, Maddie. You were always able to actually see the music around you. At least that's how you described it to me. So it's no wonder that skill translates into cooking. It's another form of your creative genius."

"Thanks," Maddie mumbled, and made a show of eating while merely pushing the food around on her plate. She hated to admit it, but her stomach was doing back flips. How long had it been since a man other than Nate had praised her in any way? And how long since she'd actually blushed like this?

They continued to eat in strained silence. Finally Tom said, "Nate tells me you've finished a new song. I'd love to hear it."

"Oh, I don't think so," Maddie said quickly. No way was she playing for Tom. "I haven't worked out all the kinks. I'm still struggling a bit with the bridge."

"Isn't the band coming out tomorrow to record it?" Nate asked.

Maddie stared at her son, willing him to stop talking. Too late.

"The band?" Tom asked with feigned disinterest. "Really? Anyone left over from the old days?"

"Ned, Charlie, and Andre, right, Mom?"

"Yes," Maddie said in a strangled whisper.

"Wasn't there another woman who sang backup? What was her name?" Nate looked at Maddie at the same time Tom caught her gaze.

"Emilia. Her name was Emilia, and no, she won't be coming," Tom answered for Maddie, his voice soft, his eyes kind as he looked at her.

How long had it been, Maddie wondered, since she'd had a man—had Tom—to guide her around the rocky bumps of life? She'd not handled Nate's questions about Emilia's letter well; had been too destroyed by that unexpected news to do more than lash out at him. And to know that Emilia, not Tom, had initiated that encounter in the dojo . . .

After all this time, did it matter? How the hell would she know? She hadn't had a moment to herself to even think since she'd walked into the cottage and found Tom Seymour standing there.

"I'm hoping they'll help me smooth out the rough spots," Maddie said now, referring to the band, to the music, to the one topic that had always steadied her, made her feel in control.

"I know we haven't worked together in years, Maddie," Tom said casually, not looking at her, "but I still know my way around an arrangement. I'd be happy to help."

"No," she said quickly. "Not a good idea."

"Okay," he said, pushing his stool back and bringing his plate to the double sink. "Just thought I'd offer as a way to repay your kindness for letting me stay through the storm."

Nate stood as well and began to clear the dishes before Maddie stopped him, suddenly overwhelmed to have them both here in her kitchen. "I'll do those, Nate. Go give your father that tour," she said.

"Really?" He sounded surprised, but added quickly, before she had a chance to change her mind, "Great! C'mon, Dad. I'll get the album of 'before' pictures so you'll have a sense of the monumental job Mom took on when we moved in."

"I think I already have a good understanding of that." Tom's gaze locked with Maddie's for a brief moment, his deep green eyes intense, before he followed Nate out of the kitchen, one arm slung around his son's shoulder.

Maddie quickly began clearing the rest of the plates and food from the countertop, hoping to regain her bearings by keeping busy. She had spent so many years hating Tom, building walls to keep him away after that afternoon in the dojo. Now Emilia had sent her a message from the grave and Tom was here in her house. Maddie's whole world was suddenly upside down, and she felt as if she were sinking in quicksand. If she didn't find some sort of lifeline soon, she'd be smothered.

She began to put the leftovers in containers and stow them in the refrigerator. The rote movements were hypnotic, soothing. As she rinsed the dishes and stacked them in the washer, she wondered if the shrink who was coming to the house on Monday could help her sort through her jumbled feelings about Emilia, about Tom, even if she couldn't get her to leave the property. Maybe Maddie should be thankful after all that Nate had arranged for Dr. Jennings to come.

Finished with the dishes, Maddie stoked the fire before filling the kettle and placing it on the burner. She put some white lotus flower tea bags on a pretty yellow plate, filled a matching pitcher with milk, pulled some mugs and the sugar bowl out of the cabinet, and placed them on the counter with fresh napkins. Opening the Tupperware container with the leftover cookies she had baked the night before, she set it on the countertop and went to find her son and his father to offer them dessert. She needed to wrap up this visit. She was exhausted and craved the kind of sleep that erased all thoughts and memories.

Monday morning dawned brightly, with a cloudless, cornflower-blue sky. If it wasn't for the two feet of snow on the ground, no one would have known they'd just experienced a major Nor'easter. Maddie yawned and pulled herself from under her warm comforter to get ready for her band's arrival. The snow had delayed them for three days after all, and while Maddie wasn't sure when they'd get there, she wanted enough time to ensure that Nate put Tom on the train back to the city.

It wasn't until she was almost out of the shower that she remembered: the therapist Nate had found for her was coming today to begin working on her agoraphobia. *Not a moment too soon*, Maddie thought. The snow had continued to fall well into Saturday evening, piling up in deep drifts, trapping them in its natural beauty—such a calm landscape in contrast to her inner turmoil. In fact, it had been hell sitting across from Tom at dinner that first night and then putting up with his mere presence after that, although Tom had obligingly stayed in the cottage the rest of the time.

But even knowing he was on her property had frayed Maddie's nerves unbearably.

And then, of course, there was the matter of Nate's wedding and the fact that Maddie knew she *must* attend—assuming that Sasha Jennings could work some magic in order to get her there. Cursing under her breath, Maddie threw on her jeans and a sweatshirt and headed downstairs to make coffee.

"Good morning, Mom."

She turned and smiled as Nate joined her in the kitchen. "Hey, sweetie, how'd you sleep?"

"Pretty well considering Dad and I stayed up late talking."

"What time is his train?"

"I haven't even checked if they're back on a regular schedule." Nate picked up the remote for the television mounted on the wall and found the local news station.

Maddie could feel anxiety building from her toes to her head, like a million electric jolts coursing through her. What was she going to do if the trains weren't running yet? If Tom had to spend more time here invading her space, she wasn't certain she could cope.

When she heard the announcer say that workers were still busy shoveling snow off the tracks and that full rail service to the eastern tip of Long Island would probably not be restored until early evening, she felt sick. Another day with Tom in the cottage, the shrink on the way, and the band arriving whenever they could get here. It was too much all at once, and her hands shook as she tried to pour herself a cup of coffee. Cursing, she set the French press down with a loud thud.

Nate's head snapped up. Quickly, he took the empty mug from her and filled it, then seated her gently on a stool at the counter. It was something he hadn't had to help her do in a long time, but it was still all too familiar to them both.

Maddie took a deep breath. "I'm sorry, Nate. I guess the weekend was a little much for me. I'll be fine once I drink this." She nodded weakly as she took her first sip. "Thanks. It's perfect."

Nate sat down on the stool next to hers, and for a few minutes neither of them spoke. The news announcer droned on, filling the room with mindless chatter as people being interviewed gave their inane opinions about the snowstorm. When Maddie stood up to pour herself more coffee, Nate said quietly, "If you want, I'll drive Dad back to the city after breakfast."

Tears pricked Maddie's eyes at his tone. How many more times was her son going to have to pick up the pieces of her life? She had tried so hard to make a safe haven for him, to keep him happy, to be both parents to him, and she had always been able to tell herself that she had overcome the odds and that Nate had grown into a successful and independent man—the true proof that she'd done her job well. But, she had to admit, seeing Nate with Tom had made her realize that despite all her efforts, he needed his father in his life. She just wasn't enough.

"Thanks for offering, but no," she said, feeling defeated. "We'll just wait till the trains are running. What time is that doctor coming? I can't remember what she said."

"You told me yesterday she'd be here around one." Nate glanced at his phone. "It's only eight thirty." He got up to refill his own mug. "If this doctor is as good as her online reviews say, maybe she can help you, Ma."

"I wish I could be so certain. But there's just so much I'd rather forget, Nate, not dredge up for a total stranger."

"Can you at least try?"

"I will. I want to be at your wedding."

Nate gathered a few pieces of fruit from the bowl Maddie kept on the counter. "For Dad's breakfast. He must be pretty bored with toasted bagels by now," he said sheepishly. "Unless you mind?"

"No, go ahead. There's oatmeal in the pantry if he feels like cooking." She sighed. "I'm going to sit here for a while."

Nate shoved everything into a shopping bag, then kissed her cheek and went into the mudroom to put on his coat. When the door closed behind him, Maddie turned to the windows at the back of the kitchen to watch the waves hit the beach and carry some of the snow out to sea. But for once the sight of the ocean did not calm her. Even though Tom had been respectful and stayed in the cottage all weekend, she continued to feel unsettled, uneasy. It was almost as if the life she'd been hiding from in Montauk all these years had finally found her, and all she wanted was to be lost again, to be left alone in the peace and solitude she'd created for herself.

The doorbell rang precisely at one o'clock that afternoon. Maddie, who had walked upstairs to splash some water on her face in the hopes that it would help soothe her nerves, took one final look at herself in the mirror and went down the wide front staircase that led to the marble-floored entry. From the bottom step she saw Nate taking the coat of a young, dark-haired woman who was now walking toward her. Aside from her youth, Dr. Jennings looked the role. In her prim navy blue pencil skirt, coordinating jacket, and sleek black boots, she presented herself as a package of assured professionalism. It was a pleasant surprise to Maddie when she gave her a genuinely warm smile.

"Ms. Ellis, this is a real honor."

"Please, Dr. Jennings, call me Maddie."

"Only if you'll agree to call me Sasha. I like to work more informally anyway, if that's okay with you. I think it fosters a more open communication, gives us the chance to really get to know one another," she said, addressing both Maddie and Nate.

"All right, Sasha."

"Ma, why don't you take Sasha to the music room? I promise to stay out of the way."

Maddie couldn't help smiling at Nate's eagerness. He knew that the music room was the most private and sacred space in the house to her, the place where she was most comfortable. She was touched by how much he wanted this to work. For his sake, she'd do her best.

"How beautiful," Sasha said as Maddie guided her to one of the chairs before sitting down on the couch. The doctor gestured at the piano. "Is this where you work?"

"Yes, along with my studio out back. I've written a lot of songs on that beauty," Maddie said, looking lovingly at the piano. "It was one of the few things I first brought with me when Nate and I came out to Montauk. The whole time I was waiting for the movers, I stressed over whether or not it would fit through the door. But it did. Perfectly."

"When was that, Maddie?"

"In 1995. Nate was eight years old, and I had just left his father. We came out to Montauk to start over, and I've been here ever since."

"Is that when you developed agoraphobia?" Sasha asked, pulling a notebook and pen from her briefcase. The question seemed abrupt to Maddie, despite knowing that this was the real reason for the doctor's visit.

"No, no, that happened when Nate was in high school." She paused. "Listen, Sasha, you need to know that I'm not unhappy with my present life. But Nate's getting married, and I want to be there."

Sasha's mouth set in a firm line. "Nate mentioned that he wanted you and your ex-husband to sing together at his wedding. Is that something you want to do?"

"Not really. I don't think so. Oh, I don't know. If you had asked me a week ago, I would have said absolutely not. But then Tom showed up . . ."

"Your ex? Tom Seymour? He's here?" Sasha began to scribble on the open page in front of her.

"I know it sounds crazy, but yes, he's in my cottage at the back of the property. Nate brought him out here to try and convince me to sing at the wedding." *And to tell me about Emilia,* Maddie thought, but she wasn't ready to share that piece of information with the doctor.

"How do you feel about him being here?"

"I was furious at first, but it was so important to Nate. He's rarely seen us together, or at least not that he remembers."

"Interesting. How long will Tom be here?"

"He'll be heading back to the city as soon as the trains are running. Sometime later today, I hope. Why do you ask?"

"It might be helpful to bring him into one of our sessions after you and I have had a chance to get to know each other. How do you feel about that?"

"I don't really see how it will help."

"I understand, Maddie, but my objective is to get you to a point where you're able to leave your property to attend your son's wedding. Having your ex here to work with you is a great way to achieve that end."

"I don't see why we have to bring Tom into it," Maddie said darkly. The last thing she wanted was another reason to have Tom infiltrate her life.

Sasha paused before speaking, as if carefully choosing what to say next. "Maddie, I think something happened to you, something that makes you want to stay inside this safe place you've created for yourself. Tom might be able to shed some light on that, especially if you can't identify it."

"I got tired of his constant womanizing, that's what happened," Maddie snapped. "He never understood why that might have been an issue for me. I guess you could say we had different views on what it means to be in a committed relationship."

"Yes, but that can't be what's stopping you from venturing off your property, because you were able to function in the world after you initially separated. It's got to be something else."

"And you can figure that out?" Maddie said, smirking a little bit.

"I can try, but to be successful, you've got to open up to me. There's an old saying, maybe you've heard it? *Our secrets make us sick.* You've got to deal with what you hide deep within. If you face your pain head-on, I can help you walk through it to the other side, where the entire world will be open to you again. How does that sound? Are you willing to give it a go?" Sasha smiled with such confidence that Maddie could only nod her head yes whether she believed it or not.

"Good." Sasha sat back in her chair. "Now, where should we begin? Why don't you tell me how it feels to have Tom here after all this time?"

Maddie mulled Sasha's words over in her mind before answering. "Strange. It feels strange. I had so fully written him off, put that whole part of my life on the shelf. If I didn't have Nate as absolute proof of our relationship, I could have probably convinced myself that it didn't happen at all."

"Then how would you explain the music you made together? You created a classic American songbook with him."

"Right, but that day in the dojo, the day when he and Emilia—"

"Emilia? Who's Emilia?"

Seeing the determination in the younger woman's eyes, Maddie realized she'd been backed into a corner. No way would Sasha let her drop this topic, whether Maddie was ready or not. And God knows she wasn't ready. Would probably never be. And yet . . .

Nate, she reminded herself fiercely, *do this for Nate*. She drew in a shaky breath and took Emilia's letter from her back pocket. "You better get really comfortable, Sasha. I've got a long story to tell you . . ."

An hour and a half later, Maddie had finished telling Sasha everything she could remember about her life with Tom. By this point she was exhausted from the effort, but it had been cathartic too. Much more so than she had expected. She fell silent and watched as Sasha put her pen and notebook back in her briefcase and sat up straight.

"Okay, Maddie, I think I've heard enough for today. I'd like to come back out tomorrow to continue this, if that's okay with you. Nate made it clear to me that time is of the essence. You've got some big decisions ahead."

Maddie nodded in agreement, too emotionally wrung out to say anything.

"And I don't know if you're ready to have Tom join us, but since he's here, I really think it would help. Can you think about it until I come back?"

Again Maddie could do nothing more than nod her head.

Sasha stood up and reached for Maddie's hand. Grasping it, she said softly, "This was a great beginning. I'm convinced we can get you back out into the world if that's what you want. Of course, if that isn't something you're interested in, no one can force you to go. I just want you to know you have options."

Maddie felt the warmth radiate from the doctor's strong grip and wanted badly to believe what she said. "Thank you, Sasha. Let me walk you out." She led Sasha into the hall before stopping midway to the front door. "This is as close as I can go today. Sorry."

Sasha smiled warmly. "No problem, Maddie. We'll work on it together." She took her coat from the hallway closet and gently shut the front door behind her, chilly air sweeping inside in her wake.

Maddie pulled her sweater tightly against her body and went back into the music room. Perching on the window seat, she watched as Sasha carefully walked down the slick driveway to her car. When she was gone, Maddie leaned her head against the cold glass as if to brace herself before rising to prepare for her band's arrival. They had called earlier to let her know they would be there before dusk, and she wanted to work on the bridge of her new song before then.

She walked over to the piano, her fingers gracing the polished keys, and felt herself get lost in her music. It was always that way: her music could always save her. She willed the melody to sweep away the remnants of her session with Sasha, so much buried emotion that Tom had stirred up, the confusion she felt at his mere presence.

Just as she was finally working through the roughest part of the piece, she heard Nate's voice in the doorway.

"Ma, sorry. Don't mean to interrupt you, but the band's here. Everyone's out in the cottage."

Maddie glanced up at the clock over the fireplace and saw that it was nearly five. "Where's your father?"

"Out there with them. Quite a reunion going on."

"Wow. This is just not what I had in mind," Maddie said, shaking her head.

"I'm really sorry it turned out this way. I never meant to cause this much hassle."

"It's okay, Nate," Maddie made herself say. "Tell them I'll be right there."

She could see his worry lifting instantly. "Great!" He went to the door, but stopped and turned back to her. "What did you think of Dr. Jennings?"

"Who, my new BFF Sasha?"

"Huh?" Nate looked puzzled.

"Well, she's convinced there's something I'm not remembering or have pushed down into the depths of me somewhere, and that's the thing that keeps me housebound. I'm not so sure."

"It's not unreasonable—" Nate began, but she cut him off.

"Please, sweetie, can we not go over this just now?"

"Sure, Mom, sorry. But you'll meet with her again?"

In spite of herself, she had to smile at his persistence. "Yes, Nate, I promised you I'd try, and that's what I'll do. However, there is one small twist I didn't see coming."

"A twist?"

"She wants to speak with your dad as well. I hope he's up for it." Not that she was, but she'd given Nate her word.

Nate smiled broadly. "He told me he wants to do whatever it takes to get you to sing with him at the wedding. You've got him just where you want him."

"That's the problem, my love. I don't think I want him."

She instantly regretted her words. She had always been so careful not to denigrate Tom in front of Nate. And to her surprise, for the first time in years, she suddenly doubted if what she'd said was actually true.

Nate sighed heavily. "I know, Ma, I know. You and Dad. It's been over for a long time. Whatever." He turned away, the slump of his shoulders wounding Maddie to the heart. Tears sprang to her eyes and she busied herself organizing the sheet music so he wouldn't hear the quaver in her voice as she called after him, "Be there in a minute, Nate. I just want to organize my thoughts."

"Okay, Ma. I'll let everyone know you're on the way."

As soon as she heard the back door slam, Maddie let herself go with heaving sobs, as if the pain of everything she had told Sasha earlier that day was surging out of her body. For a long time she sat on the piano bench sniffling, watching the sky darken outside her window.

Eventually she stirred, dabbed her face with a tissue, and thought, *crying twice in two days, that's the Tom Seymour effect*, and gave a broken little laugh. "C'mon, Maddie," she said aloud, "time to go face the music. Literally."

A soft knock sounded on the door, and she stood up to find Tom standing there.

"Maddie," he said softly, seeing the trail of tears she was trying to conceal by wiping them away with her sleeve. "I hope it's okay I came into the house. We were starting to worry that you'd changed your mind about recording the song."

"I guess it depends on your definition of 'okay.' You showing up here with Emilia's letter and the news of her death, well, it's more than a little overwhelming."

"I know. And I'll go tonight, or as soon as the trains are running. I never meant to upend your life like this."

"You never did, Tom," Maddie whispered. "It's just always what happened."

A look of pain crossed his handsome face, and she realized she'd wounded him. How was this possible? In the past he had always laughed when she accused him of anything, made a snide remark or cursed her, or, worst of all, simply shrugged and turned away.

She struggled for some sort of equilibrium. "I was doing just fine before you showed up with your letter from Emilia and your, your . . ."

"My what, exactly, Maddie?" he challenged as she fell silent.

Your impossible good looks, your charisma and green eyes, the gentleness you show to Nate, she wanted to say, *that same kindness you once showed to me . . .*

"Never mind. I'll be out in a minute," she snapped.

"Are you sure?" He was frowning at her, searching her face, and she panicked at what was starting to build inside her.

"Yes, I'm sure! I am fine! Go on, Tom, please!"

"God, Maddie, you are so far from fine, stuck inside this beautiful prison you've created for yourself. For chrissakes—" He turned away so that she couldn't see his face.

"We gave up on each other a long time ago, Tom," she shot back. "I adjusted to that, created a whole new reality for myself."

"I know, Maddie," he replied without turning around. "It's my biggest regret, losing you to that reality."

His words jolted through her. Was he feeling it too? That old connection, the electricity between them? Is that what it was? She took a moment to consider this, and as she did so, Tom let out a long sigh and moved without speaking toward the door.

"My new therapist wants to meet you," she said quickly, not sure why but not wanting to let go of this moment. "She seems to think you can help me fill in the blanks. I'm not so convinced."

Tom turned and walked back to her. Any emotions he might have been feeling were hidden now, and Maddie was annoyed with herself for being disappointed. "Maybe I can. I've been in therapy as long as I've been sober. Six years, and I'm still trying to get my life right, Maddie."

"Dr. Jennings—Sasha—is coming back tomorrow, and she asked if you could sit in on our session."

"That would mean I'd have to stay another night. Is that okay with you?"

No, it wasn't. But for Nate's sake, she would allow it.

"We really need to do this for our son, Maddie."

"I'm not the one who's let him down time after time," Maddie said sharply, hating that he could still read her thoughts so easily.

"No? Do you think it doesn't worry him in the least that his mother refuses to leave her house? That she hasn't in years? Do you think that's okay with him, Maddie? No burden? No cause for concern?"

She turned her back to him as tears clogged her throat.

"Maddie," he said softly, standing right behind her now, "I've repaired my relationship with our son. I will continue to work on it, even if it means doing a solo set at his wedding to Sophie." He paused. "But I want you to do the same. Work on it, for Nate's sake. And yours. You've come so far already. You've let me in, talked to me, allowed me to stay another night . . ."

"I didn't ask you here!"

"No, but now that I am—" His voice grew husky; his breath tickled the hair at the nape of her neck. "C'mon, Maddie. Isn't it obvious?"

She whirled around to find his green eyes upon her, and the angry retort she was about to make died on her lips as her heart began to pound double-time. "Is—is what obvious?" she stammered.

"C'mon, Maddie," he said again. "You know."

She put one hand behind her to support herself on the edge of the piano. So he felt it too. That familiar magnetic attraction. "Stop it, Tom." The words had no force whatsoever, but she was relieved when he immediately took a step back.

Still, being Tom, he didn't relent. "Maddie. The girl I once knew, the woman I was married to a hundred years ago, the mother that I know you to be wouldn't miss Nate's wedding day for anything. Let me stay while you work through your issues, at least as they relate to me. Let me help you. For Nate."

She looked up into Tom's pleading eyes as he continued, "I won't cause you any new pain, I promise." Again he took a few steps toward her, as if he couldn't help himself, but stopped before he got too close. "Will you let me try to repair some of the damage I've done?"

"Will you be honest with Dr. Jennings?" she asked defensively.

"It's the least I can do to prove I want to make amends for my past behavior. If it makes you more comfortable, I'll see if there's a hotel room in town, now that the storm has passed."

She felt some of the tension leave her shoulders. Crossing her arms over her chest, she sighed. "No, you can stay in the cottage." She paused, then said, "And I'm not sure if the storm is over. Just wait until Sasha Jennings gets a hold of you!"

He grinned. "Was that an attempt at humor, Maddie? If it was, I'll take it as a good sign."

She picked up her sheet music and said sharply, "We've kept the band waiting long enough. Are you coming?"

"Is that all right?" He looked surprised. "I'd love to hear what you've got."

She nodded. "Everything is upside down, and my life is so out of control right now, I don't think your presence matters. Just don't take over the session, okay?"

"I wouldn't dare. Believe me."

"Believe you? I'm not sure I'm ready to do that again, Tom."

"Got it. So I'll leave it at 'scout's honor,'" he said and smiled at her.

Maddie actually felt herself go a little weak in the knees for a moment, but recovered enough to say, "Let's go then."

"After you. This is your album, not mine."

"That's right, it is," she responded. "Try, please just try, to remember that."

It was like old home week in the cottage. The original members of their old band—Ned, Charlie, and Andre, the three musketeers, as Maddie liked to think of them—were waiting for her with warm hugs and a big bag of bagels from Murray's in Chelsea, the first store to reopen once the snow stopped. These men, these troubadours, had been there for Maddie from the beginning; and while they might be a little older, a little grayer, and somewhat wider around the middle, deep down they were the same wonderful artists she'd met in the park all those years ago.

Maddie's female backup singers, Jessie and Shanna, had accompanied them from the city. They had joined the band later, after her divorce from Tom and after many rounds of auditions with hundreds of singers that Maddie had arranged when she needed to put together her first solo album, the one she had to deliver to appease the label when Tom could not fulfill his end of the bargain he'd made with them. Maddie was sure Tom had told all of them about Emilia by now, and she was grateful that none of them mentioned her name.

When Maddie stepped into the cottage's kitchen to put the bagels into a basket, Jessie and Shanna followed her.

"Is that really your ex?" Jessie, the curvy, full-busted one, asked, peering around the corner for a better view of Tom. "He and the guys have been catching up on old times. We couldn't get in a word edgewise, and neither could Nate. What's he doing here?"

"Yeah, Maddie, I thought you guys don't speak. How long has it been since you've seen him?" Shanna, all sharp angles and flawless mocha skin, peeked around the doorway as well. "He's damn fine looking, if I do say so myself."

"Watch out for him, Shanna. He'll have your panties off before you've even been introduced," Maddie deadpanned.

"So does he want to reunite?" the younger woman asked.

"Or is he fair game?" Shanna chimed in.

"And this is why we broke up—" Maddie began before Jessie cut her off.

"I'm sorry, Maddie. For some reason I thought he was dead. He hasn't had a hit song in ages, right? Lots of drugs, no?" She crunched loudly on a pretzel, waiting for Maddie's answer.

"Tom stopped recording years ago, and I haven't seen him since Nate's high school graduation. Now he's here to try and convince me to sing with him at Nate's wedding."

Shanna brightened. "Oh yeah! Nate told us. That's awesome, Maddie!"

"Wish I felt the same way."

"But Maddie, it's for Nate. You've got to consider it," Shanna implored.

Maddie handed each woman a bowl of salsa and chips to bring to the group. "I'm mulling it over, but no promises." She walked into the living room and said, "Sorry for the delay, guys," as she placed some napkins down on the coffee table. "The new song is still pretty rough. I'm struggling with the bridge. I wanted to have it ready by the time you got out here, but with the storm . . ."

"No big deal, Maddie. Let's hear what you've got. We can work out any kinks," Ned said encouragingly.

She walked over to the baby grand piano in the corner of the room, a smaller version of the one she had inside the house, and began to play. There was not a word exchanged until after she was done.

Andre was the first to speak. "Nice! I love the hook, Maddie."

"So do I," Charlie added, applauding, "but I agree, the bridge is a let-down. It falls off too much."

"No man, that's not it. It's the tempo," Ned interjected.

"It's neither of those," Tom said softly. "Is it okay if I say something, Maddie?"

"Dad, maybe it would be best if you didn't," Nate blurted, watching his mother's face. She sat still on the piano bench, clearly stunned by Tom's intrusion, especially after she had warned him not to get involved.

"It's okay, Nate. Let your father speak," Maddie said. "If I know him at all, he'll make his opinion known one way or another."

All of the heads in the room swiveled to watch the two of them spar, but Tom wasn't taking the bait. Instead he said in the same soft tone, "It's pretty clear, Maddie. You need to ramp up the drama of the bridge with a key change. Your voice isn't as high as it used to be, your register is much lower. Don't get me wrong, the tone is still beautiful, but you're struggling with it."

"I think you're right, Tom," Andre said, nodding slowly. "I hope you're not mad, Maddie, but I think a simple key change will make a huge difference. Why not try it?"

Maddie turned back to the piano. In her heart, she knew Tom had hit on the very crux of the problem. All those years ago when they wrote music together, he had been the one more schooled in technique and had the keenest ear. And he had always been able to make those small but perfect fixes right away.

The question that now flashed through Maddie's mind was whether or not this was a sign of the old version of Tom, the man she had once been so desperately in love with, the man she thought she'd never live without. The clarity of his thoughts, his ability to see exactly what was wrong . . .

Quickly she began to play the song's introduction again, to give herself time to settle before having to sing. When she got to the bridge, she lowered the key.

It was perfect.

"Oh man, that's pure genius!" Charlie shouted. "We've got to record that just as it is. I love this tune!"

There was a lot of high fiving and hugging as Maddie played it again, this time with Jessie and Shanna improvising some of their backup vocals. Tom took this good cheer as a signal that it was all right for him to become even more involved, and promptly began punching up the arrangements with Andre and working out a short solo for Ned. Maddie watched him while pretending not to, knowing she should be angry, resentful, and yet feeling that everything was suddenly so . . . normal, so *right*.

Apparently Nate felt the same way. Unable to stop smiling, he called in an order for six pizzas from Gino's, and before Maddie even realized what was happening, she had her next number one single recorded in her home studio.

It was close to three in the morning before Maddie, Jessie, Shanna, and Nate bundled up and walked back to the main house while Tom and the rest of the band camped out in the cottage. By the time she got to bed, Maddie was so tired that she basically passed out, blinking awake only when the sun crested over the ocean and shone between the curtains she had neglected to draw closed the night before.

In that netherworld between being asleep and fully awake, Maddie drifted off into a dream. She and Tom were back in her dorm room at NYU, wound around each other in her bed, and he was singing softly in her ear while running his fingers up and down her naked back. It was both peaceful and erotic, and when she finally opened her eyes to the morning light, she felt disoriented, not sure where she was and, for the first time in years, sorry to be alone. *Shit!*

She hurriedly showered and dressed before going down to make a huge pancake breakfast for her guests. It was the least she could do since they had so kindly accommodated her needs by coming out here to lay down the tracks for her work, knowing that she would never go to the city to do so. Besides, she desperately needed the distraction. She felt all hot and bothered, fully out of sorts.

Once in the kitchen, she got into the groove of assembling the ingredients she'd need for breakfast. As she stepped out of the walk-in pantry, she saw Tom exiting the cottage and heading toward the house. She was standing to the side of the picture window, so he hadn't spotted her yet, and she was able to observe him unguarded. Although he was certainly older now, he was just as handsome as ever with his rugged features and piercing green gaze.

Mostly, though, she couldn't help but notice that the spark of his spirit, the spring in his step, was back. It was so familiar to her, despite the fact that it had been missing for years even before their separation. She'd noticed it first when she found him in the cottage with Nate, and it seemed more intense, more a part of him now, in his unguarded state as he came up the path, hands in the pockets of his parka. It was both comforting and unsettling, and it put Maddie even more on edge.

She heard the mudroom door open and felt the cold air sweep across her stocking feet. Tom hung his jacket on one of the pegs and stepped into the kitchen, his hair still wet from a recent shower.

"Good morning," he said with a smile. "I was hoping to find some coffee here. The guys are still sleeping off last night, and I didn't want to wake them by rummaging around the kitchen."

"Of course." Maddie busied herself with finding two mugs and pouring milk into a small pitcher. "It's the first thing I do when I'm up in the morning. Coffee prep."

"I know," he said softly. "I remember."

For some reason, Tom's presence was making it difficult for Maddie to concentrate on getting the various parts of the French press to fit together.

"Can I do that for you?" Tom asked with an amused smile.

She pushed it to him across the counter, relieved to be rid of the obvious signal of the raw state of her emotions.

By the time the kettle whistled, Tom had the whole thing assembled and filled with ground beans. Pouring the boiling water over the top of the press, he let the coffee brew a bit before pressing down on the top to fully saturate the grounds. Maddie watched him, mesmerized by his swift and simple actions. She could not take her eyes off his hands or deny the sudden vivid memory of them caressing her body, the firmness of his grip when he held the back of her neck while kissing her. It was the second time this morning she'd felt that unwanted rush of desire for him, and she quickly crossed the kitchen to open the refrigerator door, pretending to look for something inside.

Tom filled both mugs and sat down at one end of the counter, pushing Maddie's over to where she stood. "Still drink it black?" he asked. She barely nodded. The tone of his voice and the way he was looking at her made it clear that he knew what kind of reaction he was eliciting from her and that he was enjoying it.

Annoyed, Maddie concentrated on her coffee, letting the caffeine do its magic, finishing more than half her mug before Tom broke the silence. "Can I help put breakfast together for the crew?"

"Actually you could help me get the urn from the basement. It's on a high shelf."

"Lead the way," he said, getting up from his seat.

Flipping on the light switch, Maddie headed down the basement staircase. "Watch your step," she called. "It's sort of a minefield down here."

They navigated around a number of boxes and past the wine cellar to a long corridor with a large storage closet at the end. Maddie opened it, revealing oversized lobster pots, extra sheet pans, and stacks of serving platters. The coffee urn was on the top shelf.

"Hang on a minute," Maddie said. She went halfway down the corridor and returned with a small stepladder. "This should help."

It took Tom no time to pass the urn down to her. "Let me carry that for you," he said, folding the ladder away and taking the urn from her hands.

"Thanks."

As they walked back into the corridor, Tom gestured to a partially open door across from them. "So what's in there?"

"Oh," Maddie said uncomfortably, "just some stuff from when we were young."

He stared at her. "What stuff?"

"Stuff I could never seem to throw away, I guess."

"Can I see?" He walked toward the doorway.

"Tom, no—" If she had known the door was ajar, she would never have asked him to come down and help her. "Everyone should be up soon," she added quickly, trying to put him off. "I need to get breakfast ready."

"Breakfast can wait," was all he said, already pushing the door fully open. For a moment he stood frozen. "Holy shit, Maddie," he finally breathed. "You kept everything . . ."

The walls were covered with framed newspaper reviews of their early concerts, articles about their wedding, Nate's baby pictures, his birth announcement, and their first awards. The guitar Tom had played when they first stepped out onstage together sat against one wall in the far corner of the room. Their commemorative platinum albums as well as their Grammy statues were crammed on a shelf beside it. It was like a mini museum of who they'd once been.

Tom strode into the middle of the room, the coffee urn cord trailing behind him. "How come you kept all of this? Why?" was all he could ask.

"Because I knew one day Nate would be curious. He's been in and out of the basement a million times, but it's been years since he ventured in here. As a kid, I guess he thought of this as junk. As an adult, maybe he's not been ready to look at it, or maybe he just forgot it exists. I'm not sure. What I do know is that I never expected to see you in here. When I took it all out of the loft after moving here with Nate, you never asked for any of it, so I was pretty sure you didn't care."

Tom drew in a deep breath. "It's not that I didn't care. I wasn't even aware of any of it back then. Maddie, you have to realize that I walked around stoned all the time. Like a zombie."

"I know, Tom, I was there, remember?" And for the first time she realized that perhaps he actually *didn't* remember. That he had simply not been present back then. He'd been somewhere else, distant and vacant.

Tom set the coffee urn down and walked slowly over to a shelf to pick up a framed photograph of the three of them taken years ago on the beach with Russell's house in the background.

"Oh my God, Maddie, that's us with Nate, the time we went to some beach house. That's when you found out I'd committed you to that first solo album. Where were we? It looks so familiar . . ."

"You really don't know?" Maddie asked incredulously.

His expression was pained. "So much of my memory is wiped out, Maddie," he said hoarsely. "I'm sorry. No. I don't remember."

"We were standing about a half mile down the beach from where we are right now, Tom. That's Russell's house in Montauk. It was the last place I felt truly happy with you and Nate, our little family. That's why it was the only place I could think of to run to after Nate's birthday party. I told the driver to keep going until he hit the ocean." Her voice was thick with tears. "You know the rest."

They stood in the small room without speaking until Tom stepped closer, still holding the picture. "Oh God, Maddie," he choked out as he placed his free hand on her face in an impossibly light caress.

Maddie stood still, stunned by his touch, her heart racing. She was afraid he might kiss her and, even worse, that she might kiss him back.

Above them a door slammed. "Hey! Anybody home?"

Andre's voice, then others'. Maddie quickly stepped away from Tom, leaving an ache in the distance between them. "They're up. If you want to look around some more, go ahead. I'm going to make pancakes."

She grabbed the urn on her way out, aware that to stay here this close to Tom when they were both so vulnerable was too dangerous. She quickly made her way back upstairs to the safety of her kitchen, leaving Tom alone with their past.

XVI

Fixing breakfast was a blessing for Maddie. It gave her something to concentrate on other than her conflicting feelings for Tom. She put the large cast-iron griddle over the two center burners of her Viking range top, and before long she had whole- wheat pancakes sizzling in butter, turning the perfect circles as they browned on each side. The bacon strips were frying, and she knew that their smell would waft upstairs and bring Nate running. The urn was brewing an enormous amount of coffee to help with any hangovers. She cut some fruit into a large glass bowl, filled a smaller bowl with Greek yogurt drizzled with honey, and set out a ceramic container of granola. Then she pulled out silverware, mugs, and heavy stoneware plates with matching cloth napkins to round out the buffet.

She was filling a large carafe with orange juice when Tom finally came back upstairs, his expression unreadable.

"Can we talk about that room later?" he asked in a quiet tone.

"I'll talk to you about it when we both sit down with Dr. Jennings," she answered. The subject of her life with Tom was still too volatile for her to consider tackling with him alone.

"If that's what it takes, fine. But we need to discuss—"

"Mom! Dad!" Nate spread his arms wide as he came around the corner. "Good morning!"

"Glad to see somebody is wide awake," Maddie teased as she hugged him, hoping like hell he didn't think that there was anything going on between her and his father. Because there wasn't.

"Nate, hey." Andre thumped Nate on the back as the rest of the band trickled in, bleary-eyed.

Maddie poured coffee and filled plates, and when everyone was settled, she lifted her mug. "Hey, guys, I just want to say thanks. I couldn't have recorded that song without you."

"We know," Ned joked.

"Took long enough," Charlie agreed.

"Face it, Maddie," Andre added, "you need us. You love us. You can't live without us."

"So when we going on tour?" Charlie asked, smiling.

"Since when do I tour?" Maddie countered more sharply than she intended.

His smile faded. "Um, I just thought since Tom's here, maybe the old band will get back together."

Nate threw a napkin at his head. "Cut the crazy talk, Charlie. My mom and dad aren't reuniting. Unless it's to sing at my wedding to Sophie!"

"Holy crap, man!" Andre yelled. "Nice to let us know that small detail before now!"

"Nate told us yesterday," Shanna confessed. "It's a wonderful idea!"

Andre turned to Maddie and Tom. "Are you going to do it? Are you guys going to sing together?"

Maddie smiled weakly. "No decision yet."

"I expect you all to be there," Nate added quickly.

Aware that Nate was once again shielding her from awkwardness, Maddie clapped her hands and said as gaily as she could, "Please, people, the food's getting cold. Now eat!"

The mood lightened as they obeyed, chattering away about industry gossip and who was sleeping with whom.

"It's getting late," Charlie said at last. "Need to head back to the city. Got a gig to get ready for."

"I'm with you," Ned said, pushing back his chair with Andre doing the same. "Ladies?" he asked Jessie and Shanna.

Maddie took this as her cue to begin clearing away the remnants of breakfast, but Tom stood up. "Why don't you leave this to me and Nate?

We can handle the cleanup; you go upstairs and prepare for Sasha. I know you'll want to gather your thoughts."

Maddie tried not to show her surprise at Tom's helpfulness, so she smiled and said to all, "No one leave without finding me to say good-bye, okay?"

"We would never!" Ned said with mock horror. They all laughed, and Maddie went upstairs to compose herself before Sasha's arrival. Once in her room, she sat down on the edge of the bed and pulled Emilia's letter out of her back pocket. She had taken to carrying it around with her, afraid that if she put it down somewhere it would disappear. It was almost as if the letter brought Emilia back into her life so that she could finally sort out her feelings about the woman who had once been her dearest friend.

This time as she read the now familiar words, she was filled not only with sadness but with regret. How could she not have realized that Emilia had been in such trouble? She had known for years that Emilia did more than dabble in drugs, that her use of illegal substances was a large part of her daily life. What she never considered was that as an addict, Emilia would do anything for the high she craved, including trading a sexual favor with Tom for one more hit. So, Maddie wondered suddenly, should she consider Emilia's letter a final gift, a way to finally forgive her? To let her anger at Tom go and move on and be made whole again?

Sitting in the calm solitude of her bedroom, Maddie put her face in her hands. She was suddenly exhausted, and the worry about Nate's wedding and the fact that Tom was downstairs in her kitchen right now made her feel like screaming. Not to mention his wanting to talk to her about the things he had seen in her basement, and never mind, too, the rekindled attraction she now felt for him. She wished she could just pull the blanket over her head and make all of her troubles disappear like a child's game of peek-a-boo.

On the other hand, what was so wrong with her present life? Maddie asked herself defensively. She, for one, was quite happy with it.

So what if I never want to leave my property? Maddie internally argued. *It's the one place I've created for myself, and if Nate wants me at his wedding, he'll just have to have it here.*

Maddie sat straight up, filled with new resolve. When Sasha came, she'd tell her to move on to some pathetic patient who really needed her help, because Madeline Ellis was just fine. She was done trying to make everything all right for everyone else. She was going to continue being happy on her own terms.

She drew in a deep breath. *Who am I kidding?* Shoulders slumping, she turned to look at the bedside clock. An hour until her session. Sasha was probably already on the way, and it was simply too late to do anything about it.

When Sasha arrived, she and Maddie spent a long time probing possible root causes for why Maddie had become agoraphobic. Sasha said they needed to get straight to the bottom of the problem, and she was pretty sure it had to do with Tom.

"You know, Maddie, the human brain is pretty incredible. We forget the painful things in our pasts as a form of self-protection. You've been through a lot of stress, and staying inside your house makes you feel safe." She sat back in her chair. "So tell me—how has it been for the last few days with Tom around?"

"If I had to sum it up in a word, I think I'd say it's been confusing."

"In what way?" Sasha questioned.

"Well, I didn't expect to have, for lack of a better description, 'warm feelings' for him." Maddie felt herself blush.

"What do you mean? Do you think you're softening your stance?"

"Um. Not sure. But I'm feeling a definite sexual attraction to him again." There. It was out in the open. Maddie's blush deepened.

"Interesting," Sasha replied. "Care to elaborate further?"

Maddie shifted uncomfortably. "I gave up on him so long ago. The drinking, the drugs . . ." Her voice trailed off.

"Go on."

"But he's sober now, and he's Tom again. I mean my Tom . . . the Tom I knew."

"How do you know he's really sober now?"

"Both Tom and Nate told me. He's been straight for six years. And like I said, he's, I don't know, different. I had no idea it's been that long.

Even though he and Nate have had a relationship for a while, I never really wanted to hear about it. My son and I don't discuss his father."

"Why do you think that is?"

"I guess I never wanted to risk losing myself again. It was just too hard the last time."

Sasha smiled. "I can understand why you'd feel that way. But why is he still here, Maddie? Especially if you're experiencing sexual feelings and are afraid of being caught up with him again? The trains are running now. He could certainly go home."

"I realize that . . . and I told you I'm confused! And you said to bring him into a session."

"I know I did. But I think we have more work to do together before we're ready for that. He can always come back out here, can't he?"

"I guess so," Maddie said, her voice faltering at the thought of him leaving.

"Do you want him to stay?"

Maddie put her head in her hands. "Lord, Sasha, I'm just not sure. Nate is so damned happy he's here. Me? I'm really mixed up." She looked at Sasha. "It seems the more you and I speak, the more confused I get."

The younger woman chuckled. "I hear that a lot. Well, no need to send him away just yet. You'll know what to do about that, Maddie. As for us, let's pick up again tomorrow. You've got enough to ponder for one day."

The next morning when Maddie came into the kitchen, she saw Nate and Tom sitting on the porch of the cottage bundled up in their parkas, sipping coffee. She opened the sliding glass door and stepped out onto the deck. "Did you guys have breakfast yet?" she called over the lawn.

"Is that an invitation?" Nate joked back, but Maddie could hear the strain in his voice. She felt a stab of guilt, knowing she was responsible. After Sasha left, she'd spent the rest of the day in her music room, trying not to think about Tom and yet doing so all the same. When Nate knocked to ask about dinner, she'd told him she needed more time alone, and he had respected her wishes—but only after delivering a pasta dish from Gino's and a glass of wine to her door. She'd been so touched by the gesture that she'd cried all over again.

Now she forced herself to call lightly, "Yeah. I guess it is."

Tom and Nate looked at each other, then sprinted quickly over to her.

Maddie couldn't help but smile. "Wow. Guess you're hungry. Omelet sound good?"

"Better than good," Tom said, opening the sliding glass door for her as Nate's phone rang and he stopped on the deck to take the call.

Maddie quickly gathered ingredients and pulled her large skillet out of the drawer underneath the range top. She could feel Tom's eyes on her all the while, making her wish that she'd put on something other than her old sweatshirt and jeans. As she whisked the eggs, she asked, "Mushrooms and swiss?"

"My favorite," Tom said softly.

"It seems not everything's changed," she replied.

He cleared his throat. "Listen, Maddie, I've been thinking. I'd love to have my old guitar back, if that's okay with you. I saw it in that room downstairs."

She stopped whisking and looked at him guiltily. "Of course. It's yours. I should never have taken it out of the loft."

"I'm glad you did. Who knows what I might have done to it when I was using? Probably sold it or wrecked it. I did a lot of that. You saved it for me."

"Good morning, Ma." Nate was smiling broadly as he came in, and it occurred to Maddie that she'd never seen her son look quite this happy.

Don't! she told herself fiercely. She had enough emotional baggage to work through and didn't want to add crushing maternal guilt to the mix.

"Sophie says hi. She'll be here on Friday." Nate turned to his father. "Will you still be around? I can always bring her into the city to see you if you go back before then."

Maddie felt her throat tighten at Nate's words. Sasha was right. She knew what to do. "Um, Tom, I think I'm close to having you join a session. Maybe you should just stay in the cottage for a bit more? At least to see Sophie . . ."

His green eyes met her hazel ones, and the look in his threatened to melt her heart. "Thanks, Maddie. I'd be happy to wait until you're ready for that."

She nodded and turned her attention back to the eggs, hoping neither of them noticed the blush staining her cheeks.

After breakfast, Tom loaded the dishwasher, then opened the basement door.

"What're you doing, Dad?" Nate asked.

"Your mother kept my guitar downstairs for safekeeping. I think I can handle having it back now."

Nate looked at Maddie, surprise registering on his face. "You did?"

"Actually, I kept a whole lot of stuff from when your dad and I recorded together. It's been in the basement forever."

Nate looked stunned. "I always thought that was stuff left over from all those estate sales you dragged me to! I never really went in there to look around. You never told me you'd saved anything from the loft."

"It never came up," Maddie said, trying to sound casual, "and it was easier for me when you forgot about it after you left home. That you didn't ask questions."

"Do you mind if I take a look with Dad?" Nate asked eagerly.

Maddie sighed. "No."

"Come with us, Ma. Maybe there'll be something cool you can give me to put in my office in LA."

They ventured downstairs, where Maddie pushed open the heavy door.

"Holy shit," Nate said softly as she switched on the light.

"Do you mean to tell me that all the time you've lived here, you never went in this room?" Tom asked.

"Like Mom said, I never came down here after I left for college— except to visit the wine cellar." Nate grinned. "And I just thought this was all junk Mom never unpacked."

"Unbelievable," was all Tom could say.

For the next half hour Maddie watched from the doorway as Tom and Nate opened boxes and pored over old photos and press clippings. She wasn't sure who was more excited about them: Nate or his father.

"Holy shit," Nate kept repeating, wiping the dust off a tarnished Grammy award. "I always assumed your agent had these displayed in his office, Dad. It never occurred to me to ask."

Tom's guitar was badly out of tune, and they all laughed as he strummed a few off-key notes. "Just like old times," he joked. His eyes met Maddie's, and a sudden silence fell.

Maddie drew in a deep breath. "Tom. We need to tell Nate about Emilia."

"Oh yeah." Nate was busy putting things back into boxes. "I've heard that name before, and she's listed in the liner notes on your old albums as a vocalist. I don't remember her at all, though. What happened to her? Is she the one who died?"

As Tom began to repeat the story in its entirety to their son, including the extent of his and Emilia's addictions and the painful truth of what had happened in the dojo on Nate's eighth birthday, Maddie stepped outside. She stood in the dimly lit corridor, hugging herself with her arms and trying not to cry.

"Are you okay, son?" she finally heard Tom ask.

"I need some time to think," Nate answered in a voice Maddie had never heard before.

"Well, I could use some more coffee," she said brightly, stepping quickly inside. "Anyone else want some?"

Tom cleared his throat. "Me."

"I'll be up in a bit," Nate said without looking at them.

In unspoken agreement, Maddie and Tom headed upstairs, giving Nate the space they knew he needed to process what he had heard.

When he finally appeared in the kitchen, he found his parents sitting at the counter with their mugs filled, waiting. Maddie's heart sank as she looked at him.

"I really don't believe it's for me to judge, but that's a pretty messed-up story, don't you think, Dad?" Nate's voice quaked with anger. "My whole life changed in one moment. Mom had to leave New York, I had to leave all my friends, my school, and for what? A blow job?"

"Nate—"

"It makes total sense now. It always seemed to me there was something everyone else knew that I didn't. I saw that picture on the Internet years ago. I just never knew who the woman was. But I never googled you guys again after that. I was scared of what else I'd find. So I concentrated on the good stuff." His voice shook. "Thank God there was more of that."

"Nate," Tom tried again, but his son swung on him, his features twisted with outrage, with pain.

"How could you do it, Dad? How could you do that to Mom?"

"It was a long time ago," Tom answered quietly. "I'm not that man anymore. I'm trying to make amends—"

"Dad, really? Like you even can? Mom spent years holed up in this house because of what you did!" Nate spat.

"That's not your call to make, Nate. It's mine," Maddie interjected. "You can be mad at your father, and me, for that matter, for a whole lot of things. You just can't take on our past as your battle."

There was a muffled sound from Tom, and Maddie turned to see tears coursing down his cheeks. Even Nate was stunned into silence. For a moment no one said anything, then Tom choked out, "I'm sorry. So sorry. For everything. And to think Emilia took her own life and I might be responsible . . . I—I don't know if I'll ever get over that. I can't blame the drugs or drink anymore. Only myself."

"What are you saying, Tom?" Maddie whispered.

He looked down, shielding his face from them both. "I told her she couldn't sing backup for me, and just like that she was dead. I should have done something."

Maddie could only stare at him, speechless. She hadn't been aware before this moment that Tom felt in any way responsible for Emilia's death. But she knew instantly that the drunken, drug-addled Tom wouldn't have cared, while the old Tom, *her* Tom, would have felt this way about any member of their band—they had been a family, and Tom had looked after them all.

In that moment she also knew that her instincts about *this* Tom and his insistence that he was sober were right. Impulsively she reached for his hand, and when he clasped it tightly, she drew in a breath. "Nate," she said lovingly to her son's stiffly turned back, "I know this is a shock, but you're an adult now. It was time to hear the whole awful truth. To know what brought us out to Montauk all those years ago."

Nate didn't respond.

Maddie hopped off the stool and enfolded her son in her arms. "What matters now is your wedding, Nate. I want to get better, and like it or not, your wedding is forcing me to face my problems, my hurt. All of it. Not just what happened on your birthday all those years ago."

She drew in a deep breath. "And the letter Emilia wrote? By asking your dad to bring it to me, maybe she was hoping once I read it we might take a leap of faith and trust one another again. Maybe she gave me the chance to try and finally move on with my life. I owe it to her—to you—to make that happen."

Nate stepped back. "But all of those wasted years, stuck in this house . . ."

"I don't consider them wasted, Nate. I wrote some great music over the last decade, don't you think? And I'm beginning to realize that my time at home also gave me the chance to heal. And lately, to reevaluate the importance of connection." Maddie looked directly at Tom as she said this, and some of the pain etched in his face eased as he looked back at her.

Maddie finally felt Nate grow less rigid, and then he drew her into a hug of his own. Sighing deeply, he opened up the embrace to include Tom. The three of them stood locked together—as a family, Maddie realized, for maybe the very first time. She forced herself to live in the moment, willed herself to commit it to memory, and hoped that for all of them, true healing had finally begun.

For the rest of the week, Maddie and Sasha met every day, making slow but steady progress as they went through the details of Maddie's life, trying to unearth the source cause of her issues. By Thursday's session, the doctor lowered the boom.

"Listen," she said. "I think it's time to bring in Tom. From what I've heard so far, I think your ex might actually shed more light on your problem than you realize."

Now that the moment had actually come, Maddie needed time to collect her thoughts. Things had been going well for the last few days, with Tom staying mostly in the cottage and being helpful and sweetly upbeat when they were together in the house. But while they seemed to be working their way back to each other, Maddie continued to find herself nervous and unsure.

"I'll go make us some tea. Be right back," she said and fled to the kitchen. *What are you so scared of? You knew this was inevitable.* She had to confront Tom about the past. If she didn't, they'd never have a future—if that's what she wanted. *Was* it what she wanted?

She felt somewhat calmer when she returned to the music room with steaming tea, a plate of cookies, some linen napkins, a sugar bowl, and a small glass pitcher of milk on a wicker tray.

She held the tray out to Sasha, who picked up a mug.

"Are you ready to resume our talk now? Can we bring Tom into the session?"

"I don't know if it will help," Maddie replied, stalling. "Tom's the first to admit that his drug use clouded his memory, and I'm not sure he's got anything new to offer. Plus we've formed this crazy unspoken truce. I don't want to mess that up."

"Let's give it a shot," Sasha persisted. "If I think it's not productive, I'll cut it short."

"Promise?" Maddie said, recalling the heat in Tom's caress the other morning in the basement, when he had first discovered all that she'd saved.

"Promise."

"Okay." Maddie picked up the landline that sat by the piano bench. She had an intercom system that allowed her to reach the studio, and after two rings, Nate picked up.

"Is your dad there?"

"Yeah, you want to talk to him?"

"Just ask him to join Sasha and me over in the music room, if you don't mind."

The momentary pause before her son responded made Maddie even more nervous. "Sure, if that's what you want."

"It is. Thanks." She quickly replaced the receiver on its base before she lost her nerve and told Nate to forget it. "Okay, Sasha, he's coming, but I mean it. If we start circling the drain here, please, please pull the plug."

"I will," Sasha replied brightly, clearly energized by the chance to work with the two of them together.

Much too quickly for Maddie, Tom appeared in the doorway, knocking gently before entering.

"Hi," he said. "You called?"

"Come in, Mr. Seymour. I'm Sasha Jennings, Maddie's doctor. Thanks for offering to help out."

"It's the least I can do, Dr. Jennings. I have a lot to make up for."

"Please, call me Sasha. And this isn't about recrimination, Mr. Seymour—"

"Tom," he interjected.

"Okay, Tom. I've brought you into this session to see if we can make some headway into the causes, or the trigger, for Maddie's agoraphobia. I'm hoping you can shed some light on it for us. Let's talk about what you remember about your relationship and if you saw signs of this condition while you were still together."

"Did she tell you about the stage fright?" Tom asked.

"We touched briefly on it in our last session. What do you recall exactly?"

"At the very beginning, Maddie was terrified of performing live. It didn't matter where; the very thought made her literally shake with fear. I came up with a mantra, *Trust in me, trust in the music,* and we would hold hands and repeat it before we'd go onstage. That seemed to help some."

"I hadn't thought about that in years, Tom. I can't believe you remembered!" Maddie said, surprised at how the memory pulled on her heartstrings.

"Of course I remember that. I was in a panic that you'd refuse to perform after I booked that first gig. I knew I had to get you out there, and you seemed to respond to having something to hold on to. The mantra gave you the courage to believe in yourself, in us as a duo."

"I think it's interesting that you can recall the mantra, Tom. Maddie tells me your memory is faulty from years of drug abuse," Sasha said bluntly.

"Not everything is clouded. I remember the early years. I didn't do heavy drugs back then. It was only later—"

"You mean when Nate was born?" Maddie asked.

"No, actually, it was before that," Tom answered.

"When exactly? When did you really start using?" Sasha asked gently.

Tom dropped his gaze. "After our wedding. That's when things started to really spiral out of control for me."

"Why do you think it happened after you married? You were highly successful and had been a couple for a number of years by that time. You'd lived together. What changed for you?" Sasha asked.

"It's taken me years to figure that out. Lots of therapy," Tom answered, directing his words to Sasha, "and I still don't really know. My memory is shot. I honestly don't remember most of what happened."

"Wow. There it is. That's our problem, Sasha," Maddie snapped, feeling a sudden rush of anger that jolted her back to reality. "Tom can't remember the things about our relationship that I can't forget. It's a little too convenient, don't you think?"

"That's the essence of all this, Maddie. Let's try to let Tom remember what he can," Sasha said pointedly before turning back to Tom. "Go ahead. What did you figure out?" she asked.

"It's complicated."

"I'm sure it is, Tom, and I know it's hard, but you're here to help Maddie. So try to remember," Sasha prodded.

"We were on the plane ride home after the wedding. Maddie had written a song for me and performed it at our reception. It was the most beautiful thing she'd ever written. But it—it made me feel like an imposter, like she was a star burning so brightly that I needed to look away from her or go blind. And then Russell told me they'd asked Maddie to do a solo album. I was so jealous I—"

"*Jealous?*" Maddie interjected. "Jealous of what, exactly? I didn't want to do a solo album, and I told them that. I told you that too! Of course I had to change my plans a few years later, once you sold me out . . ."

"C'mon, Maddie. Isn't it obvious?" Tom cried.

"No, Tom, forgive me, but it's not. What could you have possibly been jealous of? We shared everything . . . songwriting credits, money, a home, a bed, a child. What more did you need?"

He let out a long sigh, and when he spoke again, he sounded utterly defeated. "Your talent, Maddie. Your brilliant, raw talent. Even though I knew you were the reason for our success, I held on tight for as long as I could, but I knew that eventually the label would figure out the truth. It was you, all you. I was just along for the ride."

He covered his eyes with his hand. "It was maddening for me back then, unbearable, actually. And look, you're still doing it. The song you just recorded with the band? It's fucking perfect. Take it to the bank."

"*We* recorded. You had a big hand in that session," Maddie said, and found she had to look away from Tom, from the expression in his eyes. The pain she saw there seemed to reach down into his soul—and into hers, and she couldn't stop from adding passionately, "That other stuff you said? It's just not true. You're a talented musician, Tom, and you know it as well as I do. And more than that, without our special sound, without your marketing and negotiating skills, we'd still be playing street corners. *You* made us into an international brand."

"Now you sound like my therapist," Tom said sadly. "I didn't believe in my talents back then, Maddie, and I still don't believe much in them now. I hid behind the drugs, terrified you'd find out I was a phony. Big deal—I knew a few chords, could bang out a rudimentary tune. So what? You were the true gift, the pure talent. It's only in the last couple of years that I've even had the nerve to start writing again."

He looked away from her, and the room grew still.

"How do you feel about what Tom just said, Maddie?" Sasha asked after a while.

"I don't know," she answered, still too stunned by Tom's revelation to speak. After a few deep breaths she said, "But it still doesn't explain the women. Hundreds of nameless women. And Emilia. You stole my best friend from me!" she cried.

"Oh, Maddie." Tom sounded genuinely bereft. "It explains everything. For all the same reasons. And it spiraled down even more after Nate was born. He became your focus, not me." His voice was little more than a tremulous whisper. "I—I was jealous. Of my own kid."

"And Emilia?" Maddie burst out as the tears streamed down Tom's face.

"That wasn't a choice, Maddie, it was an opportunity. She offered, and in the moment, I knew it would hurt you. *I wanted to hurt you.*"

The breath left Maddie's lungs in a wrenching sob.

"Let's take a break," Sasha said quickly.

"No!" Tom was up now, grabbing a box of tissues from a bookshelf and offering them to Maddie. "I want you to know I'll be sorry until my last day on earth for what I did to you, Maddie. And to Nate. I was a selfish, jealous prick and didn't deserve—" He broke off, clamped his mouth shut, and breathed deeply for a moment. When he continued, his voice was stronger, filled with something Maddie hadn't heard in a long, long while. Humility. Compassion. Love.

"If nothing else, I'm here now, in front of you, telling you that I'm the man you once knew, the man you loved. I am not the guy you found in the closet that day with Emilia. I swear it. He's long gone."

Maddie was aware of Sasha's eyes on her. Of Tom standing over her, the tissue box still in his hand. "Sit down, Tom," she whispered. "Give me a minute."

"Take all the time you need," he whispered back. "I can wait."

The silence that followed crackled with tension. When Maddie finally gave a soft moan and dropped her head into her hands, Sasha began to speak, gently and convincingly. "I know this is very painful for you, Maddie, but this is your path to recovery. You can't tiptoe around it. You've got to walk right through if you'd like to begin to heal. It's going to take time. This didn't happen to you overnight, so give yourself a break and commit to the process."

Maddie sat unmoving, saying nothing.

Shifting in her chair, Sasha added more briskly, "I think we've covered enough ground for today. I'd like us all to take some time and consider what we've heard this afternoon. Tom, what are your plans? Are you headed back to the city?"

"I'd like to stay and see Sophie, but if Maddie wants me gone, I'll go."

"Maddie," Sasha said gently, "let's take the weekend and reconvene on Monday."

"Me as well?" Tom asked.

"That's up to Maddie. If she wants you here, I have no objection." Sasha stood up, gathered her notebook and briefcase. "I know the way out. See you on Monday."

Maddie and Tom sat in silence long after they heard the front door close.

At last Tom said gently, "Is there anything I can get for you, Maddie?"

She shook her head. "I just need some time to work this out."

"I'm worried about you, Maddie."

"Don't be. I have a long and proven track record of taking care of myself."

"Yeah, I know. That was part of the problem. After a while you never really seemed to need me. For anything."

"Back then you were enough for me," Maddie said, finally looking at him. "You were all I needed. All I ever wanted was to have you for myself."

"I know that now."

Once again silence fell. At last Tom said hesitantly, "If you don't mind me camping out in your cottage, I'd really like to stay and see Sophie."

"Don't ask me to make that decision right now, Tom," Maddie said wearily. "I can barely think for myself at the moment."

"I promise I won't get in your hair," Tom said softly, though he was suddenly seized by the urge to do just that, to bury his face in that glorious hair of Maddie's. He quickly thrust his hands into his pockets and rocked back on his heels, and Maddie couldn't help smiling at that familiar posture.

"Okay," she said, rising from her chair, surprised at how relieved she suddenly felt. "You win. And while you're camping out, as you termed it, I'll get the house ready for Sophie. That should be mindless enough work for me. I don't think I can concentrate on much else."

"Deal," Tom said.

They stood facing each other for what felt to Maddie like a long time, neither of them wanting to be the first to leave the room.

Then Tom reached over and took her hand, pulling her close without actually embracing her. "Let me help you work through this, Maddie. I don't want you to be my biggest regret anymore."

"You said that the other day. I don't understand what you mean."

"My biggest regret," he repeated softly. "You are the person I cared for most, and now I see the damage I've done. The fact that you don't leave this house and that what I did in our past might have something to do with it. It's tearing me apart."

"I don't think it's solely because of you, Tom. That's giving you too much credit, don't you think?" she tried to joke.

He didn't smile. "I think I fucked you over pretty much at every turn. Saying I'm sorry will never make it right."

"Tom—"

"No, Maddie. That's enough for now. Like Sasha said, take some time, okay?" He leaned in and kissed the top of her head.

Afraid the innocent gesture might turn into something more, Maddie quickly shifted gears. "If I give you a shopping list, will you and Nate get some things for me in town?"

"It would be my supreme pleasure," he quipped.

A smile tugged at the corners of her mouth. "Don't get carried away. It's just groceries."

"It's a start. What do you need?"

Wiping the last of her tears away with a tissue, she said, "I'll check the pantry." She turned, only to discover that he hadn't let go of her hand.

"Hang on. I'll come with you," he said, running his thumb over her knuckles.

Shivering, Maddie snatched her hand away. She told herself she was simply reacting to all of this unaccustomed attention. She was used to living alone, used to surviving on nothing more than the most basic of needs, used to not being touched. "If you insist," was all she could say.

When they walked into the kitchen, they found Nate sitting at the counter reading the newspaper.

"I thought you two might never emerge," he said with a hopeful smile.

"Don't get too excited," Maddie warned. "Your father and I were just too exhausted to move." She brushed the hair from her eyes. "Thank God I don't have to see Sasha again until Monday. I don't have the emotional energy for this."

"As long as it helps you get off the property, I'm on Team Sasha," Nate said.

Maddie scowled at him. "Do me a favor and go into town with your father. I want to make a nice dinner for Sophie when she arrives. She doesn't need to be drawn into this madness."

Nate's smile vanished. "Actually, Mom, she does. She's a big part of my life. She needs to know what she's getting into."

"He's right, Maddie. If she's going to join the Seymour madhouse, she ought to have her eyes wide open," Tom teased.

I will not let him charm me, Maddie told herself fiercely. Shaking her head, she took a pad and pen out of the junk drawer and began to scribble a long list of ingredients from memory. She added a few more staples and handed the list to Tom. "Good luck. Nate, do you have your car keys?"

Nate flashed her a wide smile that was so much like Tom's that Maddie caught her breath. Only now was she becoming aware of the similarities between them. "Does it ever end, Ma? I do function when I'm not with you." He dangled a rectangular fob in front of her.

"Where's the key?" she persisted.

"There are no keys," Nate said.

"No car keys?"

"No, Maddie," Tom said gently. "Everything you need to start the car or unlock it is on a computer chip now."

"It's okay, Ma," Nate added, bending to kiss her cheek. "I would say that you've really got to get out more, but we all know you're working on it!"

Chuckling, Tom slung his arm around his son's shoulders and led him out the door.

"When the hell did that happen?" Maddie asked the now empty kitchen.

Tom and Nate left the house together after breakfast the next morning—Tom to a meeting in the basement of a local church and Nate to the small regional airport in East Hampton to pick up Sophie. After a long, hot shower, Maddie dressed carefully in a charcoal-gray fitted knit sweater with tiny pearl buttons open at her neckline and a pair of black slacks. She added some mascara and blush, trying to erase the effects of her sleepless night. The emotions she felt over Tom's words, both in and after the session with Sasha, had left her totally unsettled. She could no longer deny that she felt drawn to him again, and that scared her to no end.

She ran the brush through her hair and felt confident that she looked as good as she could under these stressful circumstances, then headed down to the kitchen, where she pulled out the cookware she would need to make her favorite go-to recipe, coq au vin. Since the recipe called for a full bottle of merlot, she checked several sites on the Internet to be really sure that the alcohol in the wine would fully cook away, leaving only the flavor behind. She didn't want to be responsible for putting Tom's sobriety in jeopardy.

Once she had organized the ingredients, Maddie started putting all of the components of the meal together, knowing that keeping herself busy was the best defense against letting worries overcome her. She had already assembled an apple tart and had it bubbling in the oven, and now she began to mindlessly sing as she worked, so engrossed in chopping carrots and onions that she didn't hear Tom come in through the mudroom door. She only realized he had walked into the house when she heard him begin to sing the harmony to the song along with her. Startled, she whirled to face him, knife in hand.

"Whoa," he said. "That looks dangerous! I wasn't off-key, was I? It's been a long time since I've sung 'Always in My Heart.'"

Maddie put the knife down on the counter. "No, no, I just didn't expect you back this soon. I don't know exactly how long your meetings run." She was not about to let him know what the soaring beauty of their harmony did to her insides.

"Do you always sing while you cook?" Tom asked, and she knew by his tone that he had felt it too.

"I always sing, period. In the shower, the garden, the basement. Music is constantly around me."

"In the basement?" He quirked an eyebrow at her. "I still can't get over all of the stuff you keep in there, by the way."

"I wanted to preserve the impact you and I had on pop culture," Maddie said. "That's Nate's legacy. I had to save it for him. But if I'm being truthful, I had to save it for me too."

"What do you mean by that?"

Maddie began scraping the chopped carrots into a bowl. "I had to remind myself in my darkest time that we were real, that everything, all of it, happened, the good and the bad. I was so angry. I think a part of me will always be that way, no matter what. I can try to use Sasha's help to get out of this house, but I won't forget what happened, Tom. I can't forget."

She paused, shifting her weight from one foot to the other. "Do you ever sing to yourself? Do you sing our old songs?"

"I do," Tom admitted. "And I've actually been working on some new stuff. I'd love to play a few pieces for you later, if you'll let me."

"Sure," she said warily.

Tom must have sensed her apprehension, because he said quickly, "Like I said, only if you want."

What *did* she want? Maddie felt a touch of despair. He'd come back into her life, turned it upside down, hurt their son with the truth, made her feel things she hadn't felt in a long time—hadn't *remembered* feeling, really—and now he was standing in front of her, green eyes intense, looking too damned sexy for her liking. Nate had dropped him off at the meeting and he'd run the three miles back to the house, sweating a little, his build athletic and fit. She turned from him without speaking and resumed the task of chopping vegetables.

"Oh, Maddie." There was a catch in Tom's voice and then he was behind her, reaching around her waist to cover her hands with his. The knife clattered to the countertop as he pulled her back against him, so close that she could smell the outdoors lingering on his skin. "I love you,

Maddie. That never went away." His voice broke. "It's always been you. From that day we first met until right now, I've loved only you."

He turned her around, gently, slowly, and she didn't stop him. "I know I let you down. Time and time again. But I want to spend forever making it up to you." With that, he leaned in and kissed her, at first brushing her lips softly with his own, then building up to a deeper, more lingering kiss that made the rest of the world fade from view.

Maddie hadn't lived a nun's existence since their divorce. There had been a few men here and there when she could still leave the house on her own, but nothing serious. She had a lot of scar tissue around her heart, and her defenses were always up. She didn't bring men around when Nate was young, either, because she never wanted to confuse him with relationships she knew just didn't matter. Small wonder this kiss felt like a thousand sparks shooting off in her body all at once.

She couldn't help it: she pushed forward, kissing him back, wrapping her arms around his neck. She heard him groan, and then his hands were exploring her body in a familiar pattern. Suddenly it was as though the years of pain were stripped away and they were young again, finding each other for the very first time.

As he trailed kisses down her neck and grazed the points of her collarbone with his mouth, Maddie's head tilted back, her body opening to his embrace. If they hadn't heard the sound of a car door slam on the driveway, their son and his fiancée would have walked in to find them wrapped tightly around one another.

Maddie turned away quickly to hide her flushed face. She fought to breathe evenly and quiet her wildly racing pulse. Hopefully Nate wouldn't notice anything different, because she would never be able to explain the last few minutes to him—or even to herself. Worse, she realized that while the moment with Tom was over for now, it wasn't really over. If she could still read him, and she was pretty confident that she could, the look in his eyes as he stepped away from her spoke volumes.

Sophie and Nate burst through the door in a flurry of excitement, Sophie smiling widely, her long red hair tumbling in soft waves around her lovely face. "Maddie! It's so great to see you! It's been too long!" she said, falling into Maddie's open arms.

"It has, and I'm so happy you're here, sweetie." Maddie stepped back to admire her future daughter-in-law. "You look beautiful as always. Ooh, Sophie, did you make that scarf?" She fingered the shimmering silk. "What a beautiful print!"

"Part of my new collection," Sophie said excitedly. "I'm pretty sure there's one in my suitcase for you too." She turned on the stilettos of her Jimmy Choo boots. Tall and willowy, the heels made her almost the same height as Nate. "And Tom! I really wasn't expecting to find you here. How wonderful!" She leaned over and kissed his cheek warmly.

"It's been way too long," Tom replied. "We'll have to catch up during this fantastic dinner Maddie's been working on all afternoon." He winked at Maddie when he said this, clearly reminding her that cooking wasn't the only thing she'd been up to.

"It does smell good in here," Nate added, sounding oblivious to the undercurrent between his parents, much to Maddie's relief. He picked up Sophie's luggage. "We're going to rest a bit before dinner. See you later," he added and headed hastily up the stairs.

"He was so jumpy the whole way here from the airport. So strange," Sophie remarked, and Maddie guessed that the engagement ring Nate had with him must be burning a hole in his pocket. "Anything I need to know?" Sophie whispered into Maddie's ear.

"Um, if you mean why Tom is here, I'll let Nate fill you in," Maddie stammered. Sophie's sapphire-blue eyes twinkled at Maddie as she followed after Nate.

As soon as they were out of the kitchen Tom asked, "Do you think she suspects Nate's plan?"

"Not a clue," Maddie replied, smiling and turning her attention to the simmering pot on the stovetop.

"And are you okay?"

Maddie turned to him. "Why do you ask?"

"I guess I didn't expect the reaction I got from you just before they interrupted us. It was . . . nice."

"I didn't expect it either," Maddie confessed, and because she certainly wasn't about to discuss it with him, she added, "Now if you don't mind, I'm going to get this dinner on the table."

Tom assumed a wounded look. "You mean you're choosing dinner over another round with me?"

"Absolutely. You can help me set the table, or you can go away. But you can't distract me again."

"I could try," Tom teased.

Maddie shot him a look that let him know not to take the little joke any further. Before long, the aroma of coq au vin was in the air, and Nate and Sophie came back downstairs in sweatpants and sweatshirts, leading Maddie to believe that they had wasted no time divesting each other of their previous clothing once alone together.

Her home, which had always been a place of chaste solitude, was turning into a hedonistic palace, she thought wryly. She could never have predicted the wild turn in her life at the moment, but she surprisingly felt okay about it. Nate seemed to have set his own pain aside now that Sophie was here, and thanks to Sasha, Tom had managed to work through much of his guilt regarding Emilia's death. And no matter what demons she'd have to face herself when Sasha returned on Monday, tonight Maddie intended to bask in the glow of her family's warmth, as unexpected as it was, as imperfect as they all were.

XVII

Spring seemed to arrive at the same time Sophie did, and all at once the flowers outside the house burst into bloom. The crocuses and daffodils unfurled in hues of saffron and purple while the hydrangea bushes sprang back to life despite the late-season snowstorm, turning deeper shades of green before producing small buds that would soon morph into the beautiful blue blooms that Maddie so loved.

During the week of Sophie's visit, Maddie met with Sasha three more times. Her therapy had moved along quickly following that afternoon when Tom sat in with them and opened up about his addiction and its aftermath. Sasha had helped Maddie venture out to the edge of the deck and back again, the last place she'd been before totally shutting herself inside.

Now, with Nate and Sophie back in California and Tom once again at the Prince Street loft, Maddie and Sasha sat in the music room one sunny afternoon discussing taking a short walk past the property line and down to the beach.

"I just reclaimed my house," Maddie joked. "Now you want me to leave it?"

"You had your hands full with your family here," Sasha agreed, "but you promised them you'd try, and I told them you could do it. Don't make a liar out of me!" she teased back.

Maddie smiled as she thought of Sophie and Nate. She had thoroughly enjoyed their visit and drawn a lot of strength from being around the fun-loving, gregarious Sophie, who had been such a balm for Nate as well. In so many ways Sophie's creativity and talent reminded Maddie of Emilia, before she fell into addiction all those years ago. She couldn't have found a better match for her son if she had tried herself.

Now they were back in Los Angeles preparing for Sophie's buying trip to Paris, and Tom . . .

Maddie thought back to Tom's last night at the house, when he had played them one of his new songs, a haunting melody, with Maddie humming harmony in the background. When the last beautiful guitar chord faded into silence, Nate had given them an emotional smile, then gotten down on one knee in front of Sophie, ring in hand, and proposed.

"Oh, Nate, yes!" was all she'd said as she threw her arms around his neck.

Nate turned to his parents, who were sitting close together on the loveseat in front of the blazing fire they'd built in the hearth of the music room. "I've never heard you sing as a duo before, except on a recording," he choked, holding Sophie's hand tightly. "Please. Please do us the honor and sing at our wedding."

There was a long silence. All eyes turned to Maddie. She felt Tom's hand in the small of her back, touching her, encouraging her, without Nate or Sophie noticing. "If Sasha can get me out of the house, I will sing at your wedding."

"Seriously?" Nate asked, sitting upright.

Tom's hand was still there, and Maddie leaned into it, drawing strength from it without even being aware that she was. "Yes," she said softly.

Nate whooped and leapt to his feet. "Thank you! Thank you! I am eternally grateful. Holy shit, I have so many calls to make . . . How about we do it on New Year's Eve? It's always been Sophie's dream to get married in Paris, right, babe?" Sophie nodded in smiling assent, and Nate went back to his pitch. "That gives you plenty of time to plan, to work with Sasha, to rehearse with Dad, right?"

Maddie shot a look at Tom, knowing that he was also aware of the significance of a New Year's Eve wedding in Paris, but he didn't blink. All he said was, "Let me know when and what time. I'll be there." Again without looking at her he slipped his hand over her hip, and this time Maddie tangled her fingers through his and squeezed.

"Maddie," Tom said later when they were alone together, putting away the last of the clean dishes from the celebratory dinner the four of them had shared, "are you really ready for this? You don't even know if your therapy with Sasha will get you off of the property."

"That's true, but I'm already standing on the edge of the deck with her, and I haven't blacked out yet."

Some of the worry eased from his expression at her flippant reply. "You really amaze me, Maddie. Do you know how very, very brave you are?"

"Not as brave as you. You beat an addiction. I just have to walk to the mailbox again."

His smile faded. "I still fight that addiction every day Maddie, and some of those days are a true struggle."

"Oh, Tom," Maddie said helplessly, but he held up his hand and added huskily, "But now I'm beginning to realize I have more and more of a reason to keep up the fight."

They smiled warmly at one another for a moment before Maddie turned back to finish putting the stemware away. Tom folded the dishtowel he'd been using and placed it carefully on the countertop before stepping in front of her. When Maddie turned around, she almost crashed into his chest.

"Thanks for all of this, Maddie. For Nate and Sophie and for letting me back into your life . . ." He leaned in for a kiss, deepening it as she responded despite herself to the feeling of his mouth on hers.

"Tom," she finally murmured, pushing herself away from him, "Nate and Sophie are around here somewhere. We really shouldn't be doing this."

"C'mon, Maddie, they went over to the cottage where I'm sure they're doing exactly this. . ." He wrapped his arms around her waist. "You are still as beautiful as always. Even more. And I want you. Desperately."

He pulled her closer as he spoke, and she couldn't resist. Despite everything, he had always been and still was her soul mate. She couldn't deny herself any longer; the pull of him was just too strong. She let him take her upstairs into her bedroom, where he closed the door and slowly undressed her, keeping his hungry eyes on her all the while.

As he lifted her sweater over her head, Maddie felt a brief moment of panic at being naked in front of him after all the years that had come between them, knowing she wasn't as young as she once was and that her body, although still trim, was older as well. Her breasts weren't exactly in the same place they had been, her curves were softer, her lines rounder.

But when Tom's fingers traced lazy circles on the smooth skin of her stomach, working their magic to the center of her being, all was lost for Maddie. She no longer cared if she looked any different than his memory of her. She no longer cared about yesterday or tomorrow. There was only this moment, only Tom. And when he drew off his own clothing and stood naked in front of her and asked her, "Are you sure you're okay with this?" she just smiled and led him to her bed.

"So," Sasha said, "are you ready?"

Maddie took a deep breath, held it for a few counts, then let it out slowly and nodded. The day had come: she was finally going to step off her property. To prepare her, Sasha had spent the first half hour of their session reminding Maddie of the things they had been working on for weeks now, stressing that she believed the reason for Maddie's agoraphobia was a case of post-traumatic stress disorder, or PTSD, something Maddie thought only happened to soldiers injured in combat, but in fact, as Sasha had explained, could happen to anyone after suffering any sort of emotional trauma.

"You could only keep your guard up for so long, Maddie," Sasha had said. "All those years ago you knew something was going on with Tom, something that wasn't right, but you had to put your energy into taking care of an infant. As Tom's addiction grew more serious, you had to keep up the pretense that everything was fine, hiding what you knew was a big problem from the record label, trying to protect Tom's reputation and your band's future. You held it together as long as you could. The shock and humiliation of seeing Tom and Emilia together and the field day the media had with it was the last straw for you."

"But I didn't feel any of these symptoms for years," Maddie said confusedly.

"You were all Nate had back then, and that's a role you took very seriously. It kept you strong. Once he went off to college, that guard came down. You must have been exhausted."

"I was so tired," Maddie agreed, remembering. "I slept for the first few weeks after he left."

"And it was comfortable, wasn't it? It became easier to stay inside, to build your cocoon and live in it, right? You created your own safety net, a place where no hurt could find you. But now, Maddie, now you're a beautiful butterfly. Time to go and rediscover the world. Are you ready to fly?"

Maddie smiled at the metaphor. "I think so. What happens if I panic once we're down at the beach?"

"I won't push you. For this first time, you can keep the house in sight if you need to. I promise not to let you fail."

Maddie looked at the younger woman. They had come so far together, and Maddie didn't want to disappoint her. Again she drew in a deep breath, and then another. Then she nodded. "Let's do it."

Sasha waited patiently while Maddie grabbed a soft lavender cashmere sweater from the front hall closet, one of the gifts Sophie had brought from her new collection, and put it on to ward off the cool spring air. Then they made their way slowly through the house and into the kitchen, then stepped out onto the deck through the wide glass door. Maddie bravely matched Sasha's stride as they walked past the cottage into the bright sunlight. There were clouds gathering in the distance, but for now, Maddie felt the sun's warmth on her face and drew in the heat as a source of strength.

But once they reached the rough-milled wooden staircase that led down to the beach below, Maddie paused. This was as far as she'd gone for years. The thought of taking the first step onto the long flight of stairs was terrifying. Sasha immediately took her hand.

"You can do this, Maddie. Keep breathing. One step and then another."

Shaking, Maddie grabbed the rail and steadied herself. Closing her eyes, she did as Sasha directed, taking each step slowly, at a snail's pace, until she reached the sand with Sasha right beside her.

"Look back now, Maddie. Look and see how far you've come . . ."

Sasha's words trailed behind her as Maddie kept walking, building speed, kicking her Converse sneakers off as she went. By now she was gulping deep breaths of air, pushing back the waves of nausea and hearing her heart pound in her ears so violently she was sure it would burst right out of her chest. Fighting the fear and panic, she thought of Nate, of Tom, and of the old mantra she'd used onstage all those years ago: *trust in the music, trust in each other.* She repeated it silently as she kept going, its soothing balm washing over her. She had come this far; she had to go farther until she reached the water's edge. She wanted to feel the sea spray on her face, the seawater sweeping over her naked feet.

Opening her eyes, she saw the ocean roiling before her. As the waves built and then crested, she waited for them to surge toward her and the icy water to cover her toes. When it hit, she felt a jolt of energy so life affirming that she shouted out loud, "Wow!"

She forced herself to remain still. Waited for another wave. And another after that. Behind her, Sasha said softly, "You're doing great. Do you want to walk down the beach?"

"I just want to stay here for another minute, if that's all right."

"Of course it is. Let me know when you're ready to move on," Sasha said, stepping back.

Maddie stood at the shoreline, her pulse slowing, her breathing growing more regular, even after her toes went numb, allowing herself the feeling of accomplishment she knew she deserved. The nausea had dissipated, and in its wake was something entirely different. A strange serenity had washed over her with the sea; there was no sense of panic or a dark cloud of impending peril. She realized that she was okay, that she was still breathing and standing upright.

At long last she turned her head and looked around her. She had been inside the confines of her property for so long that even the view down the beach toward Russell's house looked different now. Many of the homes had been redone, Maddie saw, most of them larger than she remembered. So much had changed; so much was unfamiliar. Her own sense of self was evolving so quickly that all at once she felt entirely overwhelmed by her shifting emotions.

A breath of panic whispered through her, but then, suddenly, it was her reconnection with Tom, the memory of their night together, that surfaced behind it, more strongly than anything else. His touch on her skin, his lips covering her own, the weight of his body on hers. Where once the memory would have left her feeling off balance, driving her back to the closed doors of her home, she held on fast, rooted to the spot, toes in the frigid water, feeling more alive than she had in years.

And suddenly the thought hit her: She wanted to speak to Tom. Now. She wanted to tell him what she'd done, how she'd made it to the beach and beyond. To let him know that she was okay.

Smiling broadly, she turned around. "Hey, Sasha, are we finished with today's exercise? I have something I need to do."

"Something more important than what you're doing right now? What could that be?" Sasha asked with a knowing smile.

Maddie felt herself blush, but answered calmly, "I want to let Tom know that I actually put a toe in the water."

"And you did, not even metaphorically! You physically did that, and I agree, you should shout it from the rooftops. C'mon, let's head back."

They walked toward the house in companionable silence, like friends on an outing, Maddie thought, astonished, not like therapist and patient. She took in the beauty of the sand and the water and the great blue sky above her without a single twinge of unease. She felt her spirits soar, and, overcome with it all, she linked her arm through Sasha's.

Once in the mudroom, pulling off their jackets and sweaters, Sasha turned to Maddie. "Is there something you want to tell me about you and Tom?"

"I'm not sure what you mean," Maddie said, although of course she did.

"It seems to me the nature of your relationship has changed. Want to talk about it?"

"Is this on or off the record?"

"I'm not a reporter, Maddie, I'm your therapist. Just thought if you were feeling confused about anything, I could be your sounding board."

Maddie smiled at her broadly. "If I'm in need, I know where to find you."

"Okay," Sasha said, grinning back as she gathered up her things. "I'll be back Wednesday, and we'll stay out longer. Sound good?"

"Perfect, actually. I'll be ready." Full of nervous energy, Maddie walked Sasha to the door. Tom first, she thought happily, and then Nate. She couldn't wait to dial Tom's number.

He picked up on the first ring.

"Maddie?" he asked tentatively. "What's going on?"

She couldn't help laughing. "Nothing bad, Tom, it's all good. I walked down to the water with Sasha today! I put my foot in!"

She heard his indrawn breath and then his voice came stronger, filled with the same joy that bubbled in her heart. "Oh, Maddie! That—that's fantastic!"

"When Sasha comes back, we plan to stay out even longer. I really believe I can do this."

"That's such great news. I'm so happy for you."

"Thanks, Tom." Encouraged by the tenderness in his tone, she added quickly, before her courage failed her, "I have to tell you something else."

"Oh?"

Her voice dropped. "I need you to know that, well, when I was out there, I wanted you with me. And when I got back inside, you were the first person I wanted to tell." She let out a long breath, as though her confession had taken the wind right out of her.

"That's great, Maddie. I'm so glad you did, I really am."

She didn't know what kind of response she expected, but this wasn't it. She had hoped for more. He sounded . . . strange all of a sudden. "Tom?" she began, but fell silent when she heard a female voice calling his name from somewhere inside the loft.

All at once her insides went cold. As cold as her toes had been out in the water. "You obviously have company," she said woodenly, "so I'll let you go."

"No, Maddie, it—"

"No worries, Tom. Let's talk when Nate has more details about the wedding. 'Bye now." She quickly pushed the button to disconnect the call. In the kitchen, the kettle she'd put on while dialing Tom's number let out a sharp whistle. Maddie steadied herself by making tea with deliberate motions, adding the boiling water and the tea bag together into her cup, stirring in the milk.

She took a few sips, but it only left a bitter taste in her mouth. Setting it on the counter, she did the only thing she knew how to do—set off for her piano, her solace, to lose herself in the one thing that had never let her down . . . her music.

The next time Maddie looked up it was dark outside. The wind had increased, and suddenly it was raining, the force of it pounding against the windows. Maddie had been so engrossed in the evolving tune she was creating that she hadn't heard a thing.

You idiot! The moment she stopped playing, the thoughts she'd been trying to hold back crashed in. *What a fool!*

He'd played her again. All the hard work and effort to get herself to leave the property, thinking Tom would be there for her moving forward . . .

You slept with him too! That's what you get for trusting him again!

No! She wasn't going to go there! Rubbing her eyes, she began to tidy up the vast pages of sheet music, organizing them hastily before sitting for a moment with her head in her hands, breathing deeply to call back the courage, the joy, and optimism she'd felt on the beach with Sasha.

Nothing. Just emptiness.

Sighing, Maddie set the music aside. As she rose from the bench, she heard a banging in the kitchen. Shit! Had she lost another tree to a storm? The last time that happened it took out the power lines, and the house was dark for days, forcing her to buy a generator.

But it wasn't a tree at all, she realized. Someone was pounding on the mudroom door, and she thought she heard the sound of her name above the rising gale.

"Maddie!"

A man's voice. More pounding on the door. She moved cautiously across the room, phone in hand, ready to call 911. "Who's there?"

"Maddie, open up. It's Tom."

She fought against the wind that buffeted the door, and when she finally got it open, she saw him standing there dripping wet, a bunch of battered daisies in one hand, overnight bag in the other. When she made no move, he stepped inside, offering her the flowers.

"These are for you."

"You came all the way out here to give me flowers?" she asked incredulously.

"I had to. I think you may have jumped to the wrong conclusion earlier. I wanted to clear the air, to apologize."

"In a monsoon?"

He stood dripping rainwater all over the tile floor, a puddle expanding under his feet. "Can I come in and explain?"

Maddie looked at the daisies, recalling their special history. She was amazed that Tom could remember such a small detail. How could she turn him away?

"Let me get you a towel. I assume this means the trains are running?"

"They are, but the cabs are another story. I walked from the station."

"That's over a mile, Tom! Take off your shoes and socks. They must be drenched."

"No more than these flowers," he said, handing them to her. "Sorry about that."

"Tom, I don't know what to say," she stammered, looking for a vase to put them in.

He joined her in the kitchen barefoot, his hair still dripping into the collar of his shirt. "Then don't say anything, Maddie. Let me tell you what happened earlier. I had a real estate agent in the loft when you called. She'd just walked in. I've decided to sell it. The worst part of our lives together took place there, and I don't want to be reminded anymore. I should have sold it a long time ago."

"Will you buy something else in the city?" Maddie's tone was brisk as she tried to hide her astonishment at the realization that he had come all this way to explain, to make it right, to bring her flowers once again. She sat down heavily on the nearest stool, her knees suddenly shaky. From relief? From happiness to have him here?

"That will be up to you, Maddie," she heard him say. "You made it down to the ocean. Can you make it back to Manhattan?"

"What do you mean?"

He leaned down to where she was sitting so that his gaze could find hers. "I need you in my life, Maddie. I don't know how much more direct I can be with you." His tone was serious, his expression urgent. "This isn't just about Nate's wedding anymore. All those wasted years I lost to drugs and drink, all the bad things I did and the hurt I've caused you—I want to spend the rest of my life making it up to you. I want us to be together."

Maddie pushed aside her discarded teacup from earlier. Smoothing back her hair, she tried to gather her thoughts. Finally she cleared her throat and said, "That's a dream I used to have, Tom, when I first came out here. I would wake up imagining you saying those words and meaning them."

"I mean them now, Maddie."

And she saw that he did.

Impulsively she reached for his hands. "I can't make any promises, Tom. Only young people are foolish enough to do that. And after all that's happened, I need time to build on the trust you want me to have in you. And I only made it down to the beach today, Tom. That's not very far."

He squeezed her hands. "Today was a start, Maddie. You can go farther. Tomorrow."

"I'm glad you're here," she whispered.

Groaning, he pulled her up to him, kissed her tenderly on the mouth, then said as he lingered on her lips, not wanting to break contact with her, "I need a hot shower. Take one with me . . ."

"You came all this way just to use my shower?" she teased.

"I came all this way just to get you naked again," he answered, and he smiled at her, the old Tom, her Tom, shining back at her from the depths of his eyes.

XVIII

On the morning of the bitingly cold December day when they were to leave for Nate and Sophie's wedding, Maddie found herself unexpectedly afraid. It was one thing to walk down to the beach with Tom or drive into the city to do some shopping and another altogether to fly to Paris. Her anxiety was exacerbated by a number of minor self-inflicted disasters, including the fact that she had no idea what to pack. Despite having sorted out her wardrobe the night before, Maddie spent so much time stressing over her decisions that Tom finally sat her gently on the bed and neatly put all of her clothing into her suitcase. Finally he wrestled it shut, dusted his hands, and grinned at her. "All done."

Then she couldn't find her house keys. She hadn't needed them in years, and she really couldn't recall where she had left them last. Tom had threatened to call a locksmith to change the tumblers and replace the keys, but Maddie had asked him to give her time. "I know they're around here somewhere," she'd told him, rummaging through her desk drawers.

"Don't take too long," he'd warned. "We'll miss our flight."

She discovered them at last in an Imari bowl on the shelf in her music room, though she had no idea how they'd gotten there. Tom's relief was short-lived, however, as Maddie insisted on testing them on all the front and back door locks to make sure they still worked. Years of disuse and the salty air had frozen most of them, and Tom had had to oil every one, doing his best—not altogether successfully—to hide his irritation.

When she'd finally declared herself satisfied, he'd swept her into his arms, kissed her soundly, then buried his face in her hair and whispered softly in her ear, "Thank the good Lord, Maddie. Can we *please* go?"

Now Tom was outside, stamping his feet in the cold, breath freezing in the icy air, as he organized their luggage in the trunk of the limousine. Maddie stood inside the foyer facing the closed front door, knowing that all she had to do was reach for the knob and turn it. Her heart hammered. Tom was right on the other side, she told herself. She could hear him kidding around with their driver, his voice strong and vibrant.

Surely Tom alone would be enough to get her through this. He had come to mean so much to her over the last few weeks, selling the Prince Street loft and moving in right after Maddie's last session with Sasha. While Maddie still kept in close touch with Sasha, speaking on the phone at least once a week to work through new problems as they arose and preventing small bothers from becoming larger concerns, it was Tom who had helped the most . . . simply by keeping his word to Maddie.

He was there every step of the way, holding her hand as she navigated the outside world by day, sharing her bed at night. They had started with longer walks on the beach, then small excursions into town either on foot or in Maddie's old car, venturing farther every time. On one particularly beautiful day, Maddie took Tom to see the Montauk lighthouse and on another to Shelter Island, the bills of their baseball caps pulled low over their faces to protect their privacy from others as best as they could. But it didn't really prove necessary—after so many years at home, Maddie had finally given the paparazzi the slip, and they were nowhere to be found. This heady new freedom was blissful for both.

More importantly, Maddie had learned to trust Tom again. And he had proven himself worthy of that trust. As often as Tom reassured her that he was never leaving again, that she was now and always had been the only woman in his life who mattered, it was his actions that meant so much more. He had moved into her house and back into her heart. When he touched her, held her, made love to her, she knew that he meant it. She could feel the scar tissue around her heart beginning to fade with each passing day.

A few weeks ago, Tom had given Maddie a check for half of the sales proceeds of their loft—a sound investment as it had turned out—and when Maddie had protested that she didn't need it, he had urged her to put it to good use.

"How?" she had asked, lying on the couch on a chilly afternoon, feeling lazy and sated after a morning of making love.

"For anything you're interested in. Arts in education. The environment. Battered and emotionally abused women. The topics are limitless, Maddie."

And she had realized, wonderingly, how right he was . . .

It was Sasha to whom she had turned for help in starting her foundation, a source for other women suffering with agoraphobia, though the project was on hold for now because of their upcoming trip to Paris.

If we ever get there, Maddie thought, a lump rising in her throat as she stared at the closed front door. She reminded herself that she could leave her house without feeling anxious for long stretches of time, including a week-long trip in the autumn with Tom to Blue Hill at Stone Barns for long, romantic hikes through the colorful falling leaves in the Hudson Valley followed by lavish candlelit dinners. But at this moment of truth, she felt overcome by a dismaying rush of fear.

Just reach out and turn the handle, the voice inside her head cried. *You've got this! You are a strong and capable woman. Just turn the knob . . .*

Time seemed to freeze as she stood motionless, her heart in her throat. *For crying out loud, Maddie, go! Just go!*

But the thought of leaving her home and traveling so far away was overwhelming. Maddie took a few deep breaths to calm her racing heart. She just couldn't succumb to her fears once again.

Nate and Sophie are getting married! she reminded herself sternly.

Nate . . . The thought of him made her smile, remembering how excited he had been as he and Sophie worked tirelessly to make their wedding arrangements at a seventeenth-century country estate right outside of Paris. When Tom and Maddie had called Nate in August to tell him that they had decided to live together again, Nate had taken time from his busy schedule to fly to New York just to confirm the unbelievable with his own eyes.

"You can't be serious," he'd said the moment he pulled into the driveway to find Tom and Maddie waiting for him there, his father's arm wrapped tightly about his mother's waist. "After all this time? Are you sure that's a good idea?" he'd asked with a broad smile.

"We think so," said Tom, leaning in to plant a long kiss on Maddie's mouth, much to the amusement of their grown son.

"I never saw this coming," was all Nate could say.

"Welcome to my world," Maddie joked back at him.

Nate had put his arms around them both, holding them tight. "This is going to make our wedding the best ever." His voice had quavered when he spoke, and he'd added briskly, "You guys can take a second honeymoon after it's over."

"Don't put the cart before the horse," Maddie warned. "Ask me again if I actually get on the plane."

"*When* you get on the plane, Maddie," Tom said. "Which I'll make sure of. And Nate's right. Let's take some time together, maybe see the Amalfi coast."

"Just don't call it a second honeymoon. We never had a first one," Maddie replied.

"You know, you're right. I think it's time to fix that," Tom said, smiling in the way he'd always done in the past when he had a devilish plan up his sleeve.

Nate had also been there when the band came out to Montauk to help Tom and Maddie rehearse the music for the wedding. His parents' set list was intended as a surprise for Sophie, and Maddie had been every bit as nervous as Nate about the band's "official" reunion—not only playing in Paris, but rehearsing in the cottage studio for days on end. Fortunately for Maddie, having the band around was like wrapping herself in an old, beloved blanket. They in turn comforted her, supported her in her weak moments, and reminded her selflessly time and again that they were her biggest fans. They made her believe that this whole crazy scheme would go off without a hitch.

Per Nate's wishes, they would start out with "The Lyric of Memory," the song they had recorded after the unexpected snowstorm that had brought Tom back into Maddie's life, a song that had rocketed to number one after it was released in May. After that, Maddie and Tom would play one of his new songs and finish off with a few of their classic tunes.

Then Nate would lead Sophie out onto the floor for their first dance as the band played "Always in My Heart." Maddie had known then that if she made it to the point of hearing the opening chords of that song, nothing would ever block her path in life again—she would be bulletproof.

That's right, bulletproof, Maddie told herself fiercely, still standing frozen before the closed front door of her house, still listening to Tom's easy banter with the limo driver outside. Again she lifted her shaking hand to the doorknob, thoughts of Nate racing through her mind.

"This doesn't bother you, Dad, does it?" he'd asked, coming up from the basement with a bottle of wine the night of his arrival after they'd told him they were a couple again. "I don't have to open this."

"I'm fine, Nate," Tom had said firmly. "Go ahead and enjoy it with your mother."

"I intend to," Nate said with a grin. "Because I have an announcement to make, and I want you to stay and hear it too, Dad."

"Oh?" Maddie and Tom asked in unison, then laughed at each other.

"Mom," their son said, smiling and turning to face her, "I am about to grant you your wish."

"Really? What's that?"

"Sophie's pregnant!

Tom whooped and pumped his fists in the air while Maddie jumped off her stool and ran around the counter to hug him. "Oh my God! Oh God, Nate!"

Tom asked, "When's the baby due?"

"Early next spring."

"Well, if you were looking for a way to take my mind off of my stage fright, you just found it!" Maddie said.

Nate grinned. "So happy to help."

"We need to call Sophie," Tom added excitedly, reaching for the phone.

"Let me," Maddie said, smiling as she took it from him. "I want to be the first one to offer to babysit whenever Nate and Sophie need a break."

"*We* will babysit," Tom amended softly, the promise of the future burning in his eyes.

Now, with the world beckoning beyond her door, Maddie fought to remember the way Tom had made her feel back then—as if anything were possible. Yet she could still feel the sweat forming on her forehead, and for a panic-stricken moment she thought about calling Sasha. But she knew it wouldn't help, that if she was going to be able to leave, it would have to be on her own.

Once again she lifted her shaking hand and grabbed the knob. Now all she had to do was turn it slightly to the right to disengage the lock. Tom was waiting. Nate and Sophie were waiting. Her soon-to-be grandchild was waiting.

She drew in a deep breath to steady herself as she heard the tumblers turn. And all at once, to her ear, they were a symphony and she the conductor. And she knew that it would always be entirely up to her to finish the sweet music that would lead her toward her future.

Liner Notes from "The Lyric of Memory"

To you, our dearest fans,

We have so many people to thank when it comes to the making of this album. First of all, our wonderful friends, the musicians you've counted on for years to bring our sound alive. Ned, Charlie, and Andre: What can we offer you but our eternal gratitude for your great gifts?

To Shanna and Jessie: Your sweet voices complete ours. You are the harmony in our lives.

To the memory of our dear friend and colleague, Emilia Parkson: we miss you each and every day and know that it was you all along who knew we would someday reunite, even though you didn't live to see it happen. Rest in peace, dear friend.

As you know, we never planned on recording together again, but the fates intervened thanks to a rare Nor'easter, and this record is the result. But truthfully, it was you, our supporters and fans, who never let us go, clamored for more when we didn't think we had anything left to give. This was a labor of love for us, and we couldn't have done it without you. Thank you for continuing to buy our music both by download and in the stores. We love you one and all.

And we'd like to dedicate this record to our son, Nate, our daughter-in-law, Sophie, and their child, whose birth we await as we write these words to you. We are blessed.

Love always,
Maddie and Tom

Acknowledgements

There are so many people who helped bring this story to the page, and to all of you, thank you, thank you, thank you, thank you from the deepest part of my heart.

My dearest friend and editor, Renate Johnson, for all of your comments, suggestions, and gentle prodding, this was, no doubt, our full circle moment.

My oldest friend, Leslie, for making me look so good in photos and for always picking up the phone, no matter the time difference, for the last forty-five-plus years.

To the world's best writer's group: Ellen, Helen, Joan, Mary, Niki, and Paula (forever in our thoughts), you were always my first readers. I couldn't have written this without you. And special thanks to Niki for being the final proofreader and making sure all of my mistakes were corrected.

To Noelle, for figuring out what I meant and creating a spectacular cover.

To the Coffee Shop girls: Annie, Claudia, Linda, Lorraine, and, of course, Alvina. Here's to Greek salad and friendship forever.

To Meryll and Lisa and all the countless hours of exercise and therapy—everything happens for a reason.

To Fern and Florence, who always believed, no questions asked.

Hilari T. Cohen

To my sons, who I hope understand better than anyone else how deeply I love them...

And of course, to my husband Ken: you have always been the best cheer-leader a girl could ask for. This one's for you . . .

Hilari Cohen has spent her lifetime surrounded by books. First as a reader, then as an editor for renowned publishing houses such as Grosset and Dunlap, Harlequin and Zebra Books, where she worked with multiple bestselling authors before deciding to give fiction writing a try herself. She lives on Long Island with her husband. You can email her at hilari. mpp@gmail.com or visit her Hilari Cohen Author Facebook page.

Photo credit: Leslie Magid Higgins